As Kelso swam cautiously through the window of what had once been a very posh home in the L.A. suburb of Inglewood, he heard the noise of an engine, dim, but growing stronger. In one swift moment his hand swept to the mask light and switched it off. He kicked his way to the roof and peered out, treading water and listening.

As the craft crossed the Imperial Highway he could make out its dark gray outline. It was one of Polliard's boats, an observation deck bulging under its belly and its sides studded with salvage winches, arms and claws. As a go[illegible]ment agent, Polliard had the right to bl[illegible] out of the water he pleased. He'[illegible] artner a year and a half b[illegible] orking the Verdugo [illegible]

Now t[illegible] winging around t[illegible] tube. The boat bristl[illegible] ponry. Kelso had his digger, a[illegible] speargun strapped to his chest. T[illegible] nothing to do for the moment but sw[illegible] like hell....

Bantam Science Fiction
Ask your bookseller for the books you have missed

UNDER THE CITY OF ANGELS

JERRY EARL BROWN

UNDER THE CITY OF ANGELS
A Bantam Book / June 1981

ISBN 0-553-14605-X

Published simultaneously in the United States and Canada

Bantam Books are published by Bantam Books, Inc. Its trademark, consisting of the words "Bantam Books" and the portrayal of a bantam, is Registered in U.S. Patent and Trademark Office and in other countries. Marca Registrada. Bantam Books, Inc., 666 Fifth Avenue, New York, New York 10103.

PRINTED IN THE UNITED STATES OF AMERICA

0 9 8 7 6 5 4 3 2 1

para Francesca
por la fe y la animo

PRELUDE: THE DESTROYER

A shrill signal from an outguard ship, light-years beyond the empire, filled the vault-ribbed communication chamber with unimpeachable urgency.

Narrow body rigid and still, a watchkeeper listened. When the message had run its course the second time, he raised one shining arm from the folds of his robe and waved it across the communicator's face. The signal died, its strident cry replaced by the quickening metallic tap of the watchkeeper's feet moving to the corridor.

In the nearest vertical fallway, the watchkeeper was dropped past other corridors and rooms, through the labyrinthine nucleus of an underground citadel built deep beneath the planet's surface millennia ago.

On the lowest level, the watchkeeper exited directly before the vitreous entrance to the First Master's sanctum. At the august doors he bowed and gave the ritual salute in an inflectionless speech pattern like the signal that had issued from the communicator.

The Master arose from his rest niche and turned nearly irisless eyes on his subordinate. With a voice similar to that of the watchkeeper's, the natural apparatus of which had been supplanted long ago by a more durable and efficient organ, the Master demanded the intrusion be explained.

At once the watchkeeper complied.

The Perfect One listened. Appropriate synapses interconnected in his long, backward-sloping brain, the variegated cortices of which were visible inside the transparent skull. Referral data concerning the planet indicated in the message streamed through.

The problem was without precedent. Deliberation was called for. But deliberation, like equivocation, like deviation from ritual and routine, was unfamiliar, and when the Master spoke, he paused frequently.

"A trusted vigilant from the inner ranks will be selected. The one chosen will be a proven servant of the realm, one whose mind has been thoroughly purified, one from whom there is no reason to expect anything but the highest efficiency and strictest obedience, especially since he will not be able to return to Naravamintara."

The keeper of the watch bent his knees at the mention of the sacred name of the planet in which they dwelled and the stellar empire it ruled. "Yes, Excellence." His impeccable memory recorded everything the Master said.

"He will be loyal, trustworthy, competent, expendable. This is as it should be. As it must be. Given the planet in question, an outguard ship, machine-piloted, would present too great a risk of being detected if it were charged with the task. A vigilant who was born of the Adulterators' lineage, unable to attain the Perfect Order, whose birthworld and ancestral background are similar to those of the planet's inhabitants, will be the best able to adjust and respond properly to such a crude environment and the unpredictable situations sure to arise, the best able to accomplish the task without risk of detection because of his ability to pass as an indigene."

"Yes, Excellence."

"The selection procedure," said the Master, "will therefore be carried out with the utmost care. Appropriate physiological and psychological data must be gathered and transmitted from the outguard so that transformation will be flawless. Though the selectee's ancestry may ultimately be traced to origins related to that of the planet's inhabitants, individual evolution will have brought about differences that must be suppressed."

Once again the watchkeeper said, "Yes, Excellence."

"During the transformation the selectee's brain will be implanted with the necessary instructions concerning what has to be done. Success will thus be assured."

The directions came to an end. The watchkeeper lifted his eyes, gazed upon his superior, saw radiance, voiced worshipful acknowledgement, turned, and left.

In a movement almost involuntary, spurred by an impulse all but dead, the First Master stepped across the room to pass a delicate gilt-sheened hand before its wall. His tiny pupils dilated in an attempt to make out the particulars in the scene. . . .

Windswept ashen desert under fixed tempests of stars.

Bald dagger peaks of lifeless mountains serrating a horizon nearly as dark as its backdrop of space. The faraway white star of the system of which Naravamintara was the penultimate planet rising slightly above a notch in the distant mountain range. And, in the foreground, barely illuminated by that timid light, ruins of the old surface city of Nammava Trah I, which lay directly above the underground stronghold.

A brief tremor rippled through the Master's neural chain as he recalled the destruction of the old city and those who had destroyed it, and the excavation below it by beams that had vaporized the planet's crustal rock so that a new Nammava Trah could be built, a fortress impregnable and eternal.

But discipline overrode the minute disturbance, the memory, just as it had overridden the initial alarm the Master had experienced on hearing what the outguard ship had found. With a second pass of the hand, the image vanished.

He turned from the wall and moved forward to the purgation couch. There he removed his robe with a flourish facilitated by perfectly engineered limbs and, carefully laying the long cerebral ridge that ran the length of his back in its cradle atop the couch, reclined.

The purification tube rose automatically out of the floor. The First Master raised golden knees and spread them. As the tube's eye tilted toward the white, featureless nib where his ancestors' sex had been, he made lightning-swift calculations of the length, breadth, depth, of the imperial reach. He did not bother to speculate on how much more of the galaxy had to be searched, if not assimilated, before the destroyers of Nammava Trah I were found.

The beam knifed out of the eye.

He jerked spasmodically, feeling, in a body that had been conditioned and redesigned not to feel, the vestigial pang of an ancient hatred.

In the center of the luminous cell, the transformation instruments hum. The prostrate form inside the cocoon-like case is motionless, blurred and enveloped in an aura of violet. The instructions with which the autopreceptor impregnates its passively waiting brain, like the energies being fed into its metamorphosing body by the machines straddling the cocoon, are soundless and final.

Brain scanners look for tangled vines of doubt, assertions of selfhood. This, however, is the mind of a trusted soldier of the High Court, a vigilant; purification beams have been here long before, incinerating any suspect weed of anarchy they might have found. The search this time is routine and cursory over the charred terrain.

The brain sleeps, unaware of the amazement to come from the influx of data that will dictate the boundaries, the conditions, of its new existence, unaware yet of the dizzying release of gravity's iron weight and the slipping away, the receding of all that was familiar and real. . . .

Blackness smeared and festooned with the intermingling streams of a stellar gulf. Passage through wheeling cycles of time and space, form, matter and energy. A path of fringe light, a broken celestial highway becoming darker, more distant. Dwindling memories of an instilled peace in unquestioning service to absolute authority giving way, breaking down, dissolving into disarrays of contradiction and conflict, at odds with what was known before.

An inkling of being stripped naked, of being aware of nakedness as if for the first time. Of cold, of pain.

Alone. Loneliness.

Confusion. For the first time, fear.

Of being lost, wandering without root or anchor when before there had been no idea that anchor or root were needed. Of being bereft of something without a name, something taken away before memory.

The noise of winds.

Of falling. Of having fallen.

Of being cast adrift with nothing to cling to but commitment that permitted no repeal.

Hands groping in darkness to find a hold. Hands with feeling. Human hands.

And an awakening. The first awareness of a world filled with new and startling sensation, of a perception as strange as the new reality perceived. Dim resonance of something previously kept interred under ash. Latent suspicion of having been fortuitously given the code to the contents of a book heretofore sealed.

1. THE GRAVEROBBER

Fleshless jaws gaped. Hollow eyes streamed seaweed. Atop a cairn of rubble a disembodied skull sat, as if placed there by a macabre prankster, its punctured cranium sporting a dark bryozoan crust that looked like a rakish hat.

With limbs caught under twisted girders and teetering walls, they undulated in slow parodies of dance as he swam past. At times they seemed to gesture, nodding like amiable pimps, beckoning him into some hazardous crevice or overhang.

Join us, Mad Jack.

Seeing them at all any more was unusual. Most had been scattered, crushed, buried. Yet, in tightly cluttered crannies such as this, where the few remaining sharks and barracudas had trouble getting in, some of the bones were still miraculously intact, though nibbled and sucked clean by smaller appetites.

In the beginning they'd driven him more crazy than he already was. Many still had had flesh, clothes, even eyes—as if their numbers were too large for the feasting predators (numberless themselves, then) to devour all at once. When he came upon them now, they were like old friends with whom he had more in common than their living counterparts and his voice rattled in his diving mask as he raved.

"What's new, Herman? How's tricks, Sal? What were you doing when the bottom fell out, old girl?"

Of course, he could seldom tell what sex they were and didn't care. Death was as sexless as it was omnivorous. But if he addressed them, they needed names and names usually evoked gender. Like death, he had no preference for either sex in his crack-brained monologues, yet the names that popped into his head were more often feminine than masculine. Maybe this was because of the woman he'd found in the Del Rosa ruins, freakishly dry, sealed and preserved, in an apartment bedroom with an infant, both dead of starvation or suffocation or radiation poisoning—what the hell did it matter?—lying on the neatly-made bed as though asleep, emaciated, the color of wax, the woman clutching the ridiculous and predictable crucifix. Enraged, he'd taken his digging tool and smashed the apartment window, then grabbed an outside light fixture to keep from being sucked inside by the inrushing current, his guts convulsing at the thought of entering that crypt.

But probably it was because of Lisa. Because he used to think of her when he came upon a corpse, a skeleton, a heap of half-buried scraps that once had breathed, talked, walked, dreamed, hoped. He'd thought of her and his two sons caught like those he saw now, waving, beckoning . . . but more likely long since gone into the bodily processes of some absurdly glutted fish which, as a consequence of its gluttony, had succumbed to plutonium poisoning.

Rarely did he think of Lisa and the boys now; rarely did he think much of anything. He was mad, all right; admittedly. Mad to keep from going mad maybe, but mad nonetheless. Why else did he keep coming here, poking through these regions like a doomed ragpicker lost in the Styx? Did he think he might find them, as though anything could remain of them to find? Did he yet harbor a stubborn belief that he'd find evidence, after all this time, that the U. S. Government, URI, somebody, had somehow triggered the cataclysm? Did he still think he might find what the Devil's Canyon Project had really been all about? And if he did, what would he do about it?

Or was his plundering, his persistent defiance and contempt of government diver, submersible, or gunboat, of cutthroat colleagues in the illegal salvage trade who also wanted his hide, a poorly disguised deathwish? Did he secretly long to join Lisa here in this underwater charnel house?

No, he was after loot. Sure. Kelso, the grave robber. Kelso, the Reaper's lackey. Kelso, the lunatic scavenger of the deep, lifted the long aluminum digger and used its tines to rake away debris from the maw of a window. The light at the crown of his mask beamed into the interior, its penetration limited by the silt he'd disturbed. What he could make out was the usual: topsy-turvy furniture, wreckage and tatters filmed by sediment and algae, that primitive form of life that seemed to grow anywhere, even here in Mad Jack's domain.

Sagging beams and yawing walls, perforated ceiling. A shadowy scum-covered sculpture of perdition.

"Halloooo? Anybody home? Anything in there for Mad Jack Kelso?"

A small brown moray eel suddenly shot out of the window. Instinctively, he reached for his knife and kicked back, footfins striking the jagged stuff on the bottom, and the light's beam marking a zigzag course over the jumble of steel and concrete above his head.

The eel disappeared through a hole in the tangle on his left and he immediately felt regret. Morays weren't the nicest of creatures to come across but he hadn't seen a moray or anything else much larger than a crab or a sea urchin in these waters for years. The experience left him awestruck, wondering how the thing could have survived—and what kind of mutation lurked in its reproductive cells. But contamination was worse in some parts than others. Here near the old L. A. International Airport there hadn't been any nuke operations; the big reactors had been miles away, and it had been nine years since the massive meltdowns and blowups. The word leaked to the underground regarding the latest study and analysis of the water by URI chemists indicated the residual radiation fell far short of what the general populace was led to believe. Considering the resilience of life, maybe the stunted moray was healthy, had escaped the curse.

Dream on, Mad Jack. Why not take off your mask, remove your antiradiation suit and put that theory to the ultimate test?

It was then, as he moved cautiously through the window into the remains of what had once been a very posh home in the suburb of Inglewood, with his mind maundering and his mouth shut, that he heard the noise of an engine.

In one swift movement, the hand that had previously gone for the knife swept to the mask light and switched it off.

Darkness in the living room of the manse. A faint glow filtering down from the surface through the battered, split-open roof overhead. The engine noise dim, maybe a half-kilometer away, but growing stronger. Coming from the south.

Pushing upward, he held the digger out to ward off any visible protuberances in the way. At the top, where the ceiling was a ragged mess of holes and haphazardly mixed materials, he held onto the end of a broken rafter and looked out.

Above the interior shadows of the house, visibility was good for several meters; the tiny luminescent depthgauge in the upper left corner of the inside of his mask indicated 66m, not quite below the well-lit zone. He quickly estimated his whereabouts to be on the western edge of Inglewood, not far from Aviation Boulevard and the airport where he'd left the *Tiburón*. Absentmindedly, he had strayed farther from the submarine than he'd intended.

He slithered out of the roof, feeling his way gingerly with the digger. The convex faceplate in the mask provided him, for the most part, with only a frontal view. Though most buildings and other structures had been leveled for a long time in the area, the hills of debris and tangled wreckage foreshortened what visibility he would have had if he'd ascended farther. But he had to keep close to the general rubble and the bottom, despite the chance of the suit's being gouged or torn, in order to avoid being picked up on the approaching craft's sonar. He was, nonetheless, able to discern a light, or its corona, in the direction from which the engine noise came. Whatever it was, submarine or submersible, seemed to be coming up the San Diego Elway toward Kelso's position, hugging the elway track.

He stopped for a moment, treading water and listening. As the craft drew nearer, he realized he had misjudged its distance, that it was much closer than he'd thought. When he heard it cross the Imperial Highway and its searchlight suddenly angled off to the west, he could make out its dark gray outline. It was a submersible of a stubby bullet shape, an observation deck bulging under its belly, and its sides studded with salvage winches, arms and claws.

Most illegal salvage operations still carried out in the Zone employed surface boats with divers. Very few freebooters had, like Kelso, a submersible or submarine capable of both eluding the San Andreas Sea Patrol and hauling up salvage undetected. Nowadays he seldom saw anything at these depths but scientific and research craft—and an occasional member of Vincent Polliard's own private little fleet. The submersible now nosing around in his vicinity was one of these, a Polliard favorite, and Kelso knew it well.

An ex-officer in Naval Intelligence and a former diver for Universal Resources, Incorporated, Polliard was known to have retained his place on both the federal and corporate payrolls, notwithstanding his pretenses of being merely a plunderer of sunken cities, like Kelso. That Washington and

URI wanted to have an inside eye on salvage activities (legal or otherwise) in the Zone was common knowledge. And no matter how hard Vincent Polliard tried to play the outlaw, it was also common knowledge he was their man. The Naval and Coast Guard installations in the Palos Verdes, Santa Monica and San Gabriel Islands had been established there primarily to police the Zone and, though the official line claimed their security measures were for the public's own good (to keep people out of a quarantined region that was seismically unstable and radioactive), Kelso figured one reason for such "security", unofficial, overrode all the rest. Something lay somewhere here that the government and its corporate accomplice, URI, did not want a lawless renegade such as himself, or anybody else, to find—or wanted to find it first in order to bury it once and for all.

In his capacity as an "intelligence agent" Polliard had license to blow anything and anybody out of the water he pleased, and it always pleased him to do so. Behind his cover as an illegal salvage diver, he had, over the years, amassed a wealth of treasure taken from the ruins at the bottom of Angeles Bay and the San Andreas Channel. A man of varied enterprises but only one interest, the accumulation of money and power, he had turned up almost everywhere Kelso had, a hated shadow, as though the two were locked together in a bizarre death dance. He had met Polliard years ago, under circumstances that had led to a chain of events whose every link had been hate.

But uppermost in Jack Kelso's mind at the moment was the fact that credit went to Polliard and crew for having killed Kelso's partner a year and a half back, when the two were working the Verdugo Canyons. Dimitri was surprised in the top story of a Sunland jewelry store when they rammed the roof and the whole works came down with Dimitri in the middle of it. Kelso had been in another building nearby. He'd tried to reach the Greek, tried to find him while at the same time trying to avoid Polliard's searchlights. But he'd failed to locate his friend, even after the murdering sonsofbitches left and he took the *Egg* out of the *Tiburón* and attempted digging through the wreckage until he broke one of the submersible's claws and had to give up.

At the present, the powerful noselights of the *Bullet*, as he had dubbed it, were now on, and the main searchlight was coming around to light Kelso up like a neon tube. This craft, like most of Polliard's boats, bristled with exotic weaponry.

Kelso had the digger, a knife, and the speargun strapped across his chest. There was nothing to do for the moment but swim like hell.

So he did. Down under the San Diego El, seeking shadows to hide him at the same time that he sought space between the ruins to swim. He cursed himself thoroughly for having left the diving suit's small propulsion unit in the submarine.

Behind, he heard a sizzling noise, like water frying, but didn't alter his stroke to see what it was. He could guess. Seconds later, as he neared the southeast edge of the airfield, he heard the explosion, then another. Small torpedoes of some sort were blowing holes in the el where they'd caught him in their lights.

A second series of detonations thundered and he felt the shockwaves aid his speed. He was in the fairly clear avenue of Century Boulevard, dropping closer to the bottom to avoid sonar, where a lot of debris hillocks lay between himself and the *Bullet*. His lungs ached and his heart pounded. The noise of his labored breath filled the mask so that he could hear nothing else. But the situation could have been worse. Apparently the *Bullet* had no heattracking torps sensitive enough to home in on a human target, or anything else more sophisticated than what had been thrown already.

He reached the place where Airport Boulevard entered Century. A snarl of wrecked, sediment-coated cars and buses obstructed the road. He swam up and over, sensing them more than seeing them, and prayed he didn't slam headfirst into something that would knock a hole in the mask.

When he crossed Sepulveda, he heard more explosions, but much farther away. They were shooting wild, had lost him. Kelso had almost reached his last bit of strength. Considering its age, it was amazing the suit's breathing apparatus still functioned as well as it did. The indicator on the inside of the mask's brow showed the system to be working at peak efficiency.

The *Tiburón* lay in the shambles of what was known as L. A. International's "Theme Building", whose understructure had collapsed. This had caused the high, arcing superstructure to snap and fall in upon itself at grotesque angles. Kelso could not see it now, but he had seen it often before, in the *Tiburón*'s lights or in the light of the mask. And he knew, as he dimly made out distorted shapes in the murk, he would have to utilize the mask light to find the submarine. Once upon a time he would have called the Chief and the computer would have turned on the low-intensity locating light outside the airlock door. But neither the light nor the head-mask phone worked any longer. He switched on the light atop the mask.

Almost instantly, he saw the *Tiburón* lying alongside the twisted remains of a huge jetliner that had somehow careened, rolled, crashed through the south parking area and come to rest amid the broken arches of the Theme Building. The plane had been one of those monsters, designed in the latter part of the 20th century, that had had passenger compartments in the wings. One of those wings had been ripped open, exposing the interior like the inside of a doll house.

When he found the opened airlock on the port side forward of the *Tiburón*'s bridge, he swam in, opened the drains and air valves and waited, cursing the slowness of the closing door.

Once through the lock's antechamber, he flung the digger aside and ran past the berthed *Egg*. He had no time to wash the suit in the decontamination chamber; he'd do it later, if he remembered. Fins slapping loudly on the metal deck, he stumbled over bits and pieces of booty that spilled off racks into the narrow passageway in a general muddle which testified to long-term indifference and neglect.

In the storage compartment aft of the *Egg*'s berth he had to throw a number of objects out of the way to reach the locker where he kept the magnetic charges.

One was left. He let out a whoop, fell to mumbling excitedly, and, reversing himself, staggered through the junk back to the airlock with the charge cradled like an infant in his arms.

At the door he considered taking the *Egg*, but discarded the idea. The submersible would be too slow, much slower than the Polliard craft. Then he thought of moving the submarine out of its ugly airport nest and closer to the el, if the *Bullet* was still there. Against the bulkhead, behind some hanging necklaces and pendants, was a squawkhole. He tried it, unable to remember if it worked or not.

"Chief?"

No answer from the *Tiburón*'s computer. To hell with it. He didn't have time to run back to the control room. Besides, the *Tiburón* was probably safest where it lay.

He left the lock door open, the inside lights burning, and

swam out of the airport shambles. He hadn't remembered to get the minijets. Kelso, he thought, you and your operation are fast going to hell.

Adrenalin helped animate his flagging limbs. In the distance he could see a cloud of swirling debris above La Cienega Boulevard, stirred up by the torpedos. The edges of the cloud were fringed with light, indicating the *Bullet* was on the far side. He swam in that direction, along the Century Boulevard route, both hands free, the magnetic charge strapped to his waist, over his diving belt, and the speargun athwart his chest. He had left the digger behind; there wouldn't be any more scratching around for fancy geegaws today.

The Polliard craft was sticking to the elway, moving north, toward the Manchester Avenue El, its lights trained west. Kelso made his way to the edge of the San Diego tracks and swam along parallel to the old freeway bed over which the electric elway system had been built, a track for each previous car lane.

The submersible had cut its engines and was hovering over a group of partially flattened buildings to the west of the elway, its lights raking the water beyond, still looking for the quarry they'd lost.

The quarry removed the satchel holding the charge as he moved closer to the craft. He kicked up over the tracks, running the necessary risk of the lights turning aft or of sonar discovering him coming up from behind. He headed for the stern where at least the lights could not reach him, where he would be in the penumbra of the *Bullet* itself.

When about five meters directly below the target, he activated the timer on the charge. Through a rear port in the observation bucket he saw a couple of men going forward, neither of whom was Polliard. Both were in ordinary seamen's clothes, and had no diving gear on at all. Too bad. Kelso smiled inside his antiradiation mask and let the charge go.

He paddled backward, at an angle across the el to the ruins on the left, as the charge drifted up to the submersible's stern. He felt like a kid watching his kite climb the wind. The magnet in the charge hit the underside of the hull and held fast, like a leech. He saw a man inside the bucket pause, a man he recognized as one of Polliard's closest lieutenants, a fact which would indicate Polliard was aboard. The man was listening, having, no doubt, heard the slight thud when the bomb hit the hull.

Kelso swerved away, arms and legs flailing. He dived, almost rammed into a knot of fence bordering the elway, skirted this and, hugging the cracked, upheaved pavement of a side street that dead-ended at the el, swam as fast as his exhausted body would permit back in the direction of the airport. He had no choice now but to turn on the mask light; the wreckage here was too thick and too unfamiliar. But, luckily, they did not pick up either his light or his figure on their sonar, and he had put the better half of a kilometer between himself and the submersible when the charge went off.

The shock of the explosion disturbed the ruins around him, sent bits and pieces crumbling bottomward, some of which fell close to his frantically moving arms and legs. He ignored them. He laughed, would have rolled, somersaulted and cavorted like a porpoise, if he'd had the strength left. There would now be a hole in Vincent Polliard's redoubtable craft big enough to accomodate Moby Dick. If Polliard had survived the blast, he'd have to face the polluted water flooding in.

On the run from patrol boats alerted by the underwater disturbances off the Santa Monica Islands, the *Tiburón* sneaked north in the late afternoon, through the Santa Clara Narrows to open sea.

In the control room, Kelso sat with his naked back turned to the central instrument panel, becoming drunk on salvaged whiskey. The incessant murmur of the submarine's engines and the sea through which it rushed subdued the faint noises of the ticking instruments, but not the rattle of the faulty air system. Indicators, needles, scales and gauges glowed behind him, framing his disheveled salt-and-pepper comb of hair in a halo of tiny multicolored lights. Sweat beaded his forehead and ran in rivulets through the grizzled tangle of beard and chest hair. Clouds of smoke plumed up from the pipe he pulled on, to hang in the already stale air above his drooping head.

About to nod off, his chin hit his sternum and he sat upright and banged the bottle against the battered metal chair. He tried to sing, but all that came out was "Yo ho ho!"

or "Hey ho!" or "Ya ha ha ho ho he hee!" He couldn't remember any songs. Time had blanked out music as well as other things.

"Hey, Chief!" he bellowed around the stem of the pipe. "Sing me a song!"

"Songs are not within my purview, Captain," answered the bland voice of the computer at his back.

Kelso swiveled around to confront the console. "I ain't no goddamn captain. You hear that, you blockhead?"

"We've discussed this problem before. For the sake of efficiency and order it is necessary that you be addressed as 'captain'."

He belched, loud and long, removed the pipe from his mouth. "Thank you very much. Hell's howling hags. You're a bore, Chief. What's more, I think you're getting a few bats in your bits, if you know what I mean. First thing you know, you'll be as balmy as I am."

"Concerning the subject of efficiency and order, Captain, the deteriorating state of the *Tiburón* must be brought to your attention again."

With a groan, Kelso squirmed in the chair. He raised the bottle for another swig to brace himself against what he knew was coming.

"We are running low on fuel and are many kilometers from the supplier. The engines need inspecting and servicing. Stores are depleted, and most of the systems and equipment throughout the ship need repair or overhaul."

"Chief, if you don't shut that crap up, I'll pull your damned plug."

The computer fell silent.

As did Kelso, all of a sudden aware of the silence, the emptiness, around him. He thought of Dimitri, remembering how the two of them could not stand the sight of the other for days, then would have a reconciliation that stopped only short of tears. They would play endless and silly card games, get in another argument and, unless they dived, would wind up hating each other's presence all over again, like two crotchety trappers holed up in a mountain cabin all winter with no place to go but at each other's throats. But he missed Dimitri. He missed . . . something.

In spite of the whiskey, or because of it, he saw clearly the state to which he'd sunk: a misanthropic drunk babbling to a machine for company. A drunk with a deathwish who seemed to always get his ass in gear when the chips were down and manage to escape with said ass and other lugubrious parts intact. For what reason, he did not know. Animal reflex, he guessed.

Glumly succumbing to the ambient social vacuum, he stared at the dirty deck under his feet and thought again of Vincent Polliard. Hatred, it seemed, was all that kept him going. Consequently, he almost regretted Polliard's assumed demise because Polliard was such a deserving object of hatred. But then the human race had no dearth of Vincent Polliards. Another was certain to come along in due time.

For a moment this idea perversely cheered him, and he was about to laugh, wanted badly to laugh. But for no explicable reason he suddenly saw his wife years ago, young, brilliant, in the springtime of her talents, standing in the observation dome of the space shuttle that had taken them to Island One. "Our possibilities are limitless, Jack," she'd said then, the faint accent of the *barrio* she'd never been quite able to shake still in her words. He remembered the stars appropriately blazing around her rich brown hair and her face, her Spanish-Indian eyes, illuminated in the dome's semi-darkness by an internal warmth and verve he'd loved and could not emulate. "I can't imagine a better, a more exciting time to be alive. Can you?"

Ah, Lisa, he thought, feeling the memory stab like a knife, wincing with its pain. *The Reaper has the reins. I've joined him, Lisa. I'm one of them.*

Jack Kelso's head sagged to his chest and, instead of laughing, he began to weep.

2. THE AGENT

Like every other facility on Long Beach Island, the "2" Section office was being manned by a skeleton crew. One clerk busied himself at a desk, the other stood at the water fountain, looking badly hung over and diluting the contents of his coffee cup. The latter told Vincent Polliard that

Lieutenant Garret was ready to see him. He walked through the office to the back. The door was ajar.

"Come in," said a voice from inside. "Close the door behind you."

Polliard did so and met the eyes of the man at the desk across the room. Captain James Garret, formerly of the Office of Naval Intelligence, Santa Rosa Island, Southern San Andreas Zone, neither stood nor offered his hand.

"Please have a seat, Mister Polliard. Vincent, isn't it?"

"That's right." Polliard sat on one of the two fold-out chairs before Garret's desk. He wore the slacks and sportsshirt worn on the plane from Denver that morning. Garret's summons had given him no time to change into his usual "working clothes": swimsuit and diving vest.

"May I call you Vince?"

Polliard smiled thinly. "Why not?"

"Cigarette?"

"I do not smoke, Captain. Now, what did you want to see me about? And what happened to Swenson?"

If Garret was nettled by Polliard's curt tone, he did not show it. Leisurely, he tapped his cigarette on the crystal of his wristwatch, tamping the tobacco down. He was probably in his mid-forties, looked solidly built, had alert and perceptive eyes. The khaki uniform he wore was fresh but not fastidiously pressed. The desk was cluttered, and a filing cabinet behind Garret had one drawer open, with its contents looking as if a small grenade had gone off inside.

"Captain Swenson received orders to report to Honolulu," Garret said. The new intelligence chief's glance appraised Polliard. He saw a man in perfect physical shape, powerful of chest and arms, square of jaw, angular. The nose was slightly crooked, doubtless the result of some past brawl.

"Blink your eyes around here and there is a new roster," said Polliard. "Boots and shavetails, as they say. Pimply-faced kids, like the two out front. As soon as a man shows the faintest trace of a little salt in his rigging, off he goes to Fleet. They keep this up and Long Beach won't have enough personnel to launch a dinghy."

"Um hum," said Garret. "Too bad about Swenson. I understand the two of you had a fine working relationship. An 'understanding', as it's sometimes put." Garret watched for a reaction, saw none. "I suppose we could all end up in Asia the way things are going." He smiled. "Or almost all of us." With a lighter plucked from the disorder on top of the desk, Garret lit the cigarette. "I hear the test results in Denver were negative."

Polliard crossed his legs and folded his arms across his chest. A typewriter began clacking in the front room. "That is correct."

"Amazing what those antiradiation suits can do."

"Yes." A low, rattling noise came from Polliard's disfigured nose as he impatiently exhaled.

Garret gave no hint of having noticed. "What would you judge the contamination content to be in the bay now?"

"It varies. In the places where the nukes were, the contamination can still be between fifty to eighty percent. Other places, zero."

"Um hum." Garret carefully blew smoke to the side so that Polliard would not have to inhale it. "How long have you been working in the Zone, Vince?"

"Eight years."

"Quite a stint. You like it?"

Polliard was silent, contemplating his new "boss". Swenson had been easy to manipulate, lazy, sloppy, dumb. Garret might want to get in the way.

"Are you convinced there's something to be found down there besides salvage?"

"That's why I'm working for you people and URI, isn't it? To find out?"

Garret flipped ashes into his ashtray. "Supposedly. That and helping to keep the Zone free of plunderers. You've got a fairly commendable record in the latter area." The intelligence officer pushed his chair back, stood and walked to the window where he stayed, watching a couple of women, officers or nurses, swatting a tennis ball back and forth on the court east of the administrative buildings. "How is the plundering activity, by the way?"

Polliard stared at Garret's back, eyes settling on the man's broad buttocks, twin stigmata, despite the solidity of shoulders and chest, of too many years behind a desk. "Slacking off considerably. The places you can reach have been picked clean. There are a few diehards around—"

"Like Jack Kelso?" Garret continued to watch the tennis game, blowing cigarette smoke at the window glass. A small jet had just taken off from Long Beach Airfield and was banking northeast of the division supply sheds, turning out over Angeles Bay. What lay below that jet, what had formerly been the Los Angeles basin, now looked as if a gigantic fist had smashed precisely into the metropolitan core, driving the city beneath the sea and leaving, like the fragmented fringe of a sunken caldera, isleted pieces and splinters bordering the area where it had lain. The major portion of what had been L. A. and environs was now underwater, with the Santa Monica and San Gabriel Islands lying to the north and the Palos Verdes and Long Beach groups studding the southwest. At the northwest and southeast ends lay the mouths of the San Andreas Channel. From Huntington Harbor east to the channel, roughly 100 kilometers inland at that point, the land remained generally as it had been before the cataclysms, though most of the manmade structures there had been leveled. What survivors could be found in those parts of the Zone where rescue teams could land had been evacuated and relocated within a few months after the initial disaster. There hadn't been many.

Polliard had said nothing in response to Garret's mention of Jack Kelso. But a tiny ripple of tension played over his jaw muscles, and the flesh of his biceps where his hands gripped them was white.

"You and Kelso were on the *Deepfish* together, weren't you?"

"That's right."

"I've heard you have a personal grievance against the man."

Had Garret turned just then, he would have seen in Polliard's stare a hostility that included himself as well as Jack Kelso in its desire to kill. "I was what you might call very much involved in *Deepfish* and its discoveries, Garret," Polliard said, pointedly omitting the officer's rank. "Jack Kelso is responsible for sabotaging the entire voyage and everything that went with it."

"Everything?" Garret turned from the window. "I thought *Deepfish* reached the Philipines okay."

"With all her data storage destroyed. All the information, the specimens, samples, photo work, everything we'd spent months gathering—in a place and at a depth no ship had ever come close to going before—burned, shredded, smashed, thrown overboard, by that goddamned lunatic and his fellow mutineers."

"I see. An indestructible lunatic, it seems."

"No." Polliard almost lost control, almost shouted it. His arms dropped to his sides and his legs uncrossed. "You consider my job in the Zone to be two-fold. Well, I consider it to be three-fold. One of these days, and it's going to be soon, Mister Garret, I am going to have Jack Kelso's head on a stick."

The intelligence chief returned to his desk and sat down. A definite change had appeared in his face and his voice was now void of any former friendliness, genuine or feigned. He was looking straight at Polliard. "Getting Jack Kelso is part of your job only in that 'getting' any illegal diver in the Zone is part of your job. Your principle function here has no room for personal vengeance. There are others whose *primary* job is to keep the Zone free of Jack Kelsos. *Your* primary job is to find any evidence you can pertaining to what caused the quake. And you've supposedly been looking for eight years. The teams of geologists and geophysicists you've taken down haven't found a thing either. Not in the bay nor in the San Gabriels where the Devil's Canyon Project went on. In more than one case, scientists have complained in written reports of your lack of cooperation; in one case, one of them said he had the feeling you were deliberately trying to frustrate the mission." Garret smoked and thought a minute, perhaps to steady his own temper. "Maybe you were, maybe you weren't. Maybe there isn't any such evidence. What do you think about that, Vince? I've just come over from the Santa Monica research station—getting acquainted with the folks around Angeles Bay, you might say." Garret was back on his diplomatic tack again. "Over there the consensus is that the quake was the result of natural forces, put into motion by those URI scientists fooling around with nuke probes in the San Gabriels."

Polliard gave Garret one of his thin-lipped smiles. "So you're now telling me that my 'primary' job is unnecessary, that I'm looking for something that isn't there?"

The Captain leaned back in the chair. He let out a long stream of smoke, this time making no effort to keep it from wafting across to Polliard. "Just sounding you out, Vince. Trying to get your thoughts on the subject. Maybe you don't have any. Any you want to divulge, that is." Garret waited, giving the agent opportunity to offer his views. But none came. "Okay, Vince. I don't pretend to know for sure either. I once thought it patently absurd to believe a catastrophe the size of which occurred here was the result of purely natural causes. But sabotage seems just as absurd. Not we, nor the Russians, nor anybody else, as far as we know, has a weapon, or an *arsenal* of weapons, that could have done what was done here without leaving some trace of their having done it. But no such trace of any kind of sabotage has been found. The radiation, what little there is left—and the percentages you gave me were a bit old—is traceable to those underground detonations in the San Gabriels and to the meltdowns and blowups from our own nuclear facilities when the fault and basin gave way." Leaning forward, Garret snuffed out the cigarette in the already overflowing ashtray. "But maybe I—we, the U.S., national and naval intelligence, don't know everything there is to be known. Universal Resources is an international conglomerate, and Universal Resources was the principal outfit behind the Devil's Canyon Project, a project so wrapped in secrecy, I might add, that even *I* have not been able to gain access to whatever documentation exists on it, most of which was buried along with the people involved from what our intelligence can gather. Yet I've never been quite satisfied with that PR line that what URI was after in the San Gabriels was nothing more than oil." He paused again, watching Polliard, perhaps considering the wisdom of his candor. "What really puzzles me right now, though, is you, Vince."

From outside on the tennis court came a triumphant peal; someone had won a set.

"If there is any basis to my theory that URI knows something we don't and, since you are also an employee of URI as well as of the U.S. Government, you may, consequently, know something we don't, why does it appear you haven't been that concerned with finding out what caused the quake? Do you already know? Are you trying to keep those scientists from finding out? Is URI, in other words, working against our efforts here?"

Polliard's specious grin widened minutely. "You're a man with a lot of questions, Garret."

"Um hum. None of which you intend to answer, it seems. Well, maybe you can't give the answers now. Maybe answers will come in due time. Maybe there isn't anything more to you than what appearances suggest. Maybe you're only after plunder. The grapevine has it that you've squirreled away one hell of a lot of stuff you've brought up from the Zone yourself. We've all done a bit of that sort of thing, and so far none of the big boys have minded. Maybe they figure we're entitled to some kind of extra compensation for having to work in this place. But I'm talking about little stuff, Vince, weekend or offduty pickings, amateur plundering. Of course, as you say, there isn't much left to plunder, especially where the amateurs among us are concerned. But, and again as you say, there's plenty left yet in the places that are hard to get to, and I'm sure you've got a better idea than anyone else, unless it's Jack Kelso, just where those places are."

Bending forward to pull another cigarette from a depleted pack near the ashtray, Garret looked point blank at Polliard. "Let me make it straight and to the point, Vince. I run a tight ship, to use an old Navy cliché. I want every man under my supervision to do exactly what he's assigned to do, nothing more, nothing less. And while I may not know everything that's going on around here, I intend to find out. And while you may be in the employ of some big shots in Universal Resources, Incorporated, as well as Uncle Sam, I'm the one who will call the shots where a lot of San Andreas Sea Patrol work is involved, and where *all* intelligence work in the San Andreas Death Zone is involved. Those operational parameters include you, Vince."

Polliard said nothing. He sat with both hands in his lap, fingers interlaced, affecting an altogether relaxed air, though his eyes and his pulsating jaw muscles told Garret he was anything but relaxed.

"The way I see it, you've been busy with four jobs." The intelligence chief raised his right hand, index finger thrust up and the yet-to-be-lit cigarette held between palm and thumb. "One, you're supposed to be looking for some evidence of sabotage, or for whatever caused the quake; two, you're supposed to capture or destroy any unauthorized vessel or personnel you see in the Zone . . . something you're supposed to do only in the event such a vessel or persons appear in the area in which you are working at a particular time; three, you've been indulging in a personal kill hunt for Jack Kelso; and four, you've been helping yourself in a big way to that enormous salvage dump that stretches from the Sea of Cortez to San Francisco Bay."

The four extended fingers of Garret's broad hand waved before Polliard. Then middle, ring, and little fingers dropped. "One job is what I want out of you, Vince. Find some evidence of sabotage, find something to indicate the reason for the San Andreas and Los Angeles Basin catastrophes, help the scientists find it, or forget it. Go back to work full time and in full daylight for your corporate friends who were really the ones behind *Deepfish*—and who are trying to run things here. But go work for them elsewhere, not in my area of responsibility."

Polliard slowly lay his palms flat against his thighs. "Is that what you called me in here to tell me?"

The lieutenant regarded him thoughtfully and said, "I guess that's about it, Vince. Unless you want to tell me something you know and I don't." Garret waited, as before, but no comment was offered. He found the way Polliard was looking at him unsettling, and his hardened tone did not conceal his irritation. "Face it. You've gotten away with a lot because you're a good diver, you know the Zone, and you're known to have as little fear as you do scruples. Those qualities, the fact that with the personnel shortage it would be damned difficult to find a replacement, the fact you were doing some very sensitive work on *Deepfish* and, earlier, at Colnette, for some folks in very high places, and the fact you are still working for said highly placed folks, have all contributed to your having had a very free hand around here. That's over. We can't go on holding hundreds of thousands of square miles of habitable and arable land in quarantine forever. An area so damned vast we couldn't adequately police it during the best of times. We've got to find justification for the quarantine. We've either got to open the area up for resettlement or give the public a good reason why we can't. The story we continue to publicize, about the area being unstable and radioactive, has begun to wear thin. The news media are starting to make a lot of fuss in that quarter." Garret placed his hand on a stack of papers. "Here is a pile of letters, cablegrams, what have you, sent to the Zone commandant and passed on to me. From reporters, journalists, senators, crackpots, you name it, requesting to be let in to 'update' or 'reassess' the San Andreas Death Zone." Garret stopped, winded. He dropped the unlit cigarette on the desk. "You get the picture?"

Forcing his hands down along his hips, Polliard stood. "Of course. I get the picture." His lips lifted at the corners with that thin smile, eyes like an osprey's watching the slick silver wiggle of a fish just below the surface of the water seconds before the folding in of wings, the plummet, the taloned dip.

"Well, Mister Garret, I am a busy man, as you have noted. I have things to do. But permit me to shed some light on our little discussion by pointing out a fact that should be of interest to you. It should relieve you of that burdensome responsibility of which you spoke regarding my activities in the Zone. You see, those people I have worked for in the past—and work for still, as you have also noted—can be very accomodating and influential. I can easily get their ear. All I have to do is remind them that I have done things for them they would not like their stockholders, or their constituencies, to know about. All I have to do is remind them that this information is kept in a safe place, to be put in the hands of someone who will see that it becomes known to the public should I wish it, or should anything unpleasant happen to me. So I think it would be wise on your part, Mister Garret, to concern yourself with other matters." Polliard turned, stepped to the door, but could not resist turning to look at Garret one last time.

He saw what he'd expected. The naval officer's face had turned the color of chalk. Polliard slammed the door.

3. IN ISLES OF THE DAMNED

From the upper deck of the cabin cruiser she watched the boat's prow cut cleanly through the water. Sunlight whirled in the spume of its wake. The wind in her face, in her hair, helped ease the faint headache, the occasional fits of dizziness.

The doctors had let her go.

She remembered them as vague presences in white. She would suffer occasional headaches, they had said. She would sometimes be dizzy. Her illness had been severe, but she was getting over it. Her years-long convalescence, and her work as a nurse, had helped immensely. Soon she would be completely well, the doctors had said. Medication and supervision were no longer necessary; she was free to go.

Free. She let the word, its meaning, glide across her mind like the glide of the gull across the air above the boat. It seemed a strange word, with a meaning she could not quite grasp. Except for the minor headache, she felt fine; very good, in fact. But *free?* Well, free to do as she wished, to go where she pleased. That was what the doctors had meant. She had not told them to what purpose she would put this freedom, not them, nor anyone. It was her *free* choice, and she had chosen.

In the west, Restitution Island, the largest of the group, was a black mountain with a foreshortened summit looming above the sea. For the last hour she had watched it and its sister mountain to the south grow closer. Green was now distinguishable along the lower slopes. She knew about the Restitution Islands, had first heard about them in San Diego where she had bought the cruiser. Where she had hired Juan and Carlos Lavacca as sailors and bodyguards. San Diego seemed hazy, but not as hazy as Phoenix. She had been on drugs, of course, for a year. What kinds of drugs, she did not remember. Now she felt as if she were waking from sleep that had lasted years.

She turned, looked down at the stern where Carlos Lavacca had an automatic rifle apart and spread over the top of an ice chest. "Carlos," she called. "How soon will we reach shore?"

He looked up, then forward beyond the cruiser's bow to the distant islands. "In twenty minutes, *señorita.*" At once he resumed oiling the rifle parts. She saw that a tarpaulin had been improvised forward of the chest to protect the parts from the salt spray.

"Will you bring me the binoculars, please?"

Without hesitation, he dropped what he was doing, found the binoculars just inside the cabin, and climbed the ladder to the narrow upper deck. She searched his expressionless face as he gave her the glasses. "Have you been to the Restitutions before, Carlos?"

"No, *señorita.*" He remained there, standing on the top rung of the ladder, waiting in case she wished to say more. Though he looked at her expectantly, his dark eyes were void of interest.

She smiled, uncertain. "Thank you." And, after watching his chunky form descend to the stern, she turned to study the islands through the glasses, and wondered why she longed so strongly to talk to him, or his brother, to *someone* about *anything.*

The raw, rugged flanks of Restitution and Terremoto, two monsters belched from the sea, filled the lenses. She remembered picking up a book in San Diego, a book she had read in less than an hour after first leaving the coast, perhaps famished for intellectual nourishment after her long "sleep".

A fresh wave of giddiness made her bring the glasses down. She leaned against the rail, waiting for it to pass.

She concentrated on the solidity of the book to regain her equilibrium. It had said the chain of small islands 480 kilometers west of Tijuana were approximately forty years old, depending on at what stage of their development one thought of them as having been "born", and were already being reclaimed by the sea. Extruded from the ocean floor by volcanic uplift during one of the many sequences of tectonic disturbances in the latter quarter of the twentieth century, they'd hardly cooled before the first wave of land-starved adventurers invaded their porous shores. Lacking in both vegetation and beaches, the ash, tuff, and pumice that made up their soil had little resistance to the constant lash of wind and wave or heavy rainstorm. Their bizarre terrain resembled war-blasted badlands, where the simplest forms of life could no longer survive. Such drawbacks did little to discourage those who came. The ugliness of the islands aside, they were virgin lands without a native population to contend with, and without a government that could rightfully claim ownership. These facts alone goaded the first invaders into fighting over the scorched hills like carrion over a killing ground.

The attack of dizziness ebbed. She raised her head and stared at the islands in the distance, remembering the kindled curiosity started by things the book had said. The text of the book continued to move through her memory in review, almost verbatim.

Along with some haphazard attempts at self-government, there erupted a rash of schemes which took as their impossible task the improvement and preservation of these craggy isles for the purpose of tourism. Soil, sand, and vegetation were imported, much of which blew away on the wind or washed away in the rain. Some of these efforts took hold, however, and small oases of vegetation actually began to flourish for a time in the hospitable climate. Through various applications of cement, plastics, and other building materials, attempts to create artificial beaches were made, some of which showed promises of lingering, most of which disintegrated and sank. Nevertheless, in keeping with the general delirium of the age, instant spas and playgrounds sprang up wherever possible, and within two decades after their explosive births, the main islands swarmed with hedonists lured by such tantalizing invitations from promoters as "Come play in a pahoehoe paradise that was a gift from hell." The rough hardened lava on which the thus-lured pleasure-seeker would set foot would be anything but pahoehoe, but few knew or cared about such details. It sounded wicked and exotic, and that was all that mattered.

The twin volcanoes bobbed up and down in her view through the binoculars, as the cruiser sped over the gentle swells. She thought of their having risen slowly, for ages, from the sea floor, finally to explode upward into light and air, freed from the deep.

Spray filmed the lenses, and she brought them down to wipe them on the tail of her shirt. She could now make out the thin white line of a beach, the recessed shadows of a harbor. Both to the north and to the south she could see the outlines of other islands, smaller than the ones directly ahead and without mountains.

Said the book, the resulting territorial melange was nominally governed by an ad hoc council made up of both Mexican and American profiteers and allegedly policed by a gang of cutthroat louts who rarely ventured beyond the less barbarous areas of the three largest islands. These three, Restitution, Terremoto, and Las Penas sported the resort towns, the gambling strips, and tourist centers. The smaller islands served as habitats for fringe groups of every persuasion—from a colony of artists and pacifists on La Primula in the extreme north of the chain, to a band of renegades and terrorists on El Lugar de los Piratas in the southern end.

She felt suddenly hot with excitement, with the anticipation of going ashore in such a place. A hand flew, as if of its own volition, to her throat and quickly opened the top buttons of the shirt to allow more sun and salt spray on her skin.

The Restitutions were a perfect setting for the kind of man with the skills and knowledge she needed. But did *that* prospect merit this quickened heartbeat, this sudden rush of blood?

Why the confusion? Why these tangled and conflicting emotions? Her memory, the memory which was, if not restored by the natural healing processes of her own mind, then put back together by the research and coaching of the doctors in Phoenix, had brought about her decision and she would stick to it. But why these spontaneous reachings out toward things, these impulses that flew in that decision's face?

The Restitution Islands, raw, new, moribund, now filled the west.

The urgency that overcame her when they moored the cruiser at Rose Harbor stemmed from her fear that procrastination would only feed the confusion and make her vacillate. She wasted no time in beginning her search.

She talked to many people, gathering and absorbing much irrelevant information about the islands' odd and scant history and the people who came here. At night, upon returning to the cruiser, her mind alive with the day's lore, she would go to bed restless, unable to sleep, and reprimand herself harshly for being no closer to her objective than the day before.

Jobs as a prostitute, a card dealer, an erotic dancer, a model, an actress, were offered. She was jumped by three men and a horribly crippled boy who, despite her skill at self-defense (a skill she had apparently acquired somewhere, and not lost, prior to her illness) dragged her between buildings and ripped off her clothes. Fortunately, the Lavaccas, never far behind, sent the would-be rapists in headlong flight down the alley. This incident, its inexplicable violence, its savage cynicism, left her more bemused than anything else. Memory told her there had been similar incidents in the past, though the details, when she tried to remember them, were vague and dreamlike.

In her peregrinations she became adept at spotting the dangerous and unstable from a distance. She learned the language, spoken and unspoken, of the yachts and villas and streets, and she learned to move freely and easily (always accompanied by at least one of the bodyguards) through every social level the islands had evolved, but finally she had to give in to her initial suspicion that the kind of man she sought would have to be found in the lairs of the most lawless.

On the afternoon of her eighth day in the Restitutions, she steered the small cruiser for the island called Smoky, just south of Terremoto. It had one town and several outlaw camps and coves.

The town lay on the island's northern point, a premature slum of stucco, brick, stone, and other materials thrown together in slapdash fashion that showed unabashed signs of crumbling as fast as the land on which it sat. Trees or shrubbery were nonexistent.

While Juan and Carlos secured the cruiser to the pier below the point's low bluff, she changed from her coverall to a frayed gray T-shirt and old jeans. After brushing out her long, black hair, she pinned it close to her head so that she could wear the burgundy beret she'd bought in Rose Harbor. From a drawer in the small chest she removed the stunner pistol and clipped it to her belt. The navy blue windbreaker was pulled on and left open so the gun could be seen. Nothing the doctors had reconstructed of her past provided any background for the role she had to play. Yet instinct, intuition, something, dictated what she did, dispelled the earlier sense of disorientation, gave her a confidence and alertness she knew she would need.

A last look in the mirror provoked the inevitable pause. The delicately-boned face with its classic lines and contours confronted her with a hint of melancholy, of injury, around the mouth and in the lozenge-shaped green eyes. It was a beautiful yet vulnerable face which seemed subtly scarred with a subsurface conflict, a paradox that wanted to both affirm and deny the validity of the finely molded head.

"Judith DeFond," she said, forming the words carefully with her lips, her tongue, as one might enunciate a name in a foreign language. It was the name the doctors said was hers.

The longer she stared, the more strange the face became, the darker and more indefinite its surroundings, until it looked out at her from a blackness that had no limits. The eyes, the olive lines framed in their border of darkness, wavered and threatened to dissolve, threatened to become something other than what was previously seen in the mirror. . . .

Suddenly she had to hold the narrow dresser to steady herself. She jerked away from the mirror, afraid that if she stood there a second longer she would lose her precarious clutch on reality.

Holding at bay a hovering nausea, she left the cabin, mounted the ladderway and stepped onto the afterdeck. The fresh air helped and she took greedy breaths of it, glad to smell the sea.

Juan and Carlos waited at the stern, like terra-cotta sculptures whose theme was unqualified devotion. She could not recall having asked them anything about their backgrounds; indeed, she could not recall any clear details related to where and when she'd hired them. But though they never spoke in her presence unless she asked a question or made a request, they were efficient and, so far, trustworthy. They were certainly earning their pay.

Boisterous singing carried over the water from an approaching dinghy. Behind the dinghy lay a yacht anchored offshore. A few of the boats moored at the pier were occupied and Judith could feel the eyes of these people on herself and the Lavaccas. Every craft had the slightly seedy but trim look of a smuggling vessel. Her cruiser, neatly painted and spotless, was obviously out of place.

She turned for the gangway, determined to get down to the business of why she had come here. "Carlos, you will come with me. Juan will stay aboard and watch the boat."

They nodded. She watched Carlos follow, thick arms bulged at his sides, a conventional handgun on his right hip. His twin brother resumed whatever chore he'd been engaged in before she came topside.

About to step onto the pier, she noticed something off to the southwest, beyond the island chain. Hulldown on the horizon a ship's masts reflected in stark skeletal white the declining sunlight shot through a rift in a low bank of clouds. A string of barren islets, hardly more than a breakwater, lay between the Smoky Island pier and the earth's rim. Over this honeycombed barrier, with its igneous spires and spines in silhouette against the blazing cloudbanked sunset, she saw the fragmented remains of an incinerated city, a civilization whose fires, in final nova-like annihilation, had all burned out.

Transfixed by this vivid apparition, she stood as she had stood before the mirror, bewildered, unable to move. Until the rocking of the cruiser, rolling in the waves of the dinghy's wake, brought her back. She closed her eyes, opened them, saw ocean, the porous islets, the sunset. Though he was as inanimate as bronze, the silently waiting Carlos, his presence, prodded her forward. She stepped to the pier, refusing to look again to the southwest.

The path skirted the bluff and climbed upward to the waterfront street. Her canvas deck shoes stirred black dust on the evening breeze. The path was strewn with litter and, at the top, where it entered the dirt street, other odors, blanketing the sea smell, aggravated her queasiness.

Animal excrement and garbage paved the cheerless roadway. Naked children ran screeching through alleys between the taverns, brothels, and makeshift shops lining the waterfront. Outside these, men and women loitered, some drunk or drugged, a couple of the women as nude as the grimy children, sitting on the sprawled legs of men. They stared at her and Carlos, made lewd remarks and laughed. A sickly-looking mongrel barked from under a doorstoop. She was obviously not one of them. But she kept her back straight, eyes forward, the gun within easy reach.

As the light in the west faded, lights in the town's motley dwellings blinked on here and there, some faltering, as if unsure of braving the onslaught of night. Their varying strengths and yellow hues suggested the island lacked electricity as well as foliage. Like desultory campfires on a frontier where the homeless huddled, they hinted of fear, furtiveness, rather than warmth or conviviality.

The odor of frying fish, the sounds of bawdy music, drifted out on the street. In spite of the squalor, her senses were alive to every sound, sight and scent. She had been this way since leaving San Diego, maybe since leaving the hospital in Phoenix. She could not remember ever having been so keenly *alive*, but there was very little, if anything, she could remember of her life before Phoenix.

Careful to conceal, or inhibit, what she feared could become a mental and emotional whirlwind, she concentrated on affecting a calm and easy pace past *The Vipers' Den, El Volcanissimo, Rogues' Hole, The Jakes, La Suegea, La Casa de las Cabras, Happy Hannah's, Captain Blood's.*

Outside the *Last Exile* she stopped. Incongruously, a battered antiquated four-wheel-drive land vehicle sat in front beside two saddled mules that were hitched to a canting rail.

She had traveled when younger. The doctors must have told her that. She had seen much of the world, though, like everything else disclosed by the doctors for the purpose of reconstructing the personality of Judith DeFond, specific memories of those parts of the world she was supposed to have seen would not materialize out of the general blurred soup of abstraction. Maybe in time . . .

Deciding the *Last Exile* was as good a place as any to start, she drew in a breath of salty air, smelling more mule than anything else, and descended the steps to the basement-level front door. Carlos waited at the hitching rail, keeping his eight-to-ten-pace interval, as she wished.

The door banged open and two men stumbled out, hardly noticing her in the thickening darkness. They wobbled past, reeking of alcohol, stale sweat, and garlic, growling about the "wormy deal" they'd received from a "pinchgut" called Supremo.

Though the interior was not crowded, the air was murky and stagnant. It took a moment for her eyes to adjust. The murmur of conversations, the clink of glassware, only accentuated the gloom. One conversation on her left caught her ear, likely because it was the loudest.

". . . . planet's like a goddamned yoyo. Like a boat without a crew. Gone berserk, that's what. Everything flying every which way. Nothing battened down. Look at what happened to California. And tomorrow *this* glorified heap of cinders could be sinking back into the briny foam. Restitution Islands, me arse! Devil's Compensation, they should have named them." A hard slap on the table followed.

"They sink, it'll be good riddance, I'd say," said another voice, more slurred than the first.

"Bah," spat a third. "Always been like this. You humps never had the sense to notice."

"Goddamned head's full of bilge, bub. Don't you listen to them news broadcasts? Don't you pay no attention to what them scientists are saying? Look at what's happening all over. But come to think of it, it ain't happening because of the reasons them scientists give. Nossir. You want to know what's causing it all? I'll tell you! It's because they went out there and started meddling with the moon and them places! Always meddling. Always messing around—"

"Crazy things been happening since Adam found his dingus."

"I'm talking about crazy things wholesale!" Another slap of the table; bottles rattling, one falling to the floor. "Crazy things run amok! Crazy things in your stokehole and crazy things in the crow's nest with a demon down in the goddamned boilers and a maniac at the helm and a squad of blooming banshees howling alongside!"

Her eyes had become accustomed to the gloom and reluctantly she moved forward, leaving the argument behind. The room was spacious and several tables were occupied, mostly by men, but here and there a woman. All looked at her, some with curiosity, some with suspicion and open dislike. She had dressed to blend in, to appear as one who knew her way in the "underworld", and had somehow failed.

The bartender was a big man with a broad amiable face. He watched her also as she approached the bar. Behind, Carlos entered.

"What'll it be there, sweetheart?" The bartender's ample forearms rested on the bar, sleeves rolled to his biceps.

Taking a seat on the stool directly in front of him, she was aware of the few men at the bar turning to scrutinize her. One or two watched Carlos move to an old-fashioned slot machine in the corner on her right.

"I'll have a cup of coffee, please," she told the bartender.

Someone snickered. Instantly she realized that her 'please' was out of place here. She was not on her toes, not putting to use what she had learned.

With a toss of his head rearward, the bartender shouted, "Hey, Freda! Cup of *josé!*"

From the kitchen in back a woman's husky voice answered and the clatter of utensils ensued. A window situated in the wall on the right of the liquor shelves enabled a pale ocher light and smells of frying tortillas and onions to pleasantly impinge on the bartender's domain. Just as the number of taverns in the abject village seemed ridiculously disproportionate, the liquor shelves were laden with excessive amounts of liquor. But Smoky Island was a reputed terminal, a way station, and a crossroads for clandestine trading and underworld transactions of all sorts. In addition, some of the more adventurous tourists came here to get a whiff of the local color. Such a clientele required large liquor supplies, she supposed, and anyway, most, if not all, the booze was probably stolen or hauled out of the sunken liquor stores under Angeles Bay or in the San Andreas Channel.

At a metal sink behind the bar the bartender busied himself with dirty glasses but kept glancing her way. She set her handbag on the sticky bar. "Tell me," she said, loudly enough for those nearby to hear her clearly.

Every noise in the place went dead; even the kitchen stilled. The bartender turned.

She forced a smile, feeling unreality waft around her like mist, yet at the same time feeling strangely in control, removed from it all. "Do you know someone who dives in Angeles Bay?"

Something was dropped on the opposite side of the room;

a chair creaked as its owner bent to retrieve the object. The bartender straightened; a glass he'd been washing thunked on the bottom of the sink. On the window shelf behind him a steaming coffee mug was put by a shaking, flour-whitened hand from the kitchen. The bartender's heavy-browed glance raked the room briefly and returned to rest on Judith DeFond. It occurred to her that every person in the tavern could be wanted by the law for one reason or another. To them, she was a stranger, someone they could hardly trust.

"What're you talking about?" the bartender said in a low voice, wiping his soapy hands on his apron. "That entire area's under the control of the California Coastal Authority and the San Andreas Sea Patrol. They got orders to sink on sight any unauthorized boat caught in those waters. They'll do it too." His tone was fatherly, genuinely concerned. "Nobody goes in there except damfool scavengers who don't care if they're breathing come sunrise or not. They say the place still has hell's own portion of flaking fallout in the air and water both, and it's still subject to the shivers and shakes, if you know what I mean. And from what I hear," he bent closer, "the loot's getting damned thin to boot. Now you tell me something. Why do *you* want to go in there?"

"I didn't say I did. In any case, that's my business." The reply was spontaneous, without thought, as if a part of her she was not at all familiar with yet had spoken.

"Umph." He straightened up. "So it is. And so you're welcome to it, sweetie."

A man sitting several stools down the bar toward Carlos began muttering words she could not make out.

"Speak of hell's works," said the bartender as he looked over her head, "there's your man, I guess. If man he is. He knows the Zone. And every other pit that ain't fit for a human being to live in. But he's more devil than man, if you want my opinion."

She turned. Entering was a heavy-set male in a dark diving vest and swimming trunks. The inlaid jewelry of a garish tooled belt glittered in the momentary light thrown through the door by a passing vehicle outside. On the left side of the belt was a knife, on the right another sidearm that was probably a gun. He had dark, close-cut hair and long sideburns, which made his head look as if clenched in a close-fitting helmet. His face was angular, and his eyes snapped over the room like a predator's on a scent. All this she saw while the door was opened to allow three other men to come in behind him. The instant his eyes found hers the scant lips spread in a supercilious grin and the door closed, returning his face to darkness.

He came forward toward the bar, followed by the other three. The people at the tables quailed visibly as the armed quartet passed. The lull in the tavern's noise deepened.

"Who is he?" she asked, confused by the mixed emotions she felt.

"Goes by the name of Vincent Polliard," said the bartender softly. "As to who or what he is, well—claims to be a salvage diver and smuggler, but it's known he's a fed."

She saw Carlos tense at the game machines. As the four drew near, the men sitting at the bar picked up their drinks and moved off, all but the muttering drunk six stools down who, scowling at the mirror behind the bar, snorted into his grog with undisguised disgust.

The one in the vest came up and stood a little to her left. "A round of beers, Ricardo." He had a faint accent she could not remember ever having heard before.

Judith saw now that the vest was all he wore over his hairless, well-developed torso. The vest was unusually thick, probably composed of some kind of shielding material. He remained standing, one hand resting easily on the bar, his eyes wandering unceremoniously over her face, down her body. They were eyes that appeared accustomed to places of little light.

"You are the young woman who has been searching for a guide and diver into Angeles Bay." The grin spread slightly, the shape of a cutlass. "You look even better than the descriptions I've heard."

"And who are you?" She kept her face expressionless.

"Vincent Polliard at your service." He made a mock bow. "If the pay is right."

"You know the bay well?"

"Like the—well like the body of my last mistress, *mademoiselle*. A body that relinquished its every treasure to me."

The drunk six stools down cursed. No one paid any attention to him.

"Are you French?" she said, making what she supposed could be called "conversation".

"Only in the presence of a beautiful woman. No, I am from Martinique." He raised a finger to stroke his nose, whose septum, she noticed, was crooked. "Where I got my education," he said.

The muttering drunk had grown louder, banging his glass on the bar and tottering on the stool. All at once he turned. "Aye!" he yelled. "You know the Big Sink so well—tell us, *Monsieur* Polliard. What caused her, eh? What caused the big quakeroo!"

Polliard hardly gave the drunk a glance but his eyes swept around the room for a moment, as if aware for the first time he had an audience of more than one. He returned his attention to Judith DeFond.

"Why, it was God, of course," he said in answer to the drunk's question but speaking directly to her. "God is responsible. God was fed up with all the lechery and greed and perversion that went on there and he let them have it. Like he did with Sodom and Gomorrah. Too bad. But who can question God?"

No one answered. Judith DeFond waited, sensing an underlying bitterness in what the man said, in spite of the detached and derisive way in which the words were delivered. She was sure he had not finished.

He leaned on the bar, his face closer to hers, and theatrically lowered his voice. "It is fascinating to speculate on what it must have been like, *mademoiselle*. Don't you think? To imagine the sedimentary upper crust crumbling like moldy bread, the rich *cochons* of Beverly Hills and Bel Air falling under the elegant debris of their lavish mansions, or being swept away like twigs by the incoming tidal waves. Picture it, *mademoiselle*. From the southern end of San Francisco Bay across the Santa Clara Valley and the western edge of the San Joaquin, all the way down to the Sea of Cortez, runs a channel of inland sea with an average width of ten kilometers and an average depth of five hundred meters. From the San Rafael Mountains, north of the former Los Angeles Basin, to the now flooded Imperial Valley in the south, and from the San Gabriel and San Bernardino ranges westward, much of the land sank to depths of from seventy-five to three hundred meters and, in places along the main channel where the fault lay, and in the San Gabriels, to one thousand meters. Think of what must lie under the water in those places. Though the exact number will never be known, it was estimated that more than twenty million people died. Think of it, *mademoiselle*. That is a number so large that it has no meaning, just as the superquake itself defies all explanation." He straightened, grinning. "Except that one of divine intervention, of course."

The room was dead quiet. She could hear her heart, the blood pulsing in her veins. The man mystified her. She imagined that what had just been recited was a kind of religious incantation, one in which not the god of such destruction was worshiped or summoned but the simple power to destroy.

On the bar in front of Polliard, the bartender had set four mugs of beer before the unsettling speech began. Now the men each quickly grabbed a mug, as if they had been forbidden to move while it was delivered, as if even they were glad of its end. Their leader lowered himself on the stool to her left, but the others kept standing.

"I need one man," she said carefully.

"These men go where I go." He lifted his mug, swilled and licked his lips. "I have a good boat, an up-to-date U.S. Navy submersible recently 'acquired', and a crew who know the business almost as well as I do."

"What is your business?"

"I save things from oblivion, *mademoiselle*. I salvage precious things from ruins." The coal-black eyes glittered with some private irony. "And you? What is your business in the sunken basin of the dead City of Angels?"

She ignored the question and said, "Your price?" confident she could predict the answer. Her days in the Restitutions had to account for such prescience.

"That depends on where you want to go and what you want to do when you get there." His scrutiny dropped to the opening in the windbreaker. "But whatever the job, the price will include you as a, shall we say, bunkmate."

Aware of her body, its sexual strengths and its willingness to give itself gladly, if necessary, to the man she sought, she felt it instinctively recoil from this one. "Your bunkmate only?" she said. "Or would you share me with your crew?"

He laughed and raised the mug again, draining it. At his back his men nervously parroted the laughter, as though the mere suggestion of such an idea was preposterous and made them uneasy.

Evidently Polliard's theory of the quake's cause had not satisfied the lone drunk; he was beating his glass again on the bar and yelling. The first words were not comprehensible, but at last he burst forth with two that were clearly understood. "Jack Kelso!" And then: "Jack Kelso's the gob you want!" He swayed on the brink of falling, face puffed with petulance and drink, a knobby finger pointing at Polliard. "Not this guano-brained bastard!"

In an instant two of Polliard's men yanked the fellow from the stool, stuffed his coattail into his mouth to prevent him saying anything else, and dragged him to the door. At the doorway he got his mouth free briefly and bawled, "Find Jack Kelso!"

His captors hurled him out the door and followed, arms raised to flail. Cries of pain, cursing and scuffling noises, came through the quickly closed door.

Judith DeFond listened to these sounds for a moment, sorry for the drunk. "Why does that man hate you?" she said to Polliard.

The "salvage diver" shrugged. "Maybe I broke his daughter's heart. Or her head." His laugh was now mirthless.

When another peal came from outside, she looked at Carlos and was tempted to do something to save the drunk. But what? Two against four? Maybe Carlos was capable, but she did not want to risk another distraction or entanglement. Or did she? An impulse to act had her gripping the edge of the bar. "And who is Jack Kelso?" she blurted, holding back the confusion, ignoring the noises outside and the noises within.

Polliard's jaw had hardened and the lines around his mouth were compressed. The look in his eyes told her she had, with her question, opened the lid to an emotional inferno. He kept the fire contained, however, snapping only in the eyes. "Among other things, he's the doomed poltroon who murdered three of my men and destroyed one of my submersibles a few days ago. Thinking I was aboard, I am sure." The grin returned to the lips but did not reach the eyes. "But he's no one who concerns you, *mademoiselle*. Now," all at once impatient, he arose, "let's go out to my yacht and discuss the details of our business arrangement."

"No, thanks." She looked at the bartender and said, "My coffee has probably become cold sitting over there. Would you have the cook pour a fresh cup and bring it here, please?"

The bartender nodded and turned from the bar.

"What?" said Polliard.

"I said, no, thanks. I'll look around some more. I don't think you and I would be able to come to any sort of arrangement agreeable to us both." She was suddenly exceptionally calm under the circumstances, as if her mood had been pre-empted by an internal overseer who would not tolerate fear.

He bent toward her, shoving forward the face of a man who has refused to believe what he has just heard. "You're turning me down?"

About to answer, she saw his hand fly up, but wasn't quick enough to dodge it. The blow caught her across the side of her head, momentarily dazing her and making her ears ring. With the same hand, he grasped her by the hair and jerked her head back, exposing her throat. The fingers of his other hand came up and stroked the arteries and veins in her neck with feigned gentleness.

"You fool with me, bitch, and I'll throw you to the fish."

When he grabbed her hair, she had flung her left arm over the bartop to steady herself on the stool. Now she felt something being placed beside her left hand and realized the bartender had just put the coffee there. The cup was scalding hot.

"You'll get up and come with me on your own power, or I will carry you out by the hair."

Her fingers found the handle of the cup. In the same second, she dashed the steaming liquid into his face and kicked one perfectly aimed foot into his tightly compact crotch.

He crashed backward into chairs, doubling up, hands darting from his eyes to his sex and back to eyes again, as if they could not decide which was more vulnerable and which held the greatest pain.

Already on his knees, his companion fell forward against the bar, hit in the head by a shot from Carlos's silenced pistol.

"Through the back," the bartender whispered. "Quick! Those other two are out front. Through the back!"

She did not argue. She jumped over the bar and rushed through the door he held open, Carlos close on her heels. Her last impression of the *Last Exile* was a startled Freda up to her elbows in cornmeal and her expression one of open-mouthed shock.

"*Madre de dios!*" the woman cried with heavy German intonations. "Run like crazy. Run like the wind!"

She tried. And as she ran, out the backdoor of the kitchen, through garbage, a shrieking cat whose tail she mashed, a dark alley, a back street, a strange exhilaration gave her added speed. Laughter gushed up from her chest, like the water of a spring set free by a thaw, laughter she could not remember having known before. The violence of what she had done, the effectiveness with which she had done it, the outrage that had made her act, clashed and clattered about in her mind like the several trash cans she crashed through when she turned up another alley. While, weighing what had happened, her laughter could have been simple borderline hysteria, she knew it was not. And Carlos, beside her now, echoed in confirmation the noise of this inexplicable and pointless joy.

4. THE STRATEGIST

The warships lay off one of the iceworlds of the Mrirdugans. Numbering in the hundreds, they filled this pocket of the interstellar frontier like a galaxy of dark stars, multifaceted sensors sweeping the heavens for any threat of discovery or attack from an imperial outguard patrol.

In the council hall of the Prithipean command ship the leaders of the Alliance sat, lay, or stood, depending on the demands of their anatomies, in the circular tiers ringing the rotating central floor. At an oval table in the middle of this floor Abrea Acexea, Prithipean leader and supreme commander, acknowledged the hardships and risks incurred by their having come this far. He outlined, in soldier's terms, what lay ahead. Members of his audience disposed to express themselves vocally murmured, muttered, cursed. A few beat their seats, or their bodies, but the noise was generally subdued. The Prithipean giant discouraged undisciplined excess by his mere presence.

"The one who is about to speak," Acexea said, "has been the primary force behind our coming together in unity." For those who did not have auditory translators, his words flashed, changed into the necessary languages, on infoscreens placed in the tiers. "Since early years she has devoted her life to what is about to unfold. Her genius is behind our plan."

Suddenly, as was characteristic with his race, Acexea sat. The ensuing hush was dramatic.

On his right sat the Onnahlaetian woman and boy. The woman stood. She looked up, saw a confusing array of costumes and demeanors climbing, row upon row, toward the high ceiling of the hall. The rough Prithipean garment pressed against her tall, thin frame like a cloak of metal. But she could not appear before soldiers, Acexea had said, as she might on her native world where, before the Yaghattarin came, nudity had been the norm.

"Fellow allies, war is not my province." Cinara Tlii's voice seemed lost in the spaceship's immense chamber. She raised the volume of the tiny amplifier at her throat. "War is alien to me, alien to my people. Until the Deathlords came, tyranny, malevolence itself, had no place in our lifeview. That is why Onnahlaeti and its few dependent worlds fell easily so many turns ago. But Onnahlaeti has survived with much of its original integrity and uniqueness intact. And it has managed to save some of its males, so valued by the despots. This boy sitting beside me here is living proof of the cunning, the ability to elude them, for which we have become known."

Falur, the boy, sat with hands folded on the table, his steady gaze on those Tlii addressed.

"You understand war; we understand—we have come to be masters of—evasion and circumvention." She paused, aware of Falur's empathy. Uncommonly inquisitive and adventurous for an Onnahlaetian male, he had wanted to come, and the old ones had given their consent. They were right. He was as safe, perhaps safer, here with her, with the Alliance, than he had been in the mountain refuge on Onnahlaeti Ke, where the danger of discovery by the Surveillance was an everyday likelihood. And Falur would be helpful when the time came for the thoughtprobe.

"You understand war," she continued, bringing her complete attention again to bear on her audience. "But of a certain kind. Naravamintara and the subsurface stronghold of Nammava Trah II can only be taken initially by cunning rather than force, by innovative and unconventional means."

She moved away from the table, around the Prithipean commander and his lieutenants who, even sitting, dwarfed her. "You have all been given layouts of the defensive networks of Naravamintara and its underground fortress. You each have a summary of the penetration and attack plan."

Before her, between the table and the first tier of seats, appeared a three-dimensional image of the imperial planet, suspended above the floor. Its diameter equaled Acexea's height and the equator lay several hands above Tlii's head. A barely visible gridwork of lines circumscribed the hologram.

"As all of you know, the hub world of the oppressors is surrounded by what we have thought to be an inpenetrable web of annihilation fields capable of disintegrating anything alien or unauthorized trying to enter its atmosphere. But with the development of the forceshield by our comrades of Selinmea, the problem of those deathfields should be eliminated. Also, the highly effective antidetection devices recently created and tested by the Klaymrs should enable us to enter Naravamintara's atmosphere unnoticed by their powerful sensors."

She raised a hand, a signal to Acexea. A small dais lifted from the main platform, carrying her upward to a point where she could stand even with the hologram's northern hemisphere. An area several degrees north of the Naravamintaran equator glowed.

"The First Force of the salient will enter at the location that is illuminated. It will land in the great valley between these mountain ranges—called the Ancient Rift Valley by the Yaghattarin—that lies on an east-west axis at the far northern edge of the Desert of Nammava Trah."

At the table, Acexea fingered a control. The image of the planet slowly began to turn, like the floor above which it seemed to float. Another spot glowed immediately south of the first.

"The Second Force will land here, south of the mountain chain and near the equator. The Third and Fourth will fall on opposite sides of the desert. The Fifth will be deployed in smaller units over the planet in order to take the lesser cities, spacebases, and other installations. Nammava Trah II is our main objective and it will be surrounded. It is the empire's intelligence and communications center, as well as the home of those highest in the imperial hierarchy. When it falls, all of Naravamintara—the planet and the empire—will follow."

They stared down from the tiers at the hologram. They were quiet, listening now, or reading the infoscreens, taking in all she said. A number of them, she knew, did not like being led or instructed in any way by a thin Onnahlaetian female, a "whiff of witch's dust" as a Xlimoyin might say.

Resolutely she went on. "The Sixth and Seventh Forces will establish a protective perimeter offplanet, to deter any incoming retaliation from the outworlds. But I am getting ahead of my purpose."

She wanted to turn, to read in Acexea's rough face that she was doing well. This, however, would be a sign of uncertainty on her part, of weakness (she had learned such things in her furtive journeys through the empire, trying to enlist belligerents in a cause most thought futile) and, in any case, the face of a Prithipean was never readable. So she kept her eyes forward, upward, on the image and her audience. As yet she felt no particular hostility or disapproval from them, but many minds were, by their very nature, barred from hers.

"As soon as all forces are consolidated in the designated positions, as soon as all communications links have been established and it is confirmed that all have slipped in undetected, we will begin the second phase of the penetration."

The part to come would be the hardest to explain and make credible to many, especially those most warlike and physical in viewpoint.

The image of Naravamintara vanished. She confronted them from the dais, which remained raised. "My friends, we of Onnahlaeti have always believed that our ancestors enjoyed a synthesis of mind, body, and spirit that we have in some measure lost."

Murmurs arose. She waited, closing her eyes and seeking the inner meditative calm that was every Onnahlaetian's source of strength. She had introduced what most here would regard as typical Onnahlaetian arrogance and narcissism. Her people had always thought themselves blessed. Before the seizeships came, they had not known or cared to know that other worlds, and other intelligences, existed. In their ignorance of evil, Onnahlaetians had been easy prey. Blessed as they were, or had been, however, the Cosmic Benevolence they believed reigned over life did not intervene and restore their former bliss. When the existence of evil, manifested by the Deathlords, had finally been recognized, it was too late to escape it. Too late until Cinara Tlii had taken it upon herself to go against the Onnahlaetian lifeway and combat that evil—a blasphemous act that, in the Onnahlaetian view, despite the long oppression by the despots, tilted her precipitously toward becoming one with that very evil she sought to destroy.

The noises had faded. She pushed on. "We of Onnahlaeti cherish and enjoy, as best we can under Naravamintaran rule, a lifeway of intuitive knowledge and harmony, of unity and kinship, with all things on our mother planet and its sister worlds. Unlike the Yaghattarin machinarchs who remain in thrall to their own creations, we of Onnahlaeti have a strong antipathy for artificial contrivances, an antipathy that, as some of you know, has made us narrow in our thinking, unable at times to understand or sympathize with those peoples, on much harsher worlds than ours, who have had to invent elaborate ways and means to cope with their environments and survive."

There were sounds of approval for her present offering of sympathy. "But the point I wish to stress is the fundamental divergence in our lifeview and that of the Yaghattarin. Though it is said we derive from the same ancient race, we have evolved along profoundly opposite paths. The Deathlords assume they have attained ultimate ontological knowledge. They see themselves as evolution's apex, while in fact they are an evolutionary dead end." She was again on uncertain ground, unsure that, even if the translators effectively conveyed her meaning, the majority of her audience would grasp such concepts.

"They exemplify what I have come to be aware is a common malady in many aspects of existence, that of one aberrant organism wanting to assimilate all other organisms. The Yaghattarin justify this rapacity in the name of a grotesque metaphysics which, in turn, is a mask for a very old vengeance mania. As all of you know, their craze to find and destroy their ancient enemies has remained frustrated."

She noticed movement here and there in the tiers, noises of impatience. They had little use for oratory, less for an Onnahlaetian's long-winded review of a history with which they were all too familiar.

"My words have purpose," she said. "Bear with me. For centuries the Yaghattarin Lords of Death have prized Onnahlaetian males for the latter's intelligence and belief in immanent benevolence, for their eagerness to serve a higher reality than themselves. Our men are easily conscripted, indoctrinated into service for Naravamintara's perverted ideals." Again she felt Falur's gaze, and his compassion. He was the only sentient alive, other than herself, who knew of her special pain related to the loss of Onnahlaetian males.

"Yet, at the same time they covet the Onnahlaetian male, they revile all that Onnahlaeti holds dear." Especially the Onnahlaetian female, she thought. And the females of all races for that matter, or any idea of a gender capable of naturally bearing and bringing forth life. Indeed, though the Yaghattarin possessed the power, through their relentless engineerings, to transform an Onnahlaetian woman into a man, their hatred of the procreative sex was such that they would not touch one of its number for any reason. Nor would cloning suffice. In their thinking, they surmised that if they were to have genuine Onnahlaetian male slaves, males born free of Yaghattarin meddling, Onnahlaetian women had to live in order to supply them.

Tlii realized she had again strayed, said more than she intended on this topic, had let her emotions and native inclination for discourse come to the fore.

"If I may return to that original synthesis of mind, body and spirit of which I earlier spoke," She closed her eyes for a moment, seeking respite from the strain, remembering gentle hills, sunlit meadows, a world where the spirit was forever awake. . . .

A loud voice from the table filled the hall. It was Acexea, ordering silence in the tiers. In the immediate quiet Cinara Tlii heard only her own breathing. She braced herself and, determined, resumed.

"We of the Onnahlaetian race have for a long time been able to synthesize this presently fragmented trinity and communicate this synthesis through the use of mental energy by means of what I will have to call 'thought language,' through the true communion of our entire being. We lived, before the seizeships came, as one people, a people with highly developed mental powers in tune with each other and our worlds. Some of us have been captured and taken from Onnahlaetian worlds by the Deathlords, and we have reason to believe many of these function in high places as those favored, or used for amusement, by the machinarchs. It is my belief that many are in Nammava Trah II. It is my hope that I will be able to reach them and persuade them to join us by helping to revive that ability. I have spent the last four Onnahlaetian turns studying with some of the oldest of our race in a mountain sanctuary on Onnahlaeti Ke so that I may accomplish this." She fell silent and, having at last said what she most feared would be derided as sorcery, or nonsense, waited expectantly for the uproar.

It did not come. The silence grew and in it her anxiety also increased. She had spoken rapidly at the last. The translators may not have followed—

Tlii heard noises which sounded more like argument and debate than incredulity or outrage. This lasted for only a few beats of her heart. She raised her head, still refusing to look at Acexea.

"We have these things in our favor," she said, moving forward in the wake of the surprisingly subdued reaction, "our devices, which will neutralize their detection and destruction network, the telepathic means of reaching those within the citadel itself we believe are potential allies, and the monumental arrogance and complacency of those we seek to ruin. Like all despots, the Yaghattarin of Naravamintara have come to believe their own twisted logic, their lies and myths, that they are gods and indestructible. Afraid of that which refuses to fit into their sterile philosophy, they are afraid of Being itself, oblivious of Being's subtle strengths and needs. That is their blindness, their place of sleep. We will send their 'Eternal City' to sleep eternally."

A growl burst from one of the helmeted Xlimoyin. A high wail answered from a C'rimaen. These were, Tlii assumed, warcries. Soon the hall was filled with them. A shudder ran through her, like a chill caused by an alien wind. Her skin, the dark and hairless skin of the purest of her race, tingled with a strange excitement.

She had not broached the third phase of the plan. They would know what it was from the summaries they'd been given, but there were points she wanted to clarify.

The din grew, almost pushing her off the dais with its power. At last she turned.

Prithipeans did not smile; the coarse flesh of their faces forbade expression of any kind. But the yellow eyes below the ridge of bone crowning Acexea's head radiated satisfaction and, offering a sign of allegiance and respect, he lowered that massive head toward her. This caused a renewed wave of cries around the room that became deafening.

Cinara Tlii looked at the boy, Falur. His large eyes were warm and filled with questions, as if he saw in her one he had not known before. But she felt no condemnation. And in his face she saw another's as dark as her own, as sapient and beautiful as Falur's.

What would it be like now, that face? What would its mind, its heart, be like? Would that one know her? Would she know him, now that the Deathlords had had him for so long to do with as they pleased in order to make him over for their "divine" ends?

5. THE SUPPLIANT

One of his favorite hideouts was an old mountain cabin, still standing, more or less, on the eastern slope of Islip Island. From this solitary retreat he had a good view of the San Gabriel Channel. The main arm of water extending north into the San Gabriels from Angeles Bay, the channel lay over what had been San Gabriel Canyon, was one of the less difficult routes through the San Gabriel Island group and the main northern route for the San Andreas Sea Patrol because of its depth and relative lack of debris.

Kelso had found Islip by accident several years back. He and Dimitri had successfully evaded a patrol boat after being flushed out of the San Bernardino ruins which lay directly in the middle of the San Andreas Channel. They had been deep, too deep for the patrol boat to do them much harm. They'd headed west, into the San Gabriels, meandering through the hundreds of small islands in an effort to confuse the SASP sonar. It hadn't been easy in the long submarine, and more than once they'd become lost in the maze of underwater canyons, but they finally shook the patrol boat somewhere near the Telegraph Peak area. Continuing northwest, having to surface at times, when a canyon terminated in an island's slope, dive again when they regained deep water, they'd come upon Islip and decided it was a good place to hole up. Kelso had loved the place, but the crazy Greek sponge diver could not stand land for more than a day, especially if it offered no significant prizes in the way of fancy trinkets, jewels, or gold.

Like Islip, the adjacent islands, long and narrow remnants of crests and ridgelines, were deserted now, except for an occasional band of scavengers that might come in from what was now the mainland coast north of the San Gabriels and the San Andreas Channel; but even these "Mojave Magpies" were rare these days, and Kelso would easily know their whereabouts if they did materialize, because they made enough noise to wake the dead. Not that he had anything particularly to fear from them; he simply did not enjoy the proximity of his own species that much. He preferred Islip's indigenous coyotes and crows.

The solar-powered radio he'd recovered from a half-collapsed building in the old winter sports area of what had been Crystal Lake Park could pick up stations around the world. Provided its cells were regularly replenished with sunlight, it could supply him with music around the clock. But at times it aroused his wrath by broadcasting the news. On this afternoon he was too lazy to move out of the hammock to change stations or turn it off. A mistake. The news reintroduced the world and the world brought back both history and present reality.

After the commentator had run through the usual dreary list of atrocities committed in the Middle East, the states of the famines in India and Africa, riots in Europe and the Americas, the conflict along the Sino-Soviet border, crises caused by pollution, energy depletion, economic instability, crime, and the general unmitigated rot in the moral and social fabric of the "advanced" peoples of Mother Earth, she finally gave the space news. The colonies between the earth and the moon were growing, thriving, the moon was yielding its mineral wealth and the first exploratory outposts on Mars were beginning to overcome some of their initial setbacks. The contrast of peace, earnest labor, cooperation, and a sensible respect for nature *out there* and the chaos and calamity between nations and inside nations *down here* was grotesque. And probably illusory, if not downright false. Both the government and the media were currently encouraging the space program.

"Our only hope," Kelso said aloud from the sun-drenched hammock strung between two pines outside the cabin. There was little sarcasm in his voice. Lisa's words. *Only by colonizing and industrializing space will we ever solve Earth's problems.* Though he'd often argued with the romantic "New

Frontier" idea, considered it naive and saw with his jaundiced squint the human diseases of power and greed being implacably spread to the stars (he had only to point out what men had done to Antarctica, Ellesmere Island, and everywhere else they put their bloody, goddamned feet), he'd loved her optimism in spite of himself, loved her faith in life's perennial promise. A promise he'd once believed in also, so long ago it seemed another incarnation.

Lisa. A physicist. A clean-energy advocate as well as a fighter for the exploration and colonization of space. An indefatigable enemy of the fossil fuel and fission power interests. A fighter and a visionary.

The old industrialized civilizations of Earth are in decay, stagnant, rootbound, choking to death and starving on a planet of over seven billion. We need radical changes, radical new outlooks, visions, ideas. We need new worlds where we can build new societies, new civilizations, a new race.

He would never forget the sight of the earth from Island One, where he and Lisa had gone on a work-study program during the early years of their marriage. He knew then what she meant by a radical new outlook. Looking out of the habitat at the planet on which he was born, seeing it suspended like a jewel in an infinity of nothingness that was sprayed with countless and nameless stars, he'd felt strange hands plucking at his heartstrings, all right. He'd wanted to reach out, grab that beautiful and pitifully frail-looking globe in his hands, hug it in his arms, babble and weep over it like a mother with a babe—or a grown man with a terminally ill mother.

Lisa.

Along with a number of others, she'd helped yank the flagging space works out of the hands of the bumbling government bureaucrats and put them into those of private maverick groups headed by young people with the vision and vigor she sought, in her lectures, in her speeches, on her recruiting campaigns. Her courage and enthusiasm inspired them. She had even inspired Jack Kelso. Now, though he still believed she had, in essence, fought for a worthy cause—and, according to the news, time was vindicating her beyond her dreams—he no longer felt inspired. Inspiration, among other things, died when she died. And the giant corporations, the cartels and conglomerates that in reality ruled the roost, the collective monstrosities whose only reasons for being were profit, power, growth, control, were doing their dead level best to take over the space colonies as well as everything else. But the media, being owned by corporations, would not report that.

And maybe, Kelso, it isn't even so. Maybe you're the one who's full of rot, and the world, with its little islands out there in space, is coming along just fine.

Our only hope.

He got up, stalked into the cabin, picked up the radio and flung it through the glassless front window. Rummaging in his confiscated stores, he found a bottle of scotch and returned outside to the hammock.

Something skittered across the ground less than a meter away. A rat maybe. Maybe a chipmunk. Rats had multiplied to hideous numbers during the first years after the quake but, since there were no longer any kill-crazy hunters in these parts, were currently being diminished by the growing coyote population. Coyotes were fine; rats, even to Jack Kelso, were another matter.

A nice little post-catastrophe ecosystem was beginning to flourish on these islands that had been the high ground of the San Gabriel Mountains, with Mad Jack Kelso as one of the periodic denizens. Like the coyotes, a survivor.

Done with hopes, though, he told himself self-pityingly. And, as he thought this, he realized he was desecrating Lisa's memory, going against all she'd stood for.

"No hope for you anyway, Kelso." Cursing with aimless fervor, he uncapped the bottle and drank. Then, like an octopus enveloped in its own ink cloud, he lay in the hammock, swathed in an atmosphere of remorse. He dozed.

The sun was a disc of amber beyond the westernmost islands when he awoke. The bottle lay on its side next to his naked belly, half its contents having spilled through the hammock mesh to the ground. Rustling noises inside the cabin came to his ears. He knew none of these things—noisy rodents, lowering sun, spilled whiskey—had awakened him. Like his adopted land totem, the coyote, he could sense a more ominous occurrence in the air. He lay still and listened.

At first he thought the faint purring noise was that of a patrol boat coming up the channel, something that in itself would have been out of the ordinary these days. But before he gathered up his gear and made a run for the *Tiburón* he listened again. It didn't really sound like a patrol boat, didn't sound as if it had that big an engine.

He swung his feet down, pulled the tattered brim of the straw hat up, turning his back on the fading sunlight. Below, the little horseshoe-shaped inlet, horned at each end by the terminus of a spur off Islip's main ridgeline, was already in shadow. At the shadow's southern fringe, the approaching craft was crossing from sunlight into shade, coming up the San Gabriel Channel.

After jerking on his boots and lacing them up, he entered the cabin. Birds and rodents squealed and scattered. In the pile of odds and ends on the table, he found his binoculars and, standing in the doorway with them, he saw that it was a private craft without flag or insignia, a small cabin cruiser with what looked like a woman standing on the little deck crowning the cabin. She, too, held a pair of binoculars to her eyes, which were aimed in his direction. The boat was heading straight for Kelso's private cove.

He scratched his grizzled chin and looked from the oncoming boat to the *Tiburón* lying offshore about seventy-five meters below and southwest of the hillside where the cabin sat. He still had time to make a run for it. The inlet was deep enough for a shallow dive; he could be under and gone before the cruiser advanced very far into its mouth. But he didn't feel like running today if he could help it. Considering the heat and his banging head, he hardly felt like standing.

Somehow he didn't sense trouble coming, though. Could be his senses were worse than pickled with alcohol, but to hell with it, he was curious. Unmarked civilian craft had not been legally allowed in these waters since the Navy and the Coastal Authority took charge of almost everything from Frisco to the Baja. Illegal entries were still made, but they were rare, especially from Angeles Bay and in that kind of boat in broad daylight. Well, almost broad daylight. Maybe she had a special permit; maybe she was one of those few scientists the Authority let roam around the Zone without escort or supervision. Maybe he was hallucinating.

On the rocky ground in front of the cabin he proceeded to relieve his aching bladder—an act that in Kelso's mind naturally followed any thought of governmental authority. By the time he'd finished, the cruiser had entered the cove. Beyond Twin Peaks Island to the west, beyond the other islands and the half-submerged San Fernando Valley to the west of them, the solar fireball was sinking slowly into the darkening Pacific.

When he heard the cruiser's motor cut back, Kelso turned and went into the cabin for the rifle, revolver, and ammo pouch. Having availed himself of these necessary items, he started down the slope, moving over the uneven ground and through the sparse timber with practiced, long-legged strides that would put him at the bottom in plenty of time.

The *Tiburón* lay half hidden between two rocky promontories that jutted out from the shoreline. If the cruiser had any designs on his boat, it would have to alter its present course to reach the anchorage. He doubted this would happen—the cruiser seemed to know exactly where he was, and intended coming straight in to meet him—but, in case it did, he could put several high-explosive rounds from the miniature cannon he carried into the cruiser before it would come close enough to do any damage to the sub.

At the water's edge he came to a halt and sat on a corner of an upthrust slab of concrete, part of an old foundation of some sort, probably for a cabin that had fallen downslope and was now under water.

He watched the mysterious boat come in. Its prow bore the name *El Vínculo*. Having been married to a Spanish-American, he should have known its meaning, but his Spanish, like everything else, had deteriorated. He saw that, yes indeed, the person on the upper deck was a woman. She was now moving down the ladder to the cabin. A male stood inside at the wheel and a second male figure came around from the stern to stand at the forward gunwale with the mooring line in his hand. The woman came out of the cabin and stood beside this man.

She was tall, wore green shorts and white canvas shoes, a windbreaker open at the front, and a white halter top underneath. The thickening shadows concealed her eyes. Her hair was long and black, worn loose and leaping in the breeze. She stood with her hands on her hips, legs spread slightly to steady herself against the faint rocking of the boat. He saw no weapon on either her or her hefty-looking companion.

She could be lost, he thought. She could be a geologist just poking around, or the daughter of somebody high up in the SASP or the Coastal Authority, with a bizarre love for exploring the sites of past disasters.

West of Islip a few kilometers was the Waterman-Twin

Peaks-Devil's Canyon region where the Devil's Canyon Project had been concentrated. People from Universal Resources or the government still went in there and the place was probably the most tightly guarded of any in the Zone. In the early days after the quake, Kelso had sneaked in a couple of times but had found the security so thick he could uncover nothing on his own. Nor had later entries into the area gleaned him much: evidence of a number of underground nuke demolitions could be found as far south as the old bed of the West Fork of the San Gabriel River, now submerged, but such evidence merely confirmed what had long been public knowledge.

The reason the government and URI gave for closing off the San Gabriel Wilderness to the public was that oil-rich rock found under the San Gabriels had to be freed. After the widespread energy panics of the last decades, the nuclear probes beneath the continental shelf off the California coast, the idea of closing off a wilderness area for the purpose of employing nuclear detonations to free "oil-rich rock" was as acceptable to people as anything else; no matter that the allegedly precious rock lay in a seismically unstable region. Few cared what went on, so long as their bellies were full, their homes comfortable and their pursuit of happiness well greased. Those who did care were ignored or silenced.

With these thoughts burning away the alcoholic residue, Kelso sat waiting, one hand holding the rifle upright like a standard so they could see it. The quality of the light reminded him of times he'd sat on other broken shorelines looking dumbfounded at the tops of buildings sticking above the water. When the tide went out, the ruins in the higher sections of Los Angeles and its suburbs would be left partly exposed. At sunset they would often be tinted a grisly red. He remembered how, in the early days after the quake, he would find himself sitting on the edge of such a place, watching the sun go down on those mangled fragments of a shattered sunken city, trying to understand, trying to exhume some meaning from what he saw. Having once been a scientist, he'd tried to figure out the geophysical puzzles, why the San Gabriel Mountains and Pasadena sank so much deeper than the L. A. Basin, why some areas fell quickly and others sank over a period of many months, what possibly could have caused such a disaster in the first place. The nuke detonations in the San Gabriels? Accumulated tension along the San Andreas Fault? Sabotage? All of these combined?

None of these? Futile. No answers. Only suspicions that, given the extent and magnitude of the quake, if quake it could be called, boggled the mind and ultimately made little sense.

The cruiser's engine stopped. It drifted in slowly, as if she wanted time to study him. Though her face stayed in shadow, he felt her eyes trying to penetrate him like two psychic microscopes. Kelso again had the feeling, eerie this time, that she fit none of those roles he'd tried to put her in, but instead had come here specifically to find *him*. And underlying this odd notion was a mood of passage, of a phase in his life coming to an end.

What the hell was the matter with him? Why all the cerebration, which would only give him a headache? Why was that woman looking at him like that?

Unexpectedly she turned away, said something to the man, and took the line. As though they knew exactly where the water became too shallow for the cruiser's draft (there were charts of the area, of course), the man dropped a lightweight anchor five meters from shore. She threw the line, neatly lassoing a crooked length of pipe sticking out of the jagged outcrop on Kelso's left.

"Jack Kelso?" Her voice carried, distinct and vibrant, across the water, not raised above normal tone. It seemed a part of the gathering twilight.

"What's left," he said, watching the boat swing obligingly around to float parallel with the shore as if to show him that only the three people were aboard.

"May I come ashore?" she said.

"Who are you, and what the hell do you want?"

She seemed to consider his question—or her answer. "I want to come ashore." The same clear voice. "To speak with you."

"About what?"

This time her tone dropped, suggesting a weakening of patience. "May I come ashore, Mister Kelso? What I have to discuss is very important to me, and can be very profitable for you."

He thought about it. "All right," he said. "Just you. Your two friends can stay where they are."

She nodded, removed the windbreaker, and went to the starboard ladder hung over the side. Kelso watched her legs, her hips, move as she descended. It had been a while since he'd seen a woman of any kind, a longer time still since he'd seen a woman with this one's attributes. He was, he had to admit, mystified. What in blazes did she want? But not for a second did he abandon the suspicion she and her brace of goons might be up to having his head. There was a price on it, unhinged as it was, and though he no longer knew the precise amount, he was sure the sum was sizeable.

"You'd better be careful," he said as she lowered those legs into the dark water. "All kinds of crap in there that can cut up your feet." He made no move to help, however.

The water rose to her neck and she began dog-paddling in. Soon her feet found bottom, and she held onto the mooring line to aid her footing. Though the waters around the San Gabriel Islands were relatively clean, he was nevertheless a bit surprised that she had gone in with such nonchalance. Maybe she knew.

As she moved forward, rising gradually out of the water, her eyes leveled on his. When she stepped onto the shore, shorts and halter soaked and flattened to her body, a remnant of fading sunlight at the western edge of distant Waterman Island tinted her hair with a barely visible fringe of red.

"Okay," Kelso said, uncomfortable under her stare. After all, he had a gun; she didn't. What was the matter with him? "First two things I want to know is are you working for the government or URI, and if not, how'd you get by the patrol?"

She watched him steadily. "No, I'm not working for the government, or anyone else. And I got by the patrols by knowing where they'd be and coming in elsewhere."

"How'd you know where they'd be?"

"We monitored their radio transmissions and we have microsonar aboard. We came through the Huntington Narrows three nights ago and stayed close to the southern end of the bay, and worked our way carefully up here."

"From where?"

"From the Restitutions."

"A long way."

"We were lucky."

"*Maybe* you were lucky. Maybe you work for the goddamned government. Maybe you work for *some* goddamned government." Having vented his spleen, Kelso paused, trying to relax. "So what do you want, Miz—"

"My name is Judith DeFond. And I want to hire you to take me into the ruins. The Highland Park sector. I want you to help me find something very important to me."

"You're nuts. That's one of the patrol's favorite ponds."

"But you dive there."

"What?"

"I said, you dive there. You dive there frequently, or have in the past. And you've never been caught."

"Who told you that?"

"It's known—in certain circles, Mister Kelso. You have quite a reputation in certain circles." She zipped up the dripping windbreaker and folded her arms across her breasts.

Had he heard amusement in her voice? "What *circles?*" He was sorry the light was about gone. Whatever else she might be, she was definitely a pleasure to look at.

A cautious smile curved her lips. "Your cronies. The plunderers, freebooters, smugglers, scavengers, outlaws connected with your trade. They told me you often hid out in the San Gabriels. They recommended you as the man who knows more about the Los Angeles ruins than anyone alive. A few didn't think you could still be living."

Kelso eyed her coldly. "You went to rough company, didn't you?"

"What I want to find down there made it worth the risk."

"You still haven't told me what *that* is."

"Will you take me down?"

He felt foolish holding the rifle. The two men on the boat seemed to have turned innocently to routine chores, and were paying no attention to them. But he refused to relax yet. "How did you know I was here?" He stomped the ground with a foot. "Here on this exact island."

"We checked every island we passed. Carlos happened to spot that cabin up there with binoculars. We weren't sure anyone was here. But it turned out *you* were. You came down to meet us. Again we were lucky."

"Yeah. Well, you've got some filling in to do before I agree to take you anywhere." The twilight had faded and he could no longer see her eyes, or much of her face very clearly, but he sensed she still wore the smile. "What's funny?" he said.

"I've read and heard a lot about you in the last week or so. Research, you might call it. I was thinking." She shifted her weight from one leg to the other. "I was thinking how we could have been neighbors. Before—you lived in Glendale, didn't you?"

"My wife did," he said brusquely, wanting this particular digression to end. "I lived at the subsea colony off Cabo Colnette."

"Yes, I mean—"

"I know what you mean."

"I mean we could have passed each other on the street sometime, in a store—"

"I doubt it. Like I pointed out, I wasn't there much. And when I was there, you were probably a snot-nosed brat with your fist in the oatmeal. Look, as pleasant as it is chatting with you here amid the shattered grandeur of the California coast, I suggest we get down to—" He stopped.

"What's the matter?"

"Shut up."

He listened and heard nothing but knew he soon would. "Something's coming. I'll know what in a minute. But a minute may be too late." Kelso raised himself from the concrete, keenly disappointed the conversation had to be terminated this way.

"Wait," she said, seeing him bring the rifle muzzle down to point at the cruiser. "You don't think—"

"Gave up thinking much some time ago. Bad for both head and heart. Nice talking to you, though, Ms. DeFond. I have this problem, you see. Can't make up my mind whether I'm tired of living or not, but it seems when the showdown comes, I always opt for hanging around another day or two. I'll see you around. And if you or your boys out there show any sign of trying to alter my course, I'll blow you all back to the Restitutions—if that's really where you came from."

"No, wait—"

But it was too late to wait. He was running now, jumping in the lowering darkness from rock to rock, deadfall to dirt-clump. When he looked back to see if they were up to anything funny, he saw that she ran after him.

"You're wrong, Kelso!" she yelled. "Wait, please!"

Light hit the cove as a rotary aircraft came over the ridge from the east.

Kelso dived for a depression. He struck his knee on a sharp protrusion that opened the skin over the kneecap and sent him into a spasm of angry cursing. He'd had no time to see if she had some kind of concealed gizmo with which she could talk to the patrol chopper, no time to do anything but hunker in the dark of the hole and lift the rifle.

They would spy the cruiser immediately, even if they weren't looking for it. As for the sub, he wasn't sure. They would have to come low and close to nose away the shadows the little promontories threw over its narrow length. But they'd be preoccupied with the cruiser first—that is, if they didn't know it was already there and its cutie of a captain wasn't one of their own.

The chopper dropped, a big whirring mosquito with a single blinding eye (and four or five dragon-breathed nose guns that would roast Kelso like a barbecued rabbit if they discovered him in his hole). A hallowed moment, one that made him think of peasants huddled anywhere and everywhere in the world waiting to be crushed by the forces of Right and Progress. But he was one flaking peasant who would fight back. From the ammo pouch strapped to his side he took a scatter-bomb and inserted it in the snouted launcher at the end of the rifle's muzzle. The screen of light thrown out by the chopper made it impossible to see the craft, but he could shoot for the sound of the motor.

Suddenly *she* was scampering down the side of the hole. "Kelso!"

He said nothing, but she saw him—or guessed where he was.

"What are you going to do?"

"I'm going to swat a mosquito."

She crawled up, panting in his ear. Despite the circumstances, he found this extremely pleasant. "They haven't done anything yet. Maybe they—"

"*They* have orders to blast me on sight. I'm a mad dog beyond any possibility of redemption or rehabilitation, with a bankroll on my head alive or cooked and the last time I wanted to see if they were in a friendly mood, I almost fried. If those people in the 'certain circles' you say you went to told you anything, they told you about that."

"Yes—"

"Okay. So shut up about them. Now what the hell are you doing here in this hole with me?"

She ignored the question. "If you shoot that thing, you'll have the entire contingent at Corona up here."

"But I'll be gone by the time they get here."

"And me?"

He tried to make out her face in the darkness but failed. For some reason he was beginning to doubt she was one of them. "Tough. You took the risk. Maybe you'll stay lucky."

From the dropping chopper a megaphone boomed. "YOU ARE UNDER ARREST! YOU ARE UNDER ARREST! THROW ALL WEAPONS INTO THE WATER AND RAISE YOUR HANDS HIGH ABOVE YOUR HEADS!"

The command carried loudly across the water as the cruiser was flooded with the chopper's light. Over the edge of the hole Kelso could see the two men on board the boat throw what looked like rifles into the water.

"Well, Kelso, it seems everything said about you is true. Your present certainly doesn't completely fit your past."

He knew instantly what she meant and it stung. Jack Kelso, champion of whales, porpoises, and other defenseless creatures exploited by man, refused to help a defenseless woman. "If it did," he said testily, "I guess I wouldn't be here now." So what? he thought. What was "being here now" worth when it meant being huddled in a goddamned hole waiting to kill or be killed? With a "defenseless" woman? Just how defenseless was she?

The chopper continued to descend toward the water. He could see its twin guns pointing out the nose.

"We can run for it now without having to shoot," she said at his shoulder.

He turned to look at her, saw only a dark outline. "Run for *what?*"

"Your submarine."

He growled. "And if you come with me, then what the hell will I do with you?"

"Take me into Highland Park. Listen, we don't have time to sit here and argue about this."

Hell's hotspur! He didn't want to take her, and he couldn't simply leave her to be snatched by the patrol, whoever she might be. He had, it seemed, decided she was *not* one of them. "It's all working out your way, isn't it."

"It's working out for you, too. You'll see."

"And what about the two muscle men on your boat?"

"They can take care of themselves."

"I see. True comradely devotion. And you accuse me of being thick-skinned. All right. Come on then, goddammit! And keep low. They can see us from there if they happen to turn that light this way."

She was right behind him when he sprang from the hole. Sprinting was difficult over the deadfall and irregular earth. The light from the chopper, still hovering above the cruiser, distorted objects and confused perspective. At his back he could hear Judith DeFond. She did not sound tired or frightened or clumsy; her footfalls were light and sure in spite of the canvas shoes. For his part, he was damned glad he wore boots. This made him think of the cabin and what was in it but, accustomed to spur-of-the-moment departures, he'd left only a shirt, some food, a sleeping bag, some booze and magazines, all of which he could scrounge again when the opportunity presented itself. But what had she left behind? A strange one. And, he now suspected, not all that defenseless. Well, the grim chain of events of the last decades no doubt produced strange children.

He stumbled, regained his balance and heard her slow down to keep from running over him.

"HALT!" the megaphone all of a sudden roared in their direction. They'd been spotted. "HALT OR WE WILL OPEN FIRE!"

Kelso gave up keeping to the shadows. He struck out straight for the sub, running as hard as he could, knowing the chopper's guns could easily zap them from its position above the cruiser.

"Come on!" His shout was hardly necessary. She was almost beside him.

"HALT OR WE WILL OPEN FIRE!"

About ten meters ahead, a jumble of rock, scraggly pine, and scrub formed a wall that paralleled the shore where the cove turned west. Kelso tried to put this between them and the chopper but was sure they wouldn't make it. With a jolt, his right ankle hit something. He tripped and, trying to break his fall, thrust his left foot into an unseen hole. He fell face forward to the ground.

She was on him at once, her hand brushing away dirt from his face. Her hand had a deliciously soothing effect and she held something, a small bottle. . . .

"Are you all right?"

"Run for it . . . god . . . dammit." His voice sounded far-away and his jaw was hardly able to work. "I'm coming." But he didn't move. His muscles felt like jelly, his nerves and will like fluff.

Spitting noises, like silenced guns firing, came from the vicinity of the cruiser. The chopper made a funny choking sound and its light went out. An ear-splitting explosion ensued and bits and pieces of debris came flying and crashing down around them. Kelso's last sensations were the sight of her dark head over him, her face in total shadow against a background of stars, and the feel of her cool hands on his brow just before his own light went out.

6. SHIP OF GHOSTS

The rest of the submarine stank as badly as Kelso's stateroom. When she'd found the untidy quarters where he obviously slept, Judith DeFond directed the Lavaccas to carry him to the shower forward of the stateroom instead. There they laid him, still unconscious, until more pressing matters could be put out of the way.

While the Lavaccas removed to the *Tiburón* what little gear was aboard the cruiser, using the small rubber raft Kelso had had ashore at the sub's anchorage, she inspected the control room. Momentarily ignoring the clutter and hardly knowing what she was about, she discovered that the ship was run, more or less, by a computer whose main console was flanked by twin banks of gauges, dials and meters. As though her hands had done it a thousand times, she punched the proper keys on the keyboard to check the computer's performance and, watching the screen above the console for the expected readout, learned that it could talk. While she detected a slight hesitation in its response to her verbal questions and commands, likely because Kelso had his own way of addressing it, it responded nonetheless, and would probably do so to anyone's voice. The computer told her it could handle the ship's power, propulsion, sensory, and life-support systems, maneuvering, communication, and defense. All were below par, it was more than willing to tell her.

Dialogue with the computer having been established, she stood in the control room, staring about and wondering if she had been on such a ship in the past. Without consciously thinking about it, she had known exactly how to operate the keyboard, read the data on the CRT, ask pertinent questions regarding the *Tiburón's* functions, design, and layout. All this could not be explained by her research into Jack Kelso.

The entry of the Lavaccas interrupted her quandary. They had sunk the cruiser, as she had ordered, and were ready to do what next she wished. She remembered having selected them for their technological and naval backgrounds as well as their other traits, and told Juan to take charge of the control room and see that the *Tiburón* was out of the cove and under water at once, before the San Andreas Sea Patrol sent another aircraft or boat to see what had happened to the chopper now blown apart in the water off Islip Island. Then, with Carlos, she returned to the wardroom head and stripped Kelso.

The shower stall was small but they managed to squeeze him, and themselves, in. While Carlos held the man up, she turned the water on and, with a piece of soap found on the deck, began lathering him over. Carlos accepted getting drenched with the usual Lavaccan stoicism and, as Judith scrubbed, turned Kelso this way and that to make it easier for her to clean him.

As she touched the man, she was aware of currents rippling through her fingers, up her arms. He was thin and wiry, hard as rope. The contact of her skin against his was disconcertingly pleasurable, and her hands lingered in places sometimes longer than necessary.

By the time she had finished she was also soaked, and when she turned off the water and stood up, her breath came fast. She felt weak and flushed, but knew this was not from the simple physical exertion of having given the man a bath.

What she felt was understandable, natural, she told herself as she studied the lanky body held by Carlos. Understandable perhaps, but strange nevertheless, as though she'd had no such feelings before. Which had to be absurd. True, she could not clearly remember any men in her life but the doctors had said there had been several. They had tried to furnish some details for these alleged affairs and she could, if she tried, pluck bits and pieces from their accounts and assemble a plausible romance. But when she did, it seemed the bits and pieces could have derived from any one of the experiences, be shuffled around and rearranged to come up the same, as though they were all parts of a single affair, as though the men had all been cut from the same sheet of cardboard. No doubt, this was simply another aspect of her illness, like the pervasive disorientation she still felt at times.

But what did it matter? Why these nagging questions? Why should she *care*?

Turning away to find a towel, she was aware of Carlos watching her. Her confusion was, she supposed, obvious, but it had nothing to do with him and she found his solicitude annoying.

She had moved away from Kelso in order to quell the sexual excitement, to clear away the confusion, as much as to find a towel. Successful in the latter goal, she noticed, upon turning back to dry Kelso off, the excitement resurge.

Carlos took the towel and, holding the man up with one strong arm, dried him fairly well with the other. Then, hoisting Kelso across his back like a bundle of kelp, the bodyguard followed her to the stateroom where they laid the *Tiburón's* captain on his disheveled bunk.

Juan appeared to report they were safely out of the cove and, at a depth of 20 fathoms, crawling south through San Gabriel Canyon toward Angeles Bay. The *Tiburón's* computer knew the safest routes through the bay to open sea and a course had been selected that would turn them west when they were out of the San Gabriels. They would keep to the southern edge of these islands, skirt the northern fringe of the Santa Monica group and, crossing the shallow stretch of water overlying what had been the San Fernando Valley, reach the Pacific by tomorrow's dawn.

Judith thanked him for the report and told the Lavaccas to begin cleaning things up as best they could, and to repair what needed repairing as much as possible, beginning with the submarine's air system. Without hesitation, they obeyed.

Left alone in Kelso's stateroom, she took another ampule and the needle from the small pouch on her belt and gave him a second injection, one that would insure his sleeping soundly for the rest of the night and well into the next day. From her bags, which Juan had placed in the wardroom, she found a clean robe and got him into it. Then, forcibly removing herself from the room and ignoring the emotions heretofore dormant but now trying to become dominant, she resumed her inspection of the *Tiburón*.

Moving through the junk-strewn compartments and passageways was difficult. The stench of stale pipe smoke, old lubricants, dirty metal, unwashed clothes, mold, and stagnant air stifled. The after crew's quarters in the stern was full of old machine parts, tools, salvage and other rubbish that looked as if it had been there for years. The engine room was a mess, both upper and lower decks filthy, with numerous items and parts, clearly, even to her, in need of mending or replacement. The Lavaccas' mechanical abilities would be put to good use there.

The ship's thermonuclear reactor was low on fuel, the attack center above the control room full of clutter and salvage, the galley and crew's mess a tangled miscellany of the same. But above the mess, the officers' wardroom where Juan had put her gear was comparatively navigable and, forward of the wardroom, she discovered something unexpected, or upon reflection, perhaps not so unexpected, considering Kelso's past.

She stood in the doorway looking at the book-laden shelves, remembering her research into Jack Kelso. The accounts on newstapes, Navy reports, scientific journals, some in praise, many in vilification, had intrigued her, despite the fact she was supposed to have renounced interest in anything.

The small library was the most orderly room she'd encountered, was spared the dirt and clutter otherwise ubiquitous. Maybe the orderliness was the result of disuse. The dust seemed long-settled, undisturbed. Yet, looking over the rows of books shelved from deck to overhead, noting the depressions in the cushions of the sofa against the forward bulkhead, pipe ashes in an abalone shell on the sofa arm, a pair of well-worn moccasins on the floor, she was sure she had stumbled on what was once a revered and frequented retreat.

Kelso probably did not come here now. Reading was a pastime for those who felt they had some stake in the world, in life. Everything else she had seen on the *Tiburón* suggested a tomb, a floating coffin filled with decay, inhabited by a dead man who still somehow managed to move around as though alive, but took few other pains to maintain such status.

A tomb and a man with habits that should have seemed similar to and supportive of her own state of mind, but did not. Instead of accepting the neglect, the resignation, and futility in everything she'd seen as reflecting the attitude of a man who had, generally speaking, come to the same conclusion she was supposed to have about life, something in her rebelled, something deeper than that final admission of defeat she thought she had embraced. Instead of feeling as if she belonged in the tomb of the *Tiburón*, she felt suffocation; she wanted to clean and repair the ship—she wanted to change and heal the man.

Because she needed him and his ship, needed both to function well. That was all.

No. That was not all. It went deeper than that.

She backed off, again disturbed, confused by her feelings, disturbed that she should *feel* in the first place. She closed the library door, trying to close as well that internal door on her awareness that she had glimpsed some private chink in the "dead" man's armor—and her armor also—and forced herself forward to the compartments in the bow.

There the sub's torpedoes and subrocs had originally been housed. It was impossible to tell, for the piles of salvage, if these forward compartments currently held munitions of any kind. She had become superficially acquainted with fusion-powered attack-class (antisubmarine) submarines when she first learned, in the Restitution Islands, of Jack Kelso and the fact that he had stolen such a ship. The submarine could not be separated from the man, how and why he stole it, the events that led to that brash but successful theft. A return to San Diego and several days spent in a number of large libraries, with the intention of learning only what was necessary about him, had disclosed, like the library now aft, more than she needed or would have liked.

But what should it matter to her? Why, as she stood in the middle of the haphazard heaps of salvage in the forward torpedo room, did she feel so pulled between the decision she had made after being released from that hospital in Phoenix (perhaps she had made the decision long before her release; she was no longer sure) and this increasing interest in everything around her? Had that hospital itself contributed to, nourished, the shock and depression that reputedly caused her illness? Did she remember everything right? Had the doctors, the psychiatrists, put every piece of the puzzled past together properly? Could she trust her memory of what they had said? Could she trust *what* they had said? Could it be they missed something? And if they had, how much had they missed? How much of what they told her could be false?

Did it matter?

No. Unless—

Once more she moved, retracing steps aft, past the library

to the wardroom, seeking relief from these growing uncertainties.

The papers, ledgers, notebooks, and other paraphernalia littering the long table in the center of the room indicated that this area was used by Kelso as a sort of office. On a hunch, and to busy herself with something that would keep her mind on immediate, practical goals, she began searching through the cabinets beside the port bulkhead.

She was looking for a map or maps of the San Andreas Death Zone, of the submerged portions of Highland Park in particular—or so she told herself. But her eyes, her hands, kept falling on objects that did nothing but aggravate her earlier distraction and when, removing a tattered knapsack from the cabinet top to see what the large sheet of paper was beneath it, she discovered, behind where the pack had sat, a framed photograph lying on its back, the quest for maps evaporated.

The photo was a torso color shot of a young woman whose large brown eyes were luminous with vitality, whose smile was a sunburst of exuberance. The face radiated intelligence, energy, optimism, courage. She wore a graduation cap and gown and in the lower right-hand corner of the picture was printed in pen the date: June 4, 2003. Above the date was written in a large flowing hand:

Darling Jack
All my love,
Lisa

She lifted the photograph and looked at the cover of the book on which it had been lying. The cover was featureless imitation leather, about thirty centimeters square. Despite an inner warning to refrain, she opened it.

More photos. A much younger Jack Kelso with the girl of the graduation portrait sitting on a beach somewhere, both in swimsuits, Kelso's big hand up waving censoriously at whomever had taken the shot. Another photo: Kelso and Lisa on a sailboat, the latter smiling at him from midships while he held the tiller, grinning back with a face even more bushed with beard than it was now, and minus the flecks of gray.

She flipped the pages. News clippings, mementos, more photos. The bits and pieces of two lives both lionized by the press, condemned by officialdom, deified by environmentalists. Kelso and Lisa, sometimes one of them alone, at sea, on beaches, in labs, in cities, and, halfway through the book, the two in a setting that was both colorful and odd.

Judith looked closer. It was, or seemed to be at first glance, a tropical setting. A picture postcard scene with immaculate tiled walks, shopfronts, some bicyclist in the background, a fountain in the foreground, lush ferns lining the walks, trees in the distance, exotic birds in the air. But something was wrong. The horizon that lay slightly elevated above the distant trees was unusually curved, its extreme right and left sides bending upward. And the "sky" appeared latticed with some kind of gridwork, as if the atmosphere were paneled or ribbed.

She straightened up, all at once realizing she was looking at a picture taken on one of the space habitats between the earth and the moon. She closed the book, annoyed and wearied by her prying. She knew who Lisa was from her research. And she knew how and where Lisa was thought to have died.

She had to do something active, with her hands, something demanding her unvented energies, her complete attention. She turned from the cabinets and went to the companionway going down to the galley and the crew's mess. In cleaning these compartments she should be able to keep her mind on an even—and uncomplicated—keel.

But upon immediate confrontation with the galley, the need for soap, abrasives, disinfectant, declared itself. Rags would be easy to come by. But soap? As she began what she was sure would be a fruitless search in the melee, she thought of calling the Lavaccas to see if they had had any luck in finding cleaning gear. But then remembered she'd left her pocket radiophone in the wardroom. Nor was there any sign of an intercom in the galley. She was on the verge of going aft to find the twins when Carlos appeared in the crew's mess behind her, holding a cardboard box of sanitation supplies.

"I found these for you, *señorita,*" he said. "Juan and I have more for our jobs." He placed them on one of the mess tables, pushing objects aside to do so.

"Thank you, Carlos," she said, her eyes curiously on his wooden features, wondering how she knew it was Carlos and not Juan. It was not the first time she had the idea that he, they, had read her mind and acted on her wish before she could voice it. Cleaning gear was a pressing necessity on the *Tiburón*, considering the shape the ship was in, but this kind of anticipation of her needs had happened too often to easily discard it as coincidence.

"Do you want me to help you here, *señorita?*" His words were as lacking in emotion, in personality, as his face.

"No," she said. "You may resume working with Juan. I'll manage here. Thank you."

She watched him nod, turn and depart up the ladderway aft of the mess compartment. She stared at the cleaning gear, as if it might help cast light on her perplexities. The memory of where and how she had come to hire the Lavaccas was vague, unreal, like that which had been dreamed or imagined rather than truly experienced, like those alleged love affairs. . . .

But she had still been under the influence of the drugs then.

What drugs?

She could not remember. But surely there had been drugs. The doctors said. . . . She shook her head. All of it was blurred. Her illness, shock, amnesia. Phoenix, the doctors, the hospital. The memory, the life history, the doctors had reconstructed. Her decision upon learning the truth about her family.

The truth.

The Lavaccas. She had found and hired them after leaving the hospital, after she had come to her decision. She had found them in a bar in San Diego. Hadn't she?

Her first vivid memory, the first that seemed rooted solidly with detail and sensation, in reality, was of that day crossing to the Restitution Islands.

Drugs *had* to be the explanation. And anyway, what did she care? They were here. They were competent, efficient, asked nothing from her, did her bidding like devout slaves. She was extremely fortunate to have found them. The how and why did not matter. They would help her accomplish what she had to do and that was all that mattered.

Except. . . . Perhaps they had an ulterior motive for their uncannily adept service. Perhaps they figured something else lay in it for them. Perhaps they had their own reasons for wanting to help her go into the ruins. But again, any ulterior design they might have, so long as it did not frustrate her own, should not concern her. Nothing should concern her but her one goal. All else—everything—was meaningless, which was why she had decided on such a course in the first place. Wasn't it?

Something scraped against the hull of the *Tiburón*, making the deck shudder and the scattered things in the galley rattle. She thought of the desolation through which the ship moved, and of the ship, its quaint cramped little library, its captain. The *Tiburón* was like a tomb, yes, dank with secrets and ghosts.

What hovered that she could not get hold of, that lay as if in the very air around her, intangible, shadowy, elusive—*desired?*

How had she known what to do in the control room? Nothing in her past conjured up by the doctors included either ships or computers, and her research had not been that thorough or meticulous. And could they, after all, have given her the past of someone else by mistake? And if that were so, wasn't her plan then based on a falsehood?

Damn! Enough of this!

She willed away the confusion, forcing clarity and confidence to return, replacing doubt with determination. Having advanced to the box, she plunged hands in. With bottles and brushes and rags, she turned on the foul galley with zeal, making herself be fastidiously concerned, personally challenged, by the simple physical problems presented by untidiness and dirt.

7. PENETRATION I

Like a child who has strayed too far into an unknown cave deep in the bowels of the Ulia-Te Mountains, Cinara Tlii felt small and lost. The seat at the browport almost swallowed her in its Prithipean proportions. The view below of the dark wasteland of the Deathlords' world made her blood run cold.

She turned, had to push forward to see over the side of the observation seat. Falur sat on her left, as enclosed in his chair as she, hidden by the sloping, padded sides where a Prithipean would naturally rest a coarse-skinned arm.

Behind them, the varied sounds of the ship's operations center hummed and whispered. Forward, on a viewscreen beneath the browport, she could see that portion of the operations center where Acexea stood, the lateral ridge of bone at the top of his head brightly reflecting the room's nacreous light. On each side of this viewer, data constantly being gathered by the ship's sensory equipment and its communications links with the other ships of the Alliance moved across infopanels in uninterrupted array.

She did not understand the data, as she did not understand the mechanisms of the intricate weaponry, the interrelated systems of protective force fields and anti-detection shields employed by this and other ships in the fleet. She did not need to. She knew enough for her role as strategist; the commanders, such as Acexea, could take care of the rest.

Thus far Cinara Tlii and her plan had been accepted and she had no illusions why. Having fought and been a fugitive from the Yaghattarin for more cycles than many in the Alliance had in lifespans, her presence here had been her dream, her plan, from the beginning. The greater part of her life had been spent clandestinely traveling the inhabited planets in an attempt to gather a secret army that could rise against Naravamintaran rule. If it went against the nature of her people, if many of her race thought her scarred with the evil that burned in races like the Prithipeans, who hated the Deathlords to the point of its being all-consuming, if she felt like a child who had wandered far astray of its natural domain, she accepted such consequences for the time being.

If she did not know exactly how an annihilation beam effected its awesome results, she knew, had had it instilled in her too deeply and painfully for the mindscrubs of the Yaghattarin to erase, the memory handed down by her mother and her mother's mother, of freedom, of the way it was before the seizeships came. But despite the fears of her people regarding the state of her soul, she did not feel what Acexea felt for the Master Logicians. Where the Deathlords were concerned, her mind was perhaps as void of emotion as theirs. Any physical and psychic bonds they might once have had to a natural ancestry had long ago been severed, or so altered as to render them, in Tlii's view, nothing more than grotesque mutations engineered by their own monomaniacal wills. She could not hate machines. Or so she tried to reassure herself. So she hoped. As those of Onnahlaeti knew, one did not hate at all if one was to be truly free. Time, nonetheless, had exacted its price. One did not become committed to the destruction of another entity, however deserving of destruction that entity may be, without donning the destroyer's cloak. She had worn it for many turns. Would she, when this was done, be able to cast it aside?

"Cinya." It was Falur, addressing her with the more intimate form of her name.

She moved to the edge of the seat, where she could see him. He, too, had slid forward and sat on his seat's edge. His eyes, green and lifewarm as sunlight through the fronds of a bemikia tree, were on her. They were eyes that had been on the desolate world below them for a long time.

"The old ones," he said. "In the mountains. The Arkhatin. There is much they told me and much they did not. There is much that puzzles me."

"And me," she said. "But I know your meaning. You have been spared ugliness. Until now."

"I would like to know what they did not tell me. I would like to understand."

"About the Deathlords, the Yaghattarin, and the ancient star-wanderers, the Arkhalahn?"

"Yes. That and more."

How different you are, Falur, from most of our race, she thought, but refrained from sending the thought telepathically. *How different from most of your race, yet how like that other boy, the one the Deathlords took. . . .*

"I will tell you," she said. "I will take you back. It will help ready us in the preparation ritual when we begin the thought-sending."

But Falur would not be so easily placated. "The biggest mystery to me of all is this: how can beings like the Yaghattarin, who are so able and advanced in artificial ingenuity, be so lacking in intuitive wisdom? How can they not see their contradictions and their folly?"

"Because they have deified their creations and their ability to create, Falur. They have stifled all else. They have deified lifeless things that have been given, through their handiwork, the semblance of life. They have gazed upon this brilliant handiwork for so long that it has destroyed their ability to see."

Falur sat back but she could feel his lingering curiosity. She had offered an answer he had heard before in one form or another. It did not answer the ultimate *why*. Before the

Deathlords came to Onnahlaeti, few members of Falur's race had any need or desire to question things. Life itself was the answer to all. Few Onnahlaetians in that past age would even have been able to grasp the concept of an ultimate why, as few would have been tormented, like Falur now, with the riddle of the origin of evil.

She heard a voice from the operations center, and had to stand in order to see over the rear of the observation seat.

Acexea was speaking, coming up the steps from the bowl-like operations deck. She lifted a translator from her belt and, after making sure the selector was correctly adjusted, clamped it to her ear. His speech was instantly arranged into Onnahlaetian.

"We have entered the Naravamintaran atmosphere. We have come through the first detection layer. All ships are functioning perfectly."

Tlii exhaled, realizing she had not known they were that close. She nodded to indicate she understood. The shield systems were working; if they hadn't been, the entire armada, every ship, would now be storms of dust motes whirling in the sphere of Naravamintara's first annihilation field.

Towering above her, Acexea's yellow gaze swept over the infopanels under the wide browport. "We will succeed," he said. "Creation cannot forever ignore your determination and my hatred." Then, abruptly, he turned, leaving Tlii wondering how a creature so large could move so suddenly—and wondering how, from a Prithipean standpoint, "creation" was viewed. Considering the history of Acexea's embattled race and the inhospitable conditions of the Prithipean worlds, the universe was no doubt an adversary. Falur and Cinara Tlii did not really understand.

Since understanding usually derived from experience, such ignorance was, in the Onnahlaetian view, highly valued. In her own case, she knew she was much closer to understanding these things than she would ever wish the boy to be. But that traditional Onnahlaetian lifeview could be doomed. How could they ever truly go back to the way it was before the Deathlords came? Falur's quiet but unappeasable quest for answers perhaps foreshadowed a trend that could become widespread among her people. But he had left his world of warmth and accomodating life. He had looked on, was looking on now, a reality of desert, ice, and darkness. He would eventually come to see a Yaghattarin, provided the revolt was as successful as Acexea vowed it would be. Falur and Cinara Tlii were anomalies. Those who had never left Onnahlaeti could perhaps resume the old way. And, if they did, would Falur and she be welcomed there when they returned?

In the browport the black, windlashed mountains and frozen deserts grew more distinct. Still standing, she watched the details grow. A simple push of a button below one of the infopanels would give her cartographic data but, though she had never set eye or foot upon it, she knew the planet's topography well. They were descending toward the valley of the Great Rift, north of the Desert of Nammava Trah.

There it lay, her long-desired objective, the largest world of a system comprising fifteen arid planets, all of which had been put to such uses as indoctrination camps, training bases, penal colonies, mines, dumps, graves. All of which, in the inverted language of the Yaghattarin, came under the headings of Experimental Farms, Resource Sites, Purification Centers.

Falur was silent. She sought his thoughts and found him in passive meditation.

They were now penetrating into the planet's gravitational field. In the subsurface fortress of Nammava Trah II, in the outlying surface spaceports and cities, the sentinel systems of an interstellar empire would be picking up nothing out of the ordinary in the thin atmosphere. Even if a First Master had dared look out at stars he could hardly see, perhaps wishing for some sign of those beings against whom this empire had been built, he would have seen only the usual Naravamintaran exosphere, as empty and void of life as the turbulent deserts beneath it.

Cinara Tlii smiled—and wondered how deeply the stamp of the deathbringer had worked its lines into her face.

8. THE PLEA

He awoke to the sub's low throb and vibrations. A glimpse at the porthole confirmed that the ship was submerged.

He sat up—too fast. His head swam, then, by degrees, found equilibrium and cleared. He swung his legs off the bunk, winced, looked down: his left ankle was bandaged. Additional inspection revealed he'd been bathed, and his dirty khaki shorts exchanged for a robe many sizes too small. Under the robe he wore nothing else. A fresh scent wafting up from his skin convinced him the bath hadn't been a bad idea. Had *she*—how? He was underweight, he supposed, but still a load for a woman to lift.

A sliver of light bordered the bottom of the closed stateroom door. Was she in the wardroom?

What in hell had happened? Why had he passed out? From a sprained ankle? A broken ankle? He looked again at the bandaged left foot. It was badly swollen, and when he tried to move it pain immediately shot up the leg.

All right. But since when did he pass out from an injured limb, either broken or sprained? The dryness in his mouth, the faint remaining wooziness suggested he'd been sedated. To hell with it. Of more pressing importance was who had taken over the ship.

He slid out of the bunk, putting his weight on his right foot and maintaining his balance against the small desk beside the opposite bulkhead. Hopping to the door, he was relieved to find it unlocked, without knowing why he should have expected it not to be. Did he think he and his bloody ship had been shanghaied? Rather looked that way, didn't it? Bracing himself for more surprises, he opened the door.

At the long wardroom table she sat, with a cup near her hand and stacks of charts and maps taken from the wardroom cabinets laid out in a semi-circle before her. The wardroom table was otherwise uncluttered, a condition it had not enjoyed for some time.

She looked up with what he gauged was a tentative and decidedly forced smile. Kelso returned this pretense of civility with a look of unrestrained irritation, and hopped noisily to the table, having to hold the robe closed with his hand because he had forgotten to tie the waist cord.

"Where are we?" His tone was not friendly.

"About ten kilometers west of the Santa Monica Islands."

"Who got us here? Who's running the ship?"

"Juan and Carlos—and your ship's computer."

"Juan and Carlos?" he stormed.

"They are capable sailors, Mister Kelso."

"So why didn't you steal your own goddamned sub!"

"That would have been even riskier than enlisting you and yours. Besides, it's your services as a diver, as one who knows the Los Angeles ruins, that I need—and your ability to elude the patrols in this particular ship. Two areas of expertise in which no one is your peer, I was told. I double-checked thoroughly with those on both sides of the law to make sure said expertise wasn't mere legend, but indeed fact."

She sounded to Kelso like a microbiologist citing her sources on the habits of some rare species of amoeba. "Seems to me you've done a pretty good job of eluding the patrol yourself in this particular ship. Your fantastic luck still holding out, right?"

"The appearance of the patrol chopper was a fortunate accident—for me," she conceded, deftly steering the conversation onto another tack. "It got me over the hurdle of why I wanted to hire you and into the *Tiburón*."

"Not quite. But before I kick your tail into the drink, suppose you tell me what happened to those patrolmen."

"They, regrettably, had to be eliminated."

Kelso stared at her, slightly taken aback by the cold matter-of-fact way she'd said this. "You don't say." He had to grip the table's edge; his right foot was tiring, and fleetingly he wondered if he was adequately covering everything with the hand holding the robe but was too annoyed to look. "Eliminated by your two 'capable sailors'?"

"Yes."

"Amazing," he said. "The last time I looked they weren't even armed. Do you and your sailors do a lot of eliminating?"

Again she treated him to an ambivalent smile and let her

eyes fall to the map between her hands. He thought for a moment there was ambivalence in her tone as well when she answered, "Only when absolutely necessary. Would you like some coffee?"

"Yes—I mean, no, goddammit. You keep still and explain to me just why in the hell you want to go into Los Angeles!"

She sat back in the chair and for the first time he noticed she now had on coveralls, the front of which was unzipped halfway down her chest. From that exposed vee he surmised she could be as nude under the coveralls as he was under the robe. "Why don't you have a seat first. You must be very uncomfortable, standing on one leg."

"That's another thing—"

"One thing at a time, please, Mister Kelso."

He cursed and hopped to the other side of the table where he found a chair—as unusually clear of junk as the table—and sat, scowling at her over the maps and charts.

Her eyes met his levelly across the table. "My parents lived in Highland Park. That is where I grew up. They had a lot of money—both before and after the economic crises at the turn of the century. A lot of priceless art objects were in the house. The kind of stuff you have found pays so well on the black market these days. The paintings, I am sure, would be hopelessly ruined, but there were other things." Her eyes dropped, lifted again from the map. Her brow furrowed. "And there are personal reasons why I want to go down." This last, as well as what preceded it, was stated flatly, without emotion.

"Like I said before, you're nuts. Highland Park lay in the area that sank the deepest—"

"I know."

"Nobody goes down there. The depth is six or seven hundred meters in places. I know. I've been there. You can't—"

"Maybe we can. Where I want to go isn't in the San Rafael Sink." She looked once more at the map. Kelso saw that it was one of the Glendale-Pasadena sector. "It's several kilometers south of—"

"You don't know that. You don't know where in hell your parents' place might be, if that's *really* where you want to go. Things down there are turned inside out. Land sank in some places, in others, was pushed up. The lay of it is rarely anything like it was before. You'll never be able to tell where anything is by remembering how it *was*. And those maps, even though they were drawn up within the last few years, are not that accurate. They're basically a lot of slaphappy guesswork put together by a bunch of rummy geologists and incompetent San Andreas Sea Patrol cartographers. Nothing's the same as it was, and nobody knows exactly how it is now."

She regarded him silently, jaw set, eyes unfaltering. "Not even you?"

"Not even me. I don't dive for a specific ruin or locale. Unless I've come upon some place by accident, remember where it was and want to go back there for some reason. It's idiotic to try otherwise."

"There is artwork I've seen on the *Tiburón* that I am positive came from the Huntington Library Art Gallery and the Norton Simon Museum of Art."

"I doubt it. You're fishing. I've been in those places, all right, and I've brought up some items from them but that was a while ago and such stuff has likely long been transferred from the *Tiburón* to the tub of some black marketeer. In any case, I came on those places by luck, not by studying any flaking map drawn up after the bottom fell out."

"Why do you have these maps, then?"

"Because once upon a time I thought they'd be of some use."

He had the impression what he'd said hadn't made the slightest impact. This impression was proved correct when she said with unabashed irrelevance, "Change your mind about that cup of coffee?"

He pointed a finger, said irritably, "See that cupboard behind you?"

"Your liquor cabinet," she said without turning. "What would you like?"

"Whatever in hell your hand hits first."

She stood. He watched her turn to the cupboard, impressed by the ease and natural grace with which she moved. Though slender, she filled the coveralls in a way that made him realize he'd never given that kind of garment its due.

"Thank you," he grunted when she set before him a water glass with several fingers of brandy in it. He drank it in one gulp, thunked the glass down and scowled again, vaguely aware that whatever social graces he'd once seen fit to observe had long since been discarded. "Tell me something. Just where were you when the big crack came?"

She had reseated herself, hands folded reposefully over the

map. It was several moments before she answered his question, and the answer seemed to require some mental effort. "I was going to school in Mexico City," she said, with that faint trace of a frown he'd noticed previously again on her forehead. For the first time Kelso also noticed that forehead's breadth and height.

"Studying what?"

"Ancient cultures, ancient civilizations." Again, the answer came carefully, as though she were reciting and having a little difficulty in remembering what to recite. "Mayan mostly."

"So," he said, puzzled by her present near vacuous look. "Another grave robber." He watched her eyes regain focus. "You're an archaeologist?"

"No, I . . . didn't finish. When the news reached me that Los Angeles . . . that the San Andreas superquake had occurred, I tried to go home but roads, phones, airports . . . everything was in disorder. Many people in Mexico had friends or relatives in California, and were trying to reach them in one way or another." She paused, put a hand to her brow, eyes on the table now. "People could not believe what they were hearing from the media, the reports that were coming in. I . . . could not believe it. This was also during one of the many *agriculturistas'* revolts. There was unrest in Central and South America. Guerilla wars—" She ceased recounting the dismal catalog. "Needless to say, I had a great deal of trouble getting out. When I finally did, Los Angeles was no more. California was torn with widespread panic and no one except qualified help was allowed into what had by then become known as the San Andreas Death Zone." Her eyes shifted over the map, closed briefly, opened and looked at him.

Kelso found their sudden clear and steady gaze, as he had found it when he watched her approach Islip Island, unsettling. What followed came in a more sure, swift, and matter-of-fact tone, but still with that rote quality.

"I was beside myself. I collapsed, had an emotional breakdown, was found wandering aimlessly in Arizona and committed to a hospital in Phoenix where I recovered after several years' care. I helped at the hospital for a while. There were many cases similar to mine, others with different problems, but all related to the quake. Then I drifted again for some months. I could find no anchor of my own, no direction, no purpose. The need to return to Highland Park to try to find them, where they went down at the very least, became an obsession. So I began trying seriously to find a way to do it. That led me to finding and hiring Juan and Carlos, and eventually to finding you."

Kelso studied her for a long time without speaking, his jaw muscles grinding, itching for the stem of his pipe. On the face of it, her story revealed nothing out of the ordinary. Thousands of people could tell similar tales, had had similar desires; thousands of people in a perpetual state of shock roamed around in a daze all over the world because of what had happened in Southern California. Though there'd been a lot of earthquakes everywhere in the last several decades, none had remotely compared with the San Andreas catastrophe; the latter defied a label as much as it lacked a precedent in recorded history. In fact, it could not really be called an earthquake as the term was traditionally applied. The fault had given way, all right, in a rift wide enough in parts to accomodate a fleet of ships abreast, long enough to have created an inland sea channel two-thirds the length of the state. Maybe that rift could be considered the result of an earthquake if one thought in Jovian proportions. But the wholesale sinking, or dropping, of the San Gabriel Mountains and the Los Angeles Basin, neither of which was close to the main fault, made little seismic or geological sense in terms of an earthquake or anything else. So there was no wonder a mental affliction known as the San Andreas Syndrome had developed afterward. In some cases Kelso had seen—probably including his own—the desire to find lost loved ones was suicidal. No, her story was not extraordinary. It was the way she'd told it that bothered him. It rang too flat, emotionless. Maybe the years, along with a breakdown, had left her that way. Numb. Okay. Yet if she were truly consumed by this irrational desire, some of that "consumption" should show. Maybe she, in her own way like him, was simply crazy. Or maybe she was lying.

"We have a lot in common," she said abruptly, almost anxiously, as though she'd read his last thought.

"How's that?"

"We've both lost our families. But I'm sure you don't want to bring up the past any more than I do." Her smile faded and, as if to change the now-unwelcome subject, she picked up her coffee cup. "Would you like something to eat? I know where the galley is."

"Made yourself right at home, haven't you?"

"Mister Kelso." She put the cup down, voice gone somber again, with an undertone of both importunity and loss of patience. "I'm desperate. I've spent a long time trying to find someone who would take me into the ruins. I will pay you for your trouble. You won't be sorry. I regret that you feel... taken advantage of, but I was reluctant to tell you my reasons for wanting to hire you until I thought it was safe. In other words, until I was aboard the *Tiburón.* I hope you understand."

"I don't." (He wanted to understand badly all of a sudden.) "I don't understand a damned thing. What are those two goons for? Who are they? Where are they now? What are they doing?"

"They are familiarizing themselves with the submarine and seeing to various needed repairs. With your permission."

"They don't have it. They aren't needed."

"The repairs? Or Juan and Carlos?"

"Juan and Carlos!"

"I think you will find them very useful. They are very efficient technicians, sailors, and bodyguards. They have been with me for over a month. Under the circumstances, I couldn't very well fire them there in the cove. Once that chopper was missed—and I'm sure it had radio contact with Long Beach Naval HQ—that sector of the San Gabriel Islands must have swarmed with patrol craft. I had to take them along. They never would have gotten away."

Her present concern for her bodyguards certainly contradicted her former indifference to their plight when they were in the cove. Maybe she knew all along the two heavyweights were in no danger from the patrol. But how? Kelso groaned and tried to see answers in his empty glass. But before he could collect his thoughts she picked up the brandy bottle and, reaching across the maps, poured him another.

On her right wrist was a silver bracelet of possibly ancient Mesoamerican design. He discerned no inscription of any kind. Inlaid were tiny pieces of turquoise, a color that matched her eyes.

"They won't bother us," she said. "They'll stay in the old after crew's quarters—or wherever you wish them to stay."

That smile again. Had she hinted at something in what she'd just said that he'd missed, something sexual? Was she being coquettish? She was, god help him, yes, remarkably alluring with those green eyes, that immaculately proportioned face with its broad high brow, the coppery complexion, blue-black hair (pinned, now, most business-like, up in back). "And where do *you* intend to stay?"

"Wherever you wish. Wouldn't you like something to eat?"

"Yes." All at once he was ravenous.

Obligingly she stood and, taking her cup, went to the door and down the ladderway to the galley.

After tossing the second brandy down, Kelso sat looking broodingly into space. He knew he shouldn't drink, should keep his head clear at least to keep abreast of this—this what? To hell with it. He poured some more of the amber dynamite and gulped it down.

Her story smelled fishy, but why? Not her story so much as the way she had told it. Could she also be in the illegal salvage game and want to use him, use the *Tiburón*, have the two Mexican bruisers take over when the right moment arose? Maybe she had told him some of the truth, that she needed his knowledge of the Highland Park area, his skill at getting them there unscathed, which would explain why they hadn't deep-sixed him back at Islip. Worse yet—and this set his teeth on edge—could she be a goddamned government or corporate agent like his old buddy Vincent Polliard?

Newly angered, he pulled himself up and forgetfully stepped back with his left foot. The pain that shot up from the ankle sent him reeling away from the table, cursing between clamped jaws and hopping around on his right leg like an idiot. The too-small robe parted. He banged the bulkhead with his fist, hobbled back to the stateroom, found a pair of khaki cutoffs, put them on, and hobbled through the wardroom forward to the galley ladderway.

"Who undressed me?" he shouted when he'd gingerly made his way down to the galley. He stood between it and the crew's mess, which was full of piled plunder, watching her move behind the shelves and serving counter. "Who put this robe on me?"

She turned, looking at him through the space between the shelves. "I did. It's my robe. We brought our gear aboard, of course, from the cruiser. And when I couldn't find anything clean of yours, I—"

"It's too mothermucking small!" He threw the garment at the nearest junk-laden table. He knew he was being a fool but that was all he could think of to say. Then: "You take liberties. You do take liberties."

"Sorry. I didn't know you were modest."

"I'm not! I just—I just don't know what the hell's going on!"

"I'm cooking your dinner, Mister Kelso." She resumed doing it.

The prospect of an imminent meal calmed him a bit. "Where are we headed?"

"We're moving south."

"South?"

"Southwest, to be exact." She was at the stove, obviously not about to let the computer cook the meal.

He noticed she'd tidied up the galley. Things actually sparkled and shone; the litter and garbage that had been scattered all over the shelves, stove, and counter had disappeared.

"Out to open sea," she said.

"What the hell did you give me to knock me out?"

There wasn't the slightest pause in what she was doing. "I gave you something for the pain, and something to help you sleep."

"Something to help you get yourself and me on the sub without any resistance from yours truly. Sweet of you." He raked back salvage and sat on the edge of a table. "I suppose in your past experiences you acquired a nurse's training. Maybe a doctor's, even?"

"No, just a nurse's. I told you. I helped at the hospital in Phoenix." This time he thought he did detect a pause, in voice as well as in the task that engaged her at the stove. "But the ankle is properly set. It will heal and be fine."

"Wonderful. But I won't be diving for a while. Which brings us back to our favorite topic. What do you intend to pay me for my involuntary and legendary services?"

She stepped around the counter, the coffee cup in her hand, and, leaning against the bulkhead at the end of the shelves, said in her dry, matter-of-fact tone, "You will find ten thousand World Bank credits in the top drawer of your stateroom bureau. A rather messy drawer, I might add. I will pay you ten thousand more when we are in the Highland Park area, thirty thousand more when we dive, and an additional fifty thousand if and when we find what I hope to find, thus making a total of one hundred thousand credits, which comes to almost one million American dollars."

"At the dollar's current value," he mumbled. Still, it was not a sum to sneeze at, by any means.

"You will have a crew of two, who will run, repair, clean,

and restore the *Tiburón* to its original efficiency, and a woman who will cook, clean, mend, wash for you and help you while away in any way you wish whatever hours are otherwise uneventful."

Kelso's eyebrows shot up and his glance dropped to the front of her coveralls. "Such as?" His voice was thick.

"Such as—" She shrugged, a gesture that widened the gap in the coverall front several centimeters. "Such as teaching me how to dive."

He caught a glimpse of grinning white teeth as she turned back to the stove.

"You don't know how to dive?" This exclamation came close to rattling the dishes she had set on the counter.

She didn't answer at once, as though she were unsure what the answer should be, or as though she weren't sure herself of the answer. "I've dived some, but nothing like the diving we'll be doing down there."

"Well. It's reassuring that you've got some respect for the foolishness you want to undertake," he said wrily. "So where'd you get all the bloody money?"

With a tray of two steaming bowls of soup, she came around the counter. "As I told you, my parents were wealthy. There was property in Mexico, which I sold. They left me quite a lot of money in an international bank in Mexico City as well." She put the tray down beside him and pushed the clutter farther back. "We'd better eat our soup before it gets cold. And speaking of food, there isn't much of it around here."

Carefully placing his weight on his right foot, Kelso moved off the table. "What time of day is it? This dinner, or what?"

"It is dinner, as I said." She looked at the fancy wristwatch on her left wrist. "It is fifteen after ten. Or twenty-two-fifteen, if you prefer. By the time we're through with dinner it will be time to go to bed."

Having sat down, he looked at her again and saw a glint of something new in her eyes; not amusement this time, but anticipation and curiosity. "I just got up," he muttered, perturbed at the swiftness with which events were moving. Perturbed and hungry and, yes, goddammit, aware of a growing desire for something besides food.

She met his look across the soup bowls, green eyes gone subtly seductive. "Whatever you wish, Captain Kelso."

9. SEDUCTION

The soup was made from dried vegetables and imitation beef chunks that she'd found in a cupboard. The main course was shrimp curry (the shrimp had been transferred from the cruiser, and the rice was one of the few items of nourishment the *Tiburón's* galley had in any quantity, a barrel of it buried under a pile of rusty hardware). For condiments she had made do with raisins, coconut and powdered egg; there was neither cayenne nor chutney. For drink, a case of 1999 Gallo burgundy was found in the freezing compartment (which no longer worked) of the refrigerator. The *Tiburón* did not lack for alcoholic beverage. One might stumble upon it anywhere. Consequently, for dessert there was a choice between Kahlua and Cointreau.

When finished, Kelso pushed his plate aside and sat in brooding silence. Not having wolfed her food the way he had, Judith DeFond continued eating, meeting his periodic stares with questioning but cautious smiles. Beneath their feet the *Tiburón* seemed to be purring along more smoothly than usual, and outside, the night-dark sea sweeping past the portholes hinted of security rather than menace.

Beside her on the table sat a microcomputer, the type of portable electronic brain that used snap-in modules, or tiny interchangeable databanks, that contained all sorts of information. Maybe she'd used it to prepare the meal. Also on the table was a pocket radiophone that Kelso assumed she could use to communicate with her two goons aft, or wherever they were. She had probably discovered the ineptness of the *Tiburón's* intercom system.

"So you can cook well enough," he finally said, almost grudgingly. "Haven't eaten like that in years."

She swallowed her last mouthful and drained her glass of wine. "Considering the looks of you, I'd say you haven't eaten much of anything for some time."

Kelso contemplated his gaunt ribs through his nest of chest hair.

"I suggest we head for the Restitution Islands and take on stores."

"Oh, you do?"

"Yes, I do."

"You like the Isles of Paradise, do you?"

"I found them . . . rather fascinating. And I assume you and your notorious ship would be more welcome there than in San Francisco or San Diego, say. Since the Restitutions are a smuggling haven and underworld trade crossroads, we should be able to find everything we need there."

"Including a hundred or so Judas goats who'll be itching to put my head on a platter so they can deliver it up to the coastal cops for the well-advertised bounty."

"I can go in with Juan and Carlos, make arrangements to have a dependable and trustworthy supplier meet us on one of the deserted islands."

"Dependable and trustworthy supplier." Kelso snorted.

"Do you know one?" She ignored his sarcasm.

"Hell. Maybe. Look—" He squirmed in the chair, sat up with his elbows on the table. "I've been thinking about this, about what you want to do—or what you claim you want to do." He watched her closely but her eyes betrayed no uneasiness with the implication of possible treachery on her part. "The water in the Zone is polluted with strontium and plutonium and god knows what else. There were a hell of a lot of nuke installations of one kind or another in the area, some of them known, some of them kept secret. Most of them fission. They were using nuke explosives to get at oil deposits along the continental shelf as far back as the nineties. They were doing the same thing—though maybe not for the same reason—in the San Gabriels decades later."

"Yes, I know. Your wife—"

"What?" He was momentarily thrown off track.

"You and your wife fought against the corporate plutocrats, the government. When I first heard about you and started checking up, I remembered hearing your wife's name in newscasts, as well as yours, when I was a child." This was said quickly, as if to override an underlying uncertainty. "Lisa Kelso—"

"The point is this," he said, cutting her off sharply, unable to bear the mention of Lisa just now, "I have one radiation-proof diving suit. I assume when you say you want to *dive,* you mean outside a submersible."

"Yes. But I have an insulated suit, with alleviation cells and the Paaswell-Grunberg coils, like yours. So do Juan and Carlos. And, judging from the general condition of everything else on the *Tiburón,* I would be willing to wager that our suits are in much better shape than yours."

"You don't say." His glance went from microcomputer to radiophone to the wristwatch on her wrist, one of those, no doubt, that gave you the time, temperature, date, weather forecast, your goddamned biorhythms, blood pressure, heart-rate, and horoscope. "Well, that brings to mind another problem. The poor *Tiburón* happens to be almost out of fuel."

She picked up his plate and set it on top of hers. "Low on tritium, I believe Carlos said."

Kelso grabbed the wine bottle and poured himself another water glass full. "All right," he snapped. "Low on tritium. The last I heard, there wasn't any of *that* in the Restitution Islands."

"No. But there is in the undersea colony off Cabo Colnette where you worked."

He stared at her, for the moment nonplused.

"I told you. I did my research. You are, incidentally, an interesting subject of study, Captain Kelso." She stood with the plates, for some reason momentarily unable to meet his eyes. "A paradox—if that is the right word. A former marine biologist who developed an ingenious sonic code that enabled you to communicate with cetaceans, who, when you were pressured into employing that accomplishment for ends you felt inhumane, rebelled, fought back, and were summarily dismissed from Colnette. Who, along with your wife, consistently struggled for clean energy alternatives here on Earth and sensible pioneering programs in space." Her eyes lifted from the plates and looked at him again. "You consistently fought for life, for nature, and now you ride in a stolen fusion-powered submarine designed and built originally for warfare by the kinds of minds you've always abhorred, and you spend your time fighting government patrol boats and poking around in polluted waters where little has been able to live for years. And I think I know why."

"Yeah?" His intention was to cut her off once more—her observations were getting too near the quick—but she ceased speaking and turned for the counter. "Maybe you know too damned much. But do you also know how hard it is to take anything from the Colnette complex?"

Having placed the dishes on the counter and shoved them toward the galley side, she turned back to face him, folding her arms across the front coverall vee. "You should listen to the news. The conflicts in Asia and Africa are sapping U.S. domestic defenses. Like all the other military branches, the Navy has had to concentrate most of its forces abroad. I'm sure Colnette will still be difficult but, like a lot of other places, it cannot be protected now as it once was. One of the reasons I was able to sneak my cruiser into the San Gabriels was because the Coastal Authority and the San Andreas Sea Patrol have been greatly depleted in strength. You should know that."

"Yeah, I know that," he retorted, irritated with her relentless and effective arguments.

"All you have to do is show Juan and Carlos where the fusion fuel storage is located in Colnette. They will do the rest."

"Two supermen," he muttered. "They know all about nuke fuels too, huh?"

"They know a lot about most technical things. That was one of the reasons I hired them, if I remember correctly."

He looked up at the last phrase, curious. But she turned, averting her eyes and unnecessarily fiddling with the glassware on the counter. "Interesting," he said, meaning just the opposite where Juan and Carlos were concerned. The topic of her bodyguards had long ago palled. Kelso swilled wine. "Now let me see if I've got all this straight. First we go to the Restitutions and take on stores like any ordinary vessel about to embark on an extended cruise. Sure. Then we go help ourselves to the fusion trove at Colnette. Right. Then we proceed to Angeles Bay in all due haste and dive into the Highland Park ruins to locate and resurrect the lost and priceless *objets d'art*—along with some personal undisclosed valuables—of the DeFond estate. Right?"

Her reserved smile proved equal to his taunting. "That is basically correct, Captain."

"I'm not a goddamned captain." He scowled at the floor for a few moments, thinking, then lifted his head and ran a hand through his hair. "Sure. Why not. It'll be a change of routine." He was anything but agreeable, however. Removing himself from the chair, he clutched the table edge for support. "Hell's hags. I'm going to the control room, where I can think. Maybe figure out a way to retake command of this derelict."

Evidently ignoring the contradiction of his disclaiming the title of captain while at the same time wanting to retake command of his ship, she said, "Of course," and remained at the counter, watching him, her face deadpan. "Carlos and Juan are probably asleep by now in the after crew's quarters. They won't bother you."

"Carlos and Juan. Juan and Carlos. I've heard enough of those two for one night." Cursing, he hopped toward the ladderway aft of the mess.

"Would you like me to help—"

"No!" He reached the door, hopped through.

"Very well. Where would you like me to bunk then? My gear is in the wardroom. The old officers' quarters is filled with . . . salvage."

He turned back, saw the green eyes glinting, the rudiments of a smile at the corners of her mouth. "You sleep any damned place you like. I've got enough on my mind without worrying about where you sleep."

She nodded. "I'll wait until you return for you to show me how you want things arranged."

But Kelso was gone, talking irritably to himself as he hopped down the narrow passageway.

The deck of the control room had been swept, scrubbed and swabbed; wastebaskets and ashtrays emptied and washed; pencils, papers, maps, and charts placed in tidy stacks on the table in front of the instruments or put away in drawers. They hadn't even spared this, his meditation chamber! The place where he went to remind himself—when he felt the need—who, where, what he was, how he'd become that, and why. The place where he came to tell himself he was in some kind of control amid the general chaos overtaking the world. But he'd never find himself in this sterile surgeon's lab!

His anger was nonetheless short-lived and superficial. As he sank into the chair at the control console, he realized how badly the room had needed cleaning and straightening up. And, realizing this, he realized something else: he hadn't cared if the ship was dirty and disordered for a long time, but all at once he appreciated order and cleanliness. He cared. Why? Caring was an affliction, an insidious indulgence that could consume one's insides, reduce one to tatters.

He liked her. Goddammit, he did, he liked her! Worse than that, he *desired* her.

And distrusted her. Sensed a strangeness about her. Sensed something at odds with itself behind those disconcerting green eyes.

He was blown off-center by the swiftness with which things had moved. He'd lived alone, at his own slow and sloppy pace, for too long. Yeah. Kelso in his control room. In control of what? In the center of what? Just what did this crazy pseudolife he led amount to anyway that he should be so stupidly afraid of changing it? What did he have to lose by going along with her?

Well, that depended on what her real game was.

He had to sort things out. Yet even before he started he knew he wouldn't find any new answers. After nearly an hour of sitting at the main console, trying to wrestle to earth the questions flying around in his head, stumbling over ground already covered— What was he getting himself into? Did he want to get himself into it? Had she stated her true motive? Had she told him the whole truth and nothing but the truth about herself and her past?—he became once again mired in the miserable belief that the San Andreas-Los Angeles Basin catastrophe had been too horrible, too violent, vast and wholesale, to have been the result of natural causes alone.

That belief had haunted Kelso for almost a decade, and the Pandora's Box of theories still fouling the post-quake atmosphere had never done anything for his quest for truth. While scientists bickered among themselves about planetary alignments, sunspots, plate tectonics, and continental drift, militarists ranted about atomic sabotage, but couldn't agree on which country to blame, and finally couldn't or wouldn't prove their allegations. Religious nuts, of course, had made ample pay dirt of the grim event and preached that one more sign had been given that Doomsday was at hand. Environmentalists (Kelso had to include himself in this last group) contended that whatever had gone wrong, the inveterate stupidity of man surely had to be awarded a central place of responsibility. The proponents of this latter view could point out everything from the folly of constructing nuke facilities over the labyrinth of fault zones to the fact that the United States Government, in cahoots with corporate interests, had been surreptitiously blowing holes in the San Gabriels, thus certainly helping, if not initiating, the superquake. As far as Jack Kelso was concerned, any or all such theories could explain, to some degree, what had resulted. From his admittedly twisted perspective, man could as easily be the accomplice as the victim of blind natural forces. The San Andreas Fault and all its branches were put there by the indifferent hand of nature, but that potentially perilous handiwork had been widely publicized for well over half a century. Men were responsible for not heeding the years of warnings, for not even heeding the earlier, smaller quakes in the late 1900s, responsible for doing little or nothing in relocating or protecting the hundreds of thousands who lived in the Zone, responsible for keeping such things as nuke installations operating at full tilt, responsible for "Nuke probes" on land apparently unstable as quicksand or scree. What else might man, Kelso's countrymen, be responsible for? What had government and corporate agents been probing for under the San Gabriels? More mucking oil? Or something else?

The suspicion that had nagged from the beginning returned. Could she be an agent of some kind? Could she have found him, "hired" him to take her into Highland Park because he knew the area as well or better than anyone alive and could inadvertently help her find whatever *they* wanted her to find down there?

Kelso recalled the years after the cataclysms during which U.S. Government and URI personnel swarmed over the Zone. Looking for evidence of seismic sabotage, they said. For top secret records and research equipment at Cal Tech and JPL and other such places, they said. Probably they were trying to find and clean up evidence of having caused the catastrophe themselves. Probably Jack Kelso was paranoid. Yes.

No.

He shook his head, trying to force clarity into a brain that had for too long preferred to stay clouded. He drummed his fingers on the console and looked distractedly at the instruments, indicators, and sonar screens.

He punched the keyboard below the CRT. The *Tiburón* currently cruised at a depth of 120 meters and a speed of thirty knots, its position 119 degrees longitude, 33 degrees latitude, on a course for the Restitutions, which lay approximately 150 kms. due south.

So! The course to the Restitutions had been set before she'd suggested it to him!

When his ire finally cooled after this latest discovery, Kelso noticed that some of the instruments worked that hadn't for years. He could at a glance actually ascertain the *Tiburón*'s trim, the speed of the water's current, and specific gravity, stabilization readings, details of the sea bottom, what lay ahead, above, behind and below, without having to consult the computer. He tried a few switches and dials, then moved to the sonar console. The long-range scanner worked, as did the discriminator and the frequency converters. The UV searchlight and the external TV cameras were, however, still on the fritz. He had a thought and swiveled the chair to the computer console in the center of the main board.

"How you feeling, Chief?"

"I am feeling very well, Captain," answered the speaker in the console.

"How come? You haven't felt good in ages. All you do is grumble. Like me. Those two mechanical wizards fool with you too?"

"Your new human crew is a definite improvement for the *Tiburón*, Captain. They shall relieve me of my overload of work, and see to it that the ship is given the care it so badly needs."

"Those remarks smack of insubordination. Did they put funny ideas into your goddamned disks? Is there mutiny afoot?"

"No, Captain. In my judgment, your new crew, as well as myself, are totally devoted to you and *Tiburón*."

"Why? They tell you the reason for this bloody devotion?"

"No, Captain. They told me nothing. My impressions are based only upon the improvements and repairs they have made in myself and *Tiburón* during the few hours they have been aboard."

"Where'd they get the parts and stuff for repairs?"

"They improvised from odds and ends. Odds and ends are, as you know, in great supply on *Tiburón*."

Kelso ignored the dig. But did the blasted computer wonder too? It was capable of sarcasm (a trait likely learned from himself); was it also capable of suspicion? However badly he wanted a confidant, though, he doubted the Chief's abilities in the realm of intrigue.

"Nuts." He hoisted himself from the chair. "I need a drink." About to start forward, Kelso changed his mind, turned and hopped to the after passageway.

In the dimly-lit corridor between the control room and the engine room, he had to stop to rest. Leaning against the bulkhead on the other side of which lay the compartment housing the reactor, he thought of the deuterium-tritium mixture inside. That smidgen of fuel had lasted him seven years; it had been part of the original package entitled *USS Shark IV* that he'd rechristened *Tiburón*, liking the Spanish better. But the boat needed revitalized fuel if she was going to continue her exploits of infamy, and where else could he—they—*they?*—acquire the necessary stuff except out of the main power hydrodome at Colnette? Oh yeah, this Judith DeFond was a clever one, all right. Kelso had the disquieting notion he'd seen only a fraction of the intelligence contained in that elegant skull, despite brief glimpses of ambivalence or uncertainty in action or word.

The engine room reeked of cleaning fluids, fresh lubricants, metal polish. Everything glistened. The whiz kids had been here too. They must have worked like twin hurricanes while he'd been out.

The engine room was the longest leg of his hopalong circuit, and he stopped twice more before reaching the ladderway leading down to the lower compartment of the after crew's quarters. He didn't bother negotiating the ladderway; he could see into the quarters from where he stood above.

A single red nightlight burned from the base of the starboard bulkhead. Most of the junk strewn throughout the room had been neatly rearranged off to the side. The first two upper bunks held bags and bundles which had to be the bodyguards' gear; on the two bunks below these they slept as soundly as babes. Or seemed to.

Okay, he thought. Everything shipshape, everything shiny and neat. Everything rosy and cozy—on the surface.

He pulled back and, facing the ordeal of returning to the stateroom, sighed and resumed hopping, with the elements of a decision working their way into the intervals between leaving and connecting with the deck.

Well—(hop-clump) might as well string along (hop-thud), nothing better to do anyway (thud-hop), but got to keep (clop-hop-thud), my distance (hop), watch things (thud), with a chary eye (hop-clump), whoops, almost lost it that time; goddamned deck's too clean and slippery (thump)....

The officers' quarters lay forward of the wardroom. Like every other square centimeter of space in the *Tiburón* not set aside for the ship's needs, this room was crammed with old diving gear, salvage and plunder brought up from the wreckage of submerged Los Angeles. When he looked into the officers' quarters, he found it in its usual mess.

No sign of her. But he'd come through the galley and up through the wardroom and she was in neither of those places either. So where?

A hissing noise coming from the officers' head made him look in that direction. He couldn't see clearly over the piles of crap in the way, but a light fringed the head door. It was the shower he heard, and all at once it quit.

Kelso tried not to think of what she looked like sans coveralls. (Keep your distance. Watch things with a wary eye. Oh, yeah.) But the head door came open and, in the midst of the out-wafting steam, he saw.

Cramped by the small confines of the head, she had to step into the quarters to towel off. He stared in spite of himself, transfixed.

As if sensing him near, she stopped drying herself and looked up. She straightened, made no move to cover anything whatsoever. The towel hung idly from one hand. She threw it over her shoulder and stepped around the intervening obstacles toward him. The emerald eyes glowed as she confronted him point blank.

"Have you decided where you want me to sleep?"

10. FISSURE

In the darkness of the stateroom she lay, feeling the last spasms clutch and let go. Slowly the faint, almost subliminal, noises of the ship, the smells of the stateroom, the warmth of the bunk, replaced the diminishing sexual delirium.

Every cell and nerve resonated. She wanted more. But he slept, one arm thrown across her breasts.

The darkness was swollen and aswirl, like the pockets of deep space, with enigmatic nebulae. Under the soothing post-coital peace and gratification, an elusive misgiving and bewilderment moved.

The pockets of deep space. Nebulae. What did she know of such things?

Like the dark upwelling from the oceanic abyss and the waves that begin a thousand miles out at sea and come tumbling across the vast distances to break against beaches, she'd felt the waves, the storms, the peaks and eddies, throughout her body.

Her body? It did not feel as if it belonged to her—or rather its every sensation felt new, as if for the first time those sensations might be hers.

Repeatedly she'd shuddered, cried out and held him with a grip so strong her nails carved crescent wounds in his skin. From deep in her being something ancient, primordial, had risen, tried to burst into the perplexing present, fell back, had risen again to sink a final time, smothered by the very waves that awakened it.

Tears had wet her cheeks; her lips and teeth pressed to his face and neck as if she might draw more, suck to the dregs the magic that had given rise to the waves and disturbed the slumbering secret within. But after the third climax he was spent, and as she heard his contented moan and felt his body go slack, she knew it was over. For this night at least.

But what lay inside that had stirred and, lifting its vague head from the depths, tried to breathe as if for the first time?

Beside her, he snored. She listened to this noise with the same attention she would have given the call of a bird or beast not heard before. He reminded her of those thorny desert plants that grew among the ruins on the isles fringing Angeles Bay, a coarse prickly exterior concealing and protecting rich fruit. She could no longer deny it, not here and now anyway, lying beside him like this, after the intense pleasure she'd just shared with him. Those stories told about him, the material she'd studied, stirred obscure chords, started echoes vibrating within her own mind.

Her mind? As in the case of her body, she was beginning to be aware of a deep-rooted consciousness astir, seeking light, that seemed for the first time to be really hers.

Echoes? Derived from where, from what?

His snores cascaded down the scale like a broken, quixotic

horn summoning an army to arms that had never existed. He had fought, waged his own private war against those who steadfastly tried to lay waste the planet for avaricious and materialistic ends. Was that what had started the echoes? If so, why?

Answers seemed to move in the darkness, beyond her reach, shapeless, yet-to-be-formed.

It seemed she had never heard snoring, as it seemed she'd never lain with a man. She tingled with feelings, with half-formed thoughts she was becoming more and more certain had not been experienced before. But how could that be?

As she had recalled more than once, the history of her life that the doctors in Phoenix had reconstructed contained affairs, romances with men.

The history of her life that the doctors had reconstructed.

Phoenix. The doctors.

Why did it all seem false? Why did all her knowledge, experiences, the bits and pieces of a youthful life preceding her breakdown, and even the years at the hospital in Phoenix and after seem fabricated, the artificial input of an extraneous origin or source? Was this typical of amnesia, or of post-amnesia?

Her body protested that she had never felt like this before, had never felt such sensations. Her body screamed an incontestable *no.*

The possibility that the doctors made a mistake, traced the past of another Judith DeFond and gave her the history of someone else, did not seem to explain it. Because the doctors themselves appeared now to be as much a fabrication, a delusion, as that tidily arranged history. They moved like wraiths in her introspective vision, like papier maché figures withering under the light of this sudden new eye of truth gaining dominance.

Why? How?

Her eyes came open. The questions rang in her mind like gongs, alien and ominous, and she felt a tug downward toward a vortex of endlessly repeated "whys", "hows", "whats", that branched and multiplied like plankton.

Why did questioning itself seem so strange, inimical?

She sat up. Kelso stirred and became still.

She looked down at him. His face was faintly visible from the glow of the red nightlight in the outside passageway.

Why did she fear feeling so much? Why did she fear joy?

Her "Phoenix memory" offered the automatic answer. The death of her parents had been such a shock that she never wanted to feel anything for anyone again. Simple. Pat.

False.

Then why this obsession to dive into sunken Highland Park? *That* seemed to come from a deeper compulsion, a more real impetus, than anything belonging to the Phoenix "experience". Why? Did her parents really die in the cataclysm? Was their home in Highland Park? Had she really loved them so much, had their deaths been such a shock as to have destroyed her memory, such a blow as to have flattened her with the notion that God was evil, the world a vast deathhouse, life absurd? Had she loved them so much that she could see no other course but the suicidal one of finding their underwater graves and, like Kelso's suspected motive for continuing to dive in the ruins, of joining them there?

Or was she simply demented?

No. Somehow she knew the internal turmoil could not be resolved that way. The fact that she could raise such a question convinced her of its absurdity.

She moved carefully off the bunk so as not to wake Kelso. Finding her robe on the floor, where she'd discarded it, she pulled it on and stepped into the passageway. She did not know where she was going, only knew that she had to move. But she found herself passing through the wardroom and stopping at the door of the library.

She grasped the wheel that was supposed to seal the door airtight and gave an experimental tug; it came open easily, as it had before. Her fingers found the light switch on the inside bulkhead.

The room was as it had been when she first saw it, small, den-like, crammed with books. She stood there, eyes running over titles she could make out from the middle of the room, not knowing what she looked for, not even sure she was looking for something that could be found between the covers of a book, only aware for the moment that her mind had been taken off the endless questions, the bizarre and disturbing directions her thoughts were taking her.

The books were in no kind of order. One title would suggest a subject in the field of marine biology, the next a work of fiction. There were history and philosophy titles, books on oceanography, submarine geology, sea farming, sea mining, and navigation. And there were popular nonfiction titles, like the one on which her eyes suddenly fastened.

Self-healing Through Self-hypnosis: Untying Your Kinks Without a Shrink.

She stepped to the shelf, plucked the book from its niche between the others, went to the sofa, sat down, tucked her legs under her, and opened it.

The book was read from the first line to the last. A chapter on hypnotic cure for amnesia was read twice. Kelso had obviously read the book, because passages in many places, particularly those sections dealing with depression, were underlined and bordered with scribbled notations. She ignored these for the time being, and concentrated on what the author of the book had to say. The chapter on technique was committed to memory almost verbatim. When she was satisfied she could glean nothing more from its content, she closed the book, returned it to its place on the shelf and lay down on the sofa. Following the author's instructions, she closed her eyes and willfully shed all conscious distraction, imagined a central pinpoint of light and, willing her body to relax by degrees, from her toes to her scalp and hair, she began silently to repeat the word "one" in her mind. . . .

. . . the small cabin cruiser moving through the water. Juan at the helm, Carlos cleaning a weapon in the stern. Herself above the pilot's cabin, watching the dormant volcano that was Restitution Island beginning to loom in the distance.

Her first vivid and real memory. But she wanted to go back, go deeper, much deeper than that.

She drifted, remembering the freshness of that day they landed in the Restitutions, remembering how her mind and senses were almost overwhelmed with everything she saw, smelled, heard, felt. Questions had come even then, yes.

Floating. Through images, noises, not quite real. The Phoenix "layer". Downward, backward in time, ignoring the false mnemonic fabric of this second level, falling deeper.

Through a darkness almost palpable, like the sea. Tiny points of light far away, stationary. Like stars.

Wait. They were stars. Yes. Like phosphorescent clouds. Streams of them. Her passage through them was like a comet's, or a comet's tail.

A faster-than-light particle? A faster-than-light ray?

Where were *these* concepts coming from? They seemed familiar here, at this level, at this depth. But what else was here?

Nothing but the star streams, interstellar dust clouds, infinity.

Beneath this, a barrier, a darkness that allowed no farther descent. The fists of the mind beat against its implacable iron. Futile. Over the edge of the barrier, a void, nothingness, perhaps the ultimate plunge. But a world, another world, other worlds, of hidden realities lay secreted just beneath the barrier, the black iron door floating there on the current of this interstellar sea.

The abyss beyond, below, waited. The journey down had been far, farther than previously thought possible, perhaps too far. Reality, the world of ordinary things, substance, sentience, was suddenly dear.

Upward. Back. Frantic now, afraid.

But then, coming up through the Phoenix layer, a strange light, an abrupt alteration of "setting" . . .

. . . in an earthly place she walks through broken arches. She has a clipboard in her hand, wears a pack on her back. A camera is strapped over her shoulder. On the perimeter of the broken stones is tropical forest. Pyramids, walls, stellae, courtyards, fill a clearing in the middle of the jungle. She is in Chichén Itzá? Or is it Copán? Palenque? Any or all or none of these places where she has never been?

Searching, she walks among the broken glory of a vanished race, a race that claimed celestial origins. A race that flourished, perhaps a utopian race. Depending on what was meant by *utopian.*

There is no one here but Judith DeFond and carved faces, heads, figures that watch. An occasional bird flits past, like a reincarnated spirit of someone who once lived here. The air is hot and humid and thick with the scent of vegetable life. Moss and lichen and ferns cover everything with varied shades and patterns of green. Here one could become drunk with life. And secrets.

But for the twitter and squawk of the encompassing jungle, a silence pervades. Silence but for the tap of her sandaled feet on cracked masonry and her breath coming fast as she looks.

For what?

Sharp blades of grass cut her bare legs. Cobwebs whisper

against her face, brush against her eyes. Howler monkeys call down from the high trees beyond the rubble as if to warn the silent rock-hewn gods awake.

Something draws her toward the jungle behind the last crumbled column. Whatever she seeks lies there somewhere. She stumbles over the staggered rocks. She plunges into the vegetable tangle. Brambles, limbs, vines, tear at her shirt, claw at her camera and clipboard, whip at her face and legs. Outraged by her intrusion, the howlers shriek and multicolored quetzals fly screeching. Across her path a form, black and sleek with yellow eyes, appears and vanishes into the undergrowth. Above her head, high above the forest canopy, a lone bird of prey spirals downward.

She falls, gets up, goes on. She has lost the clipboard. The camera beats against her ribs. She bleeds where the vegetation has lashed her skin. It is there, up ahead, something. . . .

The brush is a matted net with a thousand strands wrapping around her, snarling her ankles and wrists. She throws her arms up over her eyes and pushes, kicks her way through. Above, the howlers scream and gibber and rattle the branches in a frenzied cacophony that drowns out all other sound.

When at last the jungle parts, she lurches into another clearing. Before her stands a tremendous wall, a free-standing wall with a single great doorway in the center and a legend carved on the colossal lintel above the door.

It is the Gate of the Sun at Tiahuanaco, says the Phoenix knowledge.

No. It is more huge than that. And this place is not Tiahuanaco. Also, the hieroglyphs are strange, ciphers that defy her pseudo background in archaeology.

But all at once the sky is dark, the jungle behind her is gone. She is in desert that stretches limitlessly in all directions. Above the desert, stars. And the great wall remains before her.

Atop its lintel perches the bird of prey, blacker than the black sky, its eyes two pools without pupil or iris, through which she can see stars. He is the guardian of the gate, and the holder of the key to the indecipherable hieroglyphs.

Yet as she watches, numb with a cold the desert wind has beaten into her soul, the giant bird leaps from the lintel, its wings aflutter like a robe in the wind, then suddenly outspread. It drops toward her, casting its darker-than-death shadow over her like a satanic shroud. She is powerless, cannot move. Talons out for her throat, it strikes and knocks her to the ground. Its beak beats like a hammer at her brain.

She came up gasping, holding her neck, crying out at the relentless pain in her head. Dizzied, she got up from the sofa, reaching out to the bookshelves for support.

Stumbling out the door, she came to a stop for a moment in the red-lit passageway, hands pressed to her head in an effort to halt the steady pounding. Nausea welled up and she felt as if she were falling in space. Slowly the pain in her head began to subside, the nausea to ease. And in the ensuing hiatus came again the question:

Am I simply mad?

There was one question that could be answered now, this night.

She moved aft down the passageway, past the wardroom, the stateroom, past the control room, the reactor compartment, through the engine room and came to the door into the after crew's quarters where the Lavacca brothers slept. The door was open to allow better circulation. A wall fan droned softly as she stepped in. She could see, in the pale red glow of the nightlight, the sleeping bodyguards in the two lower bunks near the fan. Their breathing was regular, rhythmic. She stepped close so she could see the first one's face.

It did not help. She could not tell if it was Juan or Carlos in the low light. It shouldn't matter, unless—

Juan, she thought, concentrating, and telling herself she was being foolish at the same time. *Juan, wake up. Now!*

From the other bunk, the prostrate form became animated, threw off its sheet and grabbed the handgun that had been under the pillow. The one she had been standing beside also moved, a little more slowly than the other, but in seconds they were both standing before her, armed, expectantly waiting.

Judith stared from one to the other, a hand involuntarily climbing to clutch guardedly at the imaginary spot on her neck where the bird had struck.

Can you read my thoughts? Both of you?

Simultaneously, they nodded. In order to be certain, she turned on the overhead light and voicelessly asked the question again, and received the same emphatic gesture of affirmation she'd seen them give the first time.

How? Her mind shrieked it. *Why?*

They looked at her blankly, and shrugged.

Who are you? Where are you from?

Again a blank look. Then the one on her left, whom she now saw was Carlos, said, "We come from you, *señorita.* We are yours."

"What?" The sound of her voice startled her; it had been almost a shout. "What do you mean you came from me?"

Carlos looked at Juan and the latter returned his twin's baffled expression. "I do not know, *señorita.*"

"What the hell do you mean you do not know? Don't you have a mind, a brain of your own?"

The answer came back like a slap in the face, like a blow that had originated in her own mental tumult. "No, *señorita.*"

She was stunned, could not cope for the moment, had to grasp the side of the bunk. Another thought came: "When—what do you remember of—before we went to the Restitution Islands? What do you remember before that? Where did I find you? Where did I hire you?"

"You hired us in San Diego," Carlos said. "In a bar."

"Yes. All right. Before that. What did you do before I hired you?"

Carlos's voice was as toneless, as lacking in personality as it had always been when he said, "We did not exist, *señorita.*"

11. WARSONG

High mountains hemmed them in. An alien presence she could feel had penetrated the walls of the ship, of cold, of eternal night. On the comviewer in the captain's station of the operations bridge, the helmeted image of Phegakz, commander of the Xlimoyin, bobbed and swayed as the hidden head inside it raged.

Cinara Tlii sought consolation in the fact the planetfall

had been successful. All ships had reported in unharmed. Every landing force of the salient was down, secreted in their positions in a great ring around the Desert of Nammava Trah, the Desert of Heaven, in the Yaghattarin language.

The Sixth and Seventh Forces, led by the Xlimoyin and the Hrarghals, lay offplanet. They were supposed to wait until word reached them that the second phase of the penetration had succeeded before they made any move against enemy ships off Naravamintara. But patience was as foreign to the Xlimoyin as peace.

"We succeeded in penetrating the outer defenses," Phegakz said. "I say we can get through the inner ones. I say the Onnahlaetian female does not know the ways of war."

Tlii closed her eyes against the image, the glittering studded helmet that was likely not quite as hideous as the head it encased. *An ally,* she thought. A member, a leader, of one of the few races outside the imperial stranglehold who had never been subjugated by the Deathlords; one here for the pure love of killing, and for the spoils that are left in the wake of ruin. An ally. The thought bit deeply into her heart.

"I say the thought-language will fail. I say you will sit there in that valley until those mountains squash your ships to pebbles before she is able to communicate with anyone in that underground fortress through the means of her obscure wizardry."

Acexea stood before the comviewer, immobile as iron. His shadow was cast against the far wall of the ship, gigantic, remote as Prithipea. "You have seen Cinara Tlii's powers demonstrated, Phegakz. Your doubts were, we were assured, allayed. You agreed to the plan. You agreed that we would follow it without argument. Before we left the Mrirdugans, you agreed to this. It has been her guidance, her ideas, from the beginning that put us in motion, that brought us this far. We follow her plan, as we agreed."

"She does not know the ways of the Xlimoyin!" Phegakz roared. "She is Onnahlaetian. Her people are children who run naked and are ruled by women. They do not know combat!"

Standing to the side of Acexea, Tlii called forth in her mind the green lands, the warm skies, of Onnahlaeti. She walked mid flowers and kissed the grass even as Onnah's sun kissed her skin. The mountains above the valley of the Great

Rift of Naravamintara, the snarling oaths of Phegakz, fell away.

"Commander Phegakz." It was Falur who spoke. He stood several paces back from the comviewer, but now stepped forward and stood between Acexea and Tlii, looking up at the viewer that Acexea had canted so he and Cinara could see. "With respect, I would like to point out that the kind of war you are used to and the knowledge you have of such war will not do much good until it is certain we have allies inside Nammava Trah II. We have everything to our advantage now. The Yaghattarin are ignorant of our presence. To attack by conventional force would alert them to the fact we are here. They would exert every means they have to seal Nammava Trah II and they would find a way to detect our positions and neutralize our shields."

"Is it not true, sprig, that Cinara Tlii wants to save former Onnahlaetians inside Nammava Trah II? Is that not why we must wait while she plays mind-games with the Naravamintaran wind?"

Phegakz's words were far away but she heard them. Their belligerence invaded her calm, defiled the sanctuary in her mind where she sought strength. The Rift's mountains appeared, lifeless colossi supplanting Onnah's gentle hills. An ember, small but hot, burned in her heart, fanned by cold winds and the words of Phegakz.

Falur was again answering for her. "It is true she wants to save former Onnahlaetians, as well as all who are held by the Yaghattarin. This was told you in the beginning, and you agreed to it, as Commander Acexea has pointed out."

Phegakz bellowed a curse that the translator could only pass on in the Xlimoyin original.

The ember glowed, germ of the same fire which ruled Phegakz, she knew, ignited long ago when the seizeships came. Each time she saw it, felt it, it was larger and stronger than before.

Acexea said, "We will cease this pointless argument. You complain of waiting and then make us wait on your complaints. You have your orders. Obey them." The communicator, sensitive to the nuances of Acexea's voice, blanked its viewer. The Prithipean turned and spoke a command for an aircar to be readied.

The thought of what waited outside made her shudder. But she would not use that embryonic fire at her core to keep away the Naravamintaran cold, lest it grow stronger. Warmth had to come from the memory of what was good, from Onnahlaeti.

When the aircar found the high pass and lowered to a relatively level spot among the rocks, she was the first who stood. The door opened and the wind rushed in. She pushed forward, through, onto the uneven ground, moving in the heavy groundsuit like one whose limbs were chained. Behind her, Acexea spoke a warning, and she felt his firm grasp as a blast of wind almost tore her away.

"You will not be able to withstand this wind for long," he said.

"I will. I must see them, the ruins of Nammava Trah I. I must be here where I can see."

"A rest shelter will be brought up."

Above her he loomed, yellow eyes glowing through the faceshield of his headpiece. "We will be all right," she said. "Falur and I. I am grateful for your concern but it must be done this way. Falur will help. He knows the mindmusic."

The Prithipean did not move.

What holds him thus? she wondered and tried to read his thoughts. But as always, she encountered a blank, a barrier, like the rough natural integument that protected his body from Prithipea's heat.

"We will succeed," he said at last. Then, in character, he quickly turned away and strode back to the aircar, crossing the rocks like a thing that could have been born here as well as in the fiery lands of his homeworld.

The aircar did not lift, however, until she and the boy had securely buckled themselves to the rocks overlooking the precipice. Then it vanished to the valley below, on the hidden side of the mountains.

On their side, far down the massive vertical cliffs, lay the bleakness of the desert, here and there dim clusters of lights delineating an installation or city of some kind. And in the middle of the dark wasteland, the faint darker depression which marked the ruins of Nammava Trah I.

The wind tried to intrude, pressed their suits against their bodies, tried to tug them from the rocks.

—Forget the wind, she sent to Falur. Forget all but the ancient thoughtsongs and the world of your coming-to-life.

Cleanse your mind of all other things, and I will give you a brief history that will take us deeper into our hearts, deeper into the spirit of the world whose light looks out our eyes, whose rivers flow in our veins, whose peace lives in our souls.

As she sent this, she knew such guidance and reassurance was more for herself than the boy. Her eyes fell on the faraway ruins of Nammava Trah I, and in them she saw the symbol of evil, the hole that had appeared in her universe long ago, on the other side of which lay things unimaginable. The noise of the wind receded, the walls of time fell away.

—It is not known from where the ancient ones came. From another galaxy perhaps, perhaps another universe. It is not known where they have gone. In the beginning, those from whom both the Yaghattarin and we descended were, so the legends say, one race. The ancient star wanderers. The Arkhalahn. Nor is it known why there occurred the schism that grew into a stellar war and forever separated the one faction from the other. The faction from which the Yaghattarin descended denounced the others as "adulterators", as those who had polluted their blood with the blood of lower life forms indigenous to various worlds they visited and at times colonized. It is said we of Onnahlaeti are descendants of these "adulterators."

—But it is not known for certain if they actually mated with indigenes, as the Yaghattarin claim, or if they merely cohabited with them and maybe in some instances helped them genetically or improved their evolutionary pathways. It is not known for certain if this was actually the cause of the original conflict. Most of what we have for a history has been put together from the dogma of the Deathlords and the stories and legends handed down by our own race. The old ones who taught you say that the forerunners of the Yaghattarin, the "Pure" or "Divine" Ones, as they named themselves, fled here to this system of desolate worlds and the Adulterators, the Arkhalahn, followed them. The great city of Nammava Trah I, the Place of Gods, was destroyed by the Starwanderers, and the Naravamintarans were scattered over the planet. The Ones-Who-Roam-the-Stars left and have never returned. The Naravamintarans built a subsurface fortress under the ruins of Nammava Trah and from there they proceeded to subjugate other worlds and build an empire of enslaved peoples who would support their rule and their search across the galaxy for the Arkhalahn. They have never been found, as far as we know. But Naravamintara continues to search, and to subjugate, to assimilate, to annihilate.

A dust storm swirled below on the desert. From a lake of lights far to the south, a starship rose. The placid river of Cinara's thoughtstream was discolored with bitterness. But the Naravamintaran wind remained remote, howling against that river's shores, harmless.

—One I cherish is held in Nammava Trah II.

—I understand, Falur returned. The two of you were to be one.

—Yes. He was the air I breathed. He was youth, sunlight, the crucial link in my chain with Being.

The mindriver writhed for a moment, fragmented into eddies of turbulence caused by an undertow of anguish beneath its surface, grew steady again.

—As you know, Cinara sent, for many many turns the Yaghattarin have come and taken the healthiest of our males. The females they regard as dirty, bound to life's "lowly" origins, sexual heirs, repositories, of the "adulterators'" polluted seed. But the Onnahlaetian male, despite the Deathlords' professed belief of his being descended from their ancient enemies, the Starlords, is highly prized by them. For reasons you know. The Deathlords condition the Onnahlaetian males to worship them as gods.

—The women of Onnahlaeti have always struggled and fought to hide their male children from the soul-killers, with little success. You have been one of the exceptions. When the Yaghattarin killed your parents and took your brother, I managed to save you. I had taken you, a baby, into the hills that day. One of the ahni, the great birds that wander the north, came and told me a seizeship had come. Though imperceptible to my senses at the distance you and I were from your home, the ahni had felt the air's rape by the entry of the seizeship into Onnah's atmosphere. I knew better than to return to your home, though my heart knew terror for your brother. I took your father up, into the secret regions of the old ones. I saved you, but lost your brother. For he was at home, and the Deathlords took him then. Now I have come to save him after these many turns. I pain for him to live. I pray he will know me. I pray they have not been successful in reducing him to a mindless and spiritless eunuch in bondage to their will.

—Cinya. Please. It was so long ago. I do not remember my

brother, or my parents. But . . . I wish to know how my brother could still be the one you knew. How can he have escaped being transformed into what the Yaghattarin, with their arcane contrivances, desired him to be?

The thoughtstream weakened, grew chill, its current suddenly slicked with ice. The dreaded ember in her heart glowed stronger but gave no warmth, only cold. The walls of time blackened the mind's sky and the Naravamintaran wind threatened to invade before she finally sent her answer. It came out of the tiny but deathless reservoir of hope she kept close in her soul.

—It is said . . . *kie Onnah*, it is said, the Yaghattarin do not obliterate the persona and spirit of those they enslave, lest the qualities for which they seek them will also be destroyed. It is said the Yaghattarin wish their slaves to retain their basic individualities because the Deathlords wish to keep alive their loathing for traits they claim are contemptible. One of their few modes of amusement is to encourage at least rudimentary notions of self in their slaves so they can deride them and feel, in their distorted view, superior. It is my hope that somehow your brother has escaped total evisceration of self, that his original identity, his primal memory, the roots of his inner being, remain somehow safe from the limits to which the mindscrubs have been allowed to go. This is also the reason I have hope of reaching other Onnahlaetians inside Nammava Trah II and elsewhere in Naravamintara through the ancient mindmusic and our telepathic stewardship. It is my hope that they have retained their ability to be receptive to the thought-language. It is our task to penetrate the layers of ruin the Yaghattarin have laid and breathe fresh life into those realms of spirit and conscience in which the Onnahlaetian is particularly strong.

—But enough of legends and hopes, Falur. It is time we acted. We must begin, or we will have some of our allies to contend with, as well as the lords of Naravamintara, if we do not soon produce signs that our "wizardry" works. We will reach those in Nammava Trah II the way the peoples of the Onnahlaetian worlds communicated before the Deathlords came, before our people knew of star travel or the incomprehensible things that could come from the stars. Before either you or I were born.

—I am ready, Falur returned.

—I feel your confusion. I know your heart is yet troubled with questions. Perhaps we will find answers together in

Nammava Trah II. Give me your hands. Let our blood run as close together as it can through these grotesque but necessary suits. In coming here to overcome evil, let us forget that evil for now. Let us remember only the primal good, the riches and beneficence of life. Let us remember the forests and rivers of Onnahlaeti. The oceans and the two moons. Let us send forth together the mindsongs of the old ones. . . .

12. EVOCATION

They were two days out of Angeles Bay, with San Clemente Island forty kilometers to the east, when Kelso, after kicking the Lavaccas out of the control room and consulting the Chief and the newly-functioning instruments, surfaced the *Tiburón*. The day was clear and warm, the fresh air a tonic to nostrils and lungs, the sunshine a balm to the skin. The indefatigable Lavaccas had done wonders with the ship's air purification plant and the air conditioning, as well as myriad other things, but nothing could replace fresh air and sunlight.

Naked to the waist, he stood on the bridge, supported by a walking cane one of the Lavaccas had fashioned out of an old broom handle and pistol grip. He smoked the venerable briar (his other pipes, he presumed, had been mistaken for trash and thrown overboard) and watched the *Tiburón*'s prow cut through the calm water. And pondered *her*.

He could ignore neither his growing interest, nay, attraction, nor his nagging distrust. Complicating her extraordinary good looks, that body and its talents, a mind that seemed to be forever asking questions with a child's limitless inquisitiveness, those eyes that were able to look through all of his badman's blarney and see, he was sure, the emptiness within, was a vagueness or confusion of character about her that made her difficult to define, difficult to get hold of mentally. Her earlier subdued exuberance had, in the last two days, been more subdued, if not repressed. When he thought about it, he couldn't help concluding the change had occurred after their first night of lovemaking. Though too old to entertain the delusion he was any great lover, lover enough to cause such a change in any woman, his emotional antennae, however damaged, still functioned enough to tell him that something much more sinister than romance was astir in Judith DeFond. The psychological instability she'd hinted at—and which jibed with everything else she'd told him about herself—did not satisfy. He suspected deep undercurrents, violent waters kept down, hidden, that contained secrets more devious, unusual, than those that could be perpetrated by any psychological albatross. Yet all her idiosyncratic behavior could be explained by her attempts to find herself again, after the shock of her parents' death, the breakdown she'd recounted, the amnesia, the wandering. Who the hell was he to so easily discard the psychological motive? But no matter how he looked at it, he could not rid himself of the idea that something more lay at the bottom of her. Maybe the answer did lie in whatever was at the bottom of Highland Park.

He leaned against the starboard bulwark and puffed energetically on the pipe. The other perturbation originated in how cannily, how effectively, he had been seduced. Was being seduced still, if that was the word for it. Maybe there hadn't been that much craftiness required on her part, considering her physical and sexual gifts and his loneliness. Funny thing was, he hadn't realized he'd been lonely until now—or had refused to face it. In any case, she'd awakened in a mere matter of days appetites he'd thought long atrophied, defunct, had awakened in him the first desultory stirrings of emotions he no longer had any comprehensible right to feel. But in spite of that naturally suspicious and cynical nature that had probably been his since he'd come raging into the world as the first and only born of a couple of cockeyed idealists trying to eke a living out of their meager portion of a Rocky Mountain commune, he was, he had to admit, enjoying the company of this disturbing and dubious guest. Or should he think of her as the *Tiburón*'s new captain, with himself as the "guest"? That seemed a more accurate assessment of the present situation. Besides, as he had often pointed out to the Chief, he'd never thought of himself as in command of anything, let alone a goddamned submarine.

He did not know how long he'd been there on the bridge,

smoking, thinking, worrying with the question of Judith DeFond the way one might continue to scratch at an irresistable itch (he had taken the pipe from his mouth and turned slightly to tap the bowl on the rail) when his eye caught a glimpse of color on his left. He looked aft.

She stood there, back to him, arms on the after rail of the "cigarette deck". She wore shorts, not quite as brown as her skin, a rose-colored halter top. Her hair was parted, halved, up the back of her head by the wind, blown forward, over and around her face.

He'd had no hint of her presence till now and wondered how long she'd been standing there. When Kelso told the Chief to surface, she had been in the library, a place fast becoming her favorite nook.

"Well," he said more loudly than necessary, and cleared his throat. "Not a bad day topside. Sun shines brighter the closer you get to international waters—" He broke off, hearing the caution in his voice, the uncertainty, and realized the cause. She might turn, smile briefly, perfunctorily, and leave him, like a wild animal that preferred, if it could not blend in with its surroundings and avoid notice, to flee. She might sidestep his comment or query and steer him, them, on a more abstract course. She might—

But she did something this time he hadn't experienced before. When she turned to face him, he saw pain, bewilderment in her eyes. Immediately he saw she realized what he'd seen; the confusion vanished, was replaced with a smile. But, unexpectedly, a genuine warmth beamed through, and remained.

"Yes, a beautiful day," she said, and meant it.

"Clears the murkiest of moods," he said, trying to encourage a more personal drift to the dialogue. Kelso sensed that at least part of her inner disturbance was being kindled by whatever she had found to read in the library. He could not imagine what books she might have discovered that would justify the hours she'd spent there of late.

"It will be good to stretch our legs when we get to the Restitutions. I am looking forward to the diving lessons." Abruptly she frowned, as if perplexed by what she had just said. Then, placing her elbows on the rail behind her—a move that pushed her firm breasts tautly against the skimpy confines of the halter—she said, "The sun—it feels so incredibly good on the skin." And she looked down at her naked arm, as if it were a strange limb just given her. "I can feel it . . . the skin tingling, opening—" She looked up at him, then away, turned half back around, stared seaward.

Kelso studied her profile, the broad high brow, the eye he could see, the faintly oriental contours of that side of her face, partially hidden by the blowing hair. For some reason he was reminded of the ancient Greek sculpture called Winged Victory. He had come upon a replica in the ruins of a palatial house in Beverly Hills some years back. The only item of any size still intact amid all that crumbled extravagance, it had startled him, looming larger than life, as things can do only under the sea. It threw a shadow over the place, like the presence of a being eternally cursel. Why had he remembered it now? It was the wind, her blowing hair, he guessed. Yet the headlessness of the statue, the oddly hermaphroditic wings, suggested some deeper paradox parallel with hers. What? Mindless flight? Loss of mind? What exactly was *her* paradox?

Taxed with unwonted ruminations, he was on the verge of flouting all tact. "You like my library?" he blurted, aching to open doors behind that baffling beautiful mask.

"Yes," she said, not facing him. "How did you come by all the books?"

"I rescued them from here and there." He took his tobacco pouch from his shorts pocket and began refilling the pipe. "Some areas didn't fall, didn't sink, right away. Some didn't sink at all but were pushed higher up than they were before the shake-up. Some that did go down took a long time, months, doing so. Areas around the Santa Monica Mountains, like Beverly Hills, West Hollywood, Culver City, didn't go down for quite a while. Nobody knows why. Or, if they do, they're not telling." He watched her for a reaction, saw none, and wondered why he was relating all this. Fact was, he wanted to talk to her, about anything, because talk usually held her—so long as it did not become too pointedly probing into the subject of herself. "Some of those places weren't even hit by the tidal waves coming in, were protected by lands still above water to the west of them. I got to some of those places when they were still dry, when the situation was still in such a state of chaos that nobody tried to stop me." But he didn't care to tell of his attempt to reach his and Lisa's library in their home in Glendale. Glendale had been one of the first areas to go. He'd found their home all right, had even tried to save some of the books as well as other things, but the salt water had already done its work, . . . and there had been no Lisa, or their sons. He had no idea where they might have been when the disaster struck. Lisa could have been at Cal Tech where she was employed then, the boys at their maternal grandmother's in Los Angeles where they often went in the summer months. He preferred to think of it that way. Lisa busily working, happily preoccupied with research, a lecture, or a debate with colleagues, the boys having a fine time at the Griffith Park Zoo, say. He preferred to think of it happening so quickly that they hadn't had time for this alleged happiness to have been snuffed by terror. The thought of them together, clutching each other and staring at falling walls, incoming water boiling with radioactive fires—

"Find something specially interesting?" he said, refusing to carry that scenario to its grim completion. "In the library?"

She did not answer for a full minute or more, Kelso lit his pipe, waiting. When the answer finally came, it was the most direct, yet not exactly artless, of evasions.

"I think I will remove my clothes, Jack."

He was not sure the breeze had carried her words correctly. "What?"

She faced him again, the quick and brief smile now that one of sexual inducement he'd become acquainted with. He watched her undo the small knot at the front of the halter. It fell to the deck. Her perfect breasts were no lighter in color than the rest of her skin. The shorts fell. She lifted her bare feet from them and leaned against the bulwark, elbows back on the rail, neck and breasts thrown up, arched to receive the sun.

Desire flared in his loins as powerful as any he'd felt in his youth. He stared at her, speechless, knowing full well he was being offered her body as a diversionary tactic to frustrate his prying into her mind. Confronted with a beauty, an elegant sensuality that was almost palpable, that he could almost discern crossing, like an aural vibration in the air, the distance between them, and encompassing him in its heat, he could do nothing but give in, accept the offering, the diversion, and forget the rest. At least for the moment.

"I have some suntan oil in my gear." She spoke with her eyes shut, face still tilted. "Would you tell Carlos to bring it up? And—" Her head straightened and her eyes found his, "you must take off your clothes also. Feel what this is like."

Her breasts rose and fell with her quickening breath. "We will—together, we will make it perfect."

Kelso swallowed the lump of lust in his throat. Feeling not unlike a pubescent schoolboy in the company of an erotic idol, he turned, hobbled obediently to the hatch and peered down at the control room below.

Juan—or was it Carlos? Kelso would be damned if he could tell the difference between the two—was already coming up the ladder with towels, a self-inflating rubber mattress, suntan oil. He offered Kelso these items, along with one of his plastic smiles, and nodded. "How are you, *capitán?*"

Kelso grunted, surprised and irritated. He snatched the objects away and was about to close the hatch before the bodyguard stuck his head above the level of the deck when another thought came to him. "Where's your bloody twin?"

"He is in the engine room, *capitán.* He is working on some faulty circuitry in the generating compartment. Is there anything else you want?"

"No, Lavacca. You just sit down there and keep the Chief company. The two of you have a lot in common. Can't ever tell when a Navboat of some kind might be prowling around."

"*Sí.* Of course."

Kelso slammed down the hatch. "How in hell do you like that? He was bringing the stuff before I told him—"

DeFond was suddenly alert. "Oh yes," she said. "I forgot. I'd already told him to do so—when I came through the control room to come up. Here." She stepped toward him, hands reaching.

The articles in Kelso's hands fell to the deck.

He tries to uncover what I have not been able to uncover. He thinks I offer my body to elude him. He is right in part. But I also offer my body to please him—and because it pleases me to do so.

This compulsion to please him can be explained by my need of him, my use of him. He must be cooperative, must help me, so I must please him in any way I can. I know that. Somehow I know, even though I no longer know to what use I must put him.

But why, in pleasing him, did she become pleased also? Why was she so overcome with pleasure when making love to him and yet, again, why was she so afraid to feel such pleasure, to feel pleasure at all?

The Phoenix fabrication, her desire to find her parents' estate, to die there with them, to drown, would no longer serve as explanaaon for her fear of becoming emotionally and physically attached to anything, anyone, in this world. The Phoenix memory was a lie, the suicide motive false. An implanted fiction.

Put there by whom, by what? And why?

Where do I come from? Who am I? These last two questions had beaten her mind to numbness as she lay on the air mattress on the *Tiburón's* bridge.

Kelso had called down for Carlos to bring up a bottle of liquor and two cups but she had declined a drink. They'd made love again, slept in the sun, watched it set. He lay beside her now, drinking, looking at the stars. She wondered where *his* mind was and what he might think if he knew what she had been thinking. What would he think if she told him about the Lavaccas? He would not believe her. She, too, should find it hard to believe, but did not. The Lavaccas somehow were a piece that fit perfectly in a puzzle she had yet to put together. She knew that. An instinct, or intuition, was there somewhere in her psyche, powerful enough to enable her to tell the true from the false—up to a point. Beyond that point was a wall, mist, darkness.

The Lavacca brothers. Somehow they were extensions or replicas of herself. Not clones. Clones had minds independent of their parent or donor. (She'd read a book on genetic engineering found in the library, a book called *New Genesis*, and it had amazed and stupefied her, given her more puzzles, problems to ponder.) No, Juan and Carlos were more like automatons, or androids, with brains that seemed mere auxiliaries of her own. But how could they act on their own, and know things, technical and mechanical things, she did not? Somehow they had received individual knowledge—individual *programming*—yet were synced with her.

Programmed by whom? Why didn't she know? Why was her mind a blank, or fiction, where everything before her visit to the Restitution Islands was concerned? *What* had been "programmed" into her? Why couldn't she remember?

She heard the bottle clink against Kelso's cup. She said, "I should go down and fix us something to eat." It was becoming cool and they had nothing to cover with but the large beach towel Carlos had brought up.

He made a noise, guttural, indifferent.

"We have the rest of the squid Carlos speared. I could fix a stew."

"Not hungry. Drink?"

"No, thank you. I think I will go down. I'm getting cold. And hungry." She sat up, saw his eyes slide over to look at her. "How are you feeling, Jack? What have you been thinking for the last half-hour?"

He shook his head slowly from side to side, then watched her curiously. "Crazy goddamned world we live in, eh, Judith? We have spent the latter part of this day enjoying each other, giving to and taking from each other as two people who truly know each other should do. But we do not truly know each other. Do we? Crazy. Us. Life. Stubbornly clinging. Making no sense. Going to hell because we do not trust and are not open. Because we are afraid of each other. Because we are afraid."

An impulse to confide in him, and to counter the negative note, was almost overwhelming. It leapt up from some deep and tiny fountain, a timid spring whose source she would dearly like to find. In a disturbing way, she sensed that that little spring, if given half the chance, might open wide and gush forth an ocean of rejuvenated vitality, counter not only to Kelso's pessimism and distrust but also counter to whatever it was she was readied for in the Highland Park ruins.

Why did she think that? Why did she think the culmination of this journey was to be fatal?

For a moment the old vertigo returned; she was lost in space without link or line to sense or substance, adrift. Feeling this way, Kelso's present mood was a dead neutron star threatening to suck her into its massive nothingness.

She looked up at the night sky over the Pacific. Space science had been included in her current reading binge, as well as genetic engineering. She knew about neutron stars now, and supernovae and binary systems, of cepheid variables and receding galaxies and different kinds of nebulae and the unimaginable distances between stars, and of the probability, meticulously calculated and mathematically indisputable, of life on other planets besides Earth. Of the probability of other planets very much like, if not exactly like, Earth.

Why did such subjects hold her interest so? Why did it seem, as she read about them, that she was relearning things she'd known before but had forgotten?

She stood, pulled on shorts and halter, and, saying nothing to him, found her way across the dark deck to the open hatch from which glowed the light of the control room.

It took little time to prepare a stew with the remaining squid for herself and the Lavaccas. The bodyguards, androids, whatever they were, silently took theirs to the control room, leaving her to sit alone in the crew's mess. She would have asked them to remain, but she knew from previous experience that a conversation with her hands or her feet would have been as entertaining and enlightening.

She thought of sleep as an escape, but knew pills would be required to knock her out. Her mind would not rest of its own accord. The questions swam and darted like nightmarish apparitions from a world that had little to do with this one, refusing to be ignored or disbelieved.

When she had finished eating and put what was left in the warmup oven for Kelso, she found her steps taking her back to the library, a place that had become both a refuge and a flagellation chamber, a source of knowledge and a hothouse that stimulated the sprouting of new wonders and new enigmas.

The fall was fast and deep. She passed through the Phoenix fiction, saw it clearly as the lie it was, a vapor. And this time the barrier appeared almost immediately, as impenetrable as before.

On all four sides the edge promised oblivion. She had no choice but to chance going over or around it, to try finding a way under, into the depths it concealed. If she fell into a bottomless sopor from which she could not rise, if she found a truth more horrible than could be lived with, so be it. She had to have answers, no matter what those answers might be.

The barrier seemed at the same time invisible and impermeable, a door-like thereness that both revealed and concealed a void, seemed both infinitesimal and immense, seemed stationary while at the same time adrift, like her. At the same time a mirror—but without an image. She floated with it in a slow-motion water ballet, as if it and she were hopelessly coupled in an irresolvable conflict of opposites, doomed each to move counter to the other, unable to either touch or blend.

She continued in this drifting limbo for a period that had

no measurement in time, paralyzed in locked synchronous orbit with the barrier. The medium through which it and she moved was vertigo itself, a dizzying miasma that filled her brain.

She strained to break the barrier's hold. Then, without warning, it opened and she thought she was falling through. Yet, while she experienced the sensation of falling, the oblong void also fell, just beyond her grasp.

Its emptiness began to sparkle and flicker as a strange writing took shape. It was the writing she had seen on the lintel in the previous trance. And she saw now that the barrier had in fact become the lintel. . . .

The lintel pulled her now, through hydrogen hurricanes, roiling suns without histories, through stellar storms of blinding brilliance and blackness without end, across eons of emptiness where the lash of wordless winds withered her heart.

A pulsation, at first painful, like the beak of the bird of prey. But the pain subsiding, the pulsation less violent, while nonetheless insistent. Like a message coming from across the astronomical distances of interstellar space. But the pulse seemed to originate as well within her own brain, somewhere in one of its dark recesses.

The lintel coruscated, the letters lit with dazzling luminescence. The ciphers contorted like flaming snakes, changed, reformed and contorted again, coalesced into new arrangements. Letters, words, phrases, thought-units or sentences, began to be legible. It remained an alien language, its characters flickering in perfect rhythm with the strange pulse, but a language she could read.

Salieu Vidyun of Naravamintara. You have prematurely pried open the door that would have opened on its own when the proper moment arrived. You have put yourself through much discomfort for naught.

You will not remember anything about your former existence except what is needed for you to carry out your task. You may come to remember that you were Vidyun, but you will not remember who or what Vidyun was. Though you will have forgotten Naravamintara, you will remember that you are the guardian of a race beyond Earth, an exalted race untouchably advanced beyond Earth's corrupt rabble. A race whose reason for being supersedes all other entities, all other worlds. A race descended from the Pure Ones, whose duty it is to watch over those other worlds, to use them for its pur-

poses and to see that none threaten the Perfect State. Vidyun is not, was not, was never, important. Only Naravamintara is, will ever be, important. Vidyun no longer exists. Only Naravamintara and your mission exist.

My mission? What is my mission? What must I do?

You have been given a human memory, personal, racial, and sexual. You have been given a human persona for your purpose. Your mental and physical characteristics constitute a personality both attractive to and compatible with the human being who will unwittingly help you accomplish your task. On a superficial level you will become trapped in self-love and value your individuality. You will experience a confusing naiveté and will be infected with mental afflictions long ago cast off by the ones you serve. You will suffer emotional conflicts that will worry and frighten you with their intensity and power. All this will be a trying but necessary adjunct of your metamorphosis, but your new persona, engineered and guided by the ones you serve, will not allow such maladies to penetrate any deeper than your conscious mind. You must see them for what they are, use them to your advantage, and ignore them otherwise.

What is my task? What have I been charged to do?

The language on the lintel melted into a surface that was molten. The words now came through the drumming pulsations of what she suddenly realized was, had to be, an implant. They beat with the relentless power of that which could not be denied.

Remember. You have descended into a darkly troubled world unlike anything known in Naravamintara. You must constantly guard against being overwhelmed by the corrupt and chaotic human state.

You were assigned this task because you have been a staunch and devoted servant of Those-Who-Rule-And-Are-Perfect. Success means you have served your masters well and will attain peace and fulfilment in that knowledge. Failure means danger to your masters and to your race. Failure means eternal banishment and an inglorious death divested of honor and peace.

What is it I must do? Please!

The question swarmed, fighting against the despotic signals, desperate for answers.

Details will be disclosed to you as they become needed. Already you have learned more than was necessary at this stage. You must abandon these inner quests for answers. De-

votion and obedience to the masters is your answer to all questions. You will not again resort to the unnecessary indulgence of self-hypnosis, which will only cause you much uncalled-for confusion and pain.

The pulsations ceased; the lintel was the barrier once more, through which now could be seen a distant rock drifting, like an asteroid, in space.

She came out of the trance stunned. She sat staring at nothing, numb, energy drained from her body by the ordeal.

Naravamintara? An *implant* in her brain? Vidyun? A being from another world?

She rose as though drunk, hands moving to her head as if fingers might find the place where lay the internal puppeteer holding the strings to her fate.

Hers? Who was she? What had she been? Not this human female named Judith DeFond? What kind of "soul" did she have then? What sort of psychology could apply to this creature presently called *Judith DeFond?*

Remember that you were Vidyun. . . .

She staggered through the hatchway, groping, feeling the ship's steady movement through the sea, disturbingly parallel to her own prescribed and unknown course.

You serve the masters and the masters serve perfection.

Perfection. Utopia. *Naravamintara.*

She moved to the wardroom table like a sleepwalker, not knowing where she was going. The nightlight red of the roof reflected the inner shadows, the crucible-like glow of the psyche that was hers and not hers.

She untied the halter, looked down at the crimson-tinted flesh and ran her hands over her breasts, her belly, her thighs. The graceful contours mocked her now. The latent fires that smoldered under the silken skin amazed her. She dropped the shorts and examined every detail as though seeing it for the first time, seeing now with altered eyes, with the knowledge that this body belonged to *them,* whomever, whatever, they were. Was *their* ingenious product.

Cupping her breasts in her hands, she was struck by their sudden absurdity. Whereas before she had admired their beauty, they now seemed ridiculous and superfluous appendages worn by a freakish clown in a perverted comedy. Surely she would never have a child. She wore a false flesh-suit for the purpose of—what? Treachery and deceit?

For the purpose of the masters. For the purpose of the Perfect State.

So. The implant was not confined to her subconscious. It nudged her even now. *Sleep,* it said. *Sleep.*

Incredible that it seemed so credible. Uncanny the way it all seemed to fit—what few pieces she yet had to the puzzle—as though she'd known it all along and had only to find, or force her way to that subconscious door. Uncanny? What exactly was natural and unnatural in her case? What was her true nature?

Sleep. You will sleep.

Her hands touched the maps on the table, maps she'd gone over repeatedly in order to become acquainted with the shambles of Highland Park. Why? What lay there for her to find?

Naravamintara. Where? What?

Can you read my thoughts, you who sent me here? Can I reach you, speak to you?

You must constantly guard against being overwhelmed by the corrupt and chaotic human state. . . .

Like speech on a recording reel the counsel unrolled. Dictations. Prohibitions. Adjurations for fealty.

No answers. Not ultimate answers.

You will sleep.

The wardroom bulkheads swayed. Strength was ebbing from her legs.

Did they know what she thought at this moment? How could they? Who or what were *they?*

Silence within. And without—

A strange noise. Distant.

Her knees quaked. She held the table, felt the room roll but knew the ship was steady. She looked at the dark portholes on the other side of the table, listening, fighting back the hated vertigo. What had she heard? A cry of some kind.

It came again, more distinct. A deep, mournful bellowing. Then an answering and similar sound, not quite as deep or prolonged or as close as the first. A series of bellows ensuing.

The noise drew her to one of the portholes. She could not get it open; the glass was frozen to the hole by rust. But she could see, through the smeared glass, something out there, huge, churning the phosphorescent water under the thin crescent of a rising new moon.

On unsteady legs she found a pair of discarded coveralls and moved uncertainly to the control room and up the ladder to the bridge. There she saw a man's dark form against the starboard bulwark, facing the water.

"What?" she said, not sure if she was still talking to herself, to the implant, or to the man. "What is it?"

He did not move, was as rigid as the bulwark. She came up, trying to remember who the man was, eyes searching the ocean west of the *Tiburón*, searching for what she'd seen through the porthole below, as if whatever was out there would tell her who the man was.

A long wail carried over the water. She saw more streaks of phosphorescence, disturbed plankton silvering the surface like liquid diamonds. Another cry, a third and fourth. And then she saw a dark form rise from the waves it had made. She saw the low, rounded jet of vapor spout from the blowhole, heard its metallic noise, watched the creature sharply arch its back, heard it emit a low ululation before it crashed once again into the sea, its flukes barely visible in the meager moonlight before disappearing into the foam.

All at once everything came back. "Jack?" she said, remembering his name. She grabbed his arm, trying to see his face. She had never heard cries like that. Yet something stirred, like an ancestral memory. How? "Jack, can you understand them? Can you tell what they are saying?" She recalled his work with cetaceans, of the language he was said to have developed.

At last he turned to face her and she saw his glistening cheeks in the moonlight. The sea was calm, there was little wind, no salt spray. She did not know whether his tears were for the whales, for the planet on which both he and they tried to live, or only for himself.

"Humpbacks," he said thickly. "Going south."

"What are they saying?" *How have I come to be here? Why do I feel they speak to me?*

He turned his eyes back out to sea. "Listen. You'll understand them if you listen."

The ethereal cries came to them over the water, one after the other, the notes of a song that was ageless, whose theme seemed there on the other side of what she observed, hidden by the surface reality of sea, ship, man, cries, moonlight. Like the hidden truth of herself.

I want to tell you about me, Jack, she thought. *But I do not know enough to tell. You would think me indeed demented. Or would you?*

She opened her mouth to speak, not sure what she was going to say, but did not let go the first word. Dizziness seized her, filling her head with nausea and pain. She gripped the bulwark, faced the sea, inhaled. She shut her eyes, holding on desperately to consciousness.

When she opened her eyes again, the whales were still there, and so was Kelso. Lost in his own thoughts, he had not noticed her distress. She kept her face toward the water, breathing deeply, unwilling to let go the rail.

The animals stayed alongside the *Tiburón* for a long time, rising, arcing above the water, calling over the waves, splashing thunderously back into the sea. In all the time they were close, Jack Kelso said nothing more. But she could feel his anguish, and knew the whales were speaking to him in a way that transcended language, as, similarly, they spoke to her. He, too, she had come to see, sought answers behind appearances, was baffled as well as dazzled by life, sought answers concerning himself.

When at last the whales were gone and he turned and wordlessly limped to the hatch and lowered himself down the ladder, Judith DeFond was left with the dark and now silent ocean, with the cries of the humpbacks still reverberating in her ears, with the memory of what she had learned over an hour earlier through self-hypnosis.

The nausea had abated, her head was relatively clear. The attack had been severe, had come at the very moment she was about to say something to Kelso, though she was still not sure what she would have said. Did that sudden seizure of dizziness indicate the power the implant held over her?

Every star overhead posed a question. *Naravamintara?* And for every star she could see, there were millions not visible.

Where had she come from? From a place where there were likely no whales and no Jack Kelso?

She stood on the *Tiburón's* bridge until the east was pinked with dawn, mind reeling with worry and wonder, repeatedly asking why, if she were an alien, this world's beauty, and its conflicts, should touch her so deeply; why Jack Kelso could arouse emotions in her like his own, emotions that she sensed had to have been buried, repressed, so inexorably that they should never have come to life again.

13. THE AGREEMENT

Guillermo Rodríguez untied the florid red handkerchief from his neck and mopped his face as he stepped onto the patio. He had no difficulty picking out Vincent Polliard. The patio was not crowded and the latter sat alone at a table overlooking the shore. Rodríguez had never met Polliard personally, but he had heard of the man on more than one occasion. The black diving vest, the close-cropped hair, the crooked nose, the narrow eyes shaded by the limp potted palm beside the table, left no doubt this was the man.

Rodríguez creased his brow worriedly and the thin mustache above his lip twitched briefly. Polliard crooked a finger at him and pointed to the chair on the other side of the table.

Rodríguez walked over. "You wish to speak with me, *señor?*"

"Don't give me the *señor* routine, Rodríguez. I know who you are and you know who I am. Sit down."

The frown on the Mexican's face intensified as he sat. The handkerchief stayed in his hand. "You suppose we have time for a beer?" Rodríguez attempted an obsequious smile.

"I've ordered two," Polliard said. "Now let's get down to the business of why I came down here to the Baja and had my men ferret you out of your hole. I know how you make your living, and I've got enough evidence to have the U.S. Coastal Authority lock you up for the rest of your miserable days. But I won't bother you as long as you'll cooperate."

The smile had left Rodríguez's face. He nodded cautiously, still breathing heavily from his walk up the hill to the *cantina.* "I think you must have me mistaken for somebody else, *capitán.* Like I must have you mistaken for somebody else. I thought Vincent Polliard was on the, how do you say, outside of the law." He shrugged. "But I will certainly cooperate. I always cooperate with the American authorities."

Polliard ignored both the man's attempt to disclaim credit

for having one of the most successful salvage smuggling operations on the West Coast and his reference to Polliard's true colors. The beer came and Polliard tossed several pesos on the table for the waiter to pick up.

Rodríguez took his and gulped half the bottle. "The heat," he said, rubbing the handkerchief over his brow. "I prefer being on the ocean. Not so stinking hot all the time."

Polliard did not touch his bottle. "Jack Kelso is one of your suppliers," he said. "You've been buying illegal salvage from him for years." He let that sink in.

"Jack Kelso?" Rodríguez's swarthy face feigned bewilderment. His handkerchief hand fell to his lap and he sat there speechless for a moment. "I don't know," he said, shaking his head. "Much wealth has found its way down here to Mexico from the California coast, it is true. It is true I have been asked to carry cargo from the Restitution Islands down here. How was I to know that it was illegal salvage?" A smile, a shrug. "Anyway, I have merely been a, how do you say, conduit for the purpose of transferring the wealth of those dead *gringo* capitalists, those movie tycoons and people like that, to the homes of Mexicans whose traditional conditions of poverty and squalor entitle them to such treasures."

"I told you to cut the bullshit, Rodríguez. I won't tell you again. We've never been able to catch you and Kelso in a transaction. You, however, are an insignificant shrimp. I want the big shark, Jack Kelso. There's a woman with him now. I want her, too. You are going to help me get them."

Rodríguez had raised the bottle halfway to his mouth. He held it there, frozen in mid-movement, as he stared with disbelief at Polliard.

"The next time Kelso sends word to you for a buying rendezvous, and one's long overdue, according to my sources, you will let me know at once. You will get word to me where and when it will take place, in plenty of time for me to be there before either you or Kelso. We will split the reward straight down the middle, and I will see to it that you will be granted legal immunity, the freedom to come and go along the coast as you please, for the rest of your life."

A fly buzzed around Rodríguez's nose. Finally he put the bottle down and swatted the fly away. All pretense of ignorance and innocence, as well as color, had drained from his face.

"You are crazy. I have always heard you were. Now I hear it from the horse's mouth, as the *yanquis* say. The words of a crazy man. Like Jack Kelso. Both of you are crazy. But Kelso is not the shark. Kelso is the porpoise. You are the shark, Polliard. I fear the porpoise more. He has more brains."

Polliard's hand was lightning quick, and his grip around the Mexican's throat powerful enough to crush his windpipe. Rodríguez's beer bottle fell. The smuggler turned red and thrashed in the chair as Polliard held him. The other people on the patio looked on in shocked silence.

"You've got ear trouble, Rodríguez. You didn't hear what I just said about having enough evidence to put you away for keeps. But you'd better hear this. We will take your fat *mestizo* wife and your seven fat kids from that big house they live in in Mazatlán and if you don't do as I say, they will end up with a very slow and crippling disease while you rot in the Fort MacArthur lock-up on San Pedro Island." Polliard let him go.

Rodríguez fell back, holding his neck, gasping for air and coughing.

While waiting for the Mexican to regain his ability to speak, Vincent Polliard glared at the people at the other tables. One by one, they ceased looking his way and resumed their private business. A waiter came and picked up the broken pieces of Rodríguez's beer bottle but left the puddle of spilled beer for the flies.

"*Sí*," said Rodríquez hoarsely. "I hear all right." He held the handkerchief to his mouth as another spasm of coughing overcame him. "Okay," he said when the coughing subsided, "you come here to make a deal with me. Okay. We make a deal." He wiped his brow with the handkerchief, then pressed his hand to his chest, waiting for his breathing to calm. "I will capture Jack Kelso, hold him, and tell you where you can pick him up."

The agent threw back his head and laughed. He slapped the table with an open palm and his still-full beer bottle jumped. "You will catch Jack Kelso?"

'*Sí*," said Rodríguez somberly. "Me and my *compadres*. I have an advantage." A pained look crossed the Mexican's face. "He trusts me. We have done business together, as you say, for a long time. Anyway, I do not intend to call you into some place I use for my—" Rodríguez forced a smile, "business transactions. Such places are confidential. As secret as the place where you have hidden all the plunder you have brought up from Los Angeles, my friend. But I have not finished telling you my deal."

Polliard's laughter had stopped. Both his hands lay on the table, not far from Rodríguez's face.

"I will catch Jack Kelso and let you know where you can pick him up." Rodríguez touched his throat tenderly. "For that I want one half of what you have cached away, one half of the stuff you have brought up from the ruins of Los Angeles. One half of the reward, and, of course, the immunity. Also I want to know what you found in the Marianas Trench while on the *Deepfish*."

The agent's nostrils flared and his hands flattened themselves against the table top. "You goddamned fool. You see that helicopter sitting down there on the beach? How would you like to be taken up in it to a height of three thousand meters, over the Baja *cordillera*, and dropped like the sack of shit you are? I told you my terms, and that is what you'll get and nothing more. Don't put any faith in stories you hear about hidden treasures or what might have been found by *Deepfish*, Rodríguez. You're too old to be gulled by fantasies. Such fantasies can kill you."

"*Sí, sí.*" The smuggler stared morosely at the table, avoiding the agent's eyes. "No honor among thieves," he muttered. Rodríguez sighed, pushed his chair back and looked at his blackmailer. "Okay. For half the reward money and the immunity. I will catch Jack Kelso for you."

Polliard started to speak; Rodríguez waved the handkerchief. "As I said, I will not expose my places of business. Never. I must do it my way. He trusts me. We are old friends."

"All right, Rodríguez. I'll go along with you once. You get one chance. If you screw it up, and Kelso doesn't have your head, I will."

The Mexican nodded sadly. "A stinking business. You police, you government men. You are as bad or worse than anybody. You have the law to use. But you love nothing. Not honor, not people. Nothing. You respect nothing. So many like you. Everywhere. No trust. No honor. No love. Now I, Guillermo Rodríguez, must capture a friend. A stinking business."

Polliard got up. "Forget the sermonizing. You haven't the time for it. You'd better start planning right now how you're going to catch this so-called friend of yours. I want both him and the woman with him. Alive. Able to talk. No funny ideas, Rodríguez. Remember, I'm the one who wins. Because I do love something—I love winning. I love winning, vengeance, and money. And I love squashing fat greasy bugs like you. So no funny ideas, and no fuckups. I'll be waiting to hear from you. I warn you, the news had better be good, and it had better be soon." Polliard slammed his chair into the Mexican's knees when he pushed it forward. He turned from the table and swiftly moved off the patio to the stone walkway that went down to the helipad on the beach below. The two men who had found Rodríguez, coerced him into coming to the *cantina*, and then waited at another table on the patio, moved to catch up with their boss. The pilot started the helicopter as Polliard stepped aboard.

From his seat beside the pilot he could see Rodríguez still sitting at the patio table, staring out to sea, as the chopper lifted and swung over the *cantina*.

"Think he'll do it, Vince?" one of the men in back said.

"Yeah," Polliard said. "He'll try anyway. Too scared not to. But if he has any luck catching Kelso on his own, he's smarter than I think."

The chopper reached the elevation the pilot wanted and continued north, over the rocky Baja coastline.

"Why don't we put some good shadows on him?" the other man behind Polliard said.

"Tried it before, Dills. Before you joined us. Tried infiltrating his ship's crew, too. No good. Tried everything. The sonofabitch is like Kelso. Too many pals in the Restitutions and along the coast. Tight as a guerilla organization."

"Well," the man who first spoke stuck a cigarette between thick lips and fired his lighter, "we'll get him. Things are going our way what with Mister Goody Two-Shoes Garret off to duty in the Persian Gulf." The man laughed and the one named Dills joined in. "Them connections you got with URI can do wonders. We'll get Kelso. And that woman, too."

Polliard touched his groin and winced at the memory of Judith DeFond's foot slamming into his genitals. "You'd better be right," he said to the man called Fowler. "I owe her almost as much as I do Kelso." And, he thought, I'd almost give what she almost ruined to know what *her* goddamned game is.

"We'll get them," repeated Fowler. "If it don't work out with the spic, we'll get them another way. Meanwhile we got some mighty fine digging to do in that posh section of Pasadena we were finally able to get into. Right, Vince?"

"She was a strange one, that woman. Wasn't she? Didn't get a look at her much myself that night in the Exile. Busy with that drunk. But what I did see before me and Kelderman went outside—and what I've heard—"

"Sit back and enjoy the ride," ordered Polliard. "Both of you talk too goddamned much."

14. DECEIVERS

"Queer bunch you are." Puffing on a sulphurous cigar, the captain of the supply ship *P. B. Baylor* sat astraddle one of the sideposts that stuck a half meter above the pier planking. His eyes, underneath the lopsided seaman's cap, had been fastened on Judith DeFond for the last twenty minutes. "Stocking up for a long trip, are you?" he tried again.

She checked off the last crate of foodstuffs that went rolling down the ramp to Juan's waiting hands and did not answer.

"Where you headed?"

At last she looked up from the clipboard and regarded him silently.

"Hah!" he said, guessing her thought. "Do I look like I'd blow the gaff on you? Let me tell you something, girlie, I was running contraband when Jack Kelso was still dirtying his pants."

"Then you should know better than to ask such questions."

"Ah. A smart socks, are you? Got a quick tongue, eh?" Ruffled, he put the cigar back in his mouth and spoke around it. "Well I say it's damn queer, three men and a woman on a salvage sub. Queerer yet when it's Jack Kelso's sub and the other two men work like mules, don't talk, act like dummies, and the woman don't say much either, just watches everything, watches like a hawk with them green inscrutable eyes of hers. But then I've seen some queer things. Hah!"

She continued with the inventory while the captain ranted on. He seemed familiar, someone she'd seen before, but could not exactly place.

The Pacific lay calm and glittering beyond the inlet; overhead, the sky was an infinite blue dome marred only by a group of woolly cumulus to the northeast. Above the inlet, landward, the misshapen terraced slopes of the isle served as observation platforms for hundreds of birds that had come to watch and snatch whatever they could from the goods being moved from the *P. B. Baylor* to the *Tiburón.* Judith found the birds fascinating, and would have liked to sit here and watch them for the day's duration, like a child nourished by the wonders of the present, without a care or worry about what the enigmatic future might hold.

A crude wooden dock lay along the shore of the natural deep-bottomed harbor. From this jutted a ramshackle pier that ran about fifty meters out over the water. The prow of the submarine rested at the end of the pier's north side; the freighter was moored opposite.

With the cane Juan had made him, Jack Kelso walked about the narrow afterdeck of the *Tiburón* where he displayed and bartered his salvaged wares to a group of buyers who'd come down from Terremoto and Restitution. From the dock, Judith supervised the taking on of stores. As prearranged by radio, the *P. B. Baylor* had steamed from Las Penas and met them here. Food, medical supplies, equipment, munitions, batteries, books, movie canisters, and an extensive list of other materials that she and Kelso had compiled (with the help of the Lavaccas, where technical and mechanical needs were concerned) were being lifted from the cargo holds of the freighter and swung by winch to the dock where Carlos, helped by three men from the freighter, passed the stuff onto the *Tiburón*'s foredeck via a roller ramp. At the other end of the ramp, Juan stacked the goods to each side. At intervals, they had to stop this procedure and drop to the *Tiburón*'s storage compartments by elevator all that had accumulated on deck. This prevented the oncoming stores from spilling over into the outgoing salvage.

The stevedores made better headway than Kelso the merchant. Whenever Judith took her attention from the inventory to look at the *Tiburón*'s stern, Kelso and the nattily-dressed buyers were arguing hotly over the price or value of some item. Though the business was being conducted on one of the remotest of the islands, the potential danger that bounty hunter or police craft might appear was enough, in her opinion, to preclude haggling. Kelso's present indifference to possible trouble flew in the face of earlier protests against coming here but she knows now those protests stemmed from her having suggested the idea, and not much else.

A crate of books passed from Carlos's hands to the ramp. These were books she had found while shopping in Rose Harbor, the Restitutions' largest town, yesterday. Books she had carefully selected in Rose Harbor's few meagerly supplied bookstores. Books she was longing to read—and ones she preferred Jack Kelso, at this point, knew nothing about. Juan had instructions to put them below where Kelso was not likely to find them.

"Say!" The captain broke off recounting a romantic tale of his younger days. "You wouldn't be the one who kicked Vincent Polliard in the family jewels, would you? Hah! Hey, yep, you're the one all right. I was there at a table in that bar the night you done it. Whoo!" He slapped his leg. "That was a show. Girlie, I've been telling that story every place this side of Davy Jones, and everybody thinks it's a galley yarn. Eh?" Jerking the cigar out of his mouth, he squinted at her from under the cap's visor. "Now, why'd you want to go and do a thing like that to such an aboveboard bucko like Polliard? Hah! But let me tell you this, my dove. If sweet-natured Vince ever catches up with you, he'll flense you of that pretty hide, and skewer you with one of them fancy diver's guns he likes to use."

Recognition of the captain became clear. He was one of those whose conversation she'd listened to after entering the tavern. "Is Vincent Polliard a friend of yours?" She spoke this time without turning. Carlos and the captain's men passed crates of engine parts onto the ramp. She checked them off the manifest.

"Friend? Hah! That slimy no-good son of a sea witch has got no friends. I'm just telling you the way of the world, that's all."

"It is said that he's a government agent." Why did she pursue this? She recalled Polliard vividly, and recalled that she had found him strangely interesting, as though he'd triggered some deeper memory, suggested someone or something else—what? What were the myriad mysteries in her mind she had not begun to discover?

"Aye," said the captain. "That's known well enough. An agent for the government and for URI, too. One of them big outfits that's got its snout in everything of value this side of the moon. Aye." A shadow passed over the captain's wrinkled face. "It's the Vincent Polliards in this world who're the real devilfish. The ones who pretend to be something they ain't."

A prick of uneasiness made her look back at the clipboard—as if abstract figures might give reassurance that things were properly arranged here and throughout the universe.

"They're the ones who're bringing it all down on us. From the big business wheels, the corporations and conglomerates who blow a lot of bilge about having the people's best interests at heart, to the sneaky little worms like Polliard, who'll do anything under the sun and claim it's service to his damn country." The captain spat out a shred of cigar skin he'd been rolling around in his mouth. "Aye! They're the ones."

"What do you think Polliard is looking for?" Her wish to divert him from this disturbing tangent made her question brusque.

"Other than gold and silver? He could be doing two things. Trying to keep from being found whatever caused the quake, or maybe trying to find out for himself what caused it. And there's a third." He ducked his head and winked. "He could be looking for whatever them scientists were looking for when it happened."

"What do you suppose that could be?"

"Got me. What men could've done to've caused a thing like that is beyond me too. Them geologists're still trying to figure it out. But if you ask me, come to think of it, it's simple." He sucked on the cigar and stamped a foot on the planking, impatient for her to ask.

She obliged him. "How is it simple?"

"Just old Mother Earth saying she's had enough abuse, that's all. She's rebelling. All over, she's rebelling. Still, a shake-up that size—it's a wonderment all right. Sure is." The captain wondered about it for a moment. "Lots of things going on—bad things—but that one tops them all."

Checking off several items going down the ramp, she could not help commiserating with the man's bafflement. She could, she thought ruefully, give her partner in this conversation more than enough to ponder if she'd wished. Or could she? If she dared try to divulge what she knew—little that it was—would the implant stop her, inflict another fit of vertigo like the one that had prevented her from speaking to Kelso? "It does seem," she heard herself somberly murmur, "to be a time of upheaval."

"Aye. Maybe it's the time of times, if you know what I mean. The last time. I ain't never put much stock in religion, but everything's gone round the bend and nobody knows what to do about it. Any day now the daddamned fools could start throwing them wipeout warheads around enough to knock us right out of orbit. Most likely they will. A miracle's needed. A miracle to end them all." He dipped his head with emphasis, cigar cloud rising over his cap like vapor veiling an augury.

She stared at him thoughtfully, hurting to have at those books she'd bought. There was so much she did not know. She was aware, even as she longed for the knowledge in books, she would find no ultimate answers, none directly linked to her own strange plight, between their covers.

"Hah! Ask for a miracle and you get another malefactor." He raised a knobby finger and pointed out at the inlet.

Judith looked, put the clipboard on top of a half-rotted bollard and raised the binoculars that hung from her neck.

As with most vessels seen in the Restitutions, the newcomer entering the mouth of the small bay flew its own exotic flag. It appeared to be an old Coast Guard cutter, minus any observable guns, revamped and streamlined for smuggling purposes.

She brought the glasses down and looked aft of the *Tiburón*'s bridge. Kelso also watched the incoming boat. If anything happened now, they'd have to shoot their way out of the harbor and dive for the open sea, leaving what remained of the salvage and yet-to-be-stored supplies to wash from the submarine's deck and become so much jetsam for whomever might scramble to save it.

But the approaching vessel no doubt belonged to another buyer Kelso had contacted beforehand. Otherwise, she was certain, he would be doing more than merely staring at it as it entered the inlet. Several young boys from Rose Harbor had come down with them that morning, too, and Kelso had positioned them as lookouts on the rocks above the inlet. If the cutter had been one unknown to the boys, and to Kelso, an alarm would have long ago sounded.

Judith had been surprised at the number of friends he had in the Restitutions, both young and old; especially after his reference to all the "judas goats" here who wanted his head. His popularity in the islands was somewhat like the correspondence she could see sticking from the back pocket of his khaki shorts. She had never thought of Kelso as a recipient of mail, and she wondered who had written him the many letters. But when a boy had brought them to him this morning at the dingy out-of-the-way bar and restaurant where they'd eaten breakfast in Rose Harbor, she had not asked.

A voice called from the immaculate white cutter across the diminishing distance but it was still too far away for the words to be understood. Halfway into the inlet, the boat reversed engines and slowed to a gradual stop some thirty meters from the submarine's stern. Both the latter ship and the *P. B. Baylor* rose and fell on the oncoming waves caused by the new arrival.

"*¡Oye, coyote! ¿Qué tal la vida?*" the voice from the smuggler now carried clearly across the water to Judith.

Through the binoculars she saw a short, corpulent man in a yellow jacket, flanked by several sailors and standing amidships on the smuggling vessel's starboard side.

"*¡Así, así!*" Kelso yelled back. "*Tengo muchas cosas preciosas.*"

"*¡Sí, sí! ¿Muy caras, eh? ¡Para precio precioso!* Ha ha!"

"You guessed it, Guillermo. But of course, for you, I will be most reasonable."

"But of course!"

"There's you a bona fide pirate," said the captain of the freighter and cackled. "May not be as slimy as your Mister Polliard but I'd put money down he'd rob the gold from a dead man's teeth and piss in the poor bastard's mouth to boot."

"And how goes business?" Kelso called.

"Like yours, *amigo. Los grandes se comen los chiquitos.*"

"Who is he?" She threw a sidelong glance at the scabrous captain.

"Guillermo Rodríguez. Thief, smuggler, plunderer, procurer—" He spat again. "Another bringer of miracles, like Vincent Polliard."

"Why does Kelso trust him, do business with him?"

"I doubt that Jack Kelso trusts anybody. I guess Rodríguez just ain't had reason enough to try doing your good captain dirty yet."

A breeze had risen, a southwesterly wind blowing the clouds toward the islands, and she could make out only bits of what was being called back and forth between Kelso and Rodríguez. The clouds from the northeast had thickened and darkened, presaging a storm. Concern for Kelso's safety stabbed at her. Yes, she was concerned for Jack Kelso, because it fit her purpose to be concerned for him. *Their* purpose.

He had changed in recent days. Notwithstanding occasional outbursts of irascibility and bad temper, he'd become generally quieter, calmer, more meditative. Her influence? Of course. Much of his meditation consisted of his trying to figure her out, she knew, but overall things were going very well for Judith DeFond who, like Vincent Polliard and Guillermo Rodríguez, pretended to be something she wasn't. A bringer of miracles? No, in her case she could not say who or what she was.

You are a soldier of the race above races. You are a guardian of the world above worlds. You are an arm of Naravamintara. Be assured that all questions are answered, that all is right in what you do.

She looked at the approaching cloudbank. My questions, she thought. My questions are not answered. *My. Me.* What is this *me* that must have answers? *The human malady of egocentricity. An unfortunate but necessary consequence of the role you must play, of the identity you have been given in order to accomplish your task.*

The cloudrack roiled across the horizon. She watched, a faint placidity coming over her, a subtle alteration of mood she'd felt before, while reading in the *Tiburón*'s library, capable of putting her to sleep unless she fought against it. Influence of the implant? Could the implant induce the release of a calming enzyme, say, that would cause this sudden quiescence?

All at once she was aware of the captain's intent stare. She forced her attention back to the manifest.

"Eh?" said the captain. "How about you, girlie? You Jack Kelso's friend?"

She faced him with an automatic smile. "If you don't mind, I have to attend to what's going aboard the *Tiburón*."

"Oh sure." He dipped his head. "Certainly. Certainly, love. Wouldn't want you to miss a thing going on board the *Tiburón*." He got up and stalked down the pier to the gangway of his ship, muttering.

But he returned shortly before noon, when the last crate went into the submarine's forward hatch. By then it had begun to rain and the captain of the *P. B. Baylor* held a poncho over Judith as she wrote him a draft for 835 World Bank credits to be drawn on her account in Mexico City. The wind flapped the poncho about, but it also blew away the smell of the captain. He took the draft and scrutinized it carefully. She showed him several cards of identification, including a Mexican passport and a nurse's card that said she was a graduate of the Patricia Waite School of Paramedicine in Phoenix, Arizona. She had no idea how she had come by the cards, the bank account, or anything included in her personal gear. Were the cards counterfeit? Was there really money in a bank account in Mexico City that bore her name?

"Well, Joodith DeeFond!" the captain shouted above the wind. "Been nice talking to you—though it was pretty much a one-sided conversation, I'd say." He wadded up the poncho with one hand and held the draft and his cap down with the other. "But I wish you a good journey, wherever it is you go. Beware of skulkers and deceivers, mind you!" He studied her, squinty-eyed. "Look to fish like *Señor* Rodríguez. Like me, he's done business with Jack Kelso for years, but the word's getting around that there ain't much business left of that kind and the price on Kelso's head gets higher every quartermoon. If you're a friend, I'd look after the man. He's a decent lubber. Got a few rats in his forechains, but he's fought some damn good fights. Hah!" The captain turned.

She threw hair out of her eyes, pressing the clipboard against her chest to prevent the wind from snapping the pages away. "If Rodríguez wanted to try something, why hasn't he made a move by now?"

Slinging rain from his brow with a gnarled finger, the captain said, "Maybe he's been waiting till them other buyers cleared out. If you'll look, you'll see the last of them departing around yon point. Rodríguez is the only buyer left aboard. Could be I'm on the wrong tack but—well, *bon voyage* to you. I'm hauling my bones out of this daddamn wind!"

She watched him walk to his ship and shout at his men to get underway. She felt it, too. Impending danger. The captain's warning had not fallen on indifferent ears. In a way she regretted his departure and at the moment could not say why.

Protecting the pages of the manifest under her jacket, she turned her back on the *P. B. Baylor* and moved to the gangway of the *Tiburón.* A cold and calm efficiency having suddenly taken over, her mind sent a query regarding the Lavaccas' whereabouts. Immediately she became aware they were two decks below in the sub, arranging crates in the forward storehold.

Forget the stores. See that everything is secure and the ship is ready to break out of here any minute. Both of you position yourselves for trouble when that is done. The mental order was given without thought, as she might move a leg when walking. It originated in a part of her mind whose power and processes she could neither pinpoint nor fathom.

Most of the salvage had been sold. Three of Rodríguez's men were loading those items their boss had chosen for purchase onto a launch at the *Tiburón*'s stern. They worked hurriedly in the rain. Two looked up when she drew near; one lifted the cap from his head, leered, and elbowed the other.

Guillermo Rodríguez held a gold figurine in his gloved hand, waving it in the air as he argued. The intermittent gusts of wind flattened the thin jacket over his paunch and revealed a pistol strapped to his waist.

"A beauty," Rodríguez was saying. "Like the one you brought up from—what was it?—the headquarters of the Worldwide Church of God? Ha ha ha! But they say the pickings are getting slimmer, eh, Jack?"

"Maybe so."

She knew Kelso was cognizant of her presence on the afterdeck, though he gave no sign. She saw that he was careful to keep himself between the smuggler and the *Tiburón*'s bridge; his left hand gripped the handle of the walking stick with white-knuckled firmness. Obviously he, too, saw risk in Rodríguez.

"Five hundred," Rodríguez said. "Five hundred for this little statue. Two hundred for that silver dining set." He pointed the head of the figurine at a trunk disgorging plates, cutlery, and the like.

"You're loco," Kelso said. "You'll get three times that much for them in Acapulco or Caracas—wherever in hell you go."

Watching Kelso, Judith saw he was irritated, perhaps sick of the haggling, perhaps remembering the sunken homes, stores, streets, he'd ransacked for these inglorious treasures.

Rodríguez's fingers drummed nervously on his belly. "Times are hard. Nobody has the money to buy my goods. The dangers are becoming greater, always greater. The *policía* are coming farther and farther down this way. I have a lot of overhead. I have a woman in La Paz, ah, *amigo*, what a woman. I have a woman in Guadalajara, a woman in Mazatlán. My wife. They steal me blind, these women. I have to run. I have to hide. I have to pay my *compadres*. I have to pay off the *policía*. *¡La mordida es increíble!* You know how it is."

"Cut the crap, Guillermo."

"Ah. In a hurry, eh? On to something hot? Where do you go this time?"

"I've never known you to be such a goddamned yakker. You want any more of this stuff?" Kelso waved the stick.

"*Sí*. I want, I want." Rodríguez shook his head, throwing a nervous glance at the launch. "You get more—what is the word?—ornery!—each time I see you, Jack. Harder to deal with. Antisocial. I don't know how you have done it so long, living alone in those dirty islands and on your stolen U.S. Navy submarine. I don't know how you are still walking around." The smuggler pointed at the stick and laughed exaggeratedly, his wide smile strained. Then he looked at DeFond who stood a few paces behind and to the left of Kelso. "But maybe things are changing for you, eh, *amigo*? They say Jack Kelso has lived so long because he didn't care whether he lived or not. Eh? Maybe now he cares. Ha ha! Time to take care." Rodríguez's behavior was obviously odd; the man was struggling inwardly against something he did not want to do.

"Time's up, Guillermo," Kelso said. "I'm tired, wet, and out of patience. Get off my boat."

"Okay! Okay! *¡Espérate!*" Rodríguez pointed. "I'll take that and that and that—" A last glance at the launch, a quick jerk of the head, and his right hand shot into the jacket.

DeFond dropped to her knees, clipboard slamming to the deck, and, with the stunner yanked free of her belt, fired. In the same instant, Carlos yelled from the stern where he'd popped out of the after hatch.

"*¡Alto!*" His rifle was aimed at the men in the launch.

They gaped at it and froze as their leader fell over the trunk of silver dining ware, knocked out by the drug-tipped bullet from DeFond's gun.

A cry from the bridge disclosed Juan's position. The heavy automatic weapon he'd thrown across the after bulwark was trained on Rodríguez's boat, *La Dama Conchita*.

Surprised as much as Rodríguez's crew by the swiftness and concert with which DeFond and her bodyguards had acted, Kelso awkwardly pulled his own handgun and, kneeling, put the muzzle at the temple of the unconscious Rodríguez. "Okay, you *hijos de putas!*" he bellowed at the men on *La Dama*. "He sleeps, but if you don't get that tub out of here, he dies!"

For a moment they stared, at Kelso, at DeFond, at the bodyguards, at each other. They muttered, milled around, until finally, at the command of one, separated to man their respective stations in order to up-anchor and leave the inlet. The three men at the launch stood stiffly with arms over their heads, rainwater rolling down their baleful faces.

A number of minutes passed before the confused men on *La Dama* had their boat pulling away without its captain and mates at the launch. But at last it turned toward the mouth of the inlet, putting reluctant distance between itself and the pier.

Judith lowered the stunner and stood. But she remained tense and alert, and amazed at the way she had reacted to the moment's demands. Her quick and effective use of the stunner, like her aggressive reaction to Vincent Polliard in the *Last Exile*, had felt both natural and forced. In the split second when she had fired the stunner she had had an odd flash of images in her mind's eye, of firing a weapon of some kind elsewhere, at an adversary or adversaries she could not clearly make out.

"Itching to do this a long time, I guess," Kelso said. He had pulled a wad of currency from Rodríguez's shirt pocket and resumed standing over the prostrate smuggler.

"Why didn't he?" She was beside him now, her attention brought back to the present.

"Maybe he never figured the time was right. Or the price high enough. Maybe it's high enough now. Still, I've always thought Rodríguez was a basically honest guy. Never thought he might—" He looked at her suddenly, his eyes wary and thoughtful, then leaned on the broomhandle and pointed his pistol at the ones on the launch. "You two! Come over here and get your pig of a boss."

They obeyed. Carlos's rifle was trained on them as they came forward.

"Put him in the launch and get in with him. All of you."

Juan moved down from the bridge while Carlos stayed at the afterhatch. Rodríguez's men did as they were told, but there was little room for them in the laden launch. They had to lay Rodríguez over the uneven cargo and stumble through and dig holes in it for themselves.

Kelso untied their line and cast it away. The launch began to drift on the rain-lashed water.

"Okay." Kelso raised the pistol. "I want to see if you bastards have any redeeming humanity left in you."

The men in the launch yelled and frantically tried to find protection from Kelso's gun.

"I want to see which you try to save when your boat goes down. Boss or booty." He fired. Once, twice, three, four times, at the boat's waterline. Air bubbles boiled up from under.

The men screamed and cursed, thrown into a panic as the heavy launch began to sink. Not one had a lifejacket. All could likely swim, but they'd be severely burdened with either Rodríguez or whatever loot they might try to seize and pull shoreward.

Judith watched a vindictive glee spread over Jack Kelso's face as the launch slowly disappeared in the water and its occupants thrashed in a frenzied attempt to hang on to this or that relic while swimming at the same time. It looked as if Rodríguez were forgotten. Then one shouted, let go whatever he held and clutched for something beneath him. The others swam over, also relinquishing valuable objects to help the one who'd called out.

"Well, I'll be damned," said Kelso. "They've opted to save Rodríguez." He burst out laughing at the sight of the three men fighting to keep their captain up and make it to shore.

The laughter contained more than the pitiless mirth that might be derived from these men's misfortune. It was full of actual delight at seeing a "redeeming humanity" displayed; and it was infectious. She gave way to it happily, without knowing why it made her happy to do so. Then the Lavaccas, yes-men even in this, joined in.

"Can it be," Kelso howled, "can it be I've been wrong about my fellow man?"

"However that may be," Judith yelled over the noise of the rain and wind and their laughter, "and whatever their motive for wanting to take you, you've made them unappeasable enemies now for certain."

Doubled over, Kelso righted himself, wiped rain from his beard and sobered. His eyes were once again thoughtful under their dripping brows as he looked from Carlos at the afterhatch to Juan beside the bridge, to Judith DeFond. "With friends like you," he said, "I should worry?"

15. GIFTS FROM THE SEA

On the morning of the next day Kelso had the Lavaccas position the *Tiburón* a half kilometer off Isla Pequeña. With the sub resting at a depth of 15 meters on a flat area that was part of the island's undersea slope, he and DeFond left the airlock in full diving gear.

The antirad suits were restricting, and hardly necessary for diving or swimming in the uncontaminated waters of the Restitutions, but the primary purpose of this first lesson was to familiarize DeFond with the equipment (though she had a suit of her own, she'd admitted she'd never worn it, and Kelso had gone over its parts and their functions briefly before they entered the water). The thick and tightly fitting material of the suit, the twin minijets located on the lower back, the "gills" above the jets, the full headmask with its tiny gauges visible on the inside perimeter of the faceplate, the collapsible handfins and the convertible footfins, proved to be no problem getting into, and she took to the water as though she'd been born in it.

"Visibility is a lot better here than it'll be in the bay," he said into the minuscule mike below the faceplate, "and there aren't the dangers of getting snagged on pieces of metal and other junk. This is easy going around here but it's good to become used to the suit and jets without having to worry too much about anything else at first."

"Right." Her voice was clear and steady in his mask phones, without a hint of labored breathing. Obviously her respiratory system, like her suit, was in better shape than his.

The scenery was unspectacular—volcanic rock mottled with various types of algae, a sea urchin here and there—but would improve as they neared the island.

The jets were on low power, propelling them over the slope at no more than a couple of knots. A simple wave of the finned hands would lift or lower the body to accomodate the irregularity of the underwater terrain. Or the hands could be placed in front, arms extended, and used as a plane, much as the bow planes of a submarine, to maneuver up and down as the jets pushed them along. With the jets on, the footfins were automatically converted to their vertical position, jutting above the heels of the feet and pressed together by the adhesive material on the inside of each fin, to resemble the caudal fin of a fish. When the jets were not being used, the footfins could be worn forward and flat, in the old frogman manner of scuba and shallow-water divers. As he explained this to DeFond and watched her experiment with the fins, he marvelled at how easily and quickly she learned to control her movements. She negotiated the water the way she did the air above it: lithe-limbed, effortlessly graceful. Swimming slightly above her, Kelso derived both an aesthetic and sexual pleasure in watching her dark form undulate over the rock. In the suit's black sleekness, with its back humped by gills and jets, she was a svelte sea creature from a mariner's fantasy,enchanting and, perhaps, deadly. Kelso shook off the mood, afraid of enchantment.

He routinely scanned the gauges on the inside of the mask to see if everything was functioning properly, then asked Judith to do the same. She reported back that all readings were okay. The suits had been designed six or seven years ago by an outfit named Eumarine, Incorporated. Made of a light but strong synthetic that contained an intricate insulating mesh of thermal and antipressure coils, antiradiation and buoyancy cells, in the thin sheath between the flesh of the diver and the sea, they performed well enough as long as they were cared for properly. Considering Kelso's neglect of his, they were able to stand up without much care—for how long, no one knew. The "gills" had, since their invention, been the suits' most problematic item. Like the electrolung that antedated it, the gill device was intended to produce its own oxygen through the electrolysis of sea water, only more efficiently. But it had never worked the way it should, and was invariably replaced with the old electrolung, or modified. Both his and Judith's suits contained modified versions.

The worthiest improvements in the Eumarine breathing apparatus lay in its dechlorinators and pollution filters, which were much more dependable than any device preceding them in removing poison gases from the sea salt and radioactive or other toxic materials from the water. The antiradiation cells in the skin of the suit were only about forty percent effective—in areas where the level of radiation was low. According to the last promulgated Coastal Authority analysis, Highland Park contained dangerous levels of radiation that had drifted southeast from the Sunland breeder reactor. They had melted down as the underlying earth beneath the Verdugo foothills sank. But according to the Chief there was little radiation danger in the Highland Park area. Once upon a time Kelso would have paid scant attention to either the Coastal Authority's reports or the Chief's data. Now he had someone else to think of besides himself, no matter what her motives were.

He saw her come close to a rock outcrop. She swerved away just in time. He slowed his power, dropped down and fell a body's length behind her.

"Things can be deceptive underwater," he said. "Distance especially. With the jets, you can be on top of something before you know it."

"Yes." Her voice was calm, almost languid.

"Size can also be misleading. Objects always appear bigger than they actually are."

"Yes."

"Are you okay? You sound a little—dreamy."

"Yes. It is—" she undulated over a rise in the slope "—it's incredible here. Enthralling."

"Oh. Well, if we were farther out, away from Isla Pequeña, visibility would be even better. This will help you get used to a bit of the murk you'll see in the ruins. But like I said, this isn't as bad as that." If she thought the ragged undersea slope of Isla Pequeña enthralling, what would she think of diving off the Seychelles or in the South Pacific, of being lost in the spellbinding beauty of a fringing reef? Such thoughts, Kelso. A long time since you remembered such things. Like the whales that night. You had forgotten the whales. You had forgotten how to give a damn. Had this woman who had suffered amnesia, who had trouble remembering who she was, given him back that memory?

A school of yellowtails darted out of a depression in the rocks, startled by something below. For a moment the two people confused them, and the school scattered in all directions but quickly regrouped as Kelso moved past in Judith's wake. The dark spines of sea urchins were becoming more common, and here and there he saw what looked like gorgonian growths among the rocks but did not take his eyes off Judith long enough to make sure exactly what they were.

The slope had become steeper the closer they came to the island. "Do a three-sixty and move your power up a couple notches," he told her.

Judith angled her feet to the left and turned, handfins pointed forward to help keep her head up. When she'd completed the turn, she pulled thumb and forefinger from their rings on the inside of her right handfin and, fingering the dial on her belt, moved the speed control up two clicks. The jets nudged her forward, by Kelso, at a three-knot speed.

He turned around and followed, clicking his own power up. A form caught his eye on the left but when he looked, it was gone. The slope dropped beneath them again as they headed back out to sea.

"Okay," he said. "Time for some diving. You ready?"

"Yes."

"We're above a little canyon here. Bottom's about thirty meters down, or what we'll call the bottom. Actually it's only one of Pequeña's spurs. Dive, but watch for the canyon to narrow if you turn back toward the island. And cut your speed if you find yourself going too fast for comfort. Watch the reading in the upper lefthand corner of your mask for your depth. The antipressure coils can handle a lot more pressure than what you'll be under either here or in the ruins." I hope, he thought, but how could he be sure? "But it's a good idea to get into the habit of reading your gauges routinely."

"Yes," she answered.

He watched her body arc downward, fins waving only slightly as she went into the descent. He felt a pain, as one might feel upon seeing the first leaf of autumn drop. He reflected upon it, examined the pain, came up with no definite answers, or none he wanted to face at present. But that feeling of bittersweet bewitchment lingered. *Mermaid* came to mind. A dark, mysterious mermaid; a twilight creature doomed to the deeps.

"If it gets dark, turn on your headlight," he said, returning to what he had always understood to be reality.

"I've reached the bottom, Jack." Her voice floated up to him, across distances he suddenly wondered could ever be bridged or traversed. He saw the light on the brow of her mask throw its beam between the canyon walls.

"Okay," he said. "Try following the canyon on down. It should drop a lot now."

She did. He made a quick and cursory check for any sign of an unwelcome guest, like shark, ray or barracuda, hovering in the vicinity. Satisfying himself that the immediate area was safe, he homed on Judith's light and jetted downward. The anxious way he moved made him realize he did not want to lose sight of her.

After an hour of practice at depths from thirty to fifty meters, in and out of the cavernous basalt outcroppings and small branch canyons, Kelso called a halt to the diving session and led the way to Isla Pequeña. He had dived many times here (always alone before this; not even Dimitri had known of this secret place), and he knew exactly where he wanted to go. When they broke surface, they were in the small cove.

Terns and gulls sprang skyward, flew, squealing, above the rocks, their winged shadows flitting over the sunlit water. Approximately forty meters wide, thirty deep, from the narrow mouth to the small crescent beach, the cove was ringed by high rock, beneath which lay miniature caves, much like the basaltic formations they'd been swimming through for the past hour undersea.

"Welcome to, uh, Cave Cove," said Kelso, giving a name to the place for the first time. Having cut the jets before surfacing, he began to swim toward the shore.

There was no comment from DeFond but he heard her following him in. Five meters from the beach they could touch bottom and so removed the fins, stood and waded in. Judith, it seemed, had been waiting to tear off her mask before she spoke.

A gasp. "It's beautiful. You knew it was here?"

He unsnapped his own mask, yanked it away. "What did you say?"

She had thrown mask and fins at the shore and was releasing buckles, snaps, buttons. "This place. It's perfect. You've been here before. You swam straight to it."

"Yes. I used to come here and talk to the birds." Watching her come out of the suit, he saw she wore nothing underneath. She was, he concluded, the least modest woman he'd ever met, and the least vain about her body. This was even more surprising when her looks were taken into account. But immodesty, beauty, and everything else aside, it was certainly natural to cast off clothes in such a setting and Jack Kelso happily obliged nature by doing as she had done.

During their workout in the canyons she had picked up a number of specimens, and she emptied these from her diving bag. On the beach were laid several mollusks, a couple of sand dollars, a starfish. Seeing her neatly arrange these rather mediocre objects on the sand, he had difficulty relating the present Judith DeFond with the one who'd found him on Islip Island and finagled her way onto his sub, the one who had so coolly disclosed that the men in the patrol chopper had been "eliminated," the one who had expertly and swiftly knocked out Guillermo Rodríguez with a sopo gun.

She looked up at him and smiled. "Amazing," she said, pointing at her collection.

Something stabbed at him again. That pain. Her smile, the objects on the sand, what she had just said—he couldn't say what exactly triggered the sting of hope so sharply; maybe it was all these elements combined, or none of them. Maybe it was something beyond naming. Maybe it was simply one of those heart-stopping moments when it all seemed to come together, when the ugly outer fabric of survive-or-perish was torn and a glimpse was given of the true simplicity of things, the beauty and good that were really at the heart of life if only a man made the effort to *see*.

Yet he had made no effort. The moment had just happened, had been handed to him on a platter—or on a beach. He could not remember having experienced such a moment since Lisa. He hadn't deserved this one. Had he?

But suddenly her smile vanished, as if checked, wiped away by an inner reprimand. The moment was gone, not his after all. The leering demon residing in reality's heart laughed and closed the curtains. The setting, a second ago hinting of a paradisical nook outside time, turned on him with a vengeance, became a perverted illusion of what it had earlier seemed. Even their nakedness now seemed censurable.

"It's a lovely place, Jack. How did you ever find it?" She stood, looking at the high lava formations hemming them in, unwilling to meet his eyes.

"Stumbled onto it diving around here quite a while ago." His answer was automatic, almost curt.

"These islands are so young. A book in your library tells

how volcanic islands are formed. You wouldn't think—it is amazing how much life is down there."

The life was there, he thought, before the islands were. But he said nothing. The surf came in and lapped at his feet. He watched it, remembering the hour spent underwater, the reawakening of interest in everything he saw, a rekindling of his love for the sea and its riches. Spasms of this old love had occurred more frequently lately, and he knew their source, their catalyst; yet each spasm brought with it its own death, carrying like a parasite the reminder that she, that life could be, was all too often, not what it seemed, full of deception.

"Look! What is this, Jack? Come here and look."

At first he could see nothing where she pointed at the sand. But moving closer he saw a small crab, the color of the sand and presently immobile. Then, only a meter from Judith's finger, it sprang up and scuttled quickly away, disappearing into a horseshoe of rocks near the shore.

"Little early for that guy to be out," Kelso grunted, perversely reluctant to be pulled out of his depression.

"What was it?"

"Ghost crab. Rarely seen. Don't usually come out till dusk or after. Immediate descendant of the first critter to crawl from the sea. Has to jump into the water every now and then to get its gills wet. Part aquatic, part terrestrial. One of nature's first schizoid cases. Half this, half that. Like a mermaid."

He stood slightly behind her and could not see her face; but a barely discernible tension had crept into her spine and neck. He felt a sudden shame.

"How—" Her voice had altered, had the definite timbre of stress. "How did it come to be here? I saw spiders on the rocks. How did they come to be here?"

"On the wind. On the water. On logs, driftwood spilled from the mouths of rivers. In the upper atmosphere floats an aerial plankton made up of all sorts of insects, spiders, plant seeds, and whatnot. Charles Darwin took some mud from the feathers of a bird and was able to raise over eighty different plants from that smidgen of soil."

"Aerial plankton," she repeated hardly above a whisper. "Life. It's miraculous. Indestructible."

"Not quite. Courageous, tenacious, stubborn; but not indestructible. I could cite you any number of cases to prove it. Unique ecological niches and environments that it took millions of years for nature to develop have been virtually obliterated by that swaggering omnivore known as man."

She said nothing but sat at the water's edge, face toward the gentle surf. Then: "But surely a great deal of good has come of man's mastering nature, using it to his advantage. Otherwise you . . . we . . . would never have evolved—"

"Yeah." He cut her off, instantly irritated by this old argument. "Something *better* than us may have evolved. Nature never needed to be *mastered*, only understood, appreciated, revered. With that approach, a healthy symbiosis might have resulted instead of wholesale rape."

"But—it isn't too late." She fell silent again, her back still to him, knees pulled up to her breasts and her feet at the water's edge. In spite of the optimistic position she was trying to take in this worn-out debate, he detected a note of despondency in her tone.

The feeling of shame returned. Instead of indulging in his usual lament, why didn't he practice what he preached and try to understand *her*? He would, damn it all, if he could find some kind of clue, key, handle, something to get hold of that would provide a starting point, a step in the right direction.

She said, "Most of the beaches in the Restitutions are artificial. This one is real." She let some of it sift through her hand. "Why?"

He could not tell if her curiosity was genuine or if she was merely making conversation, steering them, as she did so often, onto another subject less troublesome, perhaps farther from that clue to her he sought. "Don't really know," he said. "The sand comes from the skeletons of shellfish and coral, ground to powder by the sea. Takes time to form a beach, but some of these islands could have been pushing up from the sea floor for thousands of years, enough time for a lot of wearing down of shells and skeletons. But any coral found around here will likely be only in places like this cove, where the sun can warm the water and the water is protected from the general current, because the current that comes through here is a cool one, too cool to allow coral growth. On the other hand, the waters outlying all the Restitutions are several degrees warmer than the cool water current they lie in. Some say this is caused by all the volcanic activity in the area." He stopped, unaccustomed to his new role as teacher and dispenser of knowledge, yet finding it not all that unpleasant, even if he was being manipulated away from a topic perhaps more mysterious than the sea.

"Amazing to think of the lava boiling up from the ocean floor like that, for thousands of years. All that power and force fighting to break surface, into light and air. A fascinating place, the ocean." She was watching the water come in around her legs. "The diving was like—like a dreamstate."

Kelso longed for his pipe, but hadn't brought it. He sat on the sand beside her, also watching the surf, and seeing in what she'd just said an opportunity to try prying open that door she kept under heavy key. Subtlety had never been one of Kelso's strong points, but he had had sense enough to realize some days ago the direct approach would net him nothing. "Sea's one of the oldest symbols or analogies for the subconscious. It's got all the right elements for mirroring these unplumbed depths in one's head. The deeper you go in either medium, the darker, colder, and weirder it gets."

He was aware of a change in her, and glanced over. Her face wore an intense and painful frown, and her eyes were no longer focused on the froth around her feet, weren't focused on anything. All at once she turned and met his look. For a fraction of a second her eyes revealed something plaintive, something wistful, and he had the distinct feeling she longed desperately to confide in him, to confess, to tell him what secretly ate at her. But, like the moment of joy earlier, this, too, quickly passed—so quickly that Kelso was left wondering if it had occurred at all.

She looked away. A hand went to the side of her head as if she'd just felt sharp pain there. She suddenly stood. The expression on her face was one of distress. "I'll fix us some lunch," she said, turning from the water.

The impulse to leap up, to grab her, shake her, beg, cajole, threaten, in order to force her to tell him what troubled her, what dark thing resided in *her* inner seas, made him move to intercept. But she stepped swiftly out of reach to the pack amid the parts of his diving suit.

The need to wring it from her became lost in a snarl of conflicting emotions and thoughts. He let it go and, silently succumbing to the balm of the rhythmic surf, said nothing more while she found refuge in the mundane task of preparing the lunch they'd brought.

Then, minutes later, she came over to him, her eyes strange, almost feverish. She put her hands on his shoulders and gently forced him down to the sand. Her hands ran over his face, his beard, his chest. Her breath came fast as she lay on top of him. "Make me feel, Jack. I want to forget myself—everything—with the way you can make me feel."

Speechless, he clasped her to him. A desire flamed through him that, in the moment's sudden fire, seemed to Kelso a sexual counterpart to the lava that had formed Isla Pequeña. Her disconcerting hunger, his responding passion, burned away all else. As the shadows from the rocks slanted toward the tiny beach, he knew their bodies fused, blood to blood, atom to atom, as molecularly integrated as the hydrogen and oxygen that had formed the seawater rolling into their secluded cove.

He awoke cold, alone. The impression of Judith's body on the sand, like the bits and pieces of what remained of their lunch nearby, like the receding surf pulled out by the ebbing tide, suggested time's brevity and passage, ecstatic moments gone. The cove was now blanketed by shadow and the narrow window the cove's mouth opened to the horizon told him it was nearing dusk.

He sat up, looking. She was nowhere on the beach. He stood, brushing sand from arms and back. Closer to nightfall than he'd first guessed, the sky was swiftly darkening. A couple of stars were already visible above the ring of rocks. Looking over the area where they'd left their suits, he could see that her diving gear was still there.

"Judith?" An appalling fear chilled him when he remembered her mood before lunch, her wanting to tell him something, the conflict of conscience evident in her eyes, then the sexual fever, as though it were a final and desperate rite. "*Judith!*"

An answer came over the sound of the quietened surf.

"What?" he called, almost drunk with relief. "Where are you?"

He heard it again, above him. The dark outline of rock was all he could see. He remembered the semblance of a trail going up, one he had chipped out of the rock with a knife when moved by an obscure wish to explore Pequeña's desolate span years ago.

The trail was more worn than he remembered—kids sometimes came to play here from the other islands nearby—and he found his way fairly well, but care had to be taken to avoid cutting a foot. Though swimming had proven to be little problem for the mending ankle, walking to any extent could still be painful.

When he reached the top, he saw her sitting on a ledge overlooking the water, a quiet silhouette with breeze-teased hair. He stepped gingerly to the ledge.

"I've been watching the sunset. Now the stars are coming out. It's beautiful up here." The words sounded tired and strained, with a hint of anxiety, or annoyance, at the intrusion.

"A little rough on the rump, isn't it?"

"No. It's smooth here. Feel."

He sat beside her, though a half-meter away. "It's time we were heading back, I guess."

"Yes. I know. But a while longer. Please?"

"Okay." He fell silent, thinking back on their lovemaking on the beach. A paroxysm of remembered pleasure passed through him, aggravating rather than dispelling his confusion.

"Did you like it on Island One, the space colony where you worked?"

The question surprised him without his knowing exactly why. Kelso felt knocked about like a derelict by constantly changing winds, and he knew in advance not to try to anticipate what wind might blow next. "It was interesting," he said shortly. "But overall a bit claustrophobic and artificial for my tastes. Lisa liked it. Helped make it more enjoyable for me. It was interesting, but I prefer Mother Earth. Maybe having been born in Idaho, in open country made me—but no, things were foul on Earth. I couldn't forget that, and wanted to get back to work here." Kelso bit it off, recalling Lisa had pointed out more than once that the work they and everyone were doing on Island One was for Earth, for people, and nothing else.

"You love the earth," she said without facing him.

"Yes. I suppose I do. I've never hated the earth. Only men and what men have done to it."

"Yes. I know."

"Do you? I wonder. Let me try to explain." He was annoyed, irascible, uncertain of the cause of the annoyance, "It's the wristwatch you're wearing, that'll probably sing you a bedtime lullaby if you want." He saw her head tilt to look at the watch, as though she'd forgotten she had it, or couldn't remember where it came from. "It's millions of acres of wilderness flooded so a glittering dump like Las Vegas can have enough electricity for its casinos. It's millions of acres of unique and irreplaceable wild lands ruined for the sake of our unquenchable, and in so many cases unnecessary, thirst for oil, or uranium, or coal. It's the massive meltdowns from the goddamned reactors along the San Andreas Fault that should never have been built there, or anywhere else for that matter. It's—" He felt he was babbling, being unreasonable, not saying it well at all. "Maybe like Henry Thoreau said when he'd been told about the invention of the telephone. The story goes, I think, that the bringer of such glad tidings told Hank the people in New York could now talk to the people in Texas. Hank wasn't impressed. He wanted to know what they were saying to each other through the wonderful new gadget. Being a keen observer of the conduct of his fellow man, he knew without asking. He knew what they were saying to each other over the telephone. What people always say to each other. Drivel. Inanities. Lies. Because Hank knew people had yet to learn how to *talk*, to truly communicate with each other, and he knew the telephone was only one more obstacle removing us that much farther from each other, that much farther from real communication." He knew now why he was so annoyed. He remembered his mood days earlier, after their lovemaking on the bridge of the *Tiburón*. He'd been irritated then, too, by the incredible void that lay between the pleasure they'd given each other and the reticence on her part, the distrust on his, between the lovemaking and the lies.

She spoke softly, almost too low to hear. "What do you think Thoreau would have said about your use of technology in order to communicate with whales and dolphins?"

She had done it again, made him feel like a fool. "Look, the point is that our goddamned technology hasn't moved us a centimeter closer to achieving wisdom, understanding, peace—in fact, when the tally's made, I believe we have paid dearly, perhaps irrevocably, at the expense of those qualities I just mentioned—for material claptrap, for emasculating pleasures, for self-indulgent creature comforts, and a zillion other things we would have been better off, healthier, stronger without. My point is that *we never needed as much as we took.*"

"Yes. All right. I know what you mean. Jack, I don't care to argue, but I'm—these thoughts and ideas—they're new to me—" She touched her head. "Yet they don't seem exactly new but... I can't remember. I'm still—Jack, those very things you value—wisdom, knowledge, humanistic harmony, love of nature—they arose, had to, out of man's freeing himself from the animal state and the only way he did that was by learning how to use language and tools."

"Yeah," he grunted. "Maybe. But I'm not arguing against language and tools. Look, you asked me what the whales were saying the other night when we were on the *Tiburón*'s bridge. Let me tell you what they were saying to me. They were saying that we—men—have destroyed too many things, too many unique forms of life we've judged to be of no importance. In every blessed form in which life manifests itself is a lesson, a revelation, about life and, since we are a form of life, a lesson, a revelation, about *us*. In this way, each time we destroy a species, a form of life, we destroy a part of ourselves. I don't know if anything you're reading in the *Tiburón*'s library will tell you that—or if you care." He was raving now, and knew it. "But with a population of over seven billion, Judith, who gives a damn? Who cares about wild animals and wilderness or whales in the sea? Only those who know that both are essential to the life chain, essential to the individual bodies, souls, minds, of those teeming seven-plus billion. The fact that the great majority of that seven-plus billion could not care less is the best argument that can be advanced against the continued spread of the goddamned human species!"

She said nothing and Kelso, left wallowing in the wake of his rage, was aware he'd just told his own kind of lie. What the whales had said to him that night, if they'd "said" anything to him, was a rebuke. They sang to him of his betrayal, of his having turned away from life. They sang that he had turned his back on what he had once prized, defended. They sang that she, this woman beside him now, had reawakened those values, the love and wonder of living, the miracle and mystery of life.

"Judith," he said, hoarse from his previous ire, "I'm sorry. Didn't mean to—sorry I got myself so worked up. Funny thing, my parents were back-to-the-simple-life idealists and I grew up fighting their ignorance and naiveté like hell. They blamed too much on technology and thought that by shucking it they'd find a new paradise. They almost died as a result, and I think too late they learned that selfishness, greed, lust for power, hate, all the human evils, thrived as much in a damned back-to-the-simple-life commune as they did anywhere else. Could be I'm as nutty as they were, but—"

DeFond was silent, eyes on the water below. He was about to conclude she would say nothing more and suggest they start back to the sub when she said, "You know what you were telling me earlier, before we . . . had lunch? About how life comes to develop on islands like this? About aerial plankton?"

"Yes."

"I was thinking, sitting here, before you came up, about—Jack, what do you think about the possibility of intelligent life on other worlds?"

Whatever was left of his irritation subsided. The question, banal as it was, had an odd ring coming from her. It seemed to contain both a genuine curiosity and a kind of challenge, as though she already knew the answer for herself, had made up her own mind about it, and was secretly daring him to dispute it. Dispute it, he could not.

"Yes. Of course," he said.

"What do you think it might be like?"

He thought. "Like us, and not like us. Hell, who can say? Anything and everything is possible."

"Some of the books I've been reading—I've come across ideas about the origin of life. I've read about 'interstellar space plankton', if I may call it that. Organic chemicals in interstellar dust clouds. I've read about the amino acids in carbonaceous chondrites. Of the probable ubiquity of life in one form or another throughout the universe. I've read about possible colonization of life-supporting planets by civilizations much more advanced than Earth's. I—I've read about all sorts of things. One of the most intriguing mysteries is the great gap of development between the Australopithecine and Homo sapiens, the great gap in our knowledge of what happened in that time between when first man was like the ape and the time when he began to use tools. I've come across ideas and theories of extraterrestrial intervention. I—"

Kelso was on the verge of groaning over this hackneyed topic, but out of the corner of his eye he saw her hand lift again to touch her head. He looked over at her, could not make out details in the dark.

The silence was long before she spoke. "Fascinating." But her tone had markedly changed, was strained, with an almost hysterical edge.

Both puzzled and alarmed, it occurred to him he could not

recall the books she referred to, yet supposed such books could be in the *Tiburón*'s library.

"Are you all right?" he said. "You have a headache?"

"Yes. Yes, I'm all right. I think we'd better go now." The voice was hollow, unnatural. She rose to her feet. "There could be a patrol out this way tonight." A hand rubbed her brow. She stepped backward, unsteady.

Kelso stood. He grabbed her shoulders. "Judith, listen to me. I know you're hiding something. You haven't told me all you could about yourself. Okay, so most of your past has been blitzed by amnesia. But you know something you're not telling. Have you started remembering things that the amnesia kept you from remembering before? Have you started remembering things you don't want to remember and don't want to talk about, to tell me about? Is that it?" He hated this, preferred even to think of her as a bloody agent of some kind rather than a mental case because he thought he had a better chance of dealing with an agent, whatever her mission was. The evidence, however, suggested a woman torn between reason and instability—or one torn in what she had been assigned to do.

"Let go." She recoiled from him as if now afraid of any kind of contact. "I'm all right," she said, refusing to address herself to his questions. "I'm all right. We must go down. We must return to the *Tiburón*."

She started back over the trail to the cliff, moving as if she could see every rock. Kelso knew nothing else to do but follow. Yet he felt that somewhere there in his spur-of-the-moment interrogation he had touched upon the truth, or the way to the truth. Exactly where, he could not say.

16. THIEVES

Off Cabo Colnette, Mexico, the *Tiburón* crept through the darkness below the edge of the continental shelf. Its three-knot speed, though necessary, seemed interminable. In the airlock stood Jack Kelso and his "crew". All were ready and waiting—suits, tools, weapons, fastening and binding them into costumes that bordered on the grotesque. All were strangers to these waters except Kelso.

From memory he'd drawn a map of the colony layout (it had been well over ten years since he'd worked at Colnette) and gone over it in minute and painstaking detail with DeFond and the Lavaccas. If he'd forgotten some key installation—an outpost, a guard station, nets—or remembered them in the wrong places, they could badly fumble the job.

Ten or twelve years ago prospective personnel were extensively screened before being approved for work in the undersea colonies. Entrance requirements were stiff. Once in, security and formalities relaxed, and rules became flexible. People worked in a casual atmosphere. This modus operandi worked best, because the colonists were under enough pressure, figuratively as well as literally, in other respects. Kelso gambled this was the modus operandi that yet prevailed.

He moved his ankle in the tight-fitting boot of the suit: still a little sore, but it shouldn't give him any trouble as long as no strenuous demands were put on it. Looking up, he caught her watching him. Had he seen her smile through the faceplate of her mask? Was the smile meant to reassure him? Of what? With her and her wondrous bodyguards along, how could anything go wrong? He'd seen the trio in action before. Her decisiveness and efficiency in such instances amazed him because she could be so ambivalent, evasive, vague, at other times.

Under all the gear the svelte figure of the mermaid was concealed. How many times had he felt her strange desire, her bottomless need of—what? And why, in spite of her hunger, was a part of her always somewhere else, as though that part hovered off to the side, observing with a kind of clinical yet fascinated melancholy?

The engines cut back, and the Chief's epicene tenor came over the wallphone behind them. "Drop-off in two minutes, Captain."

At his back Kelso felt a Lavacca tug at his breathing apparatus, making a final adjustment. The other Lavacca checked DeFond over. The procedure was switched, Kelso and DeFond examining the bodyguards. Everything was flawless, thanks to the whiz twins. They gave Kelso the goddamned willies, those two. He longed to smash a fist into one of those stolid jaws just to see if the head behind it could register outrage, *some* kind of emotion.

The *Tiburón* stopped and held steady. The sea valves were opened by the Chief, and the water poured in, surging and foaming around their feet, rising quickly and encircling them in its heavy grip. The airlock door cycled open, faster and smoother than it had since Kelso commandeered the sub. Before them yawned the black precipitous mouth of La Perla Canyon.

He activated the thermal and alleviation systems in his suit, watched the others do likewise. "Okay?" he said into his mike.

They each raised a thumb to indicate readiness.

He turned on his jets and was pushed into the sea. Pressing his feet together, the footfins automatically jutted upward, fanned, and sealed themselves together.

At a 150-meter depth the cliff's features were invisible; when they entered the deep vee of the canyon, the water became even darker. They had to move slowly, feeling their way. Use of the mask lights was out of the question, the risk too great that they'd be spotted by the first observation station long before they were under it.

That first observation station was their first objective, and briefly Kelso saw lights ahead before the canyon turned and the irregularity of its slope obtruded. He could recall no obstacle, such as a net or security trap, intervening here.

Jetting cautiously to the right, he felt something strike his mask and dart away. The lights reappeared as the canyon straightened. With his eyes becoming more accustomed to the darkness, he could now make out the dim forms of rock and bryozoan growths along the canyon wall. Under them passed a school of what looked like amberjack.

The others kept up easily. Maybe they had less trouble than he did seeing and maneuvering over the rough bottom. That would not surprise him. He was, in fact, or so he told himself, past being surprised by the Lavaccas or by DeFond. Did he really believe *he* led *them*? More than anything else, he felt himself to be nothing more than a disposable cog in the wheel of their obscure design. *Her* design. He was certain that whatever part the Lavaccas played was secondary. Perhaps they, too, were disposable.

Though she still gave freely and eagerly of her body, and though at times, like the day on Isla Pequeña, he had intimations of what might lie embattled inside (*what* was intimated, but remained nonetheless nameless), her mind had become increasingly closed off. At the same time, he sensed an intellectual need in her as strong as or stronger than the sexual one, an insatiable curiosity and almost desperate need to know, a desire to communicate ideas, beliefs, doubts. Kelso was haunted by that day on Pequeña when it had seemed that she was about to tell him something, confess something. But since that day she had reverted to a reticence more guarded than before, offered dialogue of only the most superficial sort, and effectively shut him out. She had been ill by the time they had suited up and started into the water, complaining of an almost debilitating headache, dizziness, and nausea, and several times had come close to passing out. He had had to help her the last hundred or so meters back to the sub, and, once aboard, she'd retired to the officers' quarters where, presumably, she had slept and recuperated. The next day she'd appeared to be all right, though she had scrupulously avoided him and refused to hear his protests that to dive into the Highland Park ruins with a recurring illness, mental or otherwise, was indeed insane.

The lights grew stronger, now illuminating with their corona the left rim of the canyon wall along which they moved. Accounting for the murk and the usual visual deceptions and distortions under water, Kelso judged them to be approximately fifty meters away. The lights would be those of the observation station: a reinforced soldenoglas dome, made of the material invented by a chemical engineer named Isaac Soldeno in the late nineties, capable of withstanding 500 kilograms of pressure per square centimeter. Thirty meters in diameter and ten meters high at the apex, the station contained a laboratory, a photo lab, a bunkroom, head, and study chamber, all encircled by an observation deck with transparent walls. No more than four or five people would—or should—be inside, all of whom would be wearing the blue coverall uniforms of the colony's highly respected and trusted scientists, uniforms which would have badges of clearance that would permit the wearers entry into the main power plant behind the large hydrodome complex. The big question: would there be any guards in or around the observation station? Kelso didn't remember any. To the best of his knowledge, the colony had never been invaded, attacked, sabotaged, or spied upon by enemy, friend or lunatic; so he hoped they relied, as in the past, only on the seacar patrols, traps, and nets for security.

When they were close enough to the station for the lights to expose the canyon floor, Kelso moved to the left, closer to the slope and its deep shadows. The rest followed him. Over their heads, just above the cliff brink, stood the observation station.

He had cut his jets, and now began the slow ascent up the wall, keeping close to the rock and coral and watching for any movement along the rim of the canyon. He glanced once southward, at the opposite side of the canyon, scanned the water above. No lights, no moving objects that he could see. So far, so good.

At the rim he stopped, treading water in the shadows of a rock overhang on his right. DeFond was beside him, the Lavaccas below. Two large sheepshead swam out of the recess under the overhang, momentarily surprising him and causing his hand automatically to drop for the knife in his knee-scabbard. Jumpy, yes.

In the northeast, the lights of a seacar or a small submersible, fuzzed by the observation station's corona, dopplered away beyond the Number Two habitat. He saw no other indication of movement. The lights of the distant main domes illuminated a square kilometer or more, but the lateness of the hour, as he had calculated, would inhibit traffic and other activity outside the domes. The observation station directly before them, and a few meters back of the cliff's edge where they waited, was as ablaze as a circus, but gave no other sign of life. Past the station to the northwest were the huge shrimp beds and, east of the beds, the pearly glow of Number One's great dome. To the southeast, across the canyon, lay Domes Four and Five, linked by conveyor tubes to their transportation terminals. Behind Four and Five lay the main power plant and the fuel stores. Northeast, the kelp farms and Dome Two. As best he could tell, everything was just as he remembered—but visibility was limited.

"The lights are going to be a problem," he said. "Swim as close to the bottom as you can without stirring up too much sediment."

As he pushed up slowly over the ledge, Kelso hugged the rocks of the overhang, careful not to rake or snare the tools and gadgetry he carried. He moved past several old fish traps and containers of one type or another, other odds and ends of abandoned hardware almost buried by silt and coral, until he came within twenty meters of the station's airlock. The seagate was closed. He looked at the wristwatch worn on the outside of his suit. Its luminous digits indicated 1750. They were on time.

DeFond drew up beside him, a dark shadow with a deformed growth on her back. "Interesting place," she said.

"Too bad there isn't time for a tour."

"Yes. How long did you work here?"

"I thought your research was thorough."

"A car is coming," one of the Lavaccas said. Kelso could no more distinguish their voices than he could their faces.

From Dome One the twin lights of a seacar, having just left the habitat, approached. The small oval vehicle dropped toward the observation station, circled it once and fell, nose first, to the airlock door. Very little sediment was stirred up from the turbulence of its jets because the area immediately around the airlock was virtually cleared of fine material by innumerable landings and takeoffs.

Since the rear of the seacar was metal, they could not see the heads of the three men in the plexiglass nose, but Kelso had counted them as they came in. He watched the seagate of the airlock open, and the car propel itself inside. The gate was soon closed.

Kelso checked his watch; the shift change should take no more than five minutes. "Only three men in that car, I think," he said. "They're working a smaller number of personnel these days, all right." As he had hoped.

"Marine scientists and technicians needed for the war effort?" DeFond's voice was soft in his earphones.

"Something like that," he muttered, thinking: that's probably where I'd be now if I'd stayed a law-abiding and sane citizen—working for the mucking war effort, whatever in hell that might mean. "Let's hope the fuel stores haven't been depleted."

"They don't seem to be very concerned about the use of lights."

"Lights are essential down here, and they have an unlimited source of deuterium."

She did not comment on the obvious. "Are all the domes fusion-powered?"

"Yes. Everything. This is one of the few places fusion has been successful, has been *allowed* to be successful. Subs, undersea colonies—"

"Allowed by the fission interests," she completed his prior thought.

Kelso wondered at her willingness to converse. She had

already said more in the last couple of minutes than she'd said in days. "How's your head? How do you feel?"

"I am fine," she answered, and he heard the immediate tension in her voice.

"The second you feel the slightest bit *un*fine, you'd better let me know. This is no place to get a headache or dizzy spells."

"I realize that," she said curtly. "The car is inside the lock. It is time we moved."

"Yeah. Okay, let's go then." Kelso pushed up, irritated by her tone. Though he had to concede there was little in it to indicate she was nervous over what they were about to undertake. He, on the other hand, could have used a stiff drink.

Staying low, they left their concealment amid the coral and quickly swam the last few meters to the airlock door. Kelso pulled his stunner from its holster and checked the dosage indicator above the grip.

The others withdrew theirs. He had forbidden exclusively lethal weapons and required that all the stunners remain on the minimum setting. San Andreas Sea Patrol police and bounty hunters were one thing; harmless scientists and technicians another. She'd given him no argument; in fact, he'd sensed her tacit approval.

As they waited, details came back how he'd departed this place. The same way he'd departed a number of other places. In a rage. In the case of Colnette, it had come as the culmination of several years' fighting against experimentation with porpoises for use in warfare, against the herding and confining of whales for slaughter. The work he had done in interspecies communications was exploited for what he could only see as inhumane ends. The showdown came when he was told—ordered—to utilize what he had learned in communicating with whales by rounding up a herd of grays for the purpose of selling them to the whaling industry for butchering. It was the final straw. Kelso went "berserk", as later official reports and news stories put it, took control of the lead submarine pursuing the herd and told the whales, through the use of his simple—and to the whales, no doubt crude—sonic code that nothing but death awaited them at Colnette. The whales fled and Mad-Jack Kelso was unceremoniously purged. Later, through the help of an old friend, he'd managed to find re-employment on the new experimental submarine named *Deepfish* by promising (in writing) to be a good boy. He'd had every intention of being a good boy—until he found out *Deepfish* wasn't diving in the Marianas Trench solely for nonmilitary and scientific purposes, as its owners, the International Sea Development Corporation, and their accomplice, the U.S. Navy, claimed. But whale slaughtering and *Deepfish*'s true *raison d'être* aside, he remembered good and peaceful times here at Colnette, remembered that some of the people he'd worked with he had liked and respected, and wondered now what had happened to them in the course of those vanished years. In a few cases he knew. They had written him, but even if their correspondence reached him—and several had taken great pains to find the proper channels through which he could be reached—he had never answered. The recent batch of letters, picked up while in the Restitutions, lay unopened in the *Tiburón*'s wardroom. He wondered what the undersea colony was like during the San Andreas/L.A. Bay calamities. Undoubtedly everyone had been confined, as they'd been on the *Deepfish*, where Kelso was working at the time, told false reasons for the tremors, sea convulsions, tsunamis, aftershocks, that followed. When the true reason was learned—pandemonium, as on the *Deepfish*? Maybe. Maybe not. There hadn't been any Mad-Jack Kelso to blow all his fuses and seize the control center and lead a mutiny against those in charge....

The station wall began to vibrate. The seagate was coming up, as slowly, it seemed, as the *Tiburón*'s before the Lavaccas worked on it. The four held on to the metal bars outside. As soon as the opening was chest high, Kelso raised the pistol and let go the bar. He kicked forward into the lock, the rest behind him.

DeFond and the Lavaccas swam to the car's cockpit, placed the muzzles of their stunners against the glass and motioned to the three surprised people (one man, two women) inside to leave all dash controls alone. The three pistols aimed at their heads no doubt looked as lethal as gamma guns, and they gave no thought to the possibility that the stunners could not penetrate the cockpit; they were scientists, not soldiers or security police.

Kelso moved to the auxiliary airlock controls in front of the car. He pushed the button that lowered the gate and opened the drain lines and the air valves. In a few tense moments the water had dropped to knee depth, and DeFond and her bodyguards vigorously motioned for the three inside the car to raise the glass and climb out. Bewildered and frightened, they complied.

As planned, Kelso's team fired point-blank, each at his individual victim's neck. The needle-thin bullets were designed to explode on contact with nerve, vein, artery, or bone, at first momentarily paralyzing the recipient, then, as the narcotic spread through the bloodstream, causing instant unconsciousness. When the bullets hit, the three scientists uttered foreshortened cries of pain (pain more imagined than real) and fell. They were caught by Kelso and the Lavaccas before they hit the floor of the lock, and pulled inside the antechamber.

Once in the antechamber DeFond joined them, and they immediately began stripping the unconscious trio of the coveted coveralls. For a full minute Kelso stood back and watched, once again amazed and a little disconcerted by the efficiency he witnessed. Then he pulled off his mask, fins and diving gear and climbed into the car to regain familiarity with the controls.

A thought struck. "Hey." He turned, saw the Lavaccas and DeFond hurriedly exchanging diving gear for coveralls. He stood, threw one leg out so he could reach into the antechamber, and grabbed the coverall Judith was about to put on. "Sorry," he said, pulling the garment on over his diving suit. "Too bad. You'll have to sit this one out in the car. And I'm in no mood for arguments."

She stared at him without speaking, her face deadpan. But the knowledge was in her eyes that she was being told to remain in the place that was safest.

It did not take long for the operation of the car to come back to him. He was surprised that there were no improvements or alterations in more than ten years. Maybe the technocrats were losing ground after all, or at least not gaining any. There he was again, picking on the toolmen, and here he sat in a gizmo even he had to appreciate. The green lights on the control board, compass, air, fuel, and power gauges, the 3D sonar screen, throttle, jet controls, joy stick—all made up a pattern of practical efficiency that belonged to a machine which would probably do exactly what it was designed to do. He hoped. Enough, Kelso. Work to do and the devil take the rest.

Once outside the station, he found the remote control

switch that closed the airlock, flipped it and turned the throttle up two notches. Without a hitch, the bullet-nosed craft moved away from the station and Kelso turned it upward with a short pullback of the attitude rod on his right, between the two front seats. Unpredictably, he felt a bit like a kid on a carnival ride.

"You should turn on the lights," she said. Her diving gear sat in her lap and she leaned forward slightly to see out the cockpit's front.

He found the light switch. The console radio crackled: "Car Alpha-Twelve calling Alpha-Four." The number stenciled in luminous orange on the face of the transceiver was Eta-Six. The Alphas were patrol craft—unless they'd changed such things; judging from what he'd observed so far, there was little evidence to suspect they had.

High above La Perla Canyon, he moved the stick to port and turned the car south. Once again he moved the throttle up. The car shot forward, crossing the gorge and heading for the colony complex on the other side.

Lights emanating from the large hydrodomes and outbuildings, lights over the kelp farms, helped to illuminate the complex but, because of fish schools, silt, and plankton, visibility was blurred by a haze that resembled fog conditions on the surface. As they neared Domes Four and Five, details became clearer, and submarines of various sizes, shapes, and functions could be seen, like giant barnacles encrusting an artifact, studding the docks on the periphery of the transportation and shipping terminal.

South of Dome Four lay the large sonic pens where the whales had been herded and kept for study and exploitation. He kept his eyes from straying that way, even though he would not have been able to see that far anyway, would have been unable to tell if any cetaceans were held within the great curtain of sound maintained by generators sitting on the sea floor. He did not even want to think about what might be in the pens. But, despite his wishes, a nostalgic pang hit him and he wondered, had he stayed, if he would have helped the whales and porpoises more by fighting the profiteers "through proper channels" instead of going bonkers and turning the animals loose. Easy to ask now, many years later, when memory had paled the cruelty, the stupidity— He shook it off.

"Is anything wrong?" she said.

Had he shaken his head? He didn't think so. "No. Why?"

"I—felt your mood."

He thought about that a minute. "This place gives me the megrims," he said and was at once sorry he'd said it. He resented telling her anything about his past, his personal conflicts, since she was so bloody secretive with hers. At the same time, he recognized in himself an impulse, growing stronger each day, to exorcise old ghosts through the timeless ritual of confession. This woman had cast a spell on him. But what kind of *spell?* He could not discount the recurring suspicion he'd been all too willing to be hexed. But while she might be a sorceress, she was also possessed. Of what, by what, he had yet to learn.

Over the complex now, he saw the central power plant coming up beneath them; he pushed the stick forward. The radio rattled: the subsea cops were over a kilometer away, in the main kelp farms, checking out an idle harvesting machine left in the middle of one of the hybrid fields; a routine problem for the cops, but one that would keep them occupied. The car dipped.

"It must have been very interesting working here," she said. "Do you know if they still—are they still working with cetaceans?"

"No. I don't know." His voice had an edge.

"I'm sorry. A bad subject."

"Right. Time to think theft." He hated cutting her off but knew from experience the conversation would not go much beyond surface generalities. Perhaps she *wanted* it otherwise; he was sure he had sensed, on a number of occasions, she had wanted it otherwise. What held her back? What was the nature of the thing that restrained her, so tortured her mentally?

He gave it up, again tossed between anger and compassion, knowing that the present task would tolerate little of either.

Like the observation station, the exterior of the power plant was void of activity. Even during "daylight" hours, most of the activity went on inside the domes, in submersibles and outranging laboratories, on the farms and mines. Every rock and mineral, every diatom and crustacean, in or around the colony, had been scrupulously examined countless times. The immediate outlying terrain held few secrets.

If memory was as reliable here as it had been thus far, the fuels would be kept in storage cells on the southeast side of the plant. He steered the car for the appropriate airlock, which was fortunately on the side least exposed to the main part of the complex, in relative darkness. At the same time, it was probably odd for a seacar to be entering this lock at 1845 hours. He wondered if he should cut the nose lights, decided not to.

The car touched the bottom. A cloud of flatfish flurried nearby and rose up the wall of the plant like a bunch of oddly deflating balloons escaped from their vendor. When he pushed the airlock remote control button, nothing happened; the door remained shut. He pushed the button again. No luck. "Hell's hounds."

From the back, a Lavacca leaned forward, between the two front seats, a tool of some kind in his hand, that looked as though it could fix anything. "Let me into the console," he said. "*Por favor.*"

"Be my guest." Kelso turned on the interior light and the hardware magician plunged into the console head first. "Be as quick as you can there, *amigo*. Somebody happens along, we're going to look a little funny sitting here."

"*Sí.*" Juan—or was it Carlos?—was now enmeshed in wires.

Against the cockpit glass DeFond's profile was a now-familiar study in elegance and mystery, in subtle strength and an occult curse; one angle of a mystifying beauty that would be, he knew, etched on his memory till death.

Aware of his stare, she turned. What he felt at that instant when their eyes met cut much deeper than nostalgia.

The door began to rise.

"Bravo," the Lavacca brother whispered. But his face, when it lifted from the console, was without expression.

As soon as the seagate was high enough to accomodate the car, Kelso accelerated, nosed it into the lock and found a berth between two other craft of similar shape. Automatically, the car anchored itself to the floor with the magnetic cups beneath its undercarriage. The seagate closed, the water began draining and the air rushed in.

"Okay." Kelso let go a sigh. "Judith, you crawl back with our diving gear to the cargo compartment in the rear. Stay there, out of sight." He opened the cockpit glass and climbed out. Drops of seawater dripped on his head from the airlock ceiling. "We shouldn't be long. We'd better not be long. Those guys we zonked at the observation station will eventually be missed at their habitats when they don't come in off duty, and there's always the chance one of those who relieved them might go to the station's airlock antechamber for some reason. Me and your whiz kids will move fast, but you stay put."

She gave him a reluctant nod, waited for Juan and Carlos to climb out, then crawled over the back seats, gathering the discarded diving gear to the rear.

He slammed the cockpit glass down and turned to the antechamber door. Opening it, he saw that both the antechamber and corridor beyond were deserted. He and the Lavaccas entered the corridor.

Up ahead a boot came around a corner, then a leg. Kelso stuck his hand into the large coverall pocket and closed his fingers around his stunner.

The guard approached, eyeing their faces curiously, their nametags and badges. He lifted his hand, palm outward. "Hold it a minute, please."

A Lavacca grabbed the guard's arm and clamped a hand over his mouth. Kelso pulled the stunner, jammed it against the man's chest and fired. There was hardly time for the guard to register astonishment. The other Lavacca took hold as he slumped and, after Kelso searched through his pockets for the master key, dragged him back to the antechamber lockers. When the guard was disposed of, the Lavacca rejoined his brother and Kelso as the latter two rounded the corner to the storage cell corridor.

Glancing at the storage cells they passed, Kelso read the labels on the doors. They leapt out at him like alchemical abracadabra, red with their own hidden fires: TRITIUM. LITHIUM. BERYLLIUM. BISMUTH.

Lights out in each cell; no evidence through the thick glass beside each door that anyone was inside. He pressed the electronic key into its door slot. The door slid into the wall. The two Mexicans stepped into the cell where the tritium was stored; the door closed behind them. Kelso would keep watch outside. It had been incredibly easy up till now. Too easy.

A few meters from where he stood, the corridor terminated in a balcony overlook. Satisfying himself that the hallway was still deserted at the opposite end, he walked over to the balcony and looked down.

Below, a group of technicians conferred beside a wide control board. Kelso pulled back, but stayed close enough to see over the rail. For some reason he found this familiar tableau interesting. It was a picture common to centers of power and knowledge all over the world. No matter that the world was coming to pieces; the technicians, the engineers, the anonymous devotees in the religion of Progress stuck to their guns. Who was he to criticize, to sneer, to denounce? What did he suggest they do, become like him? If any were to be saved, wouldn't it be on account of diligent people such as those below? Kelso wasn't sure. The same sorts of people manned the computers that hurled the missiles and bombs, didn't they? The same sorts of people succumbed to the bureaucratic diseases infesting every large-scale human endeavor, didn't they? The same people had the reins of the world in their hands and were riding it willy-nilly into the apocalypse. Weren't they? Maybe. Maybe not. Maybe those guys down there preferred exploiting the sea to incinerating cities. That was worth something. But why try to figure it out? It was as futile as trying to get to the bottom of Judith DeFond. Take the money—or in this case, the tritium—and run. He wasn't any better than anybody else. In his own way, for his own twisted reasons, he'd forsaken the only decent path, the only sane path, which was, well, fighting the "system" through its own channels. In his own way he was as much a champion of power and avarice as anybody else, just as much the self-serving ransacker and death server. He no longer fought for frugality and the reverence of life, for peace and humanistic goals. He fought for himself, fought like a cornered rat, fought for the blind stinking hell of it.

So what else was new?

His weariness with the old way. His recurring scrutiny of himself of late and the resultant self-loathing. The whalesong from the bridge of the *Tiburón* that night. Judith DeFond . . . . These were *new*.

Suddenly he turned. But no one was there. The cell doors remained shut, the corridor empty. Why had he started like that?

He walked back to the cell the Lavaccas had entered, looked inside, saw only the anteroom. What was keeping them? Did it take this long to get a few hunks of metal?

What had given him the willies all of a sudden? Something was wrong; he felt it.

Judith. He saw her face, her profile, as he had seen it framed against the plexiglas cockpit of the car. He saw himself awakening on the beach at Cave Cove alone, thinking she might have done herself in; he remembered the sudden dread—

She was in trouble. And as quick and certain as this realization had come, came the realization that he cared, that he cared more deeply than he'd cared about anybody or anything for years.

She'd felt the water surge around the seacar and fall away again as the airlock door, which had opened, cycled shut. Through a slit in the boxes and diving gear, she saw shadows on the front of the car's cockpit and heard its outside latch snap open. The beam of a handlight shot in, moving over the seats, the dash, the console, the floor in front of the seats. It swept to the back, the beam striking her retinas. She closed her eyes to protect her vision, lay motionless behind a stack of boxes, pistol in hand.

Crouched as she was, tensed and waiting, a memory flickered. It was weak, blurred, elusive, had something to do with her situation, the gun she held. She was reminded of the odd feeling of *deja vu* she'd had when she fired the stunner at Guillermo Rodríguez, of the sense of having done something similar before, of being armed, of . . . *executing others.*

"They must be in the plant somewhere," one of them said.

"Yeah. Let's check this stuff back here anyway."

Torn between what was happening there in the airlock and what was trying to make itself surface in her mind, she tried to squeeze lower, closer to the floor and behind the boxes and gear.

A hand reached behind the back seats for the box at the top of the stack.

"It's just junk those scientists haul around."

"I'm going to have a look anyway. What business an OS car's got in the power center I don't know, but I think it's irregular and I'm going to find out."

The box was pulled away. She saw the guard's dark form beyond the spray of light, could not see the other one. If she knocked this one out, the other would get away, sound an alarm, summon help, or blow her and the car to bits in sheer panic. But she had no choice.

"Well I'll be—hey!"

She fired twice, trying to hit his neck or chest. The light fell onto one of the back seats. Without crying out, the guard crumpled forward into the cockpit, and went rigid.

Knowing she had to press her advantage, she clambered over him and sprang out the cockpit's left side, thinking the other guard was there.

He wasn't.

The sudden ear-splitting noise of a weapon, the smell of scorched metal, told her where he was. She jumped away from the car, saw him standing at the rear, pumping bullets from a heavy automatic pistol straight into the tail compartment.

He looked up just as she raised the stunner. She fired several quick shots, hoping to strike a susceptible nerve or vein, but a six-meter distance intervened. Having fired, she fell behind the car's nose for whatever cover she could find.

The antechamber door crashed open.

"Judith!"

She turned. Jack Kelso stood in the doorway, an upright target as tall as a ship's mast.

"Get down!" she yelled, but it was too late.

The guard's gun opened up, and it wasn't shooting soporifics. She had failed to knock him out.

Holes exploded in the wall on Kelso's left. He clutched his thigh and fell, cursing. Judith raised to shoot at the guard again but at that instant Juan and Carlos appeared, dropped their bundles and, from crouched positions, shot at the guard. The man at last collapsed against the car's tail and rolled unconscious to the floor.

She moved to Kelso where he lay on the antechamber landing above the airlock, holding his leg and steadily muttering epithets. "Why didn't you get down?" She tried to look at the wound.

"I don't know. Dumb. Like using stunners, I guess. Dumb. Somebody could get killed."

"You, namely," she said.

Carlos was in the seacar. "We'll have to take one of the others," he called from its badly damaged tail compartment. He threw out the perforated gills of one of the suits, a blown-apart headmask of another. "We'll have to take it all the way to the *Tiburón*."

Juan had the power wide open as they climbed away from the plant. In the back seat, DeFond ripped off the leg of Kelso's coveralls, then cut into the thick leg of his diving suit with her knife. The insulating materials and the alleviation layer resisted, but finally she broke through to the bloody flesh. Had he taken off the diving suit and worn only the coveralls, the leg would probably have been cut in two.

"How come it's always me who gets hurt?" he moaned, head thrown back in the seat on her left, the wounded leg across her legs.

"I thought we'd determined the reason for that," she said straight-faced, and trained the handlight on the gaping wound, knowing it had been incurred in order to save *her*.

"Well?"

"You'll be all right, Jack. Nothing vital hit." She worked to make a compress bandage with what she could find in the car's first-aid kit.

"Dirty bastards. You'd think they'd be armed with something more humane."

"It seems nobody else worries about such things but you. Maybe they can't afford sophisticated narc guns and the like." But she knew he made conversation simply to take his mind off the pain.

"Anybody following us?" he said.

"No," Juan answered at the controls. "Not yet. But we are not going very fast. The tritium is slowing us down."

"When somebody finds those knocked-out guards and scientists all over the place down there, it should get lively."

"We'll be in the *Tiburón* soon," she said, wrapping gauze around the wound. "Hold still."

"How soon will I be able to do any diving with that leg?"

"With proper care, it won't take long to heal."

"Wonderful. Thus far it's been a hell of a lot of fun." He watched her face as she worked with the wound. "By now my curiosity knows no bounds. I wouldn't want to postpone our Highland Park picnic. I can't wait to find out what's in store for us there."

She finished securing the bandage and tidied up the torn clothing around the wound as best she could. Then she looked forward, thinking of the mnemonic glimpse she had had of herself just before the guard discovered her in the car, of an indefinable creature dispensing death. She thought about what Kelso had just said. What she saw out the cockpit was the abysmal black gorge of La Perla Canyon opening to receive them.

17. PENETRATION II

...the mountains of Arha and the forests of Urill, the grasses of Liliou and the streams of Siplor, call for you. The great river Joului, from its springs in the high reaches of Mesrica to its wide mouth where it flows into the Laeti Sea, calls for you.

The broad-winged ahni, lords of the air, and the far-wandering yirus, lords of the sea, the trees, the wind, the flowers, call to you. The paths where you walked as a child, the gardens of sunlight where you played, the fields where you sang and the bowers where you lay flushed with love... call for you.

Come home.

Where the silver roads of the two moons meet on the night water of the Sea of Ilya, the way is marked for your return. Onnah yearns to receive you as a lover longs to receive the beloved.

But take heed. The way is barred. There are those who have set themselves up as your masters. They are the ones who tore you away from this benevolent birthworld that calls for you, grieves for you.

They have thrown around your mind a net of specious webbing, have enveloped you in a darkness where darkness is the first reality, in a place where only soulkillers live. They have tried to erase forever your roots, your memory of the world of your birth, that world of warmth and light and true life. They hold a hood of oppression and darkness over your mind; they suffocate your spirit.

They bar the way.

Listen. Listen to me who speaks to you through the means of the ancient heartlyre, from a place closer to you than you would believe, from a heart dearer to you than you would remember. I am calling you back.

Come back to Onnahlaeti.
I will show you the way. . . .

Number Five Supervisor of Internal Security was about to commit himself to the purification center but the mental anomaly restrained him. Amazed, he felt it grow stronger, knowing it was something he should report. But as the images began to take conceptual shape, became words in a forgotten language, his amazement became bewilderment, then disbelief, then distrust of his disbelief and, finally, conviction that what had somehow entered his mind was neither delusion nor malady but truth.

The Commander of Pilots in the Head Inguard Fleet could no longer function. Upon returning to planetbase, he claimed the need for a short rest and a routine examination. He went to the rejuvenation center and found, as he floated in the weightless suspension chamber, that the usually somnolent environment only made stronger the aberration, deepened his passivity and receptiveness to the images and emotions now flooding in. He watched with eyes turned inward an impulse arise he had not known was there, and knew that an examination by the purification machines was out of the question.

It was in the transtube, on the way to his living quarters adjacent to the communications center deep in the interior of Nammava Trah II, that the Third Officer of Imperial Vigilance became aware he was being told, among other things, to return his thoughtpulse to the original source of the strange but hypnotic telepath . . . and he was being told how to do this.

"We are attacking Nammava Trah II. No more waiting for divine events. Try to stop us and the first phase of this war will take place here between the two of us."

Abrea Acexea contemplated the helmet-hidden visage in the comviewer on his ship's operations bridge. The picture of Phegakz, warlord of the Xlimoyin, was flanked by the leaders of the Hrarghals, the C'rimaens, and the Elyigtia.

"You may join us; you may cower there between mountains. Your choice. To be made quickly."

The Prithipean commander spoke carefully in answer.

"Phegakz, you have at last succeeded in bringing me to the point where I would as soon obliterate you as I would a First Master of the Deathlords' ranks. Since your skill with mathematics is as underdeveloped as your other mental powers, I will call your attention to the fact that you and your confederates are outnumbered eight to one by myself and the rest of us dispersed here onplanet."

"That will quickly be changed!"

"Agreed. Make a move to disrupt this alliance and its attack plan, and you and your friends will be permanently transmuted to dust. A chance the universe will, I am sure, welcome."

"Women rule Onnahlaeti!"

"You speak like a Yaghattarin, Phegakz. The Onnahlaetians do not rule anything, as you mean it. The Onnahlaetian women do, like most of us who have some degree of intelligence, value what is rare and complementary—in their case, their males."

"Commander." A sentinel's voice came over the incom.

Acexea turned to the appropriate vocalizer on the control table. "Yes?"

"Tlii Onnahle is calling."

With an instantaneous wave of one huge hand, the Prithipean leader opened his comlink to Tlii. "Cinara. What?"

"We are reaching them," she said softly, as though from much farther away than the mountain pass where he'd left her and the boy, as though from another planet, another plane of being. "We have broken through."

"Cinara, I am opening your voice to a rebellious pack of metalheads on my viewer. I want you to tell them what you have just told me."

18. ACCEPTANCE

While the *Tiburón* moved out to sea from the waters off Baja California and turned northward again, traveling slowly to allow time for Kelso's wound to heal, and to avoid coastal patrols, DeFond changed for the worse. She grew more withdrawn, preoccupied with that internal dilemma whose cause she steadfastly refused to divulge. When he tried to pry, or came upon her unexpectedly during one of these compulsive spells of melancholy, she would become annoyed and demand to be left alone. At such times another personality, another being, seemed to leap at him from the green eyes. Later, relenting, she would explain unconvincingly that these periods were temporary relapses into the depression and shock she'd suffered years ago when she received news of her family's deaths. He'd heard all this before, in one way or another, but her warning that the depressions could become worse the closer they came to the Zone and sunken Highland Park cast the already improbable venture in a shadow all the more ominous. When, angered, he demanded to know how she would be able to dive in such a state, she turned and left him without a word.

In other respects she remained as perturbing and unreasonable. Her interest in ideas, history, philosophy, and science, her capacity for pleasure, especially of the sexual kind, continued unabated, seemed even more desperate, as though her days were numbered and she wanted to drink as deeply as possible of life. This mental and physical hunger, however, she subtly and beguilingly hinted was inspired by him. At times when she told him this, it had all the earmarks of truth. Yet her knowledge from the beginning had been impressive, and, behind or beneath this limitless appetite, Kelso thought he still often perceived a coolly detached diligence in whatever she undertook to learn, study, or enjoy, as though it had little to do with her personally, as though the real ambition she served lay neither in the pleasures of the body nor the mind but in some spartan elsewhere. At the same time, this need to know and feel and experience things could precipitate one of her depressions. Without explanation, when in the middle of a book or a discussion on a subject she'd pursued almost to death, she could suddenly become silent or close the book and go off to a remote part of the ship to be alone and, afterward, never touch the book or broach the subject again, as if she'd trespassed onto territory some internal overseer had decreed prohibited.

He watched her often and closely as she pored over maps and charts of the Highland Park ruins, as she listened to him explain the operations of the salvage submersible and proper diving procedures for the Zone. Despite the fact that he received scant reward for his scrutiny, he couldn't give up trying to uncover her true thoughts. Throughout the preparatory process of showing her everything about a shallow water salvage dive he could think of, short of getting into the water again, she did not once revive the subject of her parents or anything else about her background after her explanation for the depressions and her warning that they would probably become worse. Whenever the question of her objective in Highland Park came up, she spoke only of "the estate," and this without emotion.

But in spite of, or maybe because of, these vexations, he stayed drawn to her, mystified and intrigued. That newly-awakened interest in the world, the old love of being alive, the concern over the riddles of existence she'd revived in him only grew stronger. The knowledge that he cared for things again, especially *her*, was foremost in his mind each day, all day.

They talked at length, when her mood allowed it, of the ideas and themes expressed in books she read and in the movies dug out of the film library and repeatedly watched. Her opinions on abstract principles of good and evil were about all he had to go on concerning her deeper motives. These opinions usually revolved around the central belief that service to a higher good was life's *sine qua non*. Such a belief sorely unsettled Kelso, who knew it could be used as license for any evil imaginable, and many not imaginable at all. But if he required specifics, she hedged or dodged or characteristically maneuvered the conversation around to less personal matters, or to himself—a tactic that eventually led to a fresh disinterment of his past and a head-on confrontation with her idea of devotion to a "higher good."

"Perhaps it would do you good to talk about it," she said.

They lay on his narrow bunk, her fingers tracing the ragged lines in his brow and at the corners of his eyes. He'd tried once again to ferret out something concrete in her philosophy and ended up talking about the San Andreas collapse as an example, for his side of the argument, of creation's boundless indifference to such niceties as Good or Right or Justice.

"Have you ever told anyone all of it?"

"No."

"Tell me."

"Why?"

"I think it would do you good."

He turned to look at her. "You know the story," he said, on guard.

"Not from you."

In the dim light of the bed lamp her rich hair was an arrested typhoon of waves and whirls, spun in every direction around her head. Her fingers moved to smooth his frown away. At such times she could be surprisingly disarming, but he could see no ruse in her request. An impulse to confide in her that he'd long held back made him finally open up.

He talked. It was ancient black history. The death of his soul.

They were in the galley when he finished. The ensuing silence lay in the room like a pall. He felt relieved, all right, purged, but a cold, nauseating emptiness lay in the pit of his stomach.

She had not moved for some time from the coffee urn where she stood, hands folded across her robe, watching him. Her disinclination to speak irritated, and Kelso began to feel he'd been coaxed into a confidence against his will. But that was stupid; whatever rancor remained was the aftermath of his ugly tale, nothing more. Otherwise he felt, yes, by god, relieved of an illness. Could he now put it away forever?

The coffee urn began to chug. He did not remember her having filled it.

"Jack," she finally said, and her voice was unsteady. "I—" a hand pushed a strand of hair back, a hand that shook, "I think it's good you got it out. There are things we must . . . accept. Maybe now you—"

He sat up, jerking his arms from the table as if it had suddenly become hot. "Accept?" He was dumbfounded, instantly angered. "Accept what?"

"I only meant—"

"Accept that a sane use and respect for nature *and* human nature could have prevented the overpopulation, the pollution and energy waste, the starvation and sickness and war, the poverty and crime gone wild all over the world? I'll accept that. I'll accept that too many people are controlled by greed and power and blind bondage to technology. Yeah, I'll accept that"

"I'm sorry. It's a depressing subject—"

But he was raging now, hardly heard her, because she had said things like this too many times of late. "And yes, I'll accept that the San Andreas and Los Angeles disasters were hardly due to natural causes alone. I'll accept that some heinous little scheme concocted by men for whatever miserably misguided reason—"

"Why do you think that?"

"Because of the Devil's Canyon Project. Because of nuke probes in the San Gabriels. Because if such things as planetary or celestial influences and unstable tectonic joints explain the mess, then why didn't other parts of the world where the crust is just as unstable or worse than it is in the San Andreas area suffer the same cataclysmic breaks? Why, in fact, didn't the whole bloody, goddamn planet split open like a piece of rotten fruit? But even more to the point, why did Los Angeles *sink?* Why did the San Gabriel Mountains *sink?* Neither area was in the main fault zone." He shut up, for the first time noticing her odd stare.

She quickly masked it. "You ask me that as if you think *I* know. I don't."

He searched her eyes. She looked away. "Well, maybe you can offer an opinion on the subject," he said.

Her eyes came around. "No. I've wondered too but—just the other day the captain of that freighter, the *P. B. Baylor,* talked about it, but—no, I do not know. If they weren't after oil, then what—"

"I don't know either," he said, certain that thoughts were going through her mind she was not letting him know about. "That, as the Chief says, is beyond my purview. I've tried to find out, but—" He kept watching her, decided to backtrack, try another angle. But the angle he chose instantly rekindled his ire.

"All right." Kelso ran a hand through his hair. "So what's this acceptance crap? You've said it before in one way or another. Accept. Resign yourself to some grand design. That's what you keep hinting at." His anger mounted, uncontrollable. The notion brought to mind everything in the world he hated, everything he'd fought. "How can you accept the death of someone you loved? Especially if that death was unnecessary, horrible and absurd!"

"Maybe it wasn't."

He stood, leaning on the table for support. "How could it have been anything else?" he shouted. "What do you know about that, Judith? Do you know something that would make you think they were sacrificed to some mucking *grand design?*"

"No. I don't. You keep imputing things to what I say. Things that aren't true." Her voice rose, distraught. "I'm only trying to ease your pain. Perhaps you could return the favor!" This last was spat at him with uncharacteristic venom and he recognized that strange sudden flatness and artificiality he'd heard in her voice before, as though another personality had taken over.

"Chief!" he yelled, no longer able to bear the confines of the galley.

"Yes, Captain," the computer answered from the speaker next to the door.

"What's happening out there?"

"There is nothing within detectable range at the present time, Captain. It is ten-fifty-six, clear with a surface water temperature of twenty-eight degrees celsius. A northerly wind is blowing at ten knots and the air temperature is thirty degrees."

Kelso turned and limped to the hatchway. "Take her up! I've got to have some fresh mucking air!"

Water still hissed through the scuppers when he opened the conning tower hatch.

Reality exceeded the Chief's insipid report: the sky was cloudless, a deep early autumn azure, the sea a faintly darker mirror image of the sky. In his shorts and an old sweatshirt, Kelso stood on the bridge, gazing at the calm plain of gunmetal blue, feeling the breeze, taking deep breaths to quell the wrath that had boiled up inside. No, he was not yet purged, would likely never be.

A hand passed over his short-cropped hair. Hair that she had cropped. She'd wormed herself into his ship and his bed, into his mind and heart. He'd become coddled, spoiled, disarmed. His wits and instincts floated in a viscous, ennervating soup. Most of all, he was being used for an end he could not comprehend. Goddammit, he was certain of it.

Accept.

Well, he could always simply grab her by the neck and throttle her, shake the truth out, wring that lithe lovely stalk like a dishrag if she refused to talk. Sure. He'd thought of that laudable recourse before.

But could he? If he was certain her true motive had not

been disclosed, he was also certain she had, at times, wanted to disclose it. Those attacks of dizziness, headache, nausea. What did they mean? Those sudden disconcerting alterations of voice, face, personality. Symptoms of some kind of sporadic schizophrenia, or something else?

Kelso sighed. Movement on the surface of the sea caught his eye but when he looked, he lost it. The water undulated below the arced hull of the sub, an impenetrable veil concealing myriad wonders and mónstrosities. Thousands of meters beneath that tranquil surface, in the perennial blackness of the oceanic abyss, blind creatures with grotesque mouths lurched at anything they could feel moving, lurched and snapped, lurched and snapped, and were in turn snapped up. There was *nature*, Kelso. The first law of that benign abstraction you have always professed to love is *eat or be eaten.*

Or was it? Nature, among other things, was subtle and secretive, often deceptive. Reality was often, if not always, illusion, a veil hiding truth. Perhaps life's first law was to struggle up from darkness, to escape the fight-or-die mania of the deep, to learn to live on light, to return to the light.

Accept.

A cry overhead made him shift his view from sea to sky. A high flock of birds winged their way south. Watching their rhythmic motions, Kelso felt again that stab of the old love he'd once had for things, the old faith he'd had in life's inherent beauty, order, purpose. How could he feel that way without secretly or subconsciously believing in some kind of "grand design" himself?

What time of the year was it? September? October? Far to the north the fur seals would be wandering south also, to the submerged cliffs of the continental fringe, there to dive many fathoms down for the fish of those regions. Soon the sea would be aflame with shimmering phosphorescence, the autumn blooming of the dinoflagellates. The phalaropes would be following the whales and the whales the drifting fields of plankton.

For a second he felt stirred as he had not for years. He'd lived for so long with death, wallowing in it with self-lacerating glut. Was it only his own sick cynicism that ascribed deception, malevolence, to her motives?

The birds were now tiny specks, not much more than memory against the southern sky, their cries lost to the ceaseless whisperings of the sea.

What about *her* pain? Whatever her true game, her pain was real. He'd seen it too many times, especially when he'd come upon her unannounced, when she was in one of those depressions. What was that pain's cause? The need to recover a lost estate? But what kind of *estate?* Assuming that loss of her family was the source of her problem, would whatever she wanted to find in the ruins assuage or aggravate that mental turmoil? Again he found himself wishing she were a government or corporate agent of some kind after all and was surprised to note that what lay hidden behind his cynicism was actually hope. Yet even if she were an agent of some kind, it was obvious she writhed in the throes of some mental hell. Agent or angst-ridden orphan of the superquake, he still had her odd neurosis to deal with.

Unexpectedly her head appeared in the hatch, a thermos and two cups tied around her neck by string so that her hands would be free to ascend the ladderway. He had not thought she would follow him up, had expected her to shut herself away in the library or the officers' quarters, as she often did, after their argument in the galley. He watched with an abrupt longing her dark hair lift and whip around her head as she emerged. She had put on shorts and a flannel shirt but was barefoot.

Without speaking, she set the cups on the bulwark's ledge and poured hot coffee from the thermos. Steam rose from the cuprims and immediately disappeared, like the elusive answer to an unvoiced question, into air. She handed him a cup, eyes the color of turquoise in the mid-morning light.

"I'm simply trying to sympathize with you, Jack. To give you something to . . . to . . ."

He took the cup, reflecting that confusion, being at a loss for words, ambivalence, were becoming increasingly characteristic of her—except when that other voice, that other personality took over; then there was no confusion, no ambivalence, only a vehement severity, a dictatorial certainty that her view was right.

"I only mean to say that there is perhaps an order behind this apparent chaos. Our perceptions—"

He groaned and looked away, wanting to see the birds again. What she had just said was not at all unlike what he had been thinking moments before, but an ingrained impulse rose against it.

"—a higher order than man's, I mean."

"Tell me about it," he said irritably, face to the sea. He

wanted her to do just that; he wanted to hear from her a concrete interpretation of this treacherous metaphysic.

"I can't. But I—I believe it's there."

"Nice to think so, anyway, isn't it. But I can't *accept* lives snuffed out for no reason." He knew he was being pitiless; the woman certainly had every right to reach for some sort of mooring, philosophical or otherwise, to prevent being torn apart by the mental havoc that was hers. He told himself he wanted to make sure she sought the right anchorage and believed this was true. The only problem with it was that he could not be sure *he* had found the right anchorage, or any anchorage at all.

"Maybe our perceptions aren't able to see the reasons," she said softly, almost fearfully.

He turned, no longer able to hold back the questions. "Where's this philosophy coming from, Judith? Are you just another burgeoning religious nut, or are you something else? An agent of a totalitarian government, for instance. Russia? China? The U.S.? Is one of these the higher purpose you advise serving? Is that the higher purpose that dictates acceptance of indiscriminate and wholesale murder? The country, the regime, the almighty state is everything, the individual nothing? Is that it?"

She stared at him, coffee cup suspended a hair's breadth from her mouth. "No, I—"

"What is it then? What is this higher purpose that escapes my perceptions?"

She looked away, to starboard. "I don't know."

"What?" He wasn't sure he'd heard correctly over the sound of the breeze and the sea.

"I said I don't know." The cup in her hand trembled. Her face was strained, as if she warded off—or braced herself against—some impending internal assault.

The answer baffled him. "Will you know when we go into the Highland Park ruins?"

"Possibly."

Somehow he sensed she spoke the truth, and as a result was even more perplexed than ever. In addition, he also sensed there was much she was not telling. "How!"

Turning to face him again, showing increased signs of agitation, she said, "I don't know, Jack." It was still what Kelso thought of as her natural voice, though the words had come out tremulous.

"That makes no sense!"

"It makes as much sense as what you believe."

"What do I believe, Judith?"

"You believe the same as any barbarian. Survival at all costs. Your own survival. Survival without faith in anything above or beyond yourself. Survival solely for the self."

He was thrown for a second but quickly recuperated, marveling over the fact that she had just revealed his anchorage to him. "Okay. Insofar as I believe in anything, I guess that's a reasonable summary of what I believe, yes. I believe in my *self,* for want of a better word. I believe that whatever good I'm going to find, I'll find there. But permit me to enlarge on the subject."

Once more she faced the sea but he could tell she listened.

"I believe in my own instincts and my own wits, and both say to be distrustful of all authority. There are laws that I respect because I recognize those laws as serving a common good. There are laws that I break because I see them as serving private interests. But in no case will I bow to any dictum that says I must obey or serve, in ignorance or faith, some so-called higher order because those who tell me I must do so are better or higher than myself and understand things I don't. Human history has proved that to be a collossal crock. *Nobody* is higher than anybody else in that sense, and the moment some fool or collusion of fools begins to think he—or they—*are,* then in my book they've joined the worms and should be promptly and categorically squashed."

She refused to face him. "A very egocentric and anthropocentric view."

The last adjective jarred him. "I guess so," he snapped. "But then, I don't claim to be anything other than human."

At last she turned to meet his eyes and he saw the struggle, the conflict, in her face. The antagonistic edge that had cut into her tone was replaced by a plaintive note. "Jack, this concept of self . . . it's something I've . . . it's unfamiliar to me. So much is. But it seems to me that freedom of self has to be meaningless, valueless, for its own sake. A self that is free must give itself *freely* to something higher. An isolated outlaw's glorified selfhood degenerates into narcissism, self-pity, cynicism—" She paused, swallowed, a new intensity in her expression. It was as if she knew she was on target, tasted his heart's blood and wanted more. "Jack, I met a man in the Restitutions when I first went there to find someone to take me into the Zone. He was, or posed as, a diver, a salvage diver like you. There was something about him that—sometimes I think of him when you say things. You're not the same at all. Our meeting was brief but I read him easily. The cynicism, the intransigence, the violence that lay behind his eyes like a thing wanting to kill for the pleasure of it. You're not like that, I know. You are capable of compassion, have a capacity for . . . for humility and love. But it's as if this man were a diabolical alter ego of yourself. You both *hate*, and I have a feeling you, like him, are waiting for the slightest excuse to fight, to kill."

Kelso found his tongue. "Who? What was this man's name?"

"Vincent Polliard."

He stared at her. "Polliard," he said dumbfoundedly and looked out to sea, his words his own condemnation. "I thought I killed him."

"Apparently not. You hate him then. You hate him a great deal to have wanted to kill him."

"Yes."

"Maybe you hate him so much because you see in him aspects of your self, aspects you secretly loathe. Vincent Polliard is a good example of what your glorified individualism can become." Again the acrimonious edge in her voice, the fangs showing through the mask.

He turned on her. "You're goddamned good at psychoanalyzing me, aren't you! What about you? Could it be that Mister Polliard also bears some resemblance to something in your own character? What have you put together concerning your own private imbroglio? What is Judith DeFond's secret demon? Simple depression over her parents' unwarranted deaths? Simple despair at the absurdity of events, the futility of existence? Survivor guilt? Or is it something much more complex? Are you embarked on a course where you must do something that goes against your own conscience? Do you serve an ideology, a dogma that demands strict and blind loyalty, a dogma you've come to question, to doubt? Are you assigned to do something you have begun to believe could be wrong?"

Her mouth had fallen open and the blood had left her face. "He—he—" Both her hands jerked upward, were pressed against her temples as though she were trying to squeeze out a sudden pain. Her eyes were all at once glazed and narrowed. "He—I—"

She pulled away from the bulwark and it seemed to Kelso

as if something outside her jerked her head, her body, around for the hatch. Wordless, bewildered, he watched her go. Only when he saw her head disappear beneath the deck did he realize how badly he was shaking. She had struck where it hurt, and hurt deeply, with the Vincent Polliard dagger, but what had he done to her?

Goddammit, man, if she *is* mentally unstable, you could very well push her over the brink!

He hung his head over the bulwark, sick of arguments, sick of himself. Sick of suspicions, too. He thought of going to her but stayed frozen to the deck.

At least her defense of a supernal good had something of hope in it.

I will ask it again, he thought. I will! Can it be possible she has, in fact, no other motive than the one already articulated, albeit articulated obscurely, a number of times? A pilgrimage or search for lost family artifacts or heirlooms that would somehow restore or initiate faith in an abstruse ideal?

Clutching at straws, Kelso?

He wanted to believe that, found it irresistably tempting to *hope* they might share some future together, despite present antipathies, in this unintelligible and chaotic *higher order* of things.

But no.

He gripped the bulwark ledge and closed his eyes, more sick in spirit than he could remember ever having been in his life. It was obvious that he had hit her as hellish a blow, had somehow flayed her open as certainly as she had him. He had seen the stark and unmistakeable stamp of guilt that blanched her face.

19. THROUGH THE RIFT

... running ... pursuing or being pursued. Darkness. A hollow sound underfoot. The desire to speak, to cry out, to express, to vent something, grows strong and stronger, but

there is no voice. The desire to clutch, to hold, comes, but there is nothing to hold and nothing to hold with. The darkness pervades without definition, and the realization flares that the footsteps up ahead and the footsteps far behind are the echoes of Vidyun's footsteps running on through past and future.

Eyes watch, immense and multifold, invisible and omnipresent, their surveillance immanent and indefatigable.

The footsteps alter, their cadence less frantic, more orderly, in step. They are like marching, the marching of many feet ahead and behind and on all sides. Marching feet fill the darkness. Vidyun picks it up, joins in, is marching with these thousands who seem to be Vidyun and yet seem to be others, others like Vidyun but with faces Vidyun cannot see, with bodies that cannot be seen. The drumming thuds of the marching feet lull Vidyun into a mental state free of want or pain, free of all sensation, a state in which Vidyun becomes the others and they become Vidyun, all marching in step to an exalted duty whose ultimate goal is beyond the understanding of those who march. . . .

But the thread is lost. The thud of marching feet becomes a hammering ache in her head, blotting out the vague images. Incomprehensible shapes, forms, shadows, float, flit through the darkness; geometric patterns that change, multiply, transform themselves into new patterns that likewise appear and disappear.

A chasm yawns, sucking her toward it, threatening to swallow. . . .

She forced herself up, a swimmer against a riptide, out of the self-induced trance. The sights and sounds of the *Tiburón*'s control room refilled her awareness when she raised her pounding head from the chart table. Her hands rested on maps. Her robe had come open; she pulled it together and rebuttoned it, wondering why she did this. The hour was late; she was alone; Kelso slept. Did she nonetheless feel *watched?*

If not watched, then somehow *overseen.* The implant, whatever it was, however it worked, had two ways of fighting against her efforts to learn more. The headaches could come, then vertigo, nausea that could almost paralyze—or she could be pulled toward a gulf that promised oblivious sleep. A third way of control had manifested itself in recent days, a sudden taking over of her ability to voice her own mind, to move her own body as she would have it move. The first two influences she had managed to fight with some degree of success, but the third, when it was used, seemed overpowering. She had not fought it with the will she marshaled against the other two, mainly because it usually gripped her unexpectedly, but also because, being so uncertain as to what she was truly about, she let it do so. But she suspected a restraint in this last power over her, as though its source knew that to exercise this power completely would indeed turn her into a machine even less human than the Lavaccas, and thus totally estrange Jack Kelso, make him withdraw both his sympathy and his willingness to help her in the ruins.

Trying to ignore the dull pain, a pain that always began in the frontal lobe and spread, she looked across the room at the display panels and instruments as if they might help her grasp what the "dream" had told her.

. . . the relentless marching, the ubiquitous but invisible eyes . . . the invisible but perceptible uniformity of whoever, whatever, was there.

Under her hands the top map lay wrinkled and torn in places, having been handled so much of late. She glanced at it, at the crooked northwest contour lines of the submerged areas of Glendale, Alhambra, Pasadena. She pulled out the map beneath the top one. This was the blown-up projection, more detailed, of Highland Park and the broken arteries that had run south into Los Angeles. Little was as it had been before the disaster, as Kelso had pointed out.

The map was a cryptographic analogue of her own mental enigma. She could no more read any meaning into it than she could uncover her reason for being here.

What lay there in those tortuously twisted lines for her to find, to do? And why?

Was it linked to the superquake? If the nuke probes in the San Gabriels were not for the freeing of oil, then what?

Details will be disclosed to you as they become needed.

How? Provided her theory of an "implant" in her brain was correct, was it arranged so that the information it contained would be released into her mental processes only when the proper sensory data triggered it? In other words, was the implant preprogrammed to "talk" to her, tell her certain vital things, give her the proper orders, when her eyes, ears, all her senses were taking in data that would present itself only after she had dived into Highland Park? If this were so, could she fool it, convince it she was there before she was in reality? Or did it—they—know her every move, her every thought, even now?

They. How well they had erased their fingerprints from her brain, leaving only what would serve the mission, their purpose.

Yet, had the eradication process been perfect after all? In these descents into her subconscious she'd certainly had glimpses that, from the implant's own admission, she was not supposed to have had. What now disturbed most of all was the glimpse she had just had of Salieu Vidyun.

Was Vidyun a soldier of some sort, obedient, martial, mindless?

Had Jack Kelso been right in his implacable questioning? Why had she had those brief but undeniable flashbacks of having wielded a weapon against beings who, while remaining unclear in meaning and physique, appeared defenseless?

Perhaps if she kept trying. She had to, despite the headache, or the threat of something worse....

The plunge came quickly. A moment after she began the relaxation ritual, concentrating on the rhythm of her breathing, willing away consciousness, she was diving headlong through the haze of pain, through emptiness.

Where... queer geometrical shapes reappear, coalesce, metamorphose into new configurations that suggest buildings, installations, power centers, a city perhaps. Yes, a city. There are avenues, corridors, high glimmering walls; a building then, at least a building, but one that goes on in every direction, like a city, a city complete in itself, a city that is a world. But where are the inhabitants? Where are the people who move through these endless corridors of glass or crystal?

There are domes... spires or antennae... pyramids. There are shapes that remind her of the implanted data concerning structures in the ancient earth cities of Palenque, Uxmal, Chichén Itza. Arches and architraves, pinnacles and spheres. But no vegetation and no people. No discernible windows or doors. What lies ultimately overhead is not sky but stone.

Silence, but for the growing pounding that is like the marching of thousands of feet, with each boot thudding against her head. An atmosphere of threat from without, sterility within. Within the graceful but faceless structures, a hollowness, a city of cavities. A pervading ambience of entropy.

Now she sees that the city is indeed vast, has its roots in an underground labyrinth of artificial caverns that burst and bloom in ice-like spires from the bowels of a world of rock and sand, and these spires branch and ascend and go on and on, out across space, and now there are stars and the city reaches to them with its frozen crystalline fingers.

Naravamintara?

But where are its inhabitants? Where are the "masters"?

The pounding grows, beating out a thunderous answer:

The masters keep to the imperial fortresses. The masters keep to themselves, undefiled by the imperfect rabble they rule.

THE MASTERS ARE PERFECTION AND PERFECTION IS THE MASTERS. DUTY AND ALLEGIANCE TO THE IMPERIAL UTOPIA IS THE REALIZATION OF PERFECTION FOR ALL.

The relentless voice and the thud of marching feet are replaced by another voice, other feet striking the crystal corridor, coming for . . .

Salieu Vidyun. You have been highly honored. Your devotion to the Realm, your service to Those Most High is to be rewarded. You have been chosen for a consecrated task.

They are dark figures in robes. They are tall and stiff and resemble the crested bird of prey that guarded the lintel in the broken city of her first "dream." She cannot see their faces but their heads are long, sloping backwards.

You, Salieu Vidyun, have been chosen. . . .

Are you an agent of a totalitarian government?

A fear with the grip of iron closed on her heart when these last words came unbidden out of the dark. She came up, groping, strangling for air and light. But she knew, even before she opened her eyes, that Jack Kelso was not in the room. Nevertheless, his words had rung as real, as startling, as those she suddenly realized comprised the Naravamintaran Oath. Kelso's case-hardened accusation had lain in her subconscious like a bomb ready to go off.

Alone with the ticking instruments, the murmur of the

ship, the unrelenting headache, she sat as stone, hands stiffened into map-filled fists. An alien in every sense of the word, she faced the question.

Was Naravamintara a tyranny? The language of the implant, the *influence*, was English. Was the language accurate? Was it an accurate "translation"? *Perfection, utopia, duty, allegiance, rabble, imperial, Realm—Those Most High.* Did such words mean the same *there* as they did here? How could they in every respect? If they did, they were undeniably self-damning. But would the source of such translation know that? Those words would not be self-damning to the kind of mentality that espoused authoritarian rule.

How could she have been rendered so perfectly human? What had she been before? Human-like? Or like the black-robed ones in the dreamstate?

She still had not seen Vidyun clearly, if indeed she had been Vidyun before. Was it really likely she had been humanoid? Could the race from which she had originated and Earth's race have had common origins? Was that possible?

Possible, yes. A few of the books found in the Restitutions even said it was probable; one or two treated the idea as fact and offered evidence to prove it.

There were theories of life having evolved along similar physical and mental lines on every biologically appropriate world in the universe. Such a view seemed altogether too terracentric for serious consideration. But what if it, or the seeding or tutelary theories, or all of them, were true? Could her feelings for Earth—and for Jack Kelso—be explained by this alleged common background? Such feelings could be kin to something like an ancestral memory, if she had the definition of *ancestral memory* right. But how far back in the remote past did this background go?

What was Naravamintara? Who were the masters? Who was Salieu Vidyun?

Was Naravamintara in a state of decline?

Did it fear Earth? Fear *what* from Earth? That which lay in or under the ruins of Highland Park?

This time no exercise of will was needed to erase the sensory world. Instead, almost before she commanded her mind to relax, she was pulled abruptly, involuntarily as it were, into dream consciousness.

. . . an entirely different milieu—one of earthly sights, scents, and sounds—colors and melodies . . . birdcalls . . . a

child's carousel-like world. A happy child's—a child who lived in a huge Spanish-style house with wide grounds and towering eucalypti—a villa on a hill overlooking other houses . . . a rich child's house . . . a storybook place.

A fiction, a creation of those who—

. . . when small, the child is the focal point of the family. She has no siblings. She has private tutors, a horse, a governess. The child learns piano and polo. She travels with her parents to many exotic and fascinating places. At sixteen, she earns a scholarship, another at seventeen. From nineteen through her early twenties she studied abroad, in Europe, South America, and Mexico. She has affairs, personal crises, growth-pains. She matures into a worldly-wise and canny young woman who has acquired much practical and intellectual knowledge and ability. A young woman named Judith DeFond in search of . . . her dead parents. In search of . . .

No! This was the false Phoenix memory trying to supplant all other thought, as if trying to divert her away from the depths. But its reappearance now was ridiculous, now that the implant had actually admitted she came from elsewhere than Earth. Was the implant, whatever it was, malfunctioning, out of control? Or had she come so close to the truth somewhere in these last few minutes that, in desperation, it illogically resorted to this old counterfeit biography to distract her away from the truth?

Again the question came: could she be mad? She recognized the question to be her own, was becoming increasingly adept at distinguishing what were her own thoughts and what came from the implant. But while the question was hers, she had little faith in its validity. Nonetheless, she embraced it once more, almost eagerly. Could Vidyun and Vidyun's world be the psychotic wool-gathering of a woman unwilling to accept her unhappy human past? What about her background in archaeology? Couldn't she have emerged from that hospital in Phoenix with a full-blown fantasy in order to forget or dissociate the death of her parents from herself, in order to fabricate a history more endurable?

No!

Why?

Because of her discovery she could telepathize with the Lavaccas, her realization they were something not human, auxiliaries or extensions of herself. Because of too many things that had happened. Because she *knew;* psychically or instinctively she knew.

But this certitude was encompassed in darkness, a darkness yet alive with myriad nameless eyes. She was being pulled farther into that darkness by what she instantly knew was the implant's attempt to put her to sleep.

She tried to re-surface and found she could not. Her mind suddenly felt on the verge of fragmentation. The two manifestations of her being—Vidyun and DeFond—came together, clashed, writhed, pulled apart.

Which one was she? Judith or Vidyun? Who? How could she be both? She was a fiction and not a fiction. How could she *be*?

Beside the persona she recognized as Judith DeFond another form took shape. Taller, larger, a man. Jack Kelso and Judith DeFond stood together against a sea of night. The image of Kelso burned; DeFond's reflected the flame but seemed to have no fire of its own. Yet something within DeFond cried out to burn, to live. Something reached upward through her to him, augmenting the fire, wanting to open, to tell all, discard what she'd been before and, with her own flame, emerge cleansed and new.

But another form intervened, appeared between herself and the man. This one wore a shimmering breastplate over which was draped a black cloak. He fought back the nascent flame, wrapped her in the folds of what became cold wings, wrapped her so that she could not breathe, stifling that which reached for life. This one's face was a blank but on his breast shined the name of the one chosen by the masters to do their will.

Vidyun.

What were you? What did they command you to do?

Eyes began to glow in the featureless face, eyes that were turned on Kelso's image. The latter vanished. The eyes were ones she'd seen before, here, on Earth.

The eyes were those of *Vincent Polliard.* She saw Vidyun and Polliard as the same, then. Vidyun was a killer, an instrument of death.

YOU SERVE THE MASTERS AND WILL CARRY OUT THEIR PLAN! JUDITH DE FOND IS A FICTION, AND SALIEU VIDYUN IS AN HONORED ARM OF THOSE WHO ARE MOST HIGH! BOTH, ALONG WITH JACK KELSO, WILL BE SACRIFICED TO WHAT MUST BE DONE. THE MASTERS HAVE DECREED IT TO BE SO.

What?

She was falling, falling in a dizzying spiral down the walls of a vortex that had no end.

Sacrificed?

Judith!

Vidyun!

Judith, wake up!

YOU SERVE THE MASTERS AND THE MASTERS SERVE PERFECTION.

Judith!

THERE IS NO JUDITH DE FOND. THERE IS ONLY NARAVAMINTARA, ONLY ITS WILL.

"Judith!"

She was being shaken. A voice was yelling her name. *Her* name?

Her eyes at last fluttered open. The light hurt. Strong hands gripped her shoulders. His face was before her, anxious.

"Come out of it, Judith!"

"Jack—" The here and now came back with a rush, a flood that filled and convulsed her mind.

"What the hell—"

"A nightmare," she got out. "I fell asleep in here. I was having a nightmare. I was studying the maps and I fell asleep and I—"

He released her, his expression severe. "You've looked holes in those damned maps by now." She saw that he was looking at the wrinkled map her fists had clenched.

"Yes. I was trying to—trying to be more certain where—" She gave it up, tried to rest her agonized head in her trembling upraised hands. Something in the dreamstate, at the last, she could not remember. Something terrifying. Just before Kelso woke her, brought her up from the implacable plunge. . . .

He muttered and turned away, in a manner that told her he had had all the lies and half-truths he could take. He stepped to the control board on the other side of the table and she saw he wore the robe she'd made him out of bits and pieces of old clothing. She watched him punch the viewer buttons.

Jack—Jack, I want to tell you. But I do not know what to tell. I do not know enough to tell. And in any case, I do not think they, or it, would let me tell what little I know. You would think me mad, yes. You already think it.

The computer had projected the outside perimeter of the

ship onto the group of viewscreens above the main instrument panel. Due to the work of the Lavaccas, every centimeter of the area immediately outside the *Tiburón* could be visually displayed. But Kelso did not risk the outside lights to aid the TV cameras; they were too near the patrols. The projections were of darkness, marked by an occasional undulant form coming near and disappearing back into the depths.

"Soon be in the Zone," he said, back turned to her. "Then there won't be many fish." But she knew his thoughts were not on fish.

The gloom on the viewers reminded her of the dreamstate. She shuddered, clasping her belly, feeling cold. "Our suits," she said, to be saying something, "our suits and the submersible have been meticulously gone over by the Lavaccas. All repairs have been made. Everything is ready."

What was it she had heard the implant say at the last, before Kelso woke her? What?

He stood at the instruments, saying nothing. She thought: Do I care for him because it serves *their* purpose, or do I care for him from my own heart? My own heart, what does that mean? Who is this *I* that asks this question . . . ?

He turned. "I guess—" he ran a hand through his shock of wiry hair, "a lot of things will soon be cleared up, won't they. A lot of questions answered." His look was one of weariness, and condemnation.

"Yes," she said, and looked away, afraid that he would see the anguish in her eyes, knowing she could not satisfactorily explain that anguish were he to notice and demand an explanation.

No. She was not mad. The truth exceeded the limits of madness.

20. PROBE

"I want a reading on our position." Doctor Dinah Chaney, formerly a lieutenant commander in the U.S. Navy and now head of URI's geological research branch, sat on a raised stool in the middle of a ring of instruments behind the research submarine's small control center. "I want it now."

At the plotting grid, Kelderman, Polliard's first-mate, grudgingly gave her the coordinates.

"Depth, drift, density, pressure," Chaney shot back in a bored teacher-to-schoolboy tone.

The mate mumbled an answer.

"I didn't hear you, Kelderman," Chaney snapped.

The mate shouted the readings, though he remained facing the grid.

"Stop the submarine, Mister Polliard. Right here." She let her pencil fall to the small chart table before her stool. "I trust that the large diving chamber is ready." Chaney did not bother to turn and look at Vincent Polliard, who stood beside his mate.

Light-complexioned for a Negro, her voice, her manner, her style broadcast the fact she'd had the best of education and upbringing, definitely thought of herself as "class," and was obviously proud of her position in the upper enclaves of Universal Resources, Inc. She was also one of the most voluptuous women Vincent Polliard had met, though the navy-blue smock she wore hid much of what he'd seen when he first picked her up at Long Beach Airfield almost a week ago, dressed then in fashionable and provocative street clothes.

"Of course," he said in toneless response to her last comment. "You are going down here, *mademoiselle?*"

"No. Doctor Shinn and I will remain on board. The other scientists are going down. They will stay on the bottom, directly below us, for at least twenty-four hours. They will take samples and soundings. We will continue making a small circuit in this immediate area."

"Ain't taking much more of this bitch, Vince," muttered the mate.

Chaney was too busy at her control board to hear. She now wore the same exasperated frown every time she looked at her board's central viewscreen, a screen whose information she and her colleagues had fastidiously refused to reveal to Polliard or his men.

"I've had all I can take of her and her puffed-up team of mud smellers." Kelderman jabbed a button below the gauges.

Polliard said nothing. He leaned against the main console with the sonar display screen at his back, watching Dinah Chaney. He shared the mate's sentiments. In fact, operations in general had taken a sour turn. From all accounts, Guillermo Rodríguez had fled for parts unknown. Contacts in Mexico could not, or would not, give Polliard any leads related to the black marketeer's disappearance. He'd had no better luck trying to track down Rodríguez than he had trying to find out what Kelso and the woman named Judith DeFond were up to. All he had learned about her was her name, and that had been beaten out of a drunken freighter captain Polliard had been informed sold supplies and goods to the *Tiburón*. Now he had Dinah Chaney to contend with, and Polliard suspected she was here, at URI's orders, for more than just "research". He was not such a fool as to think the *modus operandi* he'd enjoyed for so long could last forever, no matter what incriminating evidence he had on a number of the big cheeses in URI. In Dinah Chaney he smelled one of his own kind, a spy, with himself as the object of her espionage.

She was talking on the intercom with the other geologists who were in the starboard minilab adjacent to the control room. The sub's control center and most of the geological equipment, in effect the research center, were housed in a single compartment in the nose of the craft. The sub was filled with bathyscaphes, minilabs, exotic new instruments, databanks containing new data on the San Andreas and Los Angeles catastrophes, and the "earthquake experts'" gear. What that new data, and much of the old, contained, Polliard had not been allowed to learn.

He looked over at his mate. "Go help Dills and Fowler see our important guests off in their bathyscaphe."

"Aye." The mate left the navigation board and moved aft quickly, glad to put distance between himself and Dinah Chaney.

"When you've got them lowered, you and the others can go check out the Mount Wilson area in your diving suits. We're close. I'll hold the sub here."

Kelderman stopped, turned, gave him a surprised, then conspiratorial, look, said "aye," and was gone.

Geophysicist Chaney had snapped her head up as if jerked by wire. "Did you not hear what I said, Captain Polliard? This submarine will make a circuit of the immediate area while my team is on the bottom!"

Polliard pulled a toothpick from the pocket of his diving vest and pried at a food particle lodged between two molars. "I heard you, *mademoiselle*. I've heard your self-important babbling about magma surges and geomagnetism, quake lubrication, viscoelasticity, and gabbro for five days. I've heard you order me and my men around like we were third-class deck apes not fit to spitshine your shoes since the day you got off the plane at Long Beach Airfield. After hours-on-end study of line arrays on your precious data screens—line arrays whose meanings you have not condescended to disclose—your 'multiple laser probe' has produced nothing but a lot of secretive whispering and arguing between yourself and your cronies and short tempers in my crew. I've become bored with your commands and demands. Most of all, I am fed up with your refusal to discuss just what you have been doing with all this complex hardware for the last week, your refusal to discuss with me the reason for your obvious unhappiness over what that hardware has produced, your refusal to discuss what has appeared on your main screen. It's too bad if you don't like my countermanding your order, but I have other things to do."

Chaney, furious, was about to fall off her stool. "Not at the same time you are supposed to be helping me and my colleagues, Captain! I have never seen such a bunch of incompetent good-for-nothings as you and your crew. I have never encountered such a total lack of cooperation! The attitude of you and your men borders on *sabotage*. Is this Mount Wilson investigation an intelligence matter for the San Andreas Sea Patrol, or is it a new source of salvage?"

"Ah. Has someone told you I am interested in salvage?" Polliard bared his cleanly picked teeth. "And what business is that of yours if I am, Doctor Chaney? One might draw the conclusion that you are here to study and probe other things besides rock."

She swiveled around on the stool to face him squarely. "Like what?"

"Like me. Is it possible that URI no longer trusts me? Is it possible they told you to check out my activities in the Zone, say, as well as gather more data on the cause of the quake?"

She stared at him coldly. "Are you doing something that would displease URI?"

The thin-lipped grin on Polliard's dark face did not waver. "Maybe they are displeased that I have not made much progress in helping you scientists find the quake's cause. Maybe they have come to think that what I told them about Lieutenant Garret was not entirely the truth. Maybe they think that he was useful after all, that, in spite of the fact he was 'old Navy,' he had URI's best interests at heart and now they are sorry for having seen to it that Garret ended up with duty in the Persian Gulf. Maybe they believe those silly rumors about my taking illegal salvage from the ruins and hiding away millions of dollars' worth of jewels and antiques and things like that in some inaccessible place. It is a time of distrust and intrigue, *mademoiselle*. People in high positions are especially susceptible to rumors and false reports."

Dinah Chaney was too outraged to retort immediately, but when she at last found her tongue, there was a hint of admiration as well as shock in her voice when she said, "You are a most brazen man, Polliard. You would thumb your nose at one of the largest world conglomerates?"

Polliard emitted a low, rattling noise through his disfigured nose. "You and URI can both go to hell." He stepped away from the sonar console. "Now. I intend to get something by way of compensation for having had to put up with you for a week. You have brought with you a small mountain of data on the quake, have you not? Data URI has been amassing for years. Records, reports, accounts gathered from the few people who were lifted out of the Zone during the cataclysms, reports from those geophysicists and other scientists involved in the Devil's Canyon Project who happened to be in Washington, or somewhere else, when the quake occurred? You see, everyone thinks I am only interested in salvage. They are mistaken. I would also like to know what caused the quake. I have always wanted to know. I worship power, *mademoiselle,* and I am always seeking its sources. What happened here was caused by a very great power indeed. Wouldn't you agree?"

"Those reports are classified," she said, anxiety replacing her former indignation. Her hands ran over her thighs, nervously smoothing the smock's fabric. "I can tell you what you already know. Nothing more."

"What do I already know?"

She shifted her attention to the indicators and data screens for a moment, obviously trying to think of a way to divert him. "Suppose you tell me. What do you think caused the catastrophe, Captain?"

The grin spread minutely on Polliard's face at the recognition of her little verbal game. "Natural causes, of course. Isn't that the official line? The pap fed the public? Planetary alignments? Accumulated tension along the fault zone? Slip-stick nonsense? Acts of God?"

"That—or something we can't even imagine."

He threw back his head and laughed but the laughter had no more humor in it than the sun, at Pluto's remove, had warmth. "A scientist of the new school offering fantasy for a premise."

There was shouting aft, metal clanking, sea valves churning, the usual noises of putting a bathyscaphe through the lock and on its way to the bottom. Soon the only people on board the sub would be Polliard, Chaney, and Doctor Shinn, who was presently aft with the rest, persumably seeing his fellow geologists off on their twenty-four hour stay below. Kelderman had closed the hatch between the control center and the after compartments when he had gone out.

Dinah Chaney threw a worried look at that closed hatchway. "Just because we can't imagine something hardly makes it fantasy."

"No?" Polliard was parallel with her ring of instruments now. "We can't even talk about this 'something'. So how can it be real?"

Chaney rose from the stool. "We can talk about it. The same way we can talk about the farthest galaxies, and quasars. We know little, very little, about what's there but it's certainly there nonetheless. In other words, *real.*" She made a lunge for the passage between the instruments, trying to reach the door.

But Polliard was quicker. He reached the hatch and turned the lock. "So you are telling me that URI now thinks the unimaginable is here. Of course. All right, we've had our little philosophical chat. Back to the data you have gathered. Back to your mysterious data screens. I want to know all about them."

"You get away from that door, Polliard," she said, all at once openly afraid. She turned, went back inside the instrument station, fumbled with the switches at the intercom mike.

"That won't do you any good. I switched off the intercom the minute Kelderman left."

"Doctor Shinn! Can you hear me?" she yelled into the mike.

The phone was silent. The noises of the sub's inner systems, its engines holding them steady in the water, the faint murmur of the air-conditioning, seemed suddenly loud.

"Too bad, *mademoiselle*."

She faced him, eyes round, the skin around her mouth white. "You're right, Polliard," she said hurriedly. "URI no longer trusts you, if they ever did. If anything happens to me, they will have your goddamned head!"

"Ah no. You are such an amateur, Doctor Chaney. I know far too much about URI. What I know is stashed in a safe place, to be delivered into the appropriate hands if my head is had." Polliard chortled through his nose. "Speaking of heads, Doctor Chaney," his voice had dropped in tone and volume and the smile had left his face, "you are a long way from the fatuous civilization that put you in a position which obviously swelled yours to an unseemly size. You are twice a fool. A sad consequence of your sex. You have tried to ignore one of the most fundamental laws of existence . . . and you a scientist." He had taken several steps away from the hatch and was beside the instrument ring. "Civilization has indulged and pampered feminist idiocies for years, but feminism will be one of the first casualties of the coming collapse. It is men who rule and always will. No civilization here, Ms. Chaney, only ruins, so to speak. The way most of the world will soon be. Ruins. Now, what have you found out about what lies under the ruins here? Where is the data located? What have you learned from your new instruments? Why are you so disturbed by what you have seen on your screens? Are you going to tell me freely, or will I have to resort to measures that would not be considered 'civilized' back where you would priss and play the queen?"

"You keep away from me, Polliard!"

"Ah, no. No, I think you and I are going to become very intimate within the next few minutes."

She was sliding sideways along the inside of the instrument panels, eyes seeking a means of escape or something with which to defend herself. "All right. I will tell you what we know—*all* we know." She found a break in the panels opposite Polliard, stepped through, and came up against a large storage locker, cornered.

Polliard stepped calmly around the research station toward her. He wore the smile again. "Speak, Doctor Chaney."

She pressed against the locker, looked to each side, saw there was no way she could get past him now. Her words came in a tremulous rush. "When URI discovered there was oil-rich rock under the Los Angeles basin and used underwater nuclear demolitions to get at it along the continental shelf, they found a subterranean energy field whose source seemed to lie somewhere beneath the San Gabriel Mountains. They pinpointed the source at about five thousand meters below sea level, directly below the western edge of the San Gabriel Wilderness. But their instruments could not determine what it was."

Polliard had come to a stop two meters from the locker, waiting.

Chaney's breasts rose and fell with her anxious breathing. Her hand was in the right pocket of the smock. "Then they began the Devil's Canyon Project, closed off a large part of the San Gabriels, especially the wilderness area. They explained to an energy-starved public that oil had been found in the mountains, and the only way to reach it was through the use of nuclear explosives."

Polliard nodded patiently, letting her know with his look that she had better come up with much more.

"They used nuclear devices when more caution should have been exercised. They began a nuclear probe and caused the quake. It's as simple as that!"

"Really," said Polliard. "Is that all there is to it? What is in those reports you have? Those accounts of the few who were lifted out of the Zone? What did they have to say? Why haven't you been able to find that energy field again? What *kind* of energy field was it? What was the source of this mysterious energy?"

"We don't know. Accumulated data from studies over the years indicate the greatest seismic activity was in a roughly oval-shaped area stretching from the San Gabriel wilderness to Los Angeles, an area whose epicenter lay about halfway between Mount Lowe and Mount Harvard in the San Gabriels. The energy field—" She shook her head, trying to get her breath. "We don't know. That's what we have been trying to find out. We can't locate it anymore. At five kilometers our probe comes up with a blank. Our lasers are neutralized. The instruments refuse to register *anything*. There is nothing in those reports—nothing you don't already know. Death, destruction, fires, explosions, tidal waves, the falling of land and the rising of land, the sky filled with dust and vapor and steam. All the phenomena associated with vulcanism. That's *all* we know!"

Polliard thought about what she had said, found it interesting but only in a tantalizing way. "I am sure there is more—"

"No!" Chaney yelled.

Polliard stepped forward. Her hand leapt from the smock. He dived for her legs.

The gun fired and he felt the bullet graze the back of his diving vest as he slammed her into the locker and, wrenching the pistol away, knocked her to the deck with a belly blow.

She moaned, but pulled free, and was up surprisingly fast. A foot caught him on the side of the head before he could dodge. A hand chopped his neck as he tried to rise. The power of the blow was unexpected. Another foot kicked into his ribs.

He rolled, grabbed the hem of her smock. She fought to jerk loose; he tore the garment half off trying to pull her down. When her foot swung for his face, he caught it and twisted the ankle half around. She fell.

He was on her instantly, tearing the remainder of her clothes away, holding her struggling body between his thighs with a grip she could not break. With a single backhanded hit to her head, he knocked her almost senseless.

"I have learned much in my years of employment with Universal Resources, *mademoiselle*, and before that, with International Sea Development, and before that, the U.S. Navy." Polliard ripped off the last piece of underwear, flung it aside. His breathing was only slightly labored. "All venerable teachers. *Masters* in the art of removing things that get in the way of what must be done. Masters in the art of acquiring or protecting wealth and wielding the power required to keep it. The ones who rule now and will rule when the world is ruins. The kind that will eventually rule the universe." He laughed and held her jaws in the V of his hand. "Pay attention, Doctor Chaney." Her eyes came open. "I know what they know. Not science or knowledge or reason or anything else matters. Only wealth and power rule, now as always. I learned that long ago as a boy in the Caribbean. A black, maybe a distant cousin of yours, beat it into me. Every beat of his club against my head, across my face, my body, said 'Those who don't have it lose.' Like you."

She tried once more to struggle free, but he ignored her convulsive and ineffectual efforts, her hands and nails, and rammed her head into a pile of portable radio gear.

He had his satisfaction in seconds, got up, buttoned his trousers and left her there.

At the phone beside the command console, he called Kelderman.

The mate's voice finally answered. "Read you, Vince. We're not at the site yet. What's up?"

"I have a little surprise for you back here. You and Fowler and Dills. Return aboard. And, oh yes, see that, ah, Doctor Shinn, who should be somewhere back in one of the after compartments, has an incapacitating accident so that he won't try to interfere with the surprise I have. She's lying here on the deck waiting for you."

"Roger, Vince. We'll be there in a wink."

Polliard turned away from the console and moved toward the cabinet in Chaney's circle of instruments, where the classified data gathered on the quake was kept. He had a small crowbar to break the locks and force open the drawers.

21. KNOWLEDGE

Kelso discovered the box of books inside the small storage compartment beneath the library couch, and knew at once they were not his, had been put there only recently. Most of the books were softcover and secondhand, the type common in the few bookstores in the Restitutions. A couple bore the stamp of the store where they'd been purchased. "Kate's Book Shop" in Rose Harbor. It came back to him, the several hours she'd spent shopping, accompanied by one of the Lavaccas, while he had made arrangements for rendezvous with the *P. B. Baylor.*

The fact that the books had been placed in the nearly inaccessible compartment under the couch where no one was likely to find them—and Kelso would not have found them if, in his frustration, he had not been rummaging through everything in the library, trying to come upon a clue that might shed some light on her—made him irresistibly curious. He pulled out the box and began to scan the titles. What he read only fueled his bewilderment.

The titles suggested such singular subjects as matter transmission, robots, cyborgs, androids, "seeding theory," telepathy and other psychic phenomena, self-hypnosis, space travel, a book called *Escape from the Apocalypse* Kelso had read some years ago (in his opinion, a rather badly written goulash of speculations, eyewitness accounts, confused and worthless, offered by the few thousands who were helilifted out of the Zone and survived the disaster), and a book called *Evolutionary Mysteries.*

It was this last book he held, staring at its table of contents, thinking of her shutting herself away here in the library so frequently now, and for longer periods of time, her recurring attacks of migraine and dizzyness that had also become more frequent and prolonged, her silences and withdrawal, her shutting herself in here reading these books, when he became aware of her standing in the hatchway.

Her eyes were wide and glaring. Kelso sat stupefied, the book in his hands, unable to speak, feeling helpless beyond words, his brain dulled and sluggish from the booze he'd gone back to hitting heavily in the last few days. He sat there loathing himself for the drinking, cursing himself for not being able to penetrate the wall she had placed between them, telling himself, as he had done many times before, that he could abort the whole goddamned crazy thing and then asking himself could he really, asking himself if he had not passed some psychological point of no return where both she and her enigmatic purpose were concerned.

"Those are my books," she said. "Please put them back where you found them." Her voice shook.

The days spent moving north, having to change course

repeatedly, head back out to sea, come back, stop, lie silent on the bottom in efforts to avoid or evade patrol craft, glimpses of behavior in her that definitely indicated schizophrenia, had taken their toll on Kelso, and he was growing increasingly convinced that this preposterous venture awaiting them in the Highland Park ruins could well be nothing more than the result of a relapse into psychosis. In these last days, her periods of passivity and lethargy, of being lost within herself, had deepened, while sporadic fits of talkativeness, ebullience, restlessness, still sometimes came to the fore. He never knew what to expect next. She was usually distant now, hostile if disturbed or surprised, yet attempted cheerfulness, the old camaraderie of the first days, when she realized the bad way she was acting. Efforts to get her to talk about it only aggravated the situation more than ever; still, he felt that underlying desire in her to tell of a horror that had thus far, to the best of his knowledge, not been remotely touched upon. More than once he'd come upon her in what he'd come to realize was deep self-hypnosis, her face, that face too beautiful for belief, strained, lined with concentration, with dismay and fear. What in god's name did she seek in her subconscious? What was the meaning of these books?

He dropped *Evolutionary Mysteries* into the box at his feet and remained sitting on the couch, looking at her. Kelso realized, judging from the incidents they'd shared over the last two months, that, if she proved finally to be his enemy, he was in for a formidable fight. But he would fight her and her ostensibly superhuman bodyguards, fight to save her from whatever devil she struggled with, for herself, for himself.

"Are they good books?" he asked conversationally, cautiously. His spine tingled when he thought of the subjects of those titles he had read.

The green eyes seemed to expand and dilate, as if vacillating between lucidity and insanity. "They are informative," cracked that flat, mechanical, that Lavacca-like voice he'd become accustomed to during moments of tension like this.

"Informative about what? The titles, the tables of contents, are provocative, all right. Exotic subjects. But why *those* subjects, Judith?" He knew it was futile.

She stepped into the room, picked up the box, turned, and exited into the wardroom without Kelso making any move to stop her. She had gone through the entire process of retrieving and leaving with the books like a sleepwalker, rigid and silent. He heard rattling, thumping in the wardroom, as though she stumbled or were beating the box against the table or floor. He heard a cabinet open, slam shut.

He rose, stepped through the hatch just in time to see her move jerkily through the hatch to the officers' quarters, move like one fighting invisible shackles. The hatch to the officers' quarters slammed shut. She had adopted a habit of sleeping in there, or in the control room, anywhere but with him. But the library had become her sanctum and he had violated it.

He went to the cupboard and found a bottle, unable to think of anything to do but drink. Then it occurred to him she had not had the books when she disappeared into the officers' quarters. He found the box in one of the cabinets and pulled it out, wondering why she had left it here and shut herself in the other room, as though intentionally giving him a chance to read them further. Recalling the way she had moved, it seemed that a part of her had tried to go against her leaving the books where he could get at them and another part wanted him to do just that.

With the bottle on one side and the stack of books on the other, he sat at the wardroom table and began to flip through *Evolutionary Mysteries*. It promised to be a work of unanticipated richness, including chapters on the human brain, the subconscious, the conscience, ancestral memory, extraterrestrial life, the possibility of extraterrestrial intervention in Earth's remote past, cellular metamorphosis, accelerated mutation theory. Again Kelso felt his spine crawl. He was flabbergasted—and chilled. What chapters had interested her, and why? Why, if she did not want him to know she had been reading such books, had she brought them out here where he could find them again, then left, forced herself out of the room, as though she desperately wanted him to read them?

He swore, took a drink straight from the bottle, and began reading about the evolution of the human brain, soon feeling alcoholic tentacles close over his own.

The silence, the solitude of the officers' quarters pressed down upon her like the crush of frozen atmospheres. Afraid of what the implant might make her do, she had fought its hold, forced herself into the officers' quarters, hearing its pulsating command to destroy the books. She wanted Kelso to read them, wanted him to somehow know—

Know *what?*"

She knew, or feared, that if the implant so desired, it could hurl her through that door and at Jack Kelso's throat. But it would still want her to be kind to him, wouldn't it?

She almost laughed, hysterical, to think that the implant could also be as ambivalent, as torn in purpose, as she. The fine line it had to tread between totally taking her over, on the one hand, and, on the other, letting her retain some control in order to remain, to some degree, human, had to be maddening—assuming that whatever was behind the implant was capable of being maddened, driven to the verge of self-destruction as she was.

But she doubted the influence was that vulnerable, that *human.* It would likely know just when the minutest trace of her will was no longer tolerable and act accordingly. In the meantime she would display some semblance of reason, of compatibility with the man. At least until . . . and then what?

Until what?

Something came swimming up from the depths, trying to surface as it had before. Something from the Vidyun dream she'd had when Kelso awakened her in the control room.

In her mind's eye she saw broken bodies at the foot of a long flight of stone steps. Blood flowed freely over the sun-bleached stones, and there was chanting in the air. At the top of the steps stood a figure in a black robe, with a long mane of hair that, full and voluminous, swelled its back like a great spinal tumor. In fact, this growth did not seem like hair after all, more like an extension of the dark head that sloped backward and down, to be lost in the humped rear folds of the robe. She could see no face, only white irisless eyes staring down the length of the steps at the bodies lying dead on the stones. Now she saw the faces of two of those bodies. Hers and Jack Kelso's. There were others, two others at least, and she somehow recognized these stony shapes as the Lavaccas.

Suddenly it came back what the dream had told her. She and Kelso, *all,* were to be sacrificed!

Her eyes sprang open to the cold nameless silence of the room.

Sacrificed for *what?*

The inescapable overseer in her brain did not answer. *Her*

brain, yes. She had determined that much and more. She served despots, as Kelso had accused, guessed, though he had no idea of the origins or form of that despotism.

Nor did she.

Sacrificed.

No! Her heart cried out for Kelso to be spared. But how, when he was essential to her mission? And if she served despots, wasn't the mission itself evil? Could she be sure of that? Even on Earth despotism had served good causes, hadn't it? What did "despotism" mean on a world light-years from Earth, ruled by beings perhaps eons older than humanity?

How many light-years away? How many eons?

Who?

If she were not mad yet, maybe she could make herself so with these endless unanswered, perhaps unanswerable, questions! Kelso could take her to a hospital somewhere. They could lock her up for the rest of her "natural" life. That would be a way out of this godforsaken—but she knew she was being foolish again, knew the implant would not permit any such escape.

At one of the night tables next to a bunk, she sat with her fingers in her hair, the inexorable riddles pricking like needles.

Why had she come to revere Jack Kelso so much? Why had she come to love the sea, life, Earth? How had she come to *love* in the first place? Love, feelings, awe, wonder, could not have been in the implant's design. From what she had glimpsed in self-hypnosis, in her subconscious, Vidyun had not known love, or joy or pain or rage. Vidyun had been an emotional eunuch.

And Judith DeFond?

Was there another identity hidden behind or beneath Vidyun, an identity that predated both Vidyun and DeFond?

Where was the secret origin of the soul, for want of a better term?

Where did one's heart of hearts reside? Had all the clever tampering of those who sent her here failed to change some fundamental uniqueness that was truly hers? And, if so, what did that deeper self want? Was it not ultimately in conflict with what the implant wanted? It seemed to be so. If Jack Kelso was to die, it had to be so. If that was so, could she summon the strength, the craft, to go against the control and coercion of the implant?

YOU ARE BEING FOOLISH. YOU ARE BEING TEMPTED BY THE MOST FOOLISH OF DELUSIONS.

A banging on the other side of the closed door startled her. She heard a voice, his.

"Judith!" A heavy object struck the turning device on the other side. "Open this hatch! I've got to know what those books mean to you and, by god, you're going to tell me!"

A storm of fear, sympathy, uncertainty, made her jump up, then recoil and, as if the implant had automatically taken over, she felt herself telepathically summoning the Lavaccas.

In seconds they entered the wardroom. She listened to the noises of struggle, of Kelso cursing and yelling, and knew from the feedback from the Lavaccas that he was fighting savagely. One held his kicking legs, the other his arms, and they carried him thus to his stateroom.

Do not hurt him. She repeated the command aloud, hoping that by doing so she would insure the Lavaccas' obedience. They had never faltered in doing as she wished. But how could she assume they were merely witless androids, artificial extensions of herself? They too could have implants, or their entire brains could be implants, and they could have been programmed to see that their, her, mission was carried out to the end, no matter what happened. If she tried and succeeded in going against the machine in her own brain, would they follow her or *it*?

The fight Kelso put up did not end until he had hit his head on the metal bulkhead in an effort to twist free of the Lavaccas. He was knocked unconscious.

Sedate him. But not heavily. We are close to the bay. We will need him soon.

Was that her command or the implant's? Usually she knew when it was herself that spoke, thought, or telepathized, but sometimes Judith DeFond's will seemed hopelessly confused with, or identical to, the implant's.

Dear *god!* She threw herself onto the bunk, tortured head between her hands.

I must fool it, she thought, and knew she was a fool for even thinking she could.

I must *try!*

But she had tried before. She knew now beyond doubt that the device was arranged so that when the proper sensory data entered her brain, the next step in what she must do would be revealed, the next door would open on another little room that would contain the instructions for the newly presented task. But how did *they* know what would be the *proper sensory data?*

A data-gathering vessel of some kind could have gotten the information concerning what lay in and under the Highland Park ruins, precise environmental data that could have been fed into the implant in a way that would preclude her "fooling" it. Could they have been that canny? Yes, of course. She had no idea what kinds of minds lay behind her torment. Still, if such a vessel had been sent to Earth, to Angeles Bay, had gathered the necessary information for the implant's purpose, why couldn't that vessel have done the job she was sent to do? Why *her?*

YOU MUST CONSTANTLY GUARD AGAINST THE CHAOTIC HUMAN STATE. YOUR HUMAN EGOMANIA HAS GROWN TO DANGEROUS PROPORTIONS, JUDITH DEFOND. YOU HAVE SOUGHT TO OPEN WHAT MUST NOT BE OPENED UNTIL IT IS TIME. YOU HAVE BECOME DISEASED WITH THIS INCESSANT BACKWARD AND BASE PREOCCUPATION WITH A MENTAL FIGMENT YOU HAVE COME TO CALL, APING THE HUMANS BY WHOM YOU HAVE BECOME UNDULY INFLUENCED, YOUR "SELF."

Are you watching me? she thought. Then, sitting up, she screamed it.

"Are you watching me! Who are you? What are you? What is it I must do, goddamn you!" Vaguely she realized she sounded like Kelso and thus saw to what depths his rage and anguish must have reached in his life.

The despair-inducing silence which she'd come to know too well swirled round her in the room like a suffocating cloud. Within that inner room, that mental oubliette that had become as grim as any chamber in the medieval Bastille, also silence.

She threw herself back down on the bunk, her face in the blanket to help blot consciousness.

She sank, a diver descending through familiar upper zones toward the abyssal region where accumulated pressures could crush one to the consistency of the paleozoic ooze.

It was a dive of desperation, fraught with risk, for lately these self-willed plunges into her subconscious had gleaned nothing but darkness, confusion, the debilitating headaches. This time, however, she checked her fall, stopped short of going much below the semi-conscious level, and let her mind drift through the superficial waters of the old Phoenix memory, of the instilled Earth knowledge and the ritualistic exhortations of that voice she had come to call, because she knew not what else to call it, the implant. This was its incontestable domain. But she ignored the repetitious demands for loyalty, for obedience, and tried to conjure out of her imagination the crumbled and crushed deathland that would be the ruins of Highland Park.

She had yet to dive in the Zone. All her imagination had to rely upon was pictures Kelso had drawn: algae-covered wreckage of all kinds, upheaved roadways, twisted machines and machinery, mountains of broken buildings, mangled metal, square kilometers of undersea desolation. It was no good, futile. These wispy, ill- or half-formed images based on a secondhand account were no substitute for reality. She saw that she could not remotely fool the implant this way.

Her head throbbed with the old hated pain. The ineffectual images burst like bubbles, vanished, while the Phoenix rhythms ordered her out of the semi-trance, commanded her to go to the man named Kelso, to pleasure him and herself and forget these foolish and counter-productive quests for things it was not for her to know.

Another spasm of hysterical laughter shook her. She was about to give in to it, to completely let go, when an odd sensation of peace began to insinuate itself into the plague of pain and anxieties. Its fingers, timorous at first, grew stronger, coiled around the iron club that incessantly beat between her temples, held it in check, and soothed her as she could not recall having been soothed before.

Amazed, she saw other images appear against the void, replacing those false ones she had tried to paint of Highland Park. She saw water, but not the polluted murk of Angeles Bay, water that was beautifully blue and alive with sunlight. She saw crystal-clear streams that fed this water, which was now obviously sea. Along the streams, forests that were like and yet not like those of Earth's. Forests greening gentle hills, forests of variegated shades and lush fruitfulness. In spite of the underlying strangeness of this landscape, it was familiar.

This odd and unwonted tranquil influence both puzzled and pacified, and she remembered that queer mnemonic feeling she'd had when she went topside that night and found Kelso watching the herd of humpback whales following alongside the *Tiburón*. On the heels of this she then remembered, when sitting alone on the rocks above Cave Cove on the night of the day she and Jack had swum there, a pattern of vague, alien thoughts, like symbols of a language, that appeared in her consciousness, vanishing and appearing intermittently, pulsating like a faraway light that promised illumination and warmth, strangely comforting pulses coming from a source she instinctively knew did not belong to the implant or the Phoenix memory. Her mind had seemed to divide, as she watched with one part the flickering stars in the night sky overhead and, with the other, saw the flashing images of odd landscapes, strange shapes and figures—strange and not strange—in an ambience of pervasive tranquility. These images coming now, these forests, meadows, distant mountains, rolling foothills, were somehow related to that experience on the rocks that night above Cave Cove. These present images, stronger and more clearly defined and detailed, had to be the improved manifestations of those she had seen that night.

Where did they come from? From what source could such a feeling of peace originate?

How could she be sure this was not another artifice jammed into her neocortex by her anonymous overseers?

Because it was unmistakably at odds with the punitive influence of the implant, because it felt, was, totally unlike anything she'd undergone in association with the implant. Because somehow she recognized the source of these soothing images as something that held out hope, that was trying to reach her in the spirit of aid. . . .

But a sudden darkness shadowed the images, chilled the peace. The hammering head pain returned. Her brain felt pressed as between the jaws of a vise. The hammer became a scythe that beat against each side of her brain as it moved, swinging, striking, cutting away everything in its path, rendering her mind a void. She saw the scythe advancing over a field of plants and realized these "plants" were her own brain's cilia.

A noise, like that of a thousand voices screaming, burst from the field.

She pushed up, fell off the bunk, not quite conscious. Telling herself it was a dream, only a warning from the implant, nothing more, she tried to break out of the trance and move at the same time toward the door.

She could not breathe, tried to yell but nothing came out. Her hands found the hatch, fumbled with its wheel, but she dropped, with all her strength ebbing away.

Help! Her mouth opened to scream but was silent. *Help!*

The coffee tasted like ash and did little to clear her thinking. On the main sonar screen in the control room the constantly changing pattern of echoes outlining the rubble through which they passed blurred and swam in her vision. Numb and uncomprehending, she watched Carlos Lavacca—or Android A, as she had secretly come to call him—punch the console keyboard below the screen. They were now in the Zone, moving slowly toward the ruins of Highland Park. In a near stupor, she dully realized that, for a number of reasons, there was no turning back.

The implant's attack had been so acute this last time that she gravely feared any further attempt to learn what she must do. Carlos had come and opened the hatch to the officers' quarters, found her prostrate, carried her back to the bunk and gave her a sedative. She had slept for hours, a sleep without dreams, without any she could remember, anyway, and now sat at the chart table in the control room wondering if part of her brain had been somehow wiped out by the implant, because she felt that way, only partly present, half alive. She coaxed the scalding coffee down her throat like one drinking a magic potion that would restore clarity and reason to a world made of nightmare.

The coffee helped. She poured another cup from the pot she had put on the table. Carlos had told her, when after waking she managed to find her way into the control room and make coffee, that they had safely come through the Santa Monica and Long Beach Island groups in the night, were at present threading their way up the old roadbed that had been the Harbor Freeway. This was the route Jack had said would be safest. It was wide and relatively clear of debris. They could hug the bottom here and most effectively confuse or elude the sonar systems of the patrol. They would move up the freeway, over the maze of intersecting arteries north of what had been downtown Los Angeles and the Civic Center, to where Harbor became the Pasadena Freeway, which in turn would take them into Highland Park.

She had the best of the maps before her, one that Jack had

drawn up from his own knowledge of the area. The original freeway system, partially converted to elway, had remained generally as it had been before the quake—twisted, broken, sunken deeper in parts than others, but still a reliable way to travel through the surrounding shambles.

Judith looked again at the sonar screens, feeling the residual grip of the deep sleep gradually letting go. The pictures on the screens, however, still presented an exasperating array of overlapping echoes she had difficulty making any sense of. Now and then the *Tiburón*'s hull resounded as it scraped against rubble or rock when the Chief had to alter course slightly to dodge obstacles. Thus far the computer, with some help from the Lavaccas, was steering them as well as could be expected. But she knew they would soon need Kelso.

The *Tiburón*'s TV cameras and outside lights were, of course, off. She felt enveloped in darkness, a void without limit, licking like the icy tongue of nothingness, eager to devour all. She closed her eyes, shutting out the sonar screens, the lines and markings on the maps, Carlos, everything.

A lot of things will soon be cleared up. A lot of questions answered.

Yes, Jack. Soon it will be over. But will we be around for the answers?

IT IS TIME TO WAKE THE MAN. TAKE HEED, JUDITH DEFOND. THERE WILL BE NO MORE SLEEP FOR YOU, AND NO MORE ATTEMPTS BY YOU TO CIRCUMVENT YOUR PURPOSE. STAND. GO AND WAKE THE MAN.

She pushed herself up from the chart table and moved forward for the stateroom, pushed and guided by that internal goad. Her own will, like every faculty that could be called hers, stayed numb, beaten close to insensible passivity by the deadly headaches.

Only the red nightlights were on in the passageway and in the wardroom, but she knew the ship well enough to be able to move through it with even less light. Yet she almost missed the dark brooding figure sitting at the long table in the middle of the room.

"Jack," she whispered, wanting to say anything but what she was about to say. "I was on my way to wake you. We are in the Zone, nearing Echo Park." Her voice had that hard impersonal edge that derived from the implant's control. The thing inside her that longed to give full vent to her feelings, to be honest, to escape, lurched in her chest like a caged animal flinging itself against bars, was held in check, forced back and down, finally stifled. "Jack, we need your help."

He did not speak. She saw the dim red sheen of a bottle on the table. His head did not turn to face her. The *Tiburón*, hugging the bottom like a crab, struck something near the prow and the entire ship shuddered.

She grabbed the table edge for support and it slid forward under her hands. Something fell from the cabinet against the port bulkhead, breaking when it hit the deck. The bottle in front of Kelso wobbled, stabilized.

"Jack. I'm sorry for—please understand. My emotional problems. My parents' deaths. My—I have blackouts. Still not over it all. Sorry we—I've—"

She tried to say more, to get around what the implant wanted her to say, to say what she longed to say. Her head reeled. The red semi-darkness swirled, seeming to emit minute pulses of light, like coded signals being transmitted through burning cloud, in rhythm with the resurgent pounding in her brain.

"Jack! Please!" Her knees buckled.

Kelso was up and reaching before she fell.

Carlos appeared through the door just as Kelso caught her and the *Tiburón* rammed something hard that sent them all hurtling to the deck.

"Goddammit!" Kelso yelled. "Can't you muckheaded zombies keep from running into everything!" He got to his feet, leaving Judith lying. "Maybe you can at least take care of your boss." He pushed roughly past the silent Lavacca, into the passageway and aft toward the control room.

In the gloom Carlos's face seemed almost to dissolve, alter, rearrange itself in shape and substance as he knelt to lift her. Though his arms, she knew, were flesh, or a flesh-like material, they felt like iron. She imagined she could see for a moment through his skull and she saw a vacuum, at the center of which swam a solitary and vague form, a bizarre fishlike creature imprisoned in a globe of black water, doomed to swim in ever-shrinking circles until it could swim no more and would at last cease its futile writhings and ossify, an elegant oddity frozen in the heart of infinite night.

"Carlos!" She seized his shirtfront. "Do you know? What is it we have to do in the Highland Park ruins? Do you know anything I do not? Are you an extension of me, or of *them?* Who ultimately commands you?"

His eyes glowed eerily in the low red light and she remembered the white irisless eyes of the entity in her trance. His voice, when he spoke, was exactly like the demon's in her own brain, except that it had the absurd Mexican accent.

"You serve Naravamintara, *señorita.* And I serve you."

"How did you know about Naravamintara?"

"I only know it is that which we serve. It is perfection."

"What if I choose not to serve Naravamintara?" she shouted at him.

His answer came back, without emotion, without thought. "One cannot refuse the will of the masters, *señorita.* It is not possible. Their will is the will of creation. That is all that is necessary to know."

22. PENETRATION III

The Prithipean commander stood above them, with his aircar nestled in the rocks at his back. "It is time to go down," he said. "It has begun. We have reports of fighting both inside Nammava Trah II and off Naravamintara. Friend Phegakz and his confederates are happily laying waste the imperial offplanet fleets."

Exhaustion inhibited Cinara's response. Her eyes remained on the distant ruins of Nammava Trah I, as though an invisible connecting ray held them to that dark place. "Yes," she said. "Yes, but let us rest a moment. Let us come back." At last she pulled her gaze away, closed her eyes. "Falur," she said. "How is it with you, boy?"

Falur pushed himself up awkwardly in the heavy groundsuit. Acexea, ever patient despite the swiftness and suddenness with which he could move, waited. "Cinya," Falur finally said. "I can feel the—I am receiving some of—what is taking place inside Nammava Trah II."

"Yes." Tlii stirred.

"Do you think my brother—? You did not ask any of them for names."

"No. I asked for nothing not necessary to the success of the revolt. We will know in time, Falur. In time."

A faraway bloom of reddish yellow in the starlit sky overhead made all three look upward. They watched as some irradiated ship beyond the Naravamintaran atmosphere blazed briefly and vanished. Another burst near the first, darkened and was gone.

"This," asked Falur softly, "was how it was eons ago when the ancient ones fought?"

Abruptly Cinara Tlii moved to clasp the boy by the shoulders. "Listen to me, Falur. Look at me. What do you see in these things? You have wonder in your eyes. I think you marvel at what you see."

"Yes, I marvel, but not as you may fear. I wonder where the ancient ones, the Arkhalahn, originated, Cinya. I wonder where they have gone, what they sought where they went. I am not moved by the overhead spectacles, but it is difficult to understand why the ancient ones would wander. Is it not?"

"Difficult for us to understand, Falur." Tlii unclamped the harness holding her to the rocks. The wind had unexpectedly subsided some time ago. "But as the old ones teach, the universe is vast and its lifeforms legion. We have never understood the Yaghattarin's way, but they indisputably exist. That, however, will soon be corrected. Help me, Acexea."

The Prithipean lifted her from the cliff brink. "It is time to go down," he said again.

"Yes," she answered, yet did not move toward the car. "Battles are in progress throughout Naravamintara's system, and in the interplanetary spaces of other star systems ruled by the Deathlords, Acexea. In interstellar space between those systems. Battles are being waged on the planets themselves. And in the bowels of Nammava Trah II." The sudden excitement in Tlii's words was unmistakable.

"We have had reports." Acexea repeated what he had said earlier and did not bother to ask how Cinara Tlii knew of these events.

She hardly heard him. "We have been more successful than I had hoped. Because so many of the enslaved Onnahlaetians and others like them were given high-ranking positions, they have influence with subalterns and lower-level servants of the Yaghattarin. The insurrection we have kindled has leapt down the hierarchical chain like lightning. Even some of their automata, created to serve Onnahlaetian masters, are more loyal to the latter than to the ones who have ruled us for so long."

"Cinya," Falur said. The boy would say nothing disrespectful but it was obvious to him, and to Acexea, that Cinara Tlii was letting herself be swept away by the moment, despite her anxious attempt to divert Falur from becoming enchanted with the scenes of destruction and death all around. "Cinya—"

A series of deathrays streaked across the blackness above the horizon just as Cinara turned to look at Falur. The rays' brief reflection fragmented the front of her helmet with myriad fingers of splintered light.

On the smoking fringes of every Naravamintaran spaceport, city or outpost, starships seized by former prisoners, slaves, conscripts, or captives, shot above the devastation to carry the revolt to the empire's farthest reaches. Communications between the ships of the Alliance and rebel ships of the Naravamintaran space navy were established, as well as communications links with the liberators inside Nammava Trah II. Those inside the fortress who had turned on the Yaghattarin obliterated the Naravamintaran defense network. The ships of the Alliance left the Valley of the Great Rift and landed on the Desert of Nammava Trah. Entrances to the underground stronghold were opened and, led by Abrea Acexea, the armies of the Alliance poured in.

Nammava Trah II fell with little resistance. The Perfect Ones, having relied too heavily and too long on those they had enslaved and subjugated, fell easily once these former devotees to the empire revolted. Those who were indestructible, who could not die, lay dead throughout the citadel's glistening rooms and corridors. A number, of varied rank within the hierarchy, were taken prisoner pending word from Acexea regarding their fate.

Many levels below the upper wreckage, in a hidden recess Acexea and his soldiers had found, lay a cylindrical container adjacent to a wall of complex instrumentation which neither the Prithipean nor anyone else could begin to understand.

Cinara Tlii and the boy, Falur, had entered the room upon receiving summons from Acexea. Tlii's eyes instantly fell upon what had perplexed the Prithipean even more than the instruments. In a tiny transparent globe beside the cylinder, a rigid miniature replica of a former Naravamintaran guard, a "Vigilant," was suspended, like an entity frozen in air.

23. CACHE

The rap on the door was barely noticeable above the clucking of the chickens in the backyard and the grunts of the pigs in the pen just outside the window. Guillermo Rodríguez backed into the shadows of the room, the muzzle of the shotgun he held aimed at the back door whence the knock had come.

"*¿Quién es?*" Luz called from the kitchen adjoining the hut's one main room. "Who is it?" She started to move toward the door but Rodríguez waved her away.

"It is Julio. I have a message for *señor* Rodríguez."

"The password," Rodríguez whispered to Luz. "The little fool has forgotten to give the password—if it is him."

Luz sighed, moved a little closer to the door as she dried her hands on an already damp apron. "No one by the name of Rodríguez lives here," she called.

"*¡Sí, sí!*" the boy outside shouted. "He lives and hunts like the coyote, from place to place, from season to season. He lives like the hunted one."

Rodríguez relaxed, but not completely. "Okay," he whispered. "Open the door." But he did not move from the darkened corner where the hut's single dresser stood.

Wearied with Rodíguez and his penchant for such things as longwinded "passwords," Luz unlocked and opened the crude wooden door. Late afternoon sunlight fell on the dirt floor. A boy, no more than twelve or thirteen, stood in the doorway; behind him more huts and, behind the huts, in the distance, the lofty slopes of the dormant volcano called Terremoto rising into the sky.

"Come in, Julio. Quickly," Luz said. "And close the door.

Señor Rodríguez is here." As an afterthought, a mumble: "Where else would he be?"

Rodríguez lowered the gun and returned to the cot where he had been lying when he heard Julio's knock on the door. "What is it this time, Julio? No more stories. No more mistakes."

"*Sí.*" But Julio seemed hesitant. "*Señor* Rodríguez, I have listened like you told me. I have been all over Terremoto, all over Restitution, also. I have been to Smoky Island and Isla Pequeña and El Lugar de las Piratas."

"Get on with it, Julio. No preambles. I am tired. I've no time for preambles."

Julio looked toward the narrow kitchen nook where Luz had gone back to making tortillas for supper. She gave him no sign of reassurance. "*Señor*, I have heard nothing about the *señor* Kelso. Nothing. I have tried very hard. Nobody knows where he went. The man named Polliard, *señor*, it is said he is in California, back in Bahía Angeles. He has not been seen here for a long time. There have been some men asking about you on Restitution Island and here, but no one knows you are here except me and *papá* and *mamá* and a few others, like Luz here. No one will tell. You are safe."

Rodríguez groaned and lay back on the cot. "Safe," he repeated unhappily. "You do not have to eat this woman's cooking. So, is that what you came here to tell me? Why didn't you stay home, or on the streets picking the pockets of the goddamned tourists? You have already told me all this."

"*Sí.* But there is something new. Nothing new about *señor* Kelso or the bad one named Polliard, but an old man, a hermit who lives on Isla Pequeña, had something to tell me you might think is interesting."

"An old hermit," Rodríguez grumbled. "I think this is going to be one of your stories."

"No no, *señor*. Please. I will keep trying to get word to *señor* Kelso that it was Polliard who made you try to catch him. I will not give up on that. But you must listen to what the old hermit told me."

"Okay, okay. Tell it. But none of your beating around the bush!"

"*Señor*, the old hermit told me he does a lot of fishing off Isla Pequeña. He dives off a place called Los Pináculos much of the time. A very remote place. No one goes there, because it is said there are many sharks. The old man says that is a lie, but a lie that he likes because it keeps people away and he does not like people. Like your friend, *señor* Kelso."

"*Sí sí, sí, sí.*"

The old hermit told me he was diving off Los Pináculos two days ago, *señor*, and he was deeper than he had been before—he doesn't have any aqualung or anything like that. He goes down without anything but his spear and a knife. He is amazing—"

"Get on with what he told you, Julio!"

"Oh, *sí*. He told me he found a cave under the cove where he was diving, *señor*. He was chasing a big fish, and the big fish went into the cave, and the old hermit followed the big fish into the cave. The cave went very deep into the rock and curved this way and that and this way and that, and the old man was afraid he was going to become lost, and was about to turn back when the cave opened up into a big room that was only half full of water. I mean, he came up and found himself breathing air in this big underground cave-room, and this was good because he was out of air and about to drown."

"Jesus, Julio. I told you—no more *stories!*"

"*¡Sí, sí!* Please, *señor*. The old man says it is true. But that is not all there is to the—to what the old man says. The room has another cave, and this cave goes a long way deeper into the island, and there are other caves going off in many directions, but the old man kept to the main one, which climbs free of the water, but it gets smaller and smaller until a man can only crawl. He went as far as he could, and he says he does not even know why he kept trying to find what was at the end of this crazy cave that went on forever, but he finally came to a point where he could not crawl any farther. The cave was just a little hole in the rock. But through this hole he could see another room, and he could see something shining in that room because sunlight was coming through holes or cracks in the rock above the room. He says he could see what sat in the room very clearly."

"So what sat in the room, Julio!" Rodríguez yelled, exasperated.

"It was a diving submersible, *señor*. A big one. The old man could see inside, through the submersible's big front glass. He could see what was inside it."

"What? What was inside the goddamned submersible!"

"Treasure, *señor!*" Julio shouted happily. "Like the things they bring out of the ruins of Los Angeles. The old man said the submersible was filled with such things."

A tingling had started at the base of Rodríguez's spine. It climbed to his neck and raised his hair. He sat up, looking at the boy in the gloom of Luz's poor hut. "What? *What?*"

"*Sí, señor* Rodríguez. It is true! It is true!"

"If this is another one of your stories, I will skin you alive and feed you to those stinking, goddamned pigs out there!"

"*Señor,* I swear. I will take you to the old hermit. You can hear him tell you. You will know that this old man does not lie!"

"Why would this hermit tell you about all this if it were true?"

"Because he is a friend of my father's. Because he heard I was working for you. He knows you, of all men, would know how to get the submersible out of there."

"It is impossible! How does the old man even know where it is?"

'He knows Isla Pequeña well, *señor*. When he got out of the cave, he walked the island from one end to the other; and he says he knows where the submersible lies under the rock. It is at a place where some men caused a big explosion years ago, after chasing people on that part of the island away. They caused a big explosion there and some other places. The old man says they found a way through another underground passage to get the submersible into that room and then, because the room was open to the sky above, they used dynamite or something to bury the submersible. The old man says there may be other submersibles in other such rooms under Isla Pequeña, and maybe under Isla Las Penas and some of the other remote islands as well."

"Mother of God," Rodríguez muttered. He wiped his brow with his sodden handkerchief. "Where is this old man now, boy?"

"He is out there, out in the yard," Julio announced proudly and grinned. "He is sitting out there with the chickens."

Rodríguez looked over at Luz who was watching him intently, her dark eyes large, like round, old-time coins. She was the daughter of a member of Rodríguez's *La Dama Conchita* crew. The crew was scattered, hiding from Polliard's avowed wrath. Rodríguez's beloved smuggling vessel had been repainted, had its superstructure altered, and lay innocently at Rose Harbor, done up as a touring yacht which bore the prosaic *yanqui* name of *Sal.*

"Mother of God," he repeated. "I will feed you both to the pigs." Stiffly he got up and, with the shotgun, followed Julio to the door.

It was dusk, Rodríguez saw, when the door was opened. In the yard, with his back against a set-on-edge sheet of tin sheathing which served as part of the pigpen fence, sat a darkly outlined figure that looked so lean and leathery that not even Luz's voracious pigs would have found him palatable.

24. THE SEARCH

At 0700 on the last day of October, a Sunday, the *Tiburón* lay at a hundred-meter depth with all engines dead, on a relatively clear area that was part of what had been Elysian Park. Fifteen kilometers to the south lay the remains of the Los Angeles Civic Center; directly to the west, the mountain of rubble that was the Dodger Stadium ruins.

The meteorological data the Chief gave was of a chill, overcast day above the surface. The only activity in detectable range of both long- and short-range sonar scanners: a couple of patrol subs that had been previously prowling the Lincoln Heights sector, now moving south, probably on their way back to the Long Beach SASP station. The long-range sonar, however, the main source of the Chief's detection data, could pick up only moving objects; a craft lying dead on the bottom, like the *Tiburón*, would go undetected within its ten-kilometer range. The short-range scanner could more effectively discover and identify an immobile craft, but a few late-model submarines and submersibles, like Polliard's pet *Chasseur*, could emit enough sonic razzle dazzle to create an antidetection screen the *Tiburón's* pulses could not penetrate. Such a screen could, in effect, cause the incoming pulses to pass through their target as if it were not there. Thus a craft like the *Chasseur* could be near without their knowledge. For this reason, they did not use the *Tiburón*'s lights.

They had tried to find the appropriate ultraviolet filters and other equipment needed to convert the external lighting system so that it would be invisible to human eyes at least, but had no success in the Restitutions. Not even the Lavaccas had been able to improvise a UV system out of the odds and ends they had. But the *Chasseur* had UV lights as well as an antisonar screen.

Visibility through the unilluminated TV cameras was no more than a few meters. They were below the euphotic, or well-lit, zone and the overcast sky above the bay allowed little light to reach their depth.

All these factors did nothing to help Jack Kelso's mood. Mentally numbed, emotionally drained, and fighting a hangover, the thought of Vincent Polliard and the fact that he still lived was enough to put him under. What DeFond had said, likening him in her uncanny way to Polliard, had gnawed at his insides for days.

The flawless way in which the *Egg* was rolled on its track into the *Tiburón*'s airlock, the antechamber door shut, the lock filled, its door opened and the submersible launched, did little to cheer him. The two responsible for this impeccable operation remained aboard the *Tiburón* to monitor the instruments in the control room and keep up with the *Egg*'s progress, while staying alert to any possible intruder within the *Tiburón*'s sensory range.

Kelso had witnessed an unusual occurrence that morning —an argument, or its aftermath, between Judith and her bodyguards. In his alcoholic fog, stumbling into the room that housed the *Egg*, his gear hanging loosely and at odd angles from his unsteady frame, he'd first entered a scene that was silent. Yet he could sense the tension, the unvoiced dispute. After his bumbling entrance, words had suddenly erupted from DeFond but they'd sounded superfluous, as if they'd already been said and were being said again for Kelso's benefit. She had ordered, in a quaking and distraught voice, the Lavaccas to stay aboard the submarine. But they hadn't responded with their usual docile "*Sí, señorita.*" They'd stood there like twin statues, mute, but strangely resistant. Judith was obviously in a state; the distress in her tone, in the way she stood, moving a shaking hand constantly over her brow, brought Kelso out of his stupor. All at once she turned, pulled herself through the *Egg*'s side hatch and had almost closed it before Kelso, dropping coffee cup and trying to hang on to his diving suit and its paraphernalia, made it aboard.

"What the hell?" he'd blurted.

"They are worried. They wanted to come along," was all she would say, her back to him, her hands already removing the maps from their case and laying them over the small desk above the water-ballast tanks. Then she shouted for him to shut the hatch, as though afraid the Lavaccas would force their way through. He obeyed, turning to find her at the pilot-control console before the nose viewport, her mouth at the mike.

"Launch the submersible," she said into it, speaking to the Lavaccas. The command came out strained, as if she were trying to speak, as he had heard her speak before, through invisible fingers closing her throat. "Launch the submersible!" she yelled when the Lavaccas failed to react.

Stolidly and without mishap, they finally did, while Judith sat at the console holding the sides of her co-pilot's chair, her head upright but quivering. Head and hands were all he could see from where he stood at the hatch. She looked like she was having some sort of seizure.

He started forward, uncertain, and as the lock opened and the *Egg* was launched, saw her relax.

Was she afraid of the bodyguards after all? And if so, why? What did she fear they would do if one, or both, had come along?

He continued to move forward as the *Egg* slid into the water. But when he reached the pilot's seat, she rose, unwilling to show her face, and returned to the maps behind him.

Kelso slumped into the pilot's seat, eyes automatically going over the controls, flummoxed and afraid, afraid as he could not remember ever having been, because he had never been so ignorant of what he was up against. Always, it seemed, he had had his hatred and his rage to override his fear. There were other factors: he feared for her rather than for himself, feared he was going to lose her, feared she was perhaps already lost.

By now Judith had turned almost as mechanical as the Lavaccas, who, but for the fact they stood erect, walked about freely on two legs, and otherwise manipulated limbs and digits with unusual dexterity, could have claimed kinship with the Chief.

Sitting there in the pilot's seat, watching the thickening murk in the nose port, he was suddenly hit by a thought. The similarity between Judith and the Lavaccas seemed to go deeper than her current behavior patterns. He suddenly realized he had seen this all along, though he had not had the wits to reflect upon it consciously. While nothing in the Mexicans' facial features or physiques resembled hers, something in their eyes had always reminded him of Judith's. Theirs were brown, hers green. But it wasn't a matter of color, or shape for that matter—but *something*. . . .

He sighed, trying to ignore the hangover ache, and eased the *Egg*'s speed up a couple of knots. He made adjustments for trim and worked with the rudder and elevator while his mind continued to chew at this latest riddle like a dog with a new but meatless bone. There was nothing he could do but play the situation by ear, minute by minute, hope for the best and expect the worst—and the most unexpected.

"We must turn," she said, immediately obliging expectations.

He glanced at the compass. "We are heading in the right direction, Judith. North."

"We must turn around."

He swiveled the chair 180 degrees. She sat at the desk over the ballast tanks, bent over the maps with her hands at the sides of her head. "*South* is Los Angeles," he snapped. "Not Highland Park." He swiveled back to face the port, knowing he could not take his attention away from it for long without slamming into something. In fact, the view out the port was so dim that he knew he would soon have to use the lights, even at the risk of being seen by a patrol craft that might enter the area, or that might already be around and was, like the *Chasseur*, invisible to the *Tiburón*'s sonar.

He felt her coming forward.

"As you said, things have changed down here."

He looked up. Her eyes, glazed, tormented, were on the latitude-longitude indicator on the console.

"The coordinates I want are south of here. The land has inclined northeastward."

"If that's the case, then Highland Park would lie farther north, not *south*."

"Do not argue with me!" she said, eyes lifted to stare out the port. "Turn the submersible south at once." Again it was that *voice*, hoarse, choked, unnatural.

As before, out of fear he might push her over some psychotic brink, Kelso knew nothing else to do but cooperate.

The *Egg*'s short-range sonar gave back a blur of echoes, all but useless here. There was no question about it; he would have to risk the lights. But when he flipped the switch, he saw that the lights, due to the silt suspended in the water, were not going to help much. Apparently it had rained recently topside, perhaps was raining now. He could see only some ten to fifteen meters with any clarity.

He pulled the throttle back and fingered the jet reversal controls. Pushing the stick carefully to the left, he steered them slowly around, then pulled back to gain some elevation. The farther away from the hazardous bottom, the better; though, with the lights on, the higher they went, the greater the danger of being seen. To hell with it, he thought. At this point, he would almost welcome a simple and sane problem like a patrol boat trying to blow them out of the bay. Jack Kelso and Judith DeFond going down to Davy Jones. Together forever, here among the lost spirits of sunken L. A. A simple solution to a dilemma, a mystery that had just about driven him as nuts as she obviously was; and he thought he'd been nuts before ever meeting her.

But what if she is not nuts at all? What if something has control over her? What if—what if what if what if!

"How can coordinates mean anything down here, Judith?" Bullheadedly, he tried again. "Ever try to find the yolk in a scrambled egg?" Ha ha. The light-hearted approach. Levity to allay his fears. He should have brought a bottle. Sure.

"I am not looking for the yolk in a scrambled egg." She turned away from the console.

Caution forgotten, irritation winning out, he spun around. Her head was once again over the ballast tanks. This persistent study of the maps could have been only a ploy to keep from having to face him or sit beside him in the co-pilot's seat; by now she had to know the goddamned terrain by heart. "What are we looking for, Judith—exactly?"

The choked voice again, though some small part of the voice of the Judith he'd known weeks ago trying to break through. "I suspect we will both be in for some surprises."

"Wonderful. I like surprises, don't you?"

But she did not rise to the bait. Okay. Maybe she didn't know what she was after. In a sense. But in *what* sense?

Defeated, he refaced the console. Peering out the hemispherical viewport at the grim hulks of eltrains, automobiles, upheaved pavement, parts of free-standing walls, indiscriminate debris everywhere encrusted with a film of sediment and algae with which the sea-floor processes were softening and reclaiming everything for their own, Kelso remembered with longing the days spent diving off the Restitutions in waters that still teemed with life. And it hit him again: the sickness of his last nine years, his obsessed wandering through this ungodly desolation looking for ghosts. He remembered that moment in Cave Cove when it, she, him, life, everything, seemed—like something glimpsed through a hole in the mask of time—to come together. Where was it now? Gone. Perhaps forever. Why had he seen it in the first place? Why had he been resurrected from these ruins—yes, by *her*—only to return to them—with her? What fiendish power had thrown the diabolical dice that—

What was the meaning of those books she'd read?

Looming suddenly out of the haze was the cornice of a building. He shoved the stick to the right, barely avoiding a collision. The abrupt change in course sent things clattering about, though the bulk of the gear, equipment and instrumentation that crammed the *Egg*'s single small room was well battened down.

He had to keep his mind on his business, whatever his business was. The cornice of that building had belonged to the old Cathedral High School and his turn to the right put them over a street called Cottage Home. He remembered the area from dives in the past. Kelso tried for a little more elevation by blowing the ballast tanks. He moved the speed up another knot.

Below them lay the Pasadena Elway again. He considered radioing the Chief, but the submarine would have them on the sonar, and he was afraid he might have to speak to one of the zombies; he'd had all of the Lavaccas he could stand. Why had they wanted to come along so badly? From what motive did their previous incredible devotion spring? Did they now feel that Judith DeFond was trying to welsh on some deal she had with them? Were the three thrown together in some crazy treasure hunt, with himself as a mere means to get them to the site? Was that all there was to it?

No. Impossible. The whole bloody mess had been too bizarre from the start. Well soon, Kelso, oh soon you will know the truth. Hallelujah and hosanna. Oh joy and happy day.

"Here," she said. "Yes." She stood at the rear viewport, slightly bent at the waist as though with stomach pain, hands pressed to her temples. She stood that way for several seconds as Kelso sat helpless, not knowing what to do. All at once she began to sway from side to side. "All right. All right, all right."

"Judith?"

"Ahead there," she said, turning, pointing at the front viewport. "We're in the right place. There!"

He cut the jets and looked. Ahead lay what looked like a vast tangle of twisted steel and concrete where perhaps half a dozen arteries—freeways, elways—had come together and interchanged. The earth had uplifted some here, buckling, and the roadway ruins were on the western slope of the uplift at a point just below the *Egg*. He knew the place, did not have to try to see it through the murk. They were just northwest of the Civic Center area. A long way from Highland Park. No big fancy houses where a well-pampered little girl might have grown up. No houses at all standing.

"We will have to dig into that."

"Why? Your parents' house can't be under *that*."

"Yes. Yes, the land has shifted radically. They—I—did not know—miscalculated—" Her hands reached again for her head. "Jack—"

He started to get up, to reach for her, but she jerked away, wheeled around, opened the locker on the other side of the co-pilot's seat and pulled out her mask, fins, jets, and aquapak.

"We will have to find the most accessible place to dig." Her tone was cold again, her expression severe, the face of a Draconian goddess carved in rock. "You will come with me." Her hands shook badly as she strapped on the gear. It was a command.

"Sure. I'll come with you. But you're going to tell me what you're really after down there. You've lied to me from the beginning. You're not looking for any DeFond estate. Not in that mess. You're going to tell me what you mean by '*they* didn't know,' by '*they* miscalculated'!"

Having bent down to strap on the fins, she straightened. It seemed to him that her face indeed betrayed a struggle between two conflicting personalities, as he had noticed before; only this time that struggle was much more strong. Her eyes dilated, then dimmed; the corners of her mouth twitched; the flesh of her face was drawn, altered to the point of being a near death's-head mask. "Come with me," she rasped. "We will find it together." Suddenly she turned, looking out the rear viewport.

Kelso saw what she was looking at. The *Tiburón*'s prow was barely visible through the roiling water some fifty meters away. The goddamned Lavaccas had pulled the sub out of the park and followed them. But how had she known it was back there? Did she have some kind of tie with the Lavaccas that he had not detected?

The Chief's alert signal beeped three short tones over the console phone. "Unidentified submersible twelve kilometers west of your position, approaching from the Los Angeles River basin. Sonar sighting. Appears to be a research submersible of standard design, unarmed. Could be accompanied by other craft with antisonar shield and weaponry. Awaiting your instructions."

Kelso's hands had shot to the light switches the second the signal beeped. Both the inside and the outside of the *Egg* were thrown in darkness. "Get to the bottom, Chief! Don't pay any attention to those two idiots on board. Dive to the bottom and sit tight. We're going to do the same. Maybe they haven't picked us up yet." But, he mused ruefully, that was damned unlikely.

Kelso waited anxiously for the Chief to roger his message, but the roger did not come. That could mean only one thing: the Lavaccas had pulled the computer's plug.

He heard the airlock open. He turned.

"Judith!"

She stepped through as the door closed behind her. He heard her scream as she dogged the hatch from the other side. The voice was hysterical, constricted, but unmistakably Judith's this time.

"Don't—don't come, Jack! Don't follow!"

He leapt across the darkness, fell over his own diving gear and sprawled as he felt the thrum and tilt of the flooding lock.

25. THE FALL

With the footfins extended vertically from her heels, and her feet clamped together, she jetted into the snarl of roadways on the slope. Her limbs, her hands and feet, her motor nerves, were guided and controlled by the mesmerizing instructions repeated by the implant. For what it was worth, she realized that *her* will still tried, however vainly, to resist. Or, to think of it another way, there was the will of Judith DeFond, a woman of Earth who identified with all that implied, and there was the will of Salieu Vidyun of Naravamintara. For the moment, Vidyun, or the implant, had control.

Thus far it had been futile to try to fight or defy it during moments of out-and-out conflict. But then, she had not yet fought with last-ditch desperation. Or so she told herself. Questions about the objective, the mission, remained unanswered, possibly would stay unanswered, but she still harbored a hope that, if and when she reached it, at least some of those questions would be resolved.

Apparently the implant's information was not beyond error. The confusion about the coordinates for the digging site, far south of Highland Park, plagued her with the fear of other errors being made. What was the source of the implant's information? Were errors to be wished for? What was the ultimate objective? If malign, would she have time enough both to learn what it was and prevent herself from carrying it out? Would she have the will, the mental strength, to combat the implant's influence on both body and mind?

Or did her present course guarantee disaster, defeat by Vidyun? Did each step along the way mean one more closed door against possible escape, against any hope of turning back? If the implant consisted of a prearranged series of instructions, admonitions, demands, hypnosis-inducing arcana—the instructions certainly were such that she did not know exactly what would happen next and each event triggered a sequential fresh order—could it be designed so that at the final order, the ultimate event, her mind would be blown to pieces?

Why not fight it now with everything she could muster, while she still had something to fight it with?

Because she had to know what she had been sent here to do.

No matter what the price?

She was spared having to answer this last by a visual distraction on her left. A stunted octopus sprang from a crevice at the foot of the first tilted pylon, tentacles waving sluggishly as it sought a darker niche. A mutant, possibly, like her. A biological changeling darting here between the wreckage of old roadways.

But it did not matter. Those who had sent her, Vidyun's "masters," had decreed that it did not matter. Earth and everything on it could perish, and it would not matter. In fact, that was what the masters wanted. Because they were afraid. Naravamintara, whatever it was, *was* in decline, *did* fear Earth. That was why the changeling Vidyun/DeFond had been sent here, to—*to insure Earth's destruction?*

INTO THE ROADWAY RUINS. KEEP YOUR MIND ON THE TASK AT HAND. REMEMBER TO BE CAREFUL OF PROTUBERANCES, UNSTABLE OVERHANGS, HOLES, OR TUNNELS IN WHICH YOU COULD BECOME ENTANGLED OR TRAPPED. AS THE MAN INSTRUCTED. THAT PART OF WHAT THE MAN HAS GIVEN YOU IS USEFUL; THE REST IS FOOLISHNESS. QUESTIONS, DOUBTS, MYSTIFICATION WITH THE FOLLY OF SELF-LOVE, ARE CONTAGIONS CAUGHT FROM THE MAN, SYMPTOMS OF A DISEASE, A SICKNESS, VIDYUN DID NOT KNOW.

What had Vidyun known?

All she received for an answer was a resurgence of the numbing head pain.

Her senses felt drugged, but her hand moved with expert swiftness to turn off the jets, unclamp her feet and reverse the convertible footfins. Swimming on her own power now—or on the power the implant had over her—she dipped beneath the first massive pylon and switched on the headmask light.

A BRIEF RECONNAISSANCE OF THE AREA IS ALL

YOU NEED TO TELL YOU WHERE TO BEGIN DIGGING WITH THE SUBMERSIBLE.

Above, like the broken vaulted ceiling of a cathedral in which no service had ever been held save black mass, the elway and freeway superstructures stood: cracked, leaning, folded and convulsed at every angle. Every column, every buttress, arch, or slab looked as though it would give way any minute.

YOU WILL BRING THE SUBMERSIBLE INTO THESE RUINS. YOU WILL HAVE TO EXCAVATE CAREFULLY. IT WILL BE DIFFICULT, BUT YOU HAVE NO CHOICE. YOU WILL BE GUIDED. YOU WILL NOT FAIL.

Yes. Choice was something else Vidyun had not known. Happiness, unhappiness, pleasure, pain, hate, love. None of these emotions could be associated with a soldier of the Interior Guard of Naravamintara. She knew that, intuited it if nothing else. Duty, service, devotion, allegiance—if Vidyun had known happiness in any sense at all, it had to have derived from how well he (or she—or *it?*) served the *Empire.*

And "Judith DeFond?" This human persona—that had run the gamut of human emotions, it seemed, and wanted more, wanted to continue to *feel*—had to be something more than a creation of self-serving autocrats who ruled a decaying interstellar empire. Judith DeFond was perhaps the setting free of Vidyun's spirit. No matter that the masters, whoever they were, had not meant it to happen that way.

But then, had it happened? Was Vidyun, in fact, free? Was DeFond?

Unaccountably startled, she turned. Kelso was not there, though she knew he must be coming, could not be far behind.

Amazed, she saw the knife in her hand, ready for use against him and whatever else might try to interfere. The blade glinted in her headlight, irrefutable answer to the question she had just asked. The implant, or that part of her still Vidyun, had made her seize the knife even before she realized DeFond had relinquished control.

In the headlight it was Vidyun's eyes that saw the partially clear flat area, like a bench, on the side of the slope where the *Egg* could be positioned. It was Vidyun who knew this was the place. . . .

Vidyun guided the hand holding the knife to its sheath. Vidyun turned her, put her body into motion, propelled her back through the grotesquely twisted colonnade of concrete pylons that traversed the slope.

Vidyun saw Kelso, a vague form coming through the intervening rubble. Vidyun went again for the knife.

She exerted all the will she could summon to push herself upward, away from him, around him, to avoid a physical clash.

"Told you—not to come—" Her attempt to speak was strangled.

His arms shot up for her. His grasp found her belt.

"No! Let go, Jack! No time—please—for your own sake—" She writhed, trying to break free. Her foot slammed into his headmask and he let her go in order to keep the mask from being torn from his face.

The knife, guided by *her* command, however feebly for the moment, came up, slashing at the diving pack where his jets were connected. Her power over her hands waned. The knife hacked upward, trying to puncture his breathing gear.

With a thin faraway scream that was hers, she managed to kick away, out of his reach and out of danger of the knife cutting his gills; turned on her own jets and broke from the ruins for the submersible.

"Stay—stay away, Jack! I'm sorry—but—stay away!" She tried to say more but the rest was choked down, lost in garbled and incomprehensible noises that ended in a fit of coughing.

There was no response from Kelso.

When she reached the *Egg*, she forced a look back, saw him scrambling on the cloudy bottom with his headlight on, trying to find and retrieve his jets. She fought against leaving him there but her feet kicked her into the airlock and, once in, her hands closed and locked it from inside.

When the lock was drained and she entered the submersible, the switch for the interior lights was found and she went to the co-pilot's seat. Her mind was all but occluded, but her body functioned perfectly. Fingers flew to the controls. The *Egg* lurched into motion, rising, moving forward. The nose lights came on, illuminating the jagged mouth of the roadway shambles. Dark encrustations covered overhangs and protuberances, sucking up the light. The spectral shapes of several rotting oaks and eucalypti reached from the darkness on the lights' periphery, malevolent sentinels of a realm more macabre than sanity would or could accept.

Her hands continued to work. More ballast was blown; the *Egg* rose over the ruins. Manually turning the twin nose lights downward, she searched the concrete and steel thatch for an opening large enough to accommodate the submersible.

Under the criss-crossed ledges and abutments, like the menhirs and dolmens wrenched and scrambled by a crazed god, she saw Jack Kelso. Jetless, he was swimming upward, through a hole in the wreckage, toward the *Egg*. She pushed the power up but he was exiting the concrete mesh just as the *Egg* passed over him, his hands groping upward for a hold on the submersible's belly.

YOU WILL INCLUDE THE MAN. IT IS FUTILE FOR YOU TO ATTEMPT ANYTHING ELSE. IF YOU PERSIST IN TRYING TO EXCLUDE HIM, THE LAVACCAS WILL SEE THAT HE IS DEALT WITH APPROPRIATELY. WHAT YOU ARE ABOUT TO WITNESS MUST FOREVER REMAIN A SECRET, AND THE MAN HAS ALREADY SEEN TOO MUCH FOR HIM TO BE SPARED. REMEMBER THAT YOU ARE OF NARAVAMINTARA, THE SEAT OF PERFECTION. YOUR SERVICE TO YOUR MASTERS WILL INSURE YOU AN EXALTED PLACE IN THE HIGHEST OF MINDS.

Out of the painful fog in her forebrain, her own thoughts struggled into temporary focus: she wanted to keep Kelso away for his own safety, yet also wanted him with her—to help save her if that were possible, to help save her and help her save whatever it was she had to destroy, if destruction was her task. And to help her save *him*.

The mental fog intensified, stifling clarity. A remnant of reason hung on: she should stop, open the airlock, let him in, tell him everything—everything she knew at least—before she totally lost control, before the implant took over completely.

But when she tried to pull her hands away from the controls, they stayed as if frozen there, no longer a part of any volitional link that was hers.

Vidyun, you were a slave, a cipher! Your mind, your soul, was theirs!

NARAVAMINTARA IS LIFE. NARAVAMINTARA IS TRUTH AND KNOWLEDGE.

Then why fear Earth? Why destroy—

NARAVAMINTARA ADAH NAHN TALA KEO BRAH. NARAVAMINTARA ADAHKA ANDHA KAH. . . .

A chill shroud enveloped her mind, snuffing its fire. Yet eyes saw, in the twin cones of light from the Egg's nose, an opening through which it could enter. Hands cut the throttle and opened the descent-intake tanks; the submersible dropped through, port side lightly scraping a segment of concrete. Hands reached up, removed the diving mask so that eyes could see better.

The bench found earlier appeared, a few meters below and forward of the opening through which the *Egg* had dropped. A thumb jabbed the button that activated the anchor grapnels.

A cloud of silt wafted up as the *Egg* settled on the shelf. The arm-claw controls were just under the grapnel button. . . .

The steel claws bit into the rubble, scooping and lifting large chunks of mud, rock, concrete and metal, turning, one claw to the left, one to the right, and dumping their loads at the *Egg*'s flanks. The two piles already had grown large enough to crowd the narrow ledge and partially spill down the slope. The excavation into the brow of the incline deepened and widened as the piles continued to grow and spill over the shelf's edge. Storms of disturbed silt whirled in the nose lights; the arm-claw motors hummed and whined.

From a great distance, as if in a dimension no longer either corporeal or temporal, she watched the skillful manipulations of the controls. The body sweating inside the diving suit, the ache in its lower back from sitting rigidly in the co-pilot's seat for so long, were items of only the remotest concern to this dimmed, all but disembodied consciousness watching it all, controlling nothing.

She was aware as well of another scene, one unfolding outside the *Egg*, beyond the twisted roadway ruins under which it diligently worked.

The Lavaccas had taken over the *Tiburón*, allowing its computer to function only in its mechanical capacities. They had moved the submarine on a southeast course to intercept the intruding unidentified submersible which, as it had turned out, was, indeed, accompanied by another craft; a small and fast submarine with a sonar shield that, using the *Tiburón*'s powerful searchlights, the Lavaccas had now sighted visually. From descriptions given by Kelso, they identified this latter craft as Vincent Polliard's *Chasseur*. Through the implant in her forebrain, she "heard" the orders telepathed to the Lavaccas on the *Tiburón*.

DESTROY THE INVADING CRAFTS IMMEDIATELY. THEY WILL SOON BE TOO CLOSE TO THIS POSITION FOR YOU TO FIRE ON THEM WITHOUT ENDANGERING THE EXCAVATION SITE.

Numbly she felt the Lavaccas comply, saw through their eyes the *Chasseur* drop into the ruins north of the Civic Center. The slower, less maneuverable, research submersible followed but was yet above the ruins.

The bow torpedoes of the *Tiburón*, which was no more than 200 meters away, fired. At the firing buttons in the attack center, Carlos knew it was too late for a strike with the *Chasseur* and had tried for the submersible.

One charge hit the fringe of a half-collapsed building; the other struck its target just before the submersible gained the cover of the ruins. It exploded, the noise of the detonation speeding through the disturbed water to the digging site at more than a kilometer per second.

Suddenly Kelso's voice blared in the earphones of Judith's headmask where she had set it on the control console shelf.

"Idiots!" Something hard and metallic, possibly the handle of his diving knife, hammered against the outside airlock door. "The stuff we're under could fall at the slightest nudge! Order those fools on the *Tiburón* not to fire!"

Like a mere analogue of the machine in which she sat, she continued to operate its arms, digging, lifting, unloading, unable to break the implant's hold.

Kelso's head appeared in the nose viewport, ducking under the swinging right arm and its load-filled claw to get closer to the glass. Through the port, he began gesturing, pointing upward, moving his mouth, apparently thinking she could not hear him through the earphones because she had removed her mask.

NO MORE FIRING! he mouthed silently. WE'LL BE BURIED!

She stared at him, unable to speak, her face like marble.

He beat upon the viewport. OPEN THE AIRLOCK! OPEN THE AIRLOCK!

The arms, having dumped their loads, were coming around to the front again. The whirr of their motors climbed the scale. Kelso looked, as if wondering if she intended to crush him between them. But he should have known the arms could not turn that far inward.

The claws dropped again into the excavation. By now the arms were extended their maximum reach in order for the claws to bite into the pit's bottom, a depth of four meters. The forward grapnels on the rim of the hole would hold for perhaps one more claw load. To dig deeper, the *Egg* would have to move forward, down the side of the excavation. Since the excavation was into an incline, this could be done without the submersible tipping, or sliding in too far, but above them lay a massive section of elway with one of its supporting pillars footed on the very edge of the hole.

Kelso was yelling into his mike again, still beating on the viewport.

Far down in an internal darkness, she tried to reach upward toward him, tried to ascend, tried to regain command of her body, her will. She cried out to him from a place outside time or space. But her hands did not waver from the levers; her eyes stayed fastened on the work of the claws; her lips remained sealed.

YOU ARE AN ARM OF THE RACE ABOVE RACES. YOU SERVE THOSE BEYOND JUDGMENT OR UNDERSTANDING. THAT IS THE WAY IT MUST BE. THAT IS THE LAW.

Another roar from the direction of the Civic Center ruins thundered through the *Egg's* hull. The submersible wobbled. Incredibly, the arcing elway section overhead seemed to hold.

A finger pushed the buttons that released the grapnels. Her hand pulled the stick. The *Egg* crawled forward on its narrow metal tracks. Its nose tilted into the hole and Kelso, clinging to the tow-ring just under the viewport, dangled over the pit.

He let go, no doubt wearied with trying to make her listen. Dodging the newly mobile arms, he swam away from the port but kept close to the *Egg's* hull.

Jack! I'm sorry! Please try to understand. I can't—

With unprecedented effort she fought to push back the encompassing darkness, the out-of-body limbo, the stranglehold that denied her any ability to act on her own.

All at once the *Egg* shuddered; the levers quaked violently in her hands. Equipment rattled. Objects fell from cabinets and shelves. She heard an ominous crack from above, muffled but unmistakable through the thick skin of the submersible. The overhead structure was giving way!

Disturbed silt at the base of the now canting abutment on the far side of the excavation, up the slope, exploded in the lights. Chunks of concrete came tumbling from above, falling here and there around the *Egg* and into the pit. Debris slammed against the hull. Shock waves rocked the craft and, overhead, the huge slabs rumbled and groaned.

Something heavy struck the caudal section of the *Egg*, miraculously missing the vulnerable viewport in the rear, but knocking the submersible forward.

Futilely her hands clung to the levers, as if by doing so they would prevent the inevitable fall and burial. Yet as the *Egg* slid and began to plunge, she saw that the hole had widened and deepened into a cavity much larger than the *Egg* could have possibly dug.

As the subersible fell pell mell into a blackness that seemed without bottom, she was suddenly aware that the implant had relaxed or weakened its hold. Feeling returned to her hands, her body. She could think more clearly—clearly enough to feel terror replace the implant's former narcotic grip.

26. THE CITY

It didn't matter a damn that his reflective intelligence, what he had left, told Kelso the *Egg* could not be falling—every other sensation told him it *was*. Clinging to a caudal climbing rung beside the *Egg*'s after viewport, he heard a noise like wind, felt it tearing at his headmask, realized that somehow the water, the sea, had been left behind. The increasing pressure hurt his ears, pressed in upon his body despite the diving suit's alleviation cells. He fought it, trying to yawn, swallow, but became numb regardless.

Blood bubbling with narcosis, his consciousness waxed and

waned, and his hold on the rung finally failed. But when he lost it, he continued to fall—if falling was really what he did—along with the *Egg*. Occasional pieces of debris swirled around him, but nothing large enough to be dangerous. He had the nightmarish impression that he was plunging through some kind of vortical force funnel. But why didn't all the rest of the crap come tumbling? Why wasn't the bloody sea itself pulled in?

Maybe that crumbling slab that had hit the *Egg* had hit him on the head as well. Maybe he was dead and this was the inevitable descent into hell. For whatever satisfaction that might be derived from the fact, a glance at the somersaulting *Egg* below told him that DeFond was going with him.

He did not know how long he was out. When he was once again conscious, he realized that the roar was gone and he was no longer under intense pressure. He was aware, as well, of light.

Lifting his head, he saw the battered *Egg*, upright and evidently in one piece, sitting a few meters away. Beneath him lay a hard, crystalline surface that either reflected an omnipresent light or glowed with a light of its own—he wasn't sure which; at this point, he wasn't sure of anything.

He attempted to stand, and heard banging noises against the inside of the *Egg*'s dorsal hatch. The hatch creaked open, apparently having been jammed by the collapsing roadway rubble. When—how long ago was that?

His knees quivered as he pushed himself to a standing position. He stumbled around the tail of the submersible and saw her climbing out of the top, stripped of everything but a coverall, and with a pistol in her hand. Her legs, too, were unsteady as she came down the side ladder and stood beside the *Egg*, staring at what lay in the distance. He could not see her eyes.

Kelso tore his mask off and found the air slightly humid and salty, but breathable. His own vision now accustomed to the pervasive light, he saw what she stared at, what lay beyond the *Egg*.

"Hell's howling hounds," he said softly, Judith DeFond temporarily forgotten.

They were in a large vaulted antechamber, perhaps sealed

off from the sea by some kind of prodigious energy field. Behind them was an enormous black elliptical hole in the antechamber wall, the mouth of the "funnel" through which they'd been sucked, he assumed. He couldn't think that well, could not account for that "funnel" and what it had done. Nothing he had seen in reality, not in Colnette, Island One, or on *Deepfish*, could help him explain the funnel—or what lay in the other direction, beyond the antechamber.

His perceptions strove to align themselves with what needed to be perceived. In the shimmering distance stood domes, turrets, arches, obelisks. There were shapes, structures, he had no names for, forms that weren't forms, spatial relations that defied common sense. Because of the light, or the air, something, it all seemed like a mirage, not really tangible. Overall, it appeared to be a huge habitat or installation of some kind. But how?

Could this be what he'd been looking for these many years? Could this be what the U.S. Government had been probing and searching for in the San Gabriels? But they weren't under the San Gabriels now, were they? Had the government, in fact, known about this and tried to keep it hidden? Did something here cause the quakes? How could it have survived them? Hell's blazes, how could it have been constructed where it was—under a section of Los Angeles that had been, before the San Andreas catastrophe, kilometers inland?

Seeking something to grasp that would return him to the familiar and explicable, his eyes found the dented *Egg* again and came to rest on DeFond. She turned her head to meet his look with that unsettling fixed stare which was by now all too familiar, but far from being explained. For a moment, though, he thought she was trying to get past—or through—that inner fixation, whatever it was.

"Are you—are you all right?" Her voice rang and echoed loudly in the antechamber and carried out across the open area between them and the eerie structures in the distance.

"Well—" He let go a tense breath of air. "I don't buy the story we're after the DeFond jewels anymore—if I ever did." He lifted a shaking hand at the glittering architecture a hundred meters away. "Or is *this* their former nesting place?" His attempted sarcasm fell flat and meaningless against the convex ribs of the vault, ridiculous under the circumstances.

"Come with me." It was an order, clipped and brittle, yet it held a faint plaintive note. She jerked away, started for the broad, open area between the antechamber and the buildings, her body totally stripped of that natural grace and ease he'd once known, forced forward now as if made of steel and wire. Her hand seemed to clamp the pistol into its holster against a counter demand to keep it out. "Please!" she cried hoarsely. "Hurry!" When she'd left the *Egg*, she had screamed that he shouldn't follow. Now . . .

He stepped, stumbled over his footfins. After bending down to remove the fins and unharnessing the rest of his diving gear, he looked up to find her halfway across the open area. He ran. By the time he overtook her she had reached the first outlying structures.

The air, he realized, was cold, and the ambience oppressive. Overhead, the ceiling, if it could be called that, appeared to be domed, with its apex at least a kilometer above the installation's center. From Kelso's perspective, he judged that center to be many kilometers away, but because of the ceiling's luminescence, he had little faith in his judgment of its shape or size.

Preoccupied with trying to keep up with her, he hadn't much time to reflect on his surroundings but he took in what he could. Sleek, vertical walls towered above the avenue they entered, closing off what he'd had earlier of a broader view. The walls were without features of any kind, some vitreous, some opalescent, and they seemed to bend, blur, flow into each other in a vaporous vagueness that made him recall his first impression of having looked upon a mirage. Now and then the walls parted in off-street fingers, like alleyways or narrow walkways, that revealed other shapes and angles far away. Now and then something at least a little familiar crossed his vision—a pyramidal shape, an upright oblong piece like a stele with vermicated designs across its face.

"Who—" They were running and he had difficulty breathing, speaking. The oxygen content in the air could not have been high. "Where are the people who—what is this—" He had to give it up. His lungs were raw, his heart beating frantically.

She looked at nothing, said nothing. Her eyes remained straight ahead, as if mesmerized by the avenue down which they ran; her body stayed stiffly erect—though her movements were now less jerky and more rhythmic—as though every muscle and nerve were concentrated on some all-consuming purpose. He wanted to seize her, shake her, wrench from this unnerving mannikin the woman who'd rekindled in him a desire to live and to appreciate life. He wanted explanations, answers, but his hands did not move to touch her. Though he ran, he was otherwise incapable of action for the moment, stunned by the unreality of the place, the things he passed. And, as before, he feared touching her, lest she truly break—or become something with which he could not deal at all.

He did not know how long they had been running—he knew he could not have gone much farther without caving in—when the luminous street came to a Y. Directly in front of them, in the Y's fork, stood a tall, blue-black edifice more than ten meters wide, square-cornered, featureless, and fronted with a short flight of steps of the same blue-black material. Here she came to a stop.

So did Kelso. His chest heaved and he desperately inhaled the chill air while watching her.

The wooden, glazed-over expression on her face had hardly altered. She had opened the coverall at the throat. Strands of hair had come loose from their tight, swept-back arrangement, and perspiration, in spite of the cold, glistened on her brow and upper lip.

"Judith—if that is your name—" He held his side, puffing heavy plumes of vapor, still trying to get his breath.

She stepped forward, up the steps. "Come. Help me!"

"Help you? Do what?"

He saw her right hand lift to the butt of the pistol, then pull itself away.

A high, square opening appeared in the front of the building, where there had been no such opening before; the material occluding its space had simply vanished without a sound. In a panic, Kelso ran up the steps on sluggish legs in order to make it through the opening the same time as she, in case it permitted only her and closed on him. He made it; but perhaps it automatically closed when no one stood on the outside steps; in any case, it became a solid wall as soon as they stepped through.

Like the avenues and buildings they'd already passed, the interior of the structure glowed as though infused with a nacreous light. Yet there was shadow enough to delineate objects. On the high walls here were what seemed to Kelso, at first glance, strange writing, but could have been buttons, slits, indicators for instrument readings, elaborate art, anything. His disorientation became even more acute, in spite of the fact that he was "inside" a "building."

At the opposite end of the large room, between two arched doorways, sat a raised platform of horseshoe shape, in the center of which rested what looked like a horizontal wheel, a little more than a meter from the floor. To this altar-like platform DeFond walked, Kelso a few paces behind, feeling trapped and bewildered. Each time he tried to collect his wits some new oddity struck his sight, and he simply gawked, unable to comprehend.

"What is this!" he shouted at last in exasperation. He could have been in a padded cell the way the room swallowed his words. In a daze, he reeled away from the impassive walls and kept following her.

She had ascended to the platform and now, before the wheel, she stopped. When Kelso stepped onto the platform, he saw that the wall above and behind the horizontal wheel was different from the walls below. A panel of fretted slits rose over what, he now realized, would be more properly termed a disc than a wheel. These slits were bordered by rows of dogtooth design, which had to be buttons or controls. On the wall to the right was a projection, or televized picture, of the entrance antechamber and the *Egg*. In each corner of the horseshoe was a carrel-like seat, and before these were panels of diamond-pointed inlays.

Who had sat at those seats? Where were they now?

Who was *she*?

"Jack—this—" Her hands raised to touch her head. "This—" Her mouth moved but no sound came out.

As he looked, her left hand came away from her head and he saw that her face had further paled. The hand passed in front of a row of chevrons just below the fretwork, immediately above the disc. Almost imperceptibly the light in the alcove changed, dimmed, while the disc in front of her heightened its iridescence. Her back, her entire body, went as rigid as a steel beam, except for her hands, which she now brought to rest on the studded surface of the disc.

Instinct howled in Kelso to *move*.

He sprang the meter and a half between them, grabbed her by the waist, and yanked her away. Both fell from the force of his sudden lunge. Her hands fought to get at the pistol but he shoved her, belly forward, to the floor, and wrestled her arms above her head.

"Who are you?" he bellowed. "What is this place!"

She pitched and squirmed, struggled with sporadic fits of

aggression and resistance followed by lulls of passivity. Her strength at times was much more powerful than his own, and more than once she came close to overpowering him, when suddenly she would subside and be still. Strangely, she did not seem to be struggling against him so much as against something within herself. Or rather, part of her fought him and part of her fought herself. Her movements became less directed, more aimless, like one in the throes of an epileptic seizure. He knew that, had she been able to concentrate all her energy against him, he would have lost. By finally twisting her right arm behind her and almost breaking it, he forced her to stop and remain immobile.

The silence in the room was maddening. She lay limp, breathing heavily, face resting on her left cheek, eyes closed, mouth and nose slicked with sputum. He let go the arm, thrust his hand under her hip and pulled out the pistol, a stunner, and flung it away, not caring where it went.

"Now," he panted in her ear, "if you have any of your former senses left, you tell me—" He tried to catch his breath. "You tell me where we are, who *you* are. You—you tell me!"

One last attempt to break his hold was made, but he slapped her so hard across the side of her face that the tension in her body snapped like a broken stick and, with a moan, she sagged, inert.

Her mouth tried to move, her throat made choking sounds. Finally words emerged. ". . . won't fight you . . . not fighting you."

"Why the hell should I believe you?"

"Didn't fight you before. Didn't—won't—don't want to fight you. Them—"

He released her, knowing he was probably being foolish, but not knowing what else to do. Getting to his feet, he searched for the stunner and found it under the right corner carrel. He let it stay there, ready to knock her to the floor, if she tried for it.

But she didn't stand, merely sat up, rubbing her wrists where he had held them, pushing abstractedly at her hair which now fell loose.

"Yes," she exhaled wearily, eyes out of focus as though confounded by an inner image. Then her gaze steadied on the far wall. Her face was stark, an uncanny, shadowless mask above the light thrown up from the floor.

"Tried to tell—they—the implant—" Her hand darted to the side of her head in a gesture he had seen countless times. She grimaced.

"What is it?"

"I—Vidyun—"

"What?"

Her eyes blurred. She began to speak, at first so hurriedly he could not understand what she said. It sounded like rote, like mumbo-jumbo, but by an apparent exercise of will she made the words come more clearly.

"Naravamintara . . . ."

He had to bend forward to hear.

27. PLACE OF CHANGES

The dwindling noises of armed conflict continued to reach them intermittently. At times the floor quaked, as distant destructive forces were unleashed. The smoking remains of several Yaghattarin and their machine-servants lay on the floor, and Acexea, flanked by two lieutenants, still had his hand weapon bared.

"I need more light," Cinara whispered.

Falur stepped forward, pulling a pocket crystal from his cloak. She took it and played its central beam over the tiny globe, concentrating on the figure within. The light, diffracted off the outer shell of the globe, was thrown back on her face, revealing the dismay, the fear.

"Get one of them," she whispered.

Acexea bent down, his translator not having picked up what she'd said.

"One of them who knows this room—this place. Find one who is still able to make the piteous shriek they call a language. One still able to function. One who knows the workings of these things." Trembling, she indicated the cylinder, the globe, the intricate patterns of instrumentation along the walls.

Acexea straightened, spoke briefly to a lieutenant. The latter sheathed his disintegrator and moved quickly to the blast-blackened exit. Prithipean soldiers in the corridor made way for him.

They waited in silence, Tlii's stricken eyes on the rigid figure inside the globe, Falur beside her, Acexea behind them but dominating the ghostly-lit room with his mere physical bulk.

It was not long before the lieutenant returned with a Yaghattarin, selected from among the prisoners taken aboveground. The once-mighty Deathlord stood before them, a thin, wraith-like creature whose sable robe had been badly soiled and torn. Through a large rent in the robe's back could be seen the long brain that extended in a falling arc down the length of the Yaghattarin's spinal column. The variegated cortices were clearly visible through the transparent cranium.

Falur looked upon this being with a mixture of revulsion and awe. He saw a strange elegance and sinister beauty that clashed with his Onnahlaetian predilections and provincialism. Despite all he had heard about the Deathlords of Naravamintara, he was fascinated.

Tlii stood, her hand at the deflagrator on her belt. "You will explain to us what has gone on here in this room," she said, trying to speak succinctly so the Yaghattarin would understand her words. She knew no translator was needed, because the Deathlords understood all the languages of the empire, but she would run no risk of the slightest confusion. The cold fire that burned inside had spread, was spreading still.

The prisoner did not answer, did not look at any of them. The thick, gray lids of his white eyes closed. The flick of a hand through a tear in the robe's front showed that they had before them a Silver One, the next to the highest in the hierarchy.

"This is a transformation chamber, is it not?" Tlii shouted. "You will explain this room and this figure here." She pointed at the globe. "Or we will place you in that cylinder beside it. No doubt we can find one among our new comrades, your former slaves and servants, who will remember how the cylinder operates, and if you refuse to speak, we will put you in it. Immediate metamorphosis to one of those monstrosities that wander the wastelands of Strohr would be appropriate!"

Though the Yaghattarin betrayed no outward reaction except for a slight flutter of his eyelids, his terror gave off an acrid, metallic odor.

"You should find them good company," Cinara said. "They also have difficulty articulating their grotesque handiwork." She turned and signaled to Acexea's two lieutenants.

The soldiers started forward, prepared to lay hold of the Yaghattarin and force him into the cocoon-like container.

A shudder ran the lengh of his tall and heretofore static frame, shaking the tattered folds of the robe and disclosing glimpses of the silver body underneath. Though no limbs were clearly visible outside the black garment, much movement inside confirmed his agitation, as though he were physically wrestling with himself.

"Wait," he said in a high-pitched semblance of the Onnahlaetian tongue. "I will tell you. I will tell."

Tlii waved the soldiers away. "Speak quickly. We have much to do, many evils to wipe away that have been perpetrated by you and your kind. This figure here in this sphere! It is a paradigm, is it not? Where is the one whose miniaturized replica this is? What have you done with him? Speak!"

Falur reached and touched her. "Cinya. This room. It is a place of passage. Beware your fear, your virulence."

She did not look at the boy who was almost a man now, a boy who had seen the gleam of the icy, parasitic fire in her eyes, had no doubt felt it freeze her heart.

The Yaghattarin lifted his face toward the ceiling, causing the transparent cranium to fold at the point where it curved downward from its crown. The pallid eyes remained closed, as though peering backward, down the maze of serpentine circuitry contained in the long brain sac. A shrill chanting noise rose from the mouth-slit above his robe-collared neck.

As the lilting noise gradually resolved itself into Onnahlaetian words, Cinara Tlii felt the icefire leap inside, surge, climb. Her fingers curled around the handle of the deflagrator at her waist.

28. REVELATIONS

"... routine surveillance of Earth disclosed a subterranean city unaccountably left by those who built it, left by the Adulterators. Reports from the surveillance vessel said the city's location, due to recent seismic disturbances on the planet's surface and the fact that the city's automatic defenses had already caused a large-scale cataclysm that called attention to the area where it was located, placed it in a region where the danger of its being discovered by the planet's inhabitants had become extreme. It is ... imperative that the city be destroyed as soon as possible ... contains powers, information, technology ... that must not be discovered by ... must be accomplished without suspicion by the planet's inhabitants ... all participants in mission ... sacrificed. ..."

The words were like those coming from a computer, and they came from that other self in her he could not fathom. It made his skin crawl and, in spite of the need to watch her, he glanced upward, glanced around him with renewed wonder, at things he could in no way understand.

"A subterranean city ..." His words trailed off, a dried-up trickle of comprehension lost in a desert of improbability. "A city how old?" he suddenly yelled. Kneeling, he took her by the shoulders, shook her. "Built by whom? Who were 'the Adulterators'? Built how? *Whose* surveillance showed it being here!"

A revival of Judith flashed through the demonic mask. "Jack—"

"Yes," he blurted. "It's me, Jack. Nobody else here." He wondered if he could be sure of that.

Pulling away from him all at once, she got to her feet, hands moving nervously over her face as if to clear it of cobwebs, head inclining downward as if expecting the ax to fall. "They—the implant seems to have weakened—must tell while—" She lifted her head, faced him. "Instructions were to find a man who would unwittingly help me find . . . this city." Though what she said was halting, broken as though by a mental obstacle trying to divert her from this course, when the words came, they came rapidly, afraid of being cut off. "Was to charm him . . . care for him . . . ingratiate myself to him in . . . any way . . . I could to win . . . affection and trust."

You won the affection, he thought.

A tremor shook her. "When we—you and I—found this—the city—I was to go to the control center here—to the power disc—but I did not know until now—" She stopped, threw her hands to her temples. "Ahhh!"

"What is it?" He moved toward her.

She drew back against the wall. "They keep trying—to the main power disc—deactivate power that keeps city materialized—everything—"

"You mean—"

"Yes!" Pain creased her face. She clutched her midriff.

"Including us."

"Buried! We will be buried!"

"Judith!" He stepped to catch her before she fell. Her eyes had once again opaqued. Too bad, he thought, sardonically reflecting on what she had said about their being buried. *Just when I was beginning to enjoy living again.*

The spasm seemed to pass. She leaned against him, breathing deeply. "They—implanted instructions—Vidyun." She raised her head to look at him. "So much I want to tell you—they keep—I didn't know what I was to do—implant arranged so—couldn't remember who I—what Naravamintara was—reduced to arguing points that bordered on religious—clichés that meant nothing—know less now than—"

He held her to him, speaking earnestly yet placatingly, as though he were trying to coax a deadly secret out of a demented child. "What is this city? How did this Narava—this Naravablahblah know it was here? Why do they fear men finding it? You said it had something to do with the San Andreas mess, if I heard right."

"Yes!" Again he saw the pain knife her body, her hands alternately clutch her stomach and leap to her head. "It caused the superquake! Yes! Geophysicists probing for oil, other resources, picked up its location years ago under the San Gabriel Mountains—the city is huge, extends under those mountains—electronic devices recorded an energy field, but didn't know what it was, what caused it—tried to probe further—city's automatic defense mechanisms triggered—obliterated the probe—split the fault." She took a breath, swallowed, went on. "Books I got in the Restitutions—some accounts of steam and smoke coming out of the Earth seen by the few survivors helilifted out—vast clouds—energies in the city vaporized rock, anything—pieced together these things from the books, self-hypnosis. Naravamintaran surveillance learned what happened."

Kelso was stunned into silence, was remotely aware that if what she said was true, much of his hatred of the last decade could have been based on a false or flawed premise. Yet the Devils Canyon Project could have been handled more wisely, more cautiously. . . . "How—who—*what* is this Naravamintara?"

She was against the wall, sliding floorward. But when she answered, it appeared that Judith still held sway. "Interstellar empire somewhere in Earth's galactic neighborhood. It is—" She subsided to the floor, head clasped and bent between her hands.

This disclosure left him too dumbfounded to react. In a daze, he watched her come to rest at the junction of floor and wall.

"Naravamintara watching Earth for centuries—its progress toward a space culture—glad to see current decline—"

"Why? Why *glad?*"

"Jack—Jack, I was a being called Vidyun. A soldier of the High Court. Don't know what that means—don't know what I did—or where I—where Vidyun came from—but must have been things—emotions needs aspirations values—kept repressed—emotions and needs similar—yours—"

It was not an answer to his question but rather something she obviously had to get out before—

"Because they've come to life in me—you—helped bring them out. Something inside me—something deep—responded to your—past. I was fascinated—understood and commiserated with your views but—" Her voice, her face, abruptly changed. She sat up as though a rod had just been rammed up her spine. "*—but I am compelled to serve those who sent me and to whom I owe all, with whom I am one! Now and forever!*"

Involuntarily, Kelso stepped backward, badly thrown by this unsettling reversal, angered and afraid. He wanted to reach out to her, but was too shocked by the change, wanted to reach out to Judith, not the thing she'd once again become. Thus he stood with arms hanging at his sides, helpless and unable to grasp it all, unable to accept it as truth. "If you're what you claim to be, why did you need a fumbling fool like me to get you here?" The question was impulsive; he did not know what he expected for an answer, if he expected anything.

She groaned, fighting, shaking her head to and fro. When she lifted it, it was mercifully Judith who spoke. "Expense and risk—must have been too great for them to destroy city through their own presence here—don't know for certain—think that while they—while they can screen themselves from your detection—most of the time—in air or space—more difficult to do so on Earth or in your seas. Accidents happen—spy vessel may be picked up—rare—go disbelieved by people—" Her breath came faster as she tried to speak, struggling against that inner hindrance. "So close to your detection devices on California coast—might have been discovered—don't know how—don't know, don't know—all I know for certain—this the way they wanted—" (voice cracking, going flat and cold again, eyes empty but glaring, face gone ashen) "and that is the way it will be done! I am expendable! *You* are expendable!"

Totally rattled, Kelso retorted wildly. "If you're an agent from outer space, then I'm a goddamned ichthyosaur! No, there's a more mundane explanation for who or what you are and what this place is." The thought came out of the blue, and he grabbed at it as a drowning man would grab at even the illusion of a suddenly thrown life raft. "My guess is that you're either some kind of special operative working for the U.S., and this is some kind of weird government operation down here that's got to be plowed under because it's getting dangerously close to being found by somebody like me, or you're a foreign agent whose government got wind of the place, whatever in hell it is, and for your own reasons intend to send it down the tubes. Given the ingenious technology that's been developed over the years, they could have implanted some gizmo in your brain to make *you* believe your Naravamintara story. Yes, they could have mental and kinetic control over you if it comes to that!" But he seriously doubted any of this, doubted it even before he'd said it.

"Believe what you will," she said dully, with a weariness, a resignation, that wrenched his heart. "It all comes down to the same thing where we are concerned." Her eyes were on the floor.

"Could be," he said. "But you're not getting near that disc."

"Then we'll rot here." It seemed all fight had left her. "No way back out."

"There's got to be."

"None that I know."

"Seems there's a hell of a lot you don't know."

"Yes."

Compassion pulled at him. He had never seen a more dejected or defeated-looking creature in his life. He sensed she was sinking. He knew nothing to do but talk, ask questions, pull amateurish psychiatric tricks. "But what's here? What's so mucking dangerous or threatening about it that it has to be blitzed?"

She said nothing.

"Listen to me. Answer me! For god's sake, don't give up! Judith! *Think!* Keep alive whatever you have left of your own mind!"

Her face lifted, to look not at him but at the TV-like picture behind and above him. Half suspecting deception, he turned and saw that a small submarine, looking disturbingly familiar, now lay alongside the *Egg* in the entrance antechamber. A man had climbed out of its forward hatch, a heavy weapon in his hands. As soon as this one started descending the ladder on the sub's port side, another man rose from the hatch, similarly armed.

"The minisub that accompanied the unidentified submersible," she murmured. "That the *Tiburón* picked up. They must have found the excavation. Must have been pulled into the funnel."

Kelso was silent. He watched the second man who had emerged, the slick muscular torso, the sharp angular face, the close-cut dark hair. He watched this man come down the ladder to the floor of the antechamber, weapon trained on the *Egg*, as he motioned the first man to climb atop Kelso's craft and check inside.

What was it the Arabs called it? Kismet? "Of course," he said. "My nemesis. My alter ego." Kelso, he thought, looks like all your pigeons have come home to roost. "Who else would have been prowling around the ruins? Probably picked us up some time ago and followed us into the downtown area. Wonderful." She had been right. He had been locked in a deathmatch with Vincent Polliard for as long as he could remember. At Colnette, on *Deepfish,* in the underwater tombs of sunken Los Angeles, and now here, in this bizarre Atlantis beneath the rubble of that former metropolis, now also under the sea.

As he watched, two more men came down the *Chasseur's* ladder. That made four. Their attention appeared torn between investigating the *Egg* and gaping at the structures in the main dome past the antechamber. Kelso could sympathize with their astonishment.

"The *Tiburón* is all right." Her voice was low, hardly audible. "Lying still in the interchange ruins. The submersible that was with the *Chasseur* was destroyed by the *Tiburón.* But the *Chasseur* managed to find the funnel without the *Tiburón* knowing where the *Chasseur* had moved. Juan and Carlos have left the *Tiburón* in their diving suits. They are now in the vicinity of the excavation and the funnel."

He wheeled around, knowing he had heard no radio conversation between herself and the Lavaccas. He saw no evidence of a radio anywhere about her. "What are you talking about? How do you know all that?"

Like a mental patient in the throes of withdrawal, she drew up her knees, folded her arms across them in an embryonic huddle, eyes vacuous. "Juan and Carlos are extensions—of myself. They are androids, automatons, tools—of myself—or rather, of Naravamintara."

"More revelations. That one's the most believable yet." A long-practiced habit kept him affecting a coarse derision he did not feel. "Well, it looks like we're going to have a full house down here. But Polliard and his toughs didn't come for poker. They like an uglier game. Other revelations will have to wait, I think. I just hope your two 'extensions' get here pretty quick, because all we have for toys are our knives and that damned sopo gun over there."

"The Lavaccas are—against me. They obey *them,* it, the implant. They obey Naravamintara." She sounded drugged, remote.

"Oh," he said stupidly, drugged himself by all that had happened. "Well, Polliard doesn't know where we are. However, if they poke around much, they'll find us. It's my guess that that front door will open for anybody who stands in front of it, just like that funnel will likely suck anybody in that gets near it." Then why hadn't it sucked in all of Los

Angeles and the bloody Pacific besides? Stupid questions, Kelso. Nothing had made a hell of a lot of sense since that day she first found him on Islip Island.

"It doesn't matter," she said, looking at the disc.

"That point of view's beginning to get on my nerves." Kelso watched the televised scene on the wall. Polliard and louts were approaching the first outlying buildings, weapons ready, moving cautiously in a tight diamond formation, obviously expecting trouble to come from any direction. They moved a little like sleepwalkers, no doubt dazed by their present environs. "Where do those two side doors down there in the main room go?"

"It doesn't matter. We stay here. By this." She indicated the disc with an automatic jerk of the head, as if it had been yanked by an invisible string.

"No thanks. It all sounds like a tale conjured up by a lunatic, but at this point I'm taking no chances." He started for the stunner in the corner.

"Jack Kelso, you suffer from an illusion which your contemptible culture has engendered and nourished for millennia. You are a perfect example of the piteous deification of *ego!* Of inflated self-importance! You are a drunkard, a thief, a fool! You are nothing. A narcissistic pestilence only a hairsbreadth removed from animals. You are all Naravamintara loathes. Naravamintara is all. Naravamintara rules! Naravamintara is perfection!"

He had checked his step toward the gun at the first sound of that hated voice, had taken this venemous broadside without turning, but now he turned. Her drawn and contorted face suggested one caught in the grip of demonic possession. Whatever else he might disbelieve, or try to disbelieve, he had some time ago resigned himself to the fact that her mind was being overcome by something not her own, that she had fought against it, fought against it still, and, despite apparent moments of regaining control, continued to lose. But what good was this realization? What the hell could he do? Could he pull her out of this hideous duality, help Judith DeFond defeat this—Vidyun? He had to try.

"Sure!" he shouted, as enraged at his own helplessness as he was at what she—it—had just said. "I've heard it one way or another all my life. In the greater scheme of things you and I don't amount to beans. Right, Judith? Sure. Did the U.S. government or Universal Resources, Incorporated let the public know what they'd detected under the San Gabriels?

Hell no! They kept it under wraps and began to blow the area apart with nuclear detonations, didn't they! That's why my family died, at least the way I see it. In the greater scheme of things of the powers-that-be, their lives didn't amount to beans. Well I say bullshit to that. That's my philosophy. Bullshit to your greater scheme of things. Bullshit to your goddamn Naravamintara! Maybe I've survived for no other reason than to say that." He was raving, not reasoning, but what made him think reason would work?

"Yes." She nodded mechanically. "We will go together."

"Not the way you—they—have planned."

She pushed up her chin to face him, or *it* did. "Those who sent me are wiser than you," she rasped, "wiser than me. Their reason for being is much higher. The highest—"

He knelt; he took her shoulders, hoping he could revive the one he wanted, wrench her from this thing that again had hold. "Judith, listen to me. *Judith!*" He shook her. "We're the porpoise being told we should sacrifice ourselves to the almighty military mentality as kamikaze bomb carriers, so the higher purpose of homo sapiens can be served. We're the poisoned fish in the rivers, dying so the big factories can dump the wastes from their manufactured claptrap into our waters. We're the American Indian and the African Negro being told by the invading European that our way and our lives amount to little or nothing! Mulch under the heel of the Great White Race! We're anyone, anywhere, being told by the death-worshiping utopians and the greed-crazed plutocrats that we're only grist under the grindstone of their superior mill! *Their* utopia! *Their* profit! *Our* immolation!"

For an infinitesimal moment her eyes flickered with life and he thought he was getting through. Then: "You must surrender yourself to something higher," she yelled, all at once shaking violently. "You must give yourself up to a higher good!"

"There is no higher good than the self! Without the self there would be no consciousness and no conscience, and therefore no conception of any bloody higher good! Without the individual, there would be no race. Without the individual will to live, there would be no life!" He was raving again, bellowing simplicities, but it felt good to rave. If he believed in anything, he believed in this, and he would, paradoxically —and quixotically, perhaps—die to defend it.

But his eloquence had fallen on deaf ears. Her head had sagged, oblivious. He took her face, jerked it up, forced those once again vacuous eyes to look at him. He would try once more. Everything else was forgotten—Polliard, the Lavaccas, this inexplicable city without a name—and when he spoke, his words stumbled over themselves, hampered by both anger and anguish, and with even an element of prayer.

"Look. Supposing what you claim is true, how do you know that your 'race,' the ones who sent you here, aren't wrong? How do you know they aren't—how do you know they aren't some kind of evolutionary aberration, aren't in fact *evil?* If—if you can't remember them, how—then how can you remember—if you ever knew—what ends they serve? Judith? Listen to me! How do you know they don't have corrupt motives for having this place destroyed? How do you know they didn't want this place destroyed because if men found out about it, it would endanger their own designs of conquest or rule? Didn't you tell me they—"

Her throat made a gasping, choking noise; her mouth wagged, trying to speak. She seized her neck as though trying to squeeze out the words that were being held back. Her eyes swam, trying to focus; a minute but unmistakable light whirled up out of their emptiness. Suddenly wide and stricken, they glared at him. "Yes!" her voice burst out. "I—Jack—"

"What?"

"True!" It was almost a scream.

"What's true?"

"Naravamintara—a tyranny!" This was wrung from her chest as from one crumbling inside. "Yes! Yes! Yes!" she yelled at the censurer only she could hear. "An interstellar empire fraught with internal decay—fears Earth's discovery of this city because—because discovery could throw humanity into interstellar space! Jack—don't know what powers here—but they fear men finding it—yes!—fear if men found it—provide unlimited energy—food—stop war, diseases—Earth united in a stellar consciousness—radically advance man's outlook—" She fought for breath, fought to get it all out. "Wanted to—wanted you to help me save it—"

Relentless in his need to comprehend, Kelso threw her one more question. "One thing still doesn't make any sense. If the technology here is so powerful, why doesn't Naravamintara use it to help save its own neck?"

She shook her head, hair falling like a curtain around her face. "Don't know, don't know. Maybe no good . . . to them." Exhausted, she was swiftly fading. "Maybe wouldn't help . . .

them . . . their problems." She clamped her head between her hands, swaying back and forth. "Already have . . . this technology . . . won't help them. They—I don't think they— Ach! Ohh, Jack. Help me—maybe get out some way—don't know . . . how maybe . . . get out . . . tell others . . . city can save—"

Preoccupied with all she'd said, he was slow in noticing the sudden alteration. She went rigid, face cemented in pallid resolution, then sprang to her feet and dived to the corner carrel. When he realized what had happened and started to react, she had the pistol in her hand, pointed at him.

"Jack!" It was Judith's tormented voice that cried out but it was the implant's power that pulled the trigger.

29. THE TURNING

Attempts now to push back the enveloping inner darkness weakened further whatever was left of her will. The implant's control seemed to wax and wane, but it now had indisputable rule. As from a great and misty distance, she watched her body move.

REMEMBER YOUR ORIGINS, YOUR HERITAGE, YOUR RACE. REMEMBER YOUR DUTY TO YOUR RACE. THERE IS NOTHING BUT YOUR DUTY NOW, NOTHING BUT THE DISC.

Race? Origins? Of what race did . . . I . . .

THE MAN WAS NOTHING. YOU HAVE SLIPPED INTO PRIMITIVE EMOTIONALISM, INTO BASE SENTIMENTALITY AND BACKWARD CONFUSIONS, BUT YOU WILL REDEEM VIDYUN NOW. THE MAN WAS NOTHING.

The nimbus of consciousness palpitated fitfully, like an expiring heart. *And Vidyun is nothing,* the implant had said in some earlier admonition. *Vidyun is not, was never, important.* Then why should . . . failure mean anything . . . to . . .

Vidyun? How could a nothing... care about duty? How could... a nothing... care?

The question was swathed in blackness, and she continued to be propelled toward the disc.

There was motion in the wall viewer, and she saw in a vague way, from that dim distance, that Juan and Carlos were now in the antechamber, both armed and walking onto the open area at the edge of the city. Their diving gear lay near the battered *Egg;* they had descended the funnel, leaving the *Tiburón* resting on the slope outside the freeway interchange ruins. She could still read their "thoughts" but knew that, at the present, she could exert no influence on their actions at all.

But she heard that *voice* intervene, speaking to the Lavaccas through the device in her own brain, perhaps, or maybe her implant could pick up what was being sent straight to the Lavaccas, who were implants themselves.

FOUR WITH HEAVY WEAPONS. The information sent to the androids was immediate, automatic, upon their leaving the antechamber behind, and was received in the same way. *MOVING THROUGH THE OUTLYING BUILDINGS TOWARD THE CENTER.*

Vaguely, she reflected that whether they succeeded in subduing the Polliard intruders or not did not matter. All would go with the city, taking its secrets with them. All would go.

No... no... no. It was weak, but a protest. No matter. She stood now over the disc, unable to freeze her limbs. Arms moved; hands gripped its intricately designed rim.

A muffled spitting and popping noise came from outside. The Lavaccas had made contact with the *Chasseur's* crew. But she could not read the details. Instructions, pulses of data concerning the closing down of the systems linked to the disc overrode all else. Efforts to regain power over her motor nerves were in vain; her fingers only closed more tightly on the disc's rim.

Drift, that failing remnant of life that was hers whispered weakly. *Do not listen. Let go. Relax. Breathe deeply, inhale, exhale. Inhale... exhale. Relax. Your feet. Your legs... Do not obey. Drift....*

Your body. They made it what it is, but you must make it yours.

A deeper darkness; the instructions of the implant, incessantly being repeated, receding. A swim in darkness. A liquid night country. Light. Flecks of light appear and disappear. Forms trying to take shape out of the black. Eyes. Clusters of eyes. Here. There. Gone.

Another form. Summer-lit. Graceful. Moving across the night. Moving across the . . . dancing. A ballet in a tiny isolated spot of sunlight performed by a . . . girl.

Judith. Running naked, long hair streaming behind. Running upward. Running across disc-shaped crystals, ascending a crystal stairway whose steps are discs.

An alcove at the top of the steps, faintly aglow against the night. A foyer with vaulted ceiling. Mist. Something standing in the dim foyer. A form without limbs. A dark figure with no face, no eyes, no mouth. But wait. The figure is somehow familiar. It is robed, has a backward-sloping head, a humped back. No, the hump is an extension of the head. It is . . .

Vidyun? Vidyun's *master*? One of *them*?

. . . there was music in the branches and leaves of trees . . . in the fan of sunlight from the underside of cloud . . . there was music in the way your feet touched grass and the way your limbs moved as though dancing in air . . . songs in the lap of water against its shore and songs in the fall of moonlight on the seaways and this music, these songs, permeated your spirit the way the sunlight filled the grass, and you learned to sing them, learned to sing with the birds that sang to you of sky secrets, learned to sing with the land and sky creatures that carried you far upon their accommodating backs, learned to sing with the sea creatures that took you over and under the sea . . . all this was yours, and you sang in celebration of being and of being in communication with others of your kind, in a language only those of Onnah know, in a symphony that proclaimed the beauty and joy of what it is to simply be. . . .

Wait! Come back. Don't fade. PLEASE!

Whence came this strange thoughtstream, this whispering of a music, of a mindsong, of Onnahlaeti? It was the same she had felt several times before—stronger now, yet unable to sustain its strength. . . .

The foyer again. And the overpowering influence of the implant.

YES, YOU WERE A CHILD OF ONNAHLAETI. CONSCRIPTED IN THE SIXTEENTH TURN OF THAT WORLD AROUND ITS SUN. YOU WERE TAKEN TO THE IMPERIAL CITY OF NAMMAVA TRAH II AND SCHOOLED IN SOLDIERY. YOU BECAME ONE OF

THE MASTERS' FAVORITES. YOU EXCELLED IN ALL YOU UNDERTOOK. YOU EXCELLED MOST IN COURAGE AND DEVOTION TO THE REALM. YOU WERE ONE OF THE FAVORED ONES, ONE OF THE TRUSTED ONES. YOU WILL BE FOREVER KNOWN AS SUCH. YOU WILL CAST YOUR BIRTH-WORLD, ONNAHLAETI, IN EVERLASTING GLORY. YOU WILL BE REVERED THROUGHOUT THE EMPIRE.

No!

A tugging at her limbs, her flesh. Her flesh felt pulled by a force emanating from the foyer. She was pulled toward the form inside, bones becoming pliant, about to dissolve. . . .

No! Vidyun is nothing! Vidyun is dead. Naravamintara is dead!

She threw herself upon the last crystal disc. She clung to it, trying to withstand the pulling force from the foyer. She clung for an eternity.

The alcove quivered, disintegrated, whirled downward into oblivion as though swallowed by its own power to consume.

She tried to let go the crystal wheel, tried to thrash upward, fighting for light. The wheel trammeled, held her to the void. It began to turn. Round and round it spun until she was hurled away and the reeling wheel became a funnel that sucked itself into nothingness.

Feeling slowly returned to her fingers, hands, arms, legs, seeped back into her body by degrees. When at last she regained total consciousness, she found herself collapsed over the disc. Its occult figures winked and blinked in her face, painting the upper part of her exhausted and aching body in pale prismatic hues. Horrified, she saw that it had turned.

Judith pulled herself together, pushed herself up and shrank away from the coruscating patterns on the face of the disc.

Awareness grew, expanding its previously minuscule perimeters.

The gunfire outside had stopped. Juan and Carlos? The telepathic links with the twin analogues seemed severed. Had the Lavaccas killed Polliard and his men?

No answer. Nothing left of her former unbreakable bonds with the haunting androids.

And the implant, Vidyun's persona, whatever had beaten

and slashed her mind into helpless submission, also seemed to have vanished.

Why?

She stared at the flickering disc, at the strange glyphs that were the language of an intelligence more alien than she could conceive. Could she reverse it? How? Would it do any good now if she could? Which way had she turned it to begin with?

"Vince!"

She spun around, too quick. Dizziness overcame her. She swayed, groping for support. When her vision cleared, she saw, in the parted aperture in the front wall, a man in a black diving suit, his left arm ripped to the shoulder and smeared with blood. A blunt-snouted weapon jutted from his other hand. Above the black suit his face was chalk white.

"Come look what we got here, Vince!" the man said. "It's a sea sprite. Yeah! And a familiar one at that." Though he affected a brave air, it was obvious from the way his voice shook that he was either weak from loss of blood or had been scared half out of his wits by the fight he'd been through, or both.

Another man appeared, silhouetted in the aperture. Even in silhouette, she recognized him at once. He pushed anxiously past the wounded one and into the room, his sharply etched features becoming detailed in the room's eerie light, lined with fatigue, confusion and fear. Suddenly she recalled the dark black-robed figure in the alcove of her trance, the elongated cranial ridge down the back like the long beak of a carrion bird turned rearward to preen.

"You!" He raised his gun. "Who are *you*? What are you doing up there? Where are we? What is all this?"

The bitterly ironic similarity of Polliard's questions to those Jack Kelso had asked did not escape her. "It's what you've been looking for, Polliard, for many years."

"Yes? What do you know about what I've been looking for?" He started forward, then, checking himself, proceeded with more caution, looking about. The wounded one followed. "I've wondered what your game was from the beginning. You've got a lot of explaining—" He halted, seeing the prostrate form of Kelso on the platform floor to the right of the disc.

"Who is that on the floor up there?"

"Jack Kelso," she said softly.

"Kelso! What's—is he—what's the matter with him?"

"He is dead. I killed him." These words in her mouth were ash. Having said them, she realized there was no need to say anything more, to do anything more. It seemed he had been right. Evil reigned, evil won. The fight had been futile from the first.

"We wanted the satisfaction," the other man spat.

"Why did you kill him?" Polliard demanded suspiciously.

"She's got a pistol, Vince."

"I see it." Polliard raised his weapon. "On the floor. Now!"

She obeyed. The stunner clattered at her feet.

"What's that behind you?" The URI agent was unmistakably shaken by his surroundings, so much so that he overlooked the fact that she had failed to answer his question as to why she'd killed Kelso.

"This?" She turned her back on him, faced the disc and touched the intricate fretwork with her fingertips. The entire disc was now alive with iridescent pulsations that flashed up at her like malevolent eyes. Weary, numb, disoriented, defeated, all she could think of at the moment was the absurdity, the injustice, of Jack Kelso's death place having to be shared with obscenities such as these.

"I don't trust her, Vince. She's up to something up there."

"Take your hands off that!" Polliard leapt to the platform, grabbed her by the hair, and jerked her backward. The muzzle of the gun he held jabbed her in the belly.

"Spit it out! Who are you? Where are we? What does all this mean? Who put it here? What is its purpose?"

She looked up with defiance. "I don't know who put it here, and it has for many centuries been defunct."

He stared at her, confused; it was hardly the answer he'd expected. He let go her hair and struck her hard across the face with his free hand. The blow sent her staggering back against the disc but he caught her and snatched her away from it again.

"I will make good my former promise to disembowel you, with extreme pleasure!"

"Doesn't look like she'd be too bad a piece at that, Vince." The wounded man laughed nervously. "Know how to fix a mangled arm, sister?"

"Where are we?" Polliard yelled in her face. He seemed close to hysteria himself. "I knew you wanted to go into the Zone for an extraordinary reason. I *knew* it! I knew something extraordinary was up when I found out you had taken on stores and the rumheaded captain who sold them to you would not—not even after he was beaten to mush—could not tell us where you and Kelso were going or what you were looking for. But *this!* What is it? Where are we? Who put it here? Talk!"

The inside of her mouth was cut, and the blood tasted of salt. With his mention of the captain of the *P. B. Baylor*, she was reminded how she had intuited the similarities between Vincent Polliard and the creature called Salieu Vidyun, the creature she was forced to be some time ago, long before the vision she'd had of the sinister figure in the sable robe. It occurred to her that Vincent Polliard, though he would certainly not know of Naravamintara, nonetheless belonged to its dark fraternity, in spirit if not in reality, and, were the proper connections made, would have probably served its masters well. But only if it served Polliard's purpose to do so. Vidyun, she was certain, had had no purpose other than service to the masters.

"This," she said wearily, "is the place you've been coming to all your life, I suppose. As well as I." And *him*, she thought of Kelso.

As suddenly as before, Polliard released her hair and hit her in the face. This time the blow brought her down.

"Okay. We'll get it out of you one way or the other." He unsheathed a knife from his left hip. As the other man dropped his weapon and tried to pin her arms, Polliard thrust the curved blade into the material between her breasts and moved the knife downward with sufficient strength to split the coverall open and cut her skin.

She gasped with the sudden pain. A thin line of blood appeared from her sternum of her groin.

"Hey, Vince, don't damage the goods too much."

"Shut up."

She wondered if her reflexes were dead. Had the foregoing ordeal with Kelso, with the implant and the disc, so depleted her strength? Had the implant burned away all ability to react, so that she could do nothing but let this bastard knock her around and mutilate her like this? Or did she even care enough to fight, now that the disc had been irrevocably set, now that Kelso was dead?

"One more time," Polliard warned, the sweat on his face glistening in the circumambient light like oil boiling out of a melting bust of wax.

The knife point pressing against her abdomen precluded

any movement on her part, even had she the will to move. She had to ignore the pain the blade caused when she inhaled. "This is what you've been looking for for years, Polliard. What Universal Resources and the American government paid you to try to find. This is what URI geophysicists picked up on their instruments over ten years ago. This is what they set up the Devil's Canyon Project for, though they didn't know it. This is what they drilled under the San Gabriels to find." She swallowed the blood coating the inside of her mouth, wincing once when the knife cut deeper after she took a breath. "This is what—this was the cause of the San Andreas disaster, the cause of Los Angeles sinking, because when URI probed, the automatic defenses here were activated."

Polliard was for the moment unable to speak. Despite the chill, sweat continued to run down his face. He gazed up, around, dark brows raised in bewilderment.

"Sounds crazy to me, Vince."

"How do you know all this? Who are *you?*"

She felt a strange pleasue in what she was about to reply—but did not get the chance. At that moment Jack Kelso groaned.

Astonished, she did not at first believe it. Then it struck her that the dosage dial on the stunner's frame, turned to the maximum setting when she had climbed out of the *Egg*, must have been knocked off the lethal notch when Kelso threw it away. In which case, he was not dead, merely unconscious, now coming around—

A freshly alert Polliard had tossed his head in the direction of the noise. The wounded man let go of her to seize his weapon.

She tensed. All their deaths might be inevitable, but she would not sit idle and watch these two slash him to ribbons while he lay drugged. When Polliard stood to swing his gun on Kelso, she saw her opportunity and went for the one with the wound.

With the knowledge that Kelso still lived, her lethargy seemed to have evaporated. Before the man realized she'd moved, she had her own knife out of its scabbard and into his chest, plunged straight through his ribs to his heart.

"Vin—" He fell as she wrestled the gun from his hands.

Polliard swung back around, too late. On her knees, she fired. The instantaneous beam riveted him to the fretwork on the far wall. He went stiff, rising on tiptoes, eyes rolling upward into his skull. In that moment she saw again, in more detail this time, others dying before a weapon she—Vidyun—had wielded. Beings of varied shape and size, color and mien, fell numberless, nameless. And among the corpses walked several tall figures robed in black. Their hands glinted, were silver or bronze or gray in color; their white eyes pierced the darkness of the plain. Though they did not speak, they conveyed their approval of the work of Salieu Vidyun. . . .

She pulled herself back to the present and saw the irradiated husk that had been Vincent Polliard slide down the wall to the floor. It was then, when she looked up from the dead man, still dazed by the memory of thousands of others slain, that she noticed the disc had begun to turn on its own. A sudden belief she might still prevent the city's dematerialization by stopping it threw Judith DeFond at its face.

But an electrifying pain, like a million needles shooting through her brain, paralyzed her in midstride, and she crumpled.

30. ESCAPE

The vibration in the floor was his first sensation. He felt it in every nerve, every muscle. Raising himself up, squinting in the oppressively omnipresent light, he tried to clear his spinning head. Gradually, the alcove and its decorous walls, the scintillating disc, the ceiling—and three inert bodies—came into focus.

Judith sat across the alcove, back against the wall, head flung forward and disheveled hair down the front, through which he could see that her suit had been ripped open and her chest scored by a long knife wound.

Shakily, he stood, head still swimming from the fading effects of the stunner's soporific. The room tilted and veered, blurred and slowly returned to its proper order.

He heard a low, humming noise and associated it with the

vibration in the floor. He glanced at the disc. Blue and yellow patterns glowed, like St. Elmo's fire, from its rim. On the wall behind it, kaleidoscopic arrays oscillated, rearranged themselves into new configurations.

"Judith?" His voice sounded strange, unreal here.

She did not move.

Crossing the space between them in two quick steps, Kelso bent down, took her wrist and felt her pulse. It was slow but steady. He saw then that the blood along the knife cut had coagulated, that the wound was superficial.

"Judith!" He shook her.

Head lolling, she moaned. Her eyes flitted open, empty, closed again.

Kelso slapped her cheek. "Judith, come out of it!"

Unexpectedly, she rolled away, eyes opening and closing, opening again to stare at him with that glazed expression he'd seen too many times before. But this time he realized that she did not recognize him, or recognized him in some way he could not understand.

She reached sluggishly for the gun on her right. Kelso pulled her away. Her nails darted for his face. He wrestled her beneath him, clamped her arms wide to each side and pinned her body with his own. She kicked and heaved, but he was heavier and his grip was strong.

"Judith, come back!"

Her struggles subsided, and she lay breathing heavily, eyes closed. The knife cut had reopened, and now bled in several places, not profusely, but enough to warrant dressing. He looked around, tried to think of something to use. He wore nothing which could be improvised—

A loud snap made him look up. A crack had appeared in the wall above the disc. As soon as he saw it, the crack splintered into others that moved off in branches from the first. The floor, he noticed, had begun to tremble violently. He heard other cracking noises, a low rumble and thrum somewhere.

All at once the full weight of their predicament hit him. Frightened, trapped, and thinking again that if he lost her, he would once more lose it all, he rose, head raised toward the ceiling. He wanted something to materialize there, something he could fight, smash, vent his agony on.

"The old earthquake routine?" he bellowed, irrational, near collapse. "Can't you do any better than that? Goddamn you! Goddamn you to hell, whatever, whoever you are!"

Tears came. Stupidly, he shook his fists at the walls, the winking disc, cursing till his voice went hoarse and he sank to his knees, his body shaking with uncontrollable sobs.

The trembling floor finally brought him to his senses. It awakened the old animal impulse to survive, an impulse that had little tolerance for questioning the meaning of things, for impotence or despair. A life-long habit of acting, of doggedly resisting every destructive force hurled his way, made him turn, pull her to him, and stand.

He did not know what to do but, fool that he was, he thought, he would do something. Perhaps in her ambivalent mental state she had not been able to turn the disc all the way to its required position. Perhaps, given the unbelievable age of the city, the self-destructive systems no longer functioned as smoothly or as effectively as they were originally designed to do. Perhaps he had time—to do what?

There was no point in thinking about it. He hefted her to his shoulder. Taking the dead Polliard's weapon from the floor, he moved off the platform and approached the front of the room, determined to blow his way through the wall if it did not open.

It did—with an ominous hissing noise it hadn't made before.

Kelso had no idea where he was going, but supposed he was looking for an exit of some sort. From the steps at the control center, he started down the right branch of the Y, ignoring one charred body—Juan or Carlos?—in the middle of the street.

But an exit into what? Out a side door into water that had to have at least the pressure of thirty atmospheres? Or was this thing embedded under the seafloor? That was more likely.

Up the funnel then? Into radioactive water, with her suit torn open and both of them without—no, suits and masks were at the *Egg*. And it wasn't her diving suit that had been cut into, only her coverall. But how in hell could he get up that funnel without finding its controls and knowing how to reverse its power?

Structures squeaked and groaned around him. From where her head bobbed against his back Judith echoed these noises with the moans of pain or dementia. The hand that held her was sticky with her blood, and he could feel blood on his neck as well. But he could do nothing about her bleeding now.

Irrelevant thoughts came and went, like the incomprehensible arrays above the disc. What *kind* of blood was on his neck? Was her blood like his? How could she be from anywhere but Earth? How could she be anything but human? Incredible, preposterous, insane. All of it was a nightmare from which he would certainly soon awake. In the meantime, he had to find a way out of this mucking place!

His labored breath and the slap of his running feet filled the brief intervals of silence between the other ill-omened sounds. The low oxygen content of the air was presenting a problem.

In the distance he saw the street's end. There were no indications of any exits, as if he'd expected any. Nothing but blank illuminated wall. Now, he saw, the illumination was beginning to lose its intensity.

Okay, he thought, sucking in large amounts of the stingy air. Joint's coming to pieces. If what she said was true regarding that goddamned wheel, rock and sand would bury them soon. When the roof came in. Rock and sand and a trillion tons of sea.

He pivoted, and almost lost his balance. Tired and stooped under her weight, he pushed forward, retracing his steps toward the fork of the Y, back toward the city's other side and the antechamber where the *Egg* sat. He hadn't the strength to run all over, trying to find a way out that he did not believe was there. The place was too vast, the possibility of an exit, one he could deal with, too absurd. What he meant to do when he got back to the *Egg* he did not know, but he knew it was important to keep moving, important to maintain some idea of a tangible objective.

Things whispered and sighed around him as he ran, like the noises, on a much grander scale, a dying star might make. At his feet the street was cracking both lateral and parallel to its course, but the cracks seemed below the surface, dark veins shooting through the lustrous, glasslike material. The entire city was becoming filled with a deep, unnerving hum that hurt his ears and threatened to further hamper his sense of direction and equilibrium. He prayed to nameless and fickle gods even Kelso was willing to concede might be, because just now he had to believe in something beyond himself simply to keep one foot moving in front of the other. Prayed that now, after having come through all this, it would not end the way every indication promised it would end. Prayed that the force holding the huge dome's walls and ceiling held until—until what? Just what in the blazing howling hell did he think he was going to do?

Like a child seeking a security surrogate, all he could think to do was reach the *Egg*, and crawl into it. Its hull could withstand a lot of wallop, though hardly the kind that would come down when that titanic roof fell in. But he had no other choice. He had to take his—their—chances in the *Egg*. The silly name he'd given the submersible might have struck him as perversely ironic and funny, if he'd had a laugh left in him.

Humpty Dumpty beneath a wall. Humpty Dumpty squashed under it all.

He was almost at the end of the avenue when a building on his left came down with a roar. Reflexively, he dodged to the right and looked. There was no dust and no rubble. It was as if the building had become liquid and simply spilled into a pool of its own making. Yet the material still appeared to be in the solid state.

Oh, thou hast seen strange spectacles, Kelso. Thou hast seen things unnamable. Thou hast—

Another roar came from farther behind. Forward, a structure crashed into a plastic-looking puddle the color of tar. With a start, he felt the ground beneath him sag, then swell, then sag again, and saw ahead, as he tried to skirt the puddle that had flowed into the street, that the open space now between himself and the entrance antechamber was beginning to heave.

Wobbling like a storm buoy, fighting to keep his precarious balance as he trudged through the pliant stuff that moved on all sides by this time, he broke from the city's perimeter and lunged, lurched, and staggered over the undulating yard toward the *Egg*.

The span of the open area seemed endless. His agonized lungs felt on fire, and the muscles in his legs quivered and threatened to cramp.

Hissings and gurglings, thunders and groans came from behind, but he kept his attention stubbornly on the unstable ground he was trying to cross. In the distance, the *Egg* and the *Chasseur* rose up, sank down, coming close to bumping or rolling into each other as the antechamber floor swelled and troughed.

Oh, thou wouldst not believe the crazy things old crazy Kelso has seen. Old crazy Kelso doesn't believe them either.

His legs suddenly veered and, on the edge of a trough that had all at once formed in front of him, he fell. Judith rolled from his grasp. Exhausted, gasping for breath and feeling the sickening creep of fatigue snare his legs, his arms, his hands, he lay in the trough for a moment's desperately needed rest.

She moaned and, huddling into a fetal curl, was carried on the slow wave's crest along with Kelso into the next trough. The undulations were quickly becoming turbulent enough to make walking all but impossible. There was no time for rest.

He reached for her, fumbled, rolled, reached again, got hold of the torn front of her coverall, pulled her up and pushed himself erect. By moving at a low crouch with legs spread, Judith slung straight athwart his back, and bracing himself for each heave and plunge, he inched forward.

A driven animal who'd abrogated all senses save one, he was determined to reach the submersible, and kept mind and body concentrated on that purpose. He could have made it with much less difficulty, of course, had he let her go, but whatever she was, or had been, wherever she'd come from, somehow a living and revitalizing chemistry had flowed between them. Diabolical alien from a deathworld, or redeeming angel from the stars, both or neither, she had made him care and feel again, made him want to live for something other than a demented vindictiveness. He would carry her if it cost him his life, because he could think of no other reason he wanted to live in the first place.

Within a meter of the *Egg*, he fell once more. He crawled, dragging her with him, found a purchase on an outside ring and hauled himself and her to the ladderway. Mustering his last bit of strength, he lifted her over his right shoulder and climbed.

One . . . two . . . three . . . four . . . five. . . . Painfully, with each grasp of the ladder feeling as though it would be his last, he slowly ascended toward the hatch.

The *Egg* lifted and dropped, precariously canting at the peak of each swell toward the Polliard minisub. The ladderway swayed and rocked him from one side to the other, making it doubly hard to hang on.

Far off—it seemed to come from up the dark funnel beyond the antechamber wall—he heard rumbling. He had reached the hatch at last, and was sliding Judith in, holding her by the hands till her feet touched, or almost touched, the

Egg's inside deck, when, sensing something, he looked upward and saw that the antechamber ceiling had begun to contract.

He had to let go of her, hoping she would fall to the pile of life preservers behind the ballast tanks. But, as luck would have it, another swell lifted the submersible and she landed forward.

Telling himself that maybe the fall did no serious harm, he followed, closing and dogging the damaged hatch as best he could. It would not close well enough for the gasket to seal perfectly, but there was nothing he could do about that. Once inside and down the interior ladder to the deck, he realized there was nothing else he could do about anything.

At last giving in to the demands of his depleted body, Kelso collapsed in the pilot's seat and stared dully at the woman lying at the bottom of the ladder. He should have examined her knife wound, but was too spent to move.

Beyond the nose viewport, he watched the city continue to pour and heave in upon itself. Dimly, he had a momentary pang of loss as he saw something falling to ruin that would never be again, something whose origins and whose age, not to mention its builders, challenged all knowledge and belief. This astounding city under sunken Los Angeles, a city it had destroyed, was itself being destroyed. Artifact of an extraterrestrial culture, center of energies that had split the earth, no one would believe it had ever existed even if he and she, its last witnesses, could have made it to the top to tell. . . .

The distant roar had grown louder and all at once he knew what it was. Turning to look at the rear viewport, he saw a wall of debris-laden water come cascading into the antechamber from the funnel's maw. Whatever force had held the sea at bay had lost its power.

Helpless, Kelso gritted his teeth and watched it come crashing against the *Egg*. He gripped the side of the seat with one hand and reached for Judith with the other as the impact knocked him sideways and he felt the *Egg* lift and tumble in the torrent.

The water had the strength of a tidal wave. He had just thrown the submersible's pressure-system lever when he was jarred from the seat and battered from equipment to instruments like a squash ball. He grabbed at clothes, lifejackets, anything that might serve as cushions or shock absorbers, and tried to cover Judith with these scant odds and ends. Then he tried to shield her with his own wearied flesh. Though he knew it was hopeless, he would fight to his last miserable gasp to save her.

By this time totally engulfed, the *Egg* rose with the inrushing flood. Once it struck the *Chasseur* with a bone-shaking jolt. In those terrifying moments while he lay holding to the ballast tanks, the ladder, whatever came to hand that was anchored, pinning Judith under him and trying to ward off objects that careened around the interior of the somersaulting submersible, he had bleary and broken glimpses out the wheeling viewports.

He thought of Vincent Polliard, dead now, as he soon would be. He thought of an afternoon sunset off Islip Island with a young woman approaching in an unmarked boat. He thought of an island with a sunlit cove, and an afternoon of ecstasy and anguish, of questions that had been answered and of new ones raised that now would never be answered. He thought of such things as fate and secret burdens, of the storm-tossed heart not being the sole province of the inhabitants of dilemma-ridden Terra. He thought of mistakes, of guilt, and of graves.

What he saw out the viewports was churning black sea.

Rock me, he sang silently, holding on, holding on. *Rock me on the water. I'll get down to the sea somehow . . . .*

31. VICTORY

Cinara Tlii had pulled the deflagrator from her belt, but, before she could fire, Acexea's huge gloved hand covered her own.

"There is much here we may find useful," he said, forcing the weapon to be aimed at the floor. "Things here that, in themselves, are neither good nor evil, but become so through the uses to which they are put. From what this one has told us, you may find the transformation machinery of good use."

"No," Tlii said. "No.'" The desire to destroy the black-robed filth before her, the chamber, everything in it, consumed her.

"Cinara," Falur said gently. "Only through this chamber's instruments and through the Yaghattarin themselves will we be able to learn anything more."

"What more is there to learn? You heard what he said. Vidyun is dead."

"No. Altered. And not altered much, since, according to the Silver One here, the people where Vidyun was sent are similar to ourselves."

"Altered!" Tlii cried. "Changed. Changed irrevocably. Lost!"

"Perhaps not. But in destroying this place, in destroying all the Deathlords, you destroy all chance of our ever knowing otherwise." The boy retrieved the lightcrystal Tlii had dropped, and confronted the Yaghattarin who cowered against the wall of instruments.

"Can Vidyun be recalled?" Falur said. "Can you bring Vidyun back? Can we reverse the process by which you transformed him into a being like those where he was sent?"

The Yaghattarin heard, but did not answer immediately. The keening reply, when it came, was ear-splitting. "It is too late. Salieu Vidyun has been forever consecrated in service to Nammava Trah and the Eternal Imperium."

"Prove to us it is too late," Falur demanded. "Show us how and why it is too late. You have communication with the outguard ships that keep watch over the sector in which the planet is located. We want a complete and immediate report on Vidyun from the vessel nearest his location."

"It is too late," the Deathlord said again. "It is too late."

Tlii fought to raise her weapon. Acexea let her go. Beside herself, she fired. The flash was instant. The Yaghattarin flared and sank, a shrunken, smoldering shell. The section of wall behind where he'd stood exuded an acrid vapor from its blackened, half-melted face.

Having at last done something to release the grief and tension, Tlii let go the deflagrator and dropped to her knees. She folded her arms against her chest, lowered her head and began to murmur despondently.

"Cinya, please." Falur knelt beside her. "Let me tell you. I have learned many things since leaving the place of the Arkhatin. Most of all, I have learned that the universe, as the old ones say, is infinite in all aspects, is vast and diverse beyond our knowledge or ability to know. When the Yaghattarin came, we were helpless, innocent, ignorant. We are by nature passive, quiescent. It has never been our way to fight, or to doubt the basic benevolence of Being. We have accepted life as being good, a gift, in all its manifestations. But we did not know all the forms life could take, and we have suffered gravely for our ignorance." Falur took Tlii's trembling hands, continued in the same soft and earnest way. "We learned of evil, evil in the form of purity and perfection, as the Yaghattarin characterized themselves and their ideals. That purity, that evil, was one ruled by tyranny and total intolerance of other entities and lifeways. The Deathlords hated the Arkhalahn, the ones they called the Adulterators, because the Arkhalahn mixed with other races. But mixing is not necessarily evil. It is one of life's fundamental conditions. This is knowledge. We cannot succumb to intolerance the way the Yaghattarin did. We cannot let what has happened here immutably alter *us*. Even though we have had to destroy to regain our freedom, we must not become destroyers out of intolerance for things we do not understand."

Tlii tried to take her hands away.

"Please, Cinya. My words, my thoughts, are your own. There will be other Yaghattarin who have not been killed, certainly others who will know the secrets of this chamber. We will have them come here. We will have them show proof of Vidyun's death. Do you hear?"

Tlii lifted her head but did not look at the boy. "I hear. But I will not look upon another Deathlord. We will send out the mindmusic. We will search for Vidyun with our hearts."

"I think we will need the help of the Yaghattarin and their outguard ship, Cinara. Please. Do not let what has happened to us make you inflexible. It is true we have changed and can never go back to what we were before the Deathlords came to Onnahlaeti. But in throwing off their stranglehold, we must not become as they were, must not come to strangle ourselves with hate and the will to destroy."

Falur picked up the deflagrator and handed it to Acexea. The Prithipean, having patiently and silently stood aside during what could only have been to him another one of those queer Onnahlaetian exchanges concerning the states of their souls, took it and said, "The revolt here will soon be approaching its final stages. Once the remaining pockets of resistance in Nammava Trah II are eliminated, I will give permission to a number of the armies to depart Naravamintara, to return to their homeworlds so that they may remake their civilizations according to their ways. Battles will be fought in other parts of the empire for some time to come but the main tasks left onplanet will be to bring the Xlimoyin, the Hrarghals and C'rimaens under control before they have pillaged and ravaged everything and created a war within the Alliance. And," Acexea acknowledged, "to settle the question that concerns you here. I must see to the former task. I leave you with two of my lieutenants to help you in accomplishing the latter." The Prithipean bowed his head briefly, turned and, uttering commands to his soldiers, was gone.

"Cinya?"

"Send the Prithipeans away."

Falur hesitated but finally turned to the two lieutenants and said, "Please go. We wish to be alone here. We must be alone for a time, to decide what we will do."

The soldiers nodded and reluctantly moved to the charred corridor outside. But there they waited, within calling distance of the transformation chamber.

32. DELIVERANCE

Droplets of water fell at intervals on Kelso from the dorsal hatch directly above. It was this minute ablution that woke him.

He lay wedged between the ballast tanks and the attitude control cylinder. From the horrendous throb in his skull, he surmised something had hit him a heavy blow—or he had hit something. When he reached up to feel, dried blood at the hairline confirmed it. This and the many additional aches and pains throughout his body made him conclude he was indisputably and incredibly alive.

The submersible apparently lay upright and was still.

From his jammed position, he could raise his pounding head slightly and look out the rear viewport. He saw what must have been sea, with just enough light filtering through the water to indicate that the surface (or the source of light, whatever it was) could not be far away.

Only one of the interior overhead lights still worked.

He sought Judith with his hands, felt pieces of equipment, the deck, the tanks. He craned his neck, turned, looking behind him as best he could. Then he saw her.

Huddled at the foot of the co-pilot's seat, lying on her side, she had her eyes open, staring at him. But her stare was such that he did not feel she actually saw him. She had tried to pull the front of the suit together, and Kelso seized on this fact as evidence that she retained some degree, however small, of thought or reflex.

"Are you all right?" he said hoarsely, asking the impossible.

She did not answer. Her face was wan, her lips bloodless.

Kelso squirmed out of his entanglement with the gear. Every muscle and joint screamed in protest. He got up wincing, clamping his jaws against the myriad pinpricks of pain.

The *Egg*'s interior was a mess. He stumbled to the nose, rubbing a hand behind his neck in an attempt to relieve the soreness there.

"Never believed—don't see how—" But he was muttering only to himself. Her face was like stone.

The only feasible explanation he could come up with was the water that had entered the antechamber from the funnel had pushed the *Egg* upward through a rift in the splitting ceiling. This seemed damned improbable, considering the weight of the water that had to have come down from above when the ceiling collapsed. Yet if, by the time the ceiilng had begun to fall, the antechamber was already filled, and the *Egg* had consequently been pushed upward far enough.... To hell with it; it was too much for him now. He—they—were alive and it was up to him to see that they stayed that way.

A second glance at Judith, however, didn't do much to reassure him. He had yet to determine just what being alive meant in her case.

Outside the *Egg*, what he could see of the water appeared

turbid. He tried the switches for the outside lights. None of them worked. Looking up at the numerous lumps in the ceiling, the loosened wires and other paraphernalia hanging down, made him doubt that anything would work. But the leak in the hatch was not bad. Things could be worse.

He took the pilot's seat, tried the master switch. Some of the instruments on the console lit up, some didn't. The sonar was dead. He tried the ascent button, blowing ballast.

The *Egg* shuddered. The familiar whoosh of the intake tanks being cleared came up from under the deck. The submersible began to rise.

Kelso risked trying the jets. Ominous noises ensued, but finally the *Egg* rattled and gurgled forward. He tried the nose lights again. No nose lights. The tail. No tail lights. He turned on the commset.

"Chief, this is Kelso. Do you read me?"

Silence. Not even static or background noise on the receiver.

He repeated the transmission but no answer was returned.

Well, by Jesus, if he had to get out and swim every square centimeter on this side of the Pacific, he'd find that sub.

Then he remembered the Lavaccas had shut down the *Tiburón*'s computer, had at least shut down its higher level functions. His only chance then was to surface and risk being picked up by the SASP. God only knew where they were. He was assuming he was out of the city, and if his theory about having been pushed up through the opening ceiling of the dome was correct, the strength of those underwater currents created by the city's collapse could have taken them anywhere. He had no idea how much time had elapsed after he was knocked out. They could be west of the bay; they could be in the San Gabriels.

He cut the jets and was about to turn to see if he could do something for Judith's wound, when he saw a faintly flashing light ahead.

The light was flashing code. He waited, heart hammering.

A long flash, two short, a long and three short together, two short and one long.

T . . . I . . . B . . . U—

Hell's hounds! It was the submarine! But how—

He turned, was about to shout the news to DeFond, then checked himself upon seeing again her desolate stare.

Though it seemed, as before, to be fixed on him, he could tell she did not know who or what he was.

From the expression on the sweat-beaded doctor's face under the wardroom lamp, the miracles had run out.

"She has lost some blood, but not that much, not enough to account for her . . . coma. Though she is not in a coma either, really." The doctor spoke without looking at Kelso, his spectacled gaze on the gaunt face of the woman lying anesthetized on the wardroom table. The doctor had been awakened in the middle of the night in his home at Rose Harbor, had been offered an outlandish sum of money to accompany the bedraggled figure sitting across from him now to a hidden cove on Smoky Island. He'd seen the pistol in Kelso's belt, considered the obvious distraught condition of his importuner, got dressed, found his bag and followed.

"She seems to be in a severe state of shock," the doctor said, having finished dressing the knife wound and examining Judith as thoroughly as he could with what tools he had in the bag. "Reactions and reflexes are almost non-existent. It is, of course, very difficult under these circumstances to tell if there is serious brain damage, or—"

"Yeah." In his chair against the opposite bulkhead, Kelso looked at the woman's waxen face, heard the sound of rain on the *Tiburón's* deck overhead, and remembered it had rained in the Restitutions the last time they were here.

The doctor began replacing things in his bag. "I suggest you get her to a hospital where there are proper facilities to examine her further. You need a brain expert—" He stopped, at last turning to confront Kelso. He removed his eyeglasses, wiping them with a tissue he picked up from the table. A frown climbed his furrowed brow. "Of course, knowing who—guessing who you are—I might warn you that you would be taking a grave chance if you tried getting her to the hospital at Rose Harbor. There is a special San Andreas Sea Patrol contingent in the Restitutions now. Since the recent quakes in Angeles Bay, police operations have been heavily reinforced in the area and even here in the islands." He placed the glasses on his thin nose and contemplated Kelso through clearer lenses. His calm, thoughtful manner was that of a man who'd seen enough of life—and death—to be at relative ease in almost any situation. "The recent quakes were nothing big, I understand, compared to what happened before, but they have the authorities, nonetheless, concerned. Seems a very large portion of the southern San Gabriels and the northern part of Los Angeles sank farther down." He studied Kelso thoughtfully. "Perhaps you've heard about it."

Kelso said nothing. But for the fact his eyes were open and he sat erect, he seemed as lifeless as the woman on the table.

The doctor resumed packing his bag. "At any rate, the government has stepped up its police surveillance in the area, and they're after illegal salvage divers and trespassers into the Zone in a big way." He snapped the bag shut and took from his shirt pocket a pen and small notebook. Opening the latter and laying it on the table beside Judith, he wrote something.

"I have a friend in Mexico, in Mazatlán. An excellent neurologist who could be of some help. It's a long way from here, but I can't think of any other recourse, considering your . . . situation. I would suggest that you get her there as quickly as possible." He ripped the page from the notebook and left it on the table. "I will show you how to put together an apparatus that will enable you to feed her intravenously. I will show you how to care for her properly until you reach Mazatlán."

"Thanks," said Kelso, his voice thick. "Thanks very much, Doctor." He wanted to say more, but wasn't sure what he wanted to say. He wanted to talk, to tell someone, the doctor maybe—*What I have learned, what I have seen. Doctor, let me tell you . . . this woman. She—Doctor, my ideas, my prejudices, have been shaken to their roots. Doctor, I am humbled . . . what she is . . . what she's been through. Is there a soul after all, and can it be universal?*

Gibberish. The doctor would think him as much in need of a brain expert as Judith.

Kelso stirred, cleared his throat. "The money there. On the cabinet. It's yours."

The physician watched Kelso for a while. "You may need it where you're going. My Mazatlán friend could put it to good use, I am sure. Now, if you will come here and give me a hand."

At times she murmured and made noises, as if trying to speak. Nothing intelligible resulted. At times when he came to attend her, feed her, bathe her, her eyes would be open, large and luminous, watching every move he made about her bed with the look of one uncomprehending yet trying to comprehend. Once or twice he said her name, the name she'd used, anyway, but the vacuous stare he received made it plain he could just as well have spoken Zulu.

He rarely drank anymore. Liquor or anything else brought him no solace. Once safely south of the Restitutions and in international waters, the *Tiburón* stayed surfaced much of the time, and he spent many hours standing on the bridge, looking at the sea, his mind often as blank as hers might have been. Often he stood on the bridge at night with his gaze on the heavens, remembering everything she'd told him about herself, the alien city under Angeles Bay, where she originated, why she came here. He no longer found it incredible. It had happened. Unfathomable, yet irrefutable as the stars.

It was on such a night that she appeared before he knew it. He had not heard a sound; her presence alone made him turn.

"Ju—"

She remained standing beside the hatch, a dark silhouette against the backdrop of the darker sea below and behind and the star-sprayed sky above the horizon. The faint light that came up through the hatch only touched her feet and the tail of her robe. She was a dark figure with blowing hair, silent.

"Judith?" It badly disturbed him that he could not see her eyes and for no accountable reason he had the unnerving impression that she had no face.

He moved away from the bulwark toward her. One step, two. She was motionless, as if frozen.

A storm of emotions raged in him: fear her mind was gone, shame for the past years of hating and violence, for lack of faith in the good of this or any other world, and on his third step toward her he heard her speak.

Or was it the wind, the sea sighing its ageless reminder of the mystery of all life?

33. HOPE

It came again, and this time was unmistakable. She said his name.

"Judith," he answered, still doubting.

"Yes. Judith now."

He did not move, uncertain still of her state of mind, or whatever one might call being's elusive center.

"I have much to tell you," she said.

He swallowed, feeling the *Tiburón* list slightly under his feet. "I promise I'll be a good listener. Not easy for me—" He let it go.

She did not speak for several moments, perhaps trying to find the words in Kelso's language that would help her tell something that could be very nearly incommunicable.

"I have—for days I have been in the grip of the ones who had hold of me, with varied periods of control, from the beginning. I— last night something else broke through." She stopped speaking. He saw the dark outline of an arm, a hand, go to her head in a movement he'd seen all too often. But this time the movement was slow, not anxious or desperate. She took a breath. "A telepathic pulse, if that is the phrase. I recognized it as an influence that had entered, or tried to enter, my mind before. But before last night it had not been able to penetrate very deeply. It came from—"

She moved away from the hatch, a sudden eagerness and earnestness in her tone. "Jack, I know this will sound—Jack, the ones who sent me here to destroy the subaqueous city have been overthrown by a revolt led by insurgents from other—from almost every inhabited and civilized planet in their former empire. The—Deathlords—that's the best word I can think of to translate what they—the ones whose slave I was—what they are called by the insurgents—they have been overthrown by a revolt led by a—a woman. A woman who—" She stopped again, again searching for words, maybe doubting the adequacy of those she'd already used.

To Kelso the words were weighty enough. And as he stood there trying to digest their meaning, he knew it would take some time for the full implications to sink in.

Though she continued to speak with an eagerness that promised she had much to tell, there was an underlying calm, a serenity in her voice that Kelso had never heard before. The very sound of it soothed him, and he was a man who at this point badly needed soothing.

"This woman was a former friend of mine on the world where I was born, Jack. We grew up together, it seems. But no, not just a friend, a lover. You see, I was a male."

The gentle roll of the deck was suddenly almost enough to topple him. He didn't know whether to laugh or swear, yet could not help feeling that something somewhere above and beyond them saw all this as comedy. And there came a whispering in his ear, in his mind's ear, that said if the soul was anything, it was sexless.

"It was this former friend, lover, she and my brother, who reached me through what, for want of a better word, I can only call telepathy—that, along with the help of one of the Deathlords' surveillance vessels in Earth's vicinity. She told me about the revolt, the Deathlords, their history, our—Onnahlaeti's—history. She found out that the Deathlords had made me into a Terran female, implanted a—an 'overseer'—in my forebrain, and sent me here to Earth. She had the overseer deactivated, or neutralized, through that surveillance vessel whose control she seized after the revolt was victorious. She also, through the help of certain captive Deathlords and the surveillance vessel, was responsible for the *Egg*'s being safely pulled out of the city when it began to collapse. She revived the *Tiburón*'s computer—" Judith paused for breath, for the strength to tell it. He did not know if the tremor that had crept into her voice was caused by excitement or simple physical weakness from her ordeal, but his guess was both.

"The—the implant—was monitored by this ship. The implant was operated by this monitor, and the monitor received feedback from my brain and responded, would give directions to the implant. I learned to fight it somewhat, learned when its influence was strongest and could counter it—until the last. There—in the city—it directed me kinetically, blanked out my own will—but its power was sporadic because of the city's defense systems. Its influence came and went. Earlier, before the city, it refrained from taking over completely because to do so it would have erased by 'human' traits, and that would have alienated you." She paused again.

Kelso waited, not knowing what to say, judging it best not to say anything.

"But that isn't all that important right now. I—I am released." This came in a rush, and she seemed to make an effort to check her emotions lest they sweep her away. When she spoke again, she was more calm. "I am finally released from the hold the Deathlords had on my mind and body. A body that for days hasn't been able to do anything but lie comatose. I am sure I would have died if you had not fed me, cared for me the way you did—" She turned to the bulwark and leaned against its ledge. "The woman—Cinara Tlii—" The name fell uncertainly from her lips, like arcana spoken by a neophyte "—told me a great deal about my former self. We were both from the same world, as I said. A world very much like Earth, it seems, except warmer, a little closer to its sun, with a little more ocean—and two moons instead of one. Inhabited by a race that could have descended from the same celestial ancestry as yours. But that is speculation. In any case, there was a race of 'starwanderers' who once came here to Earth. The city we—there were other cities destroyed, I guess, when they left. Millennia ago. But the Deathlords, or the Deathlords' forebears, had been members of this race also. There was a war between the two factions of the galactic explorers. The Deathlords were descendants of one faction, a branch that evolved a fanatical hatred for—" Silence again, more searching. "For natural forms of life, what they considered to be lower forms. About all that was left in the Deathlords' physiology that was natural in origin, according to Cinara, was their brains, and even their brains had been extensively altered, enlarged and extended, by artificial means."

Another pause. Both the irony and the parallels in what she had just said did not escape him. Nor, he doubted, did they her. Her next words confirmed this.

"The Onnahlaetians are nature worshipers. Descendants of that other branch of the ancient wanderers. The Deathlords are—were—ultra technophiles. There is so much to sort out but—I—Onnahlaetians may be as autocratic or narrow minded, in their own way, as the Deathlords. Cinara finally had to rely on the Deathlords' surveillance vessel, and their knowledge—in other words, had to rely on what in her view was evil—to reach me."

"And you, formerly of a race of nature worshipers, have consistently argued for technology," he muttered. Again he had, in his mind's eye, the image of a cosmic joker rolling back on his heels, howling with mirth, his head in Corona Borealis, say, his fundament in Fornax.

"Yes. But—my birth on Onnahlaeti—one of the reasons I responded so—so instinctively to you."

He waited, trying to assimilate it all, watching her dark profile. Now and then he caught a glimpse, a glint, of reflected light—from the stars, or the luminescent sea—where her eyes should have been. "Judith," he said gently. "There are a thousand questions—"

"Yes. I know. I haven't told you much. I'm still trying to put it together properly, so I can tell it clearly. You see, the Deathlords had robot spaceships, very small vessels, apparently, keeping watch on worlds where intelligent species were evolving, like Earth. One of these ships discovered the ancient city under Los Angeles and the San Gabriel Mountains. I found a map a while ago, not long after I came out of the—sleep I was in. I have been awake, conscious, for an hour or more. I shaded over the area the city covered, under Los Angeles. According to Cinara's descriptions, it stretched roughly from north Los Angeles to the San Gabriel Wilderness. There were many entrances, funnels, but the one in Angeleno Heights, under the interchange—according to the data gathered belatedly by the surveillance ship—was nearest the southern power disc, was the easiest to dig into, and was one of the few funnels that still worked effectively as an entry. The way the land fell and tilted, most other entrances were buried or sealed so completely the *Egg* would not have been able to uncover them. The funnels—they could accept machines and people, but rejected everything else. I don't know how. But the confusion, the mistake about Highland Park, came about because the surveillance ship, the implant monitor, had confused the entrance with the location of the power disc. The disc was under Highland Park, the funnel entrance in Angeleno Heights, under the roadway interchange."

She took a deep breath, exhaled slowly. "Anyway, the Deathlords, the 'masters', were afraid the city would be found by men sooner or later, especially after the San Andreas superquake, and especially since men had already picked up evidence of its energy field even before the quake—"

"The Devil's Canyon Project," Kelso said, thinking aloud.

"Yes. The nuclear probes of the Devil's Canyon Project set off the quake, and the Naravamintarans knew this. Earth was far away, outside their imperial net. They had no interest in exploiting it yet. It was their belief that if left to their own machinations, men would—will—soon destroy themselves. But they feared that if men found the extraterrestrial city, Earth would be thrown forward into a highly advanced space technology and become a threat at their backs, so to speak. Cinara said they were able to jam or confuse later geological probes through the use of the surveillance ship. In the meantime, they had to have an agent, one who would pass as a Terran and one who would appeal to *you* because they knew of you, again through the surveillance vessel, through data, news reports, and so on, it could pick up—an agent who could reach that entrance, find the power center, destroy the city. This was the method thought least likely to risk discovery by Earth. Once the city was destroyed, Terrans would think the resulting seismic disturbances only another cataclysm resulting from unstable conditions in the Zone. The earlier discovery of that energy field, the Naravamintarans reasoned, would remain a mystery, and ultimately be forgotten."

She sighed again, and Kelso could almost see, like an exorcised demon rising with tattered wings, the burden being lifted from her shoulders as she related these things.

"So they chose one descended from a race similar to Earth's in order to insure the success of the mission to destroy the city," he said. "And never thought this ruse might work against them." He was half speaking to himself again. "But if they could have molded such perfect flesh, why couldn't they have made the perfect brain for their purpose, the brain that would have obeyed them totally?"

"They placed too much faith in their 'purification,' or 'mindscrubbing' techniques, according to Cinara. But did they? Maybe they were aware of the risk, of the fine line they were treading in sending a humanoid, but did not think they had a choice. You see, from what Cinara told me, they were too afraid that a robot agent, like the Lavaccas, for example, would have bungled, or somehow brought suspicion on itself.

But taking into account their complacency, it is doubtful they worried much about my turning against them. They gave me just enough Earth knowledge, through the implant, to make me Terran, but they did not foresee such things as doubt, questioning, wonder, a hunger for real knowledge, in one formerly so unquestioning, passive, intellectually dead. I was a trusted servant, a highly esteemed soldier, faithful and loyal. I was an executioner, as well. Without a conscience." Her voice changed briefly, unsteadied by remorse. "I do not know what happened when they made me over, into a Terran female. Something did. Something changed besides my physical appearance. Something was—though it didn't happen all at once and it didn't happen easily—something was *freed*. I do not think they ever thought that placing me here on Earth, with you, would have opened up and let loose something they had, as far as their world was concerned, effectively erased or suffocated. Considering what they were, it would simply not have entered their thinking that there could be an element in higher intelligences, something inviolable, that the mere reproduction or alteration of cells, of neurons, would not change. But again, maybe they knew. Maybe they knew that to change that something would kill the entity, would create only a robot in its place. Maybe they knew but had to take the risk anyway. But I do not believe they could permit themselves any doubt concerning me, any more than they were able to foresee the revolt."

Fleetingly, it occurred to Kelso once more that he could be in the presence of madness, that this intricate tale of extraterrestrial empire, despotism, decay, and revolt could be fantasy. But the thought was, indeed, fleeting. If she were mad, so was he. If all he had experienced in the last several days was nothing more than delusion and neurosis, then life itself was a hallucination, nightmare, and dream, as it could very well be. But neither he nor she could be the dreamer, and therefore could bear no responsibility for being "mad".

"Hell's harridans," he mumbled. "Looks like we—we're 'related' after all." He almost laughed, then upbraided himself. It had sounded inane; everything he said did. He felt a little drunk, light-headed. He felt like a child who suddenly found himself in a place of magic. Anything was possible, and everything was beautiful.

"I was a palace guard," she murmured. "A male. A—so strange to—"

"You're not a male now," he said, overjoyed with the fact,

yet a little anxious that it could be, weighing all that had taken place, suddenly rendered fiction.

"No. But still strange."

"Yes. But what or who isn't, when you come down to it. Judith, tell me, could they have—this Cinara Tlii—can she take you back somehow? Can they transport you from here back to—"

"To Onnahlaeti. Yes. They have the means." She became quiet, probably remembering the telepathic dialogue between herself and the female creature named Cinara Tlii, a former *lover*.

"Did Cinara Tlii want you to return?" Kelso held his breath.

"Yes. She was—I could feel her disappointment when I told her—I chose to stay here, for now at least. *I*?" She repeated the stupefying pronoun with the awe it was due.

"Well." He coughed to loosen the tightness in his throat, feeling infinitely relieved. "Welcome to the human race." He gave a mock bow, then sobered. He still wasn't sure of much. Too many things had happened; he could not make adjustments to such revelations in a mere matter of minutes, or even days. He thought he had had it all pretty well figured out but it seemed the truth always defied one's preconceptions, as well as one's imagination. He realized, seeing her dark head against the backdrop of stars, that he could no longer believe, however sardonically, that man was the dubious culmination of existence or that evil ultimately ruled. "Tell me something," he said. "Why did you choose to stay here?"

She spoke as if to the ocean. "I have felt, since my—since coming to Earth—things awakening in me that have been buried since I was a child, or buried even before my Onnahlaetian birth maybe. You have helped awaken them in me." Her head turned to look at him, though he still could not clearly see her eyes. "Don't hate your world, Jack."

"I don't. Just a sizeable number of the fools on it." The last, he realized, was said out of habit more than anything else.

"But folly is the price you pay for freedom, the freedom to do right or wrong—as opposed to doing nothing, to being dead while supposedly alive. I think that freedom is worth the price, worth the risk of folly."

Kelso felt the tensions of a lifetime of anger and despair leaving him like water being forced out an airlock by the downward press of air.

"I am fascinated with Earth, with the many things you have told me. In spite of your surface cynicism, you have communicated your love of Earth to me. I want to hear the call of the whales the way you hear it. I want to know the sea the way you do. Looking back, I realize that from the beginning, from when I first came awake on the way to the Restitutions, when they put me here, I was fascinated by Earth's contrasts, its challenges. It has awakened in me a vitality, a love of life that even paradisiacal Onnahlaeti may have repressed; has stimulated a love of adventure, conflict, quest, and, for want of a better term, conquest. It is possible that Onnahlaeti was as much a tyranny, in its own way, as Naravamintara. A paradisiacal tyranny perhaps, but a tyranny nonetheless, without complication or adversity, without challenge. That, of course, is a terracentric view."

Kelso nodded, cleared his throat. "Right. Well, Earth can be very accommodating in that quarter. Considering what you've been through, though, your desire for conflict and challenge is rather, uh, remarkable. I could do with a long rest myself."

She touched her brow. "I feel—almost delirious with release, with a feeling of newness—" She broke off, inhaled deeply, let it out. "Someday I would like to return to Onnahlaeti, perhaps with you, if that is possible and you would like to go. But for now—" She faced the sea again. "You see, Earth is where I—awoke. It is the birthplace of the 'I' that I am now—whose meaning I have yet to learn."

Again Kelso nodded, like a dummy, knowing he could not counter, or even carry further, that one. Anyway, he hadn't the vaguest desire to try.

"Jack, I haven't the knowledge that was contained in the city under Los Angeles. Nor do they, the ones who overthrew the Deathlords. Much knowledge lies in the rooms of the underground fortress on Naravamintara, but for now the entire planet is excluded from any sort of use by the victors. They are now preoccupied with restoring order and health to their own worlds."

He understood that she was telling him there would be no help for Earth from any extraterrestrial geniuses or supermen. "Yes. I see." He didn't really care that much about them at the moment, or the earth either for that matter. *She* was standing upright. *She* was rational. *She* was real.

"I am sorry. Perhaps later when—"

His turn to take a breath. He felt exhilarated enough to fly.

"Homo sapiens got himself into his current mess more or less. Maybe he can get himself out somehow. I have mixed feelings about the city being destroyed, Judith, but I think I'm generally glad it was, because the thought of what could have happened if it had fallen into the wrong hands threatens to dampen my present good mood." Cynicism again, Kelso? Or simple realism? Well he was, by nature, suspicious. How could he not be? But he also believed that in spite of evil, good still lived, in spite of death, life prevailed. There he was at the brink of the primal existential mystery, beyond which he could not go; that brink which had filled him, when a young man, with both ecstasy and *angst.*

She was speaking again. "I can communicate with Cinara—through this telepathy. Something I must work to strengthen. When Cinara, and the rest, have recovered and rectified their worlds, maybe they, she, can help tell us things we can do. But I am sworn to secrecy about my origins. I must ask you to give me your word that secret will remain with us."

He looked over at her. "Why?"

"Because Cinara, for now anyway, has too much else to deal with to face Earth's certain desire to communicate with, and eventually travel to, such worlds as were in the former Naravamintaran empire. If Earth learned such civilizations existed and could find a way to reach them, Cinara and her allies would certainly be faced with such a problem. Perhaps later."

She fell silent. Kelso thought for a long moment before he said, "Something I never told you."

Her turn to wait. He had no wish to rush into what he was about to say, was not even sure he wanted to say it, consider it as a possibility.

"There's a colony of expatriated scientists, economists, writers, thinkers, on a group of islands in Melanesia. They're from nearly every country on Earth, but all have renounced their nationalities, their governments, for one reason or another and embraced a—a sort of extranationality, and are trying to come up with solutions, workable ways, to prevent Armageddon. I know several of them; a couple were on *Deepfish.* They write me from time to time, wanting to know if I'm still alive, asking me to come down there and so forth."

"Yes." Fresh interest was in her voice. "I remember the letters you picked up when we were in the Restitutions."

Kelso ran a hand through his hair, listening to this stranger within himself speak. "We could go there. We could work there, maybe contribute something. Maybe I could resume my work in interspecies communication." Okay. He'd said it. And, having said it, he was surprised how feasible, how sensible, even attractive, it sounded.

She was looking at him now. "I like that idea very much."

"One other item. My old friend Rodríguez. I don't know if you were aware of anything then, but I went to the Restitutions after we got out of—after we were pulled out of the shambles when that place collapsed." He shuddered momentarily, remembering, feeling it in every nerve and bone. "I got a doctor to examine you—anyway, when I was there, a boy came out of nowhere, as they're wont to do. It was night, raining. I was wrapped up in an attempted disguise. He knew me though, and he gave me a note from Rodríguez. Apparently Vince Polliard had learned that Rodríguez often bought salvage from me. Polliard threatened Rodríguez, his wife and children, said they'd die unless Rodríguez helped nab me and you. Rodríguez, as he tells it, had no choice. But the note, as near as I can tell in Rodríguez's mangled English, was profusely apologetic. And he had something more tangible to offer by way of making amends." Kelso patted his shirt pocket, wanting his pipe, but the pocket was empty. He could not remember when he'd last smoked. "It seems an old hermit fisherman was diving off Isla Pequeña, not all that far from Cave Cove where we, uh, picnicked that day, at a place called The Pinnacles, which is supposed to be infested with sharks. Well, the old guy pursued his prey into an undersea cave that led to a maze of underground caverns. The place must be honeycombed with them. Anyway, he also found an underground room, could see it through holes in the cavern wall, and in it sat a submersible. The room had been sealed off, probably by explosives, but by digging he got into it, and that submersible contained enough salvaged treasure to sink the *Tiburón*, the way Rodríguez tells it. The old hermit told a boy, the boy told Rodríguez. The fisherman wants no part of any of it, but would like to see it go to the islands' poor. Rodríguez says I can have fifty percent, provided I forgive him his treachery and dispense with Vincent Polliard so he'll be out of our hair. He thinks there are other such troves on either Pequeña or elsewhere. Polliard's long-rumored secret fortune that he pulled out of Angeles Bay. I left word with the boy that Vincent Polliard would never be in anybody's hair again."

"So you could be a very rich man," she said softly.

"The people in those islands in Melanesia I told you about need every blessed cent they can scrounge. I could bring them a significant donation." He straightened up. "Hell's hounds. I feel like *I've* come through Armageddon, and for some undeserved reason been chosen as redeemable."

Silence again. The whispering sea and the mild wind coming out of the north. The brilliant streak of a meteor across Pegasus.

Her voice, low, uncertain: "Jack, I think, if I understand the signs—I am pregnant."

After all that had happened Kelso would not have thought he could ever be surprised, or shocked, again. But this latest disclosure left him speechless.

"I do not know how that can be," she said. "I suppose it is as possible as everything else about me—but what kind of offspring will I—will we—have?"

He had trouble getting the words out but they finally came. "A beauty," he said thickly. "Like you."

"You are willing to take the chance?"

He thought about that, but only for a moment. "Chance. Choice. Hazard. The human—and extraterrestrial—state of things. Like you said. Yes, I'm willing to take the chance." The stars seemed to reel. His scalp tingled. It came back to him that Lisa had believed Earth was on the brink, or in the midst, of some great evolutionary change, some collosal or catastrophic transition that would dramatically alter the course of human history, and transform the psychic mechanisms of man. He had privately ascribed this notion to his wife's more fanciful inclinations, but now felt pulled into an odd spell, in which he could no longer dismiss such an idea out of hand. What kind of offspring—who the hell was he to dismiss any idea out of hand?

So much had happened that he could still hardly believe. Life was after all miraculous, or, to put it another way, unpredictably moving on in a never-ending chronology of strange and amazing events. Life, death, birth, war, vengeance, greed for wealth and power, the old, old conflicts between good and evil, the conflicts between diverse definitions of what was good and what was evil. In short, the conflicts and unfolding of the soul seemed to be in evidence elsewhere in the universe. What he once would have regarded as peculiarly human was apparently no more limited to the predicament of Terrans that light and darkness were limited to Earth.

"Did you," he said, "did you tell your—this Cinara Tlii—did you tell her about—"

"No. I only realized—when I became fully conscious, after Cinara and I communicated. I—the genetic tampering by the Deathlords—I wonder how—let us hope—"

"Judith."

She moved a step toward him. A hand rose to touch his face. "Jack, I'm starved. For food—and other things. Everything."

Kelso said nothing, incapable of words, weary of words. He pressed her to him and felt uncertain doing so, as if a physical embrace were somehow inadequate, inappropriate. He knew then that his feelings for her would always be powerful, but also mixed, ambivalent. He would desire her, want her close, closer than flesh could come, but he would also forever see her as someone apart, ethereal and haunted, the embodiment of a reality in which only the freest of Terrans could believe. Most of all, he knew he would never be able to begin to fill the hunger she had just voiced. Nor did he want to.

ABOUT JERRY EARL BROWN

I came wailing into the world in a farmhouse near Palestine, Texas, June 24, 1940. Grew up in that East Texas locale and anxious to escape it, enlisted in the United States Marine Corps upon graduation from Palestine High School in 1958. A very indifferent student in school with a penchant for fabricating fictions in and out of the classroom, I began to do a lot of reading while in the Marines, from poetry to philosophy and everything in between. Honorably discharged in 1962, I entered a period of drifting in and out of college, from job to job and from place to place, while dabbling desultorily at the writer's craft. During that period (the sixties and early seventies), I attended Santa Ana Junior College in Santa Ana, California, Texas Technological College in Lubbock, and the University of Colorado in Boulder, majoring in philosophy and minoring in English, learning mostly from my own extracurricular reading and eventually becoming thoroughly fed up with schools and the "educational process." I worked as a freight handler, lathe operator, crane operator, lumberjack, hod carrier, chambermaid (sic), singer/guitarist, cop, janitor, and freelance writer (with stories and articles published in various men's and outdoor magazines). In 1977, I became Assistant Director of the National Writers Club in Denver, an association representing over 5,000 writers. At present I maintain that position at NWC while working on a sequel to UNDER THE CITY OF ANGELS.